Praise for
# JENNIE FIELDS and
## *CROSSING BROOKLYN FERRY*

"A novel whose heart is in the right place."
*Chicago Tribune*

"There's a wonderfully lifelike texture to this
Brooklyn neighborhood, and a real affection
for the seasonal beauties of Park Slope, not to
mention some unabashedly erotic sex scenes."
*The Baltimore Sun*

"The colors and tones of this urban landscape
are richly painted by Fields, [who] makes us
feel as if we are strolling past windows with
curtains gauzy enough for us to construe
what is transpiring within."
*New York Daily News*

"The prose often has the immediacy
of a photograph, making this probing
examination of sexuality, identity,

# CROSSING BROOKLYN FERRY

## JENNIE FIELDS

AVON BOOKS NEW YORK

AVON BOOKS, INC.
1350 Avenue of the Americas
New York, New York 10019

Copyright © 1997 by Jennie Fields
Inside cover author photo by Jerry Bauer
Published by arrangement with William Morrow and Company, Inc.
Visit our website at **http://www.AvonBooks.com**
Library of Congress Catalog Card Number: 96-45315
ISBN: 0-380-73168-1

First Avon Books Printing: November 1998

AVON TRADEMARK REG. U.S. PAT. OFF. AND IN OTHER COUNTRIES, MARCA REGISTRADA, HECHO EN U.S.A.

Printed in the U.S.A.

WCD  10  9  8  7  6  5  4  3  2  1

*For my parents, Belle and Ira Fields,*
*And always, for my daughter, Chloe*

# ACKNOWLEDGMENTS

I would like to thank my wonderful agent, Lisa Bankoff, and my friends Susan Spano, Penny Kaganoff, and Elliot Figman for their very valuable early readings. Thanks to Dr. Sarah Hartman for her information on depression and the recommended drugs, and psychologist Mimi Meyers for her unique insightful advice on child psychology. Thanks also to Dora Capers for always making our lives easier.

# CROSSING BROOKLYN FERRY

## an excerpt

(from "Leaves of Grass" by Walt Whitman—1891)

*1.*

Flood-tide below me! I see you face to face!
Clouds of the west—sun there half an hour high—I see
    you also face to face.

Crowds of men and women attired in the usual costumes,
    how curious you are to me!
On the ferry-boats the hundreds and hundreds that cross,
    returning home, are more curious to me than you
    suppose,
And you that shall cross from shore to shore years hence
    are
    more to me,
And more in my meditations, than you might suppose.

2.

The impalpable sustenance of me from all things at all
    hours of the day,
The simple, compact, well-join'd scheme, myself
    disintegrated,
    every one disintegrated yet part of the scheme,
The similitudes of the past and those of the future,
The glories strung like beads on my smallest sights and
    hearings, on the walk
    in the street and the passage over the river,

The current rushing so swiftly, and swimming with me
    far away,
The others that are to follow me, the ties between me
    and them,
The certainty of others, the life, love, sight, hearing of
    others.
Others will enter the gates of the ferry and cross from
    shore to shore,
Others will watch the run of the flood-tide,
Others will see the shipping of Manhattan north and west,
    and the heights of Brooklyn to the south and east,
Others will see the islands large and small;
Fifty years hence, others will see them as they cross, the sun
    half an hour
      high,
A hundred years hence, or ever so many hundred years
    hence,
    others will see them,
Will enjoy the sunset, the pouring-in of the flood-tide,
    the falling-back to the sea of the ebb-tide.
I too lived, Brooklyn of ample hills was mine,
I too walk'd the streets of Manhattan island,
    and bathed in the waters around it,
I too felt the curious abrupt questionings stir within me,
In the day among crowds of people sometimes they came
    upon me,
In my walks home late at night or as I lay in my bed they
    came
      upon me.
I too had been struck from the float forever held in
    solution.

# ONE

———◆———

One by one, beneath an April evening sky, the brownstones and butcher shops and vegetable markets of Park
Slope, Brooklyn, begin to light. The Lucky Pub's manager
plugs in the aging neon Budweiser sign with the lop-eared
dog. At the Korean market, the owner switches on the bell-
shaped lanterns that sway from his red-and-white awning.
Commuters spill from the subway onto Seventh Avenue
and stop for a moment at the top of the stairs to breathe
in the evening air. It is as though the air of Brooklyn is
perfumed with relief, the scent of home. Not much has
changed since the subway was built in 1930, rattling the
cellars beneath Ninth Street. Cordeiro's Market has been
there for fifty years. And the Lucky Pub recently put in
new paneling, but the crowd hasn't changed in character
since World War II. Nor has the display behind the bar:
faded shamrocks, pressed between glass and cotton, that
Paddy Dunfey found in Prospect Park somewhere between
1930 and 1950.

But now, in 1989, there are new stores, which cater to
the recent arrivals in the neighborhood. A video store. A
cheese store with fresh mozzarella and sun-dried tomatoes.
A muffin shop. A comic-book store. Already their awnings
have tarnished in the city air, their windows are cluttered
in a familiar way. And though not many houses have sold
in other neighborhoods since the market crashed two years

ago, in Park Slope real estate is still moving, and every third store along Seventh Avenue is an agency displaying slick pictures of renovated brownstones.

If you turn right at the Lucky Pub you'll be on Eighth Street. Walk into its silence. Feel it: the rich solidity of the hundred-year-old bluestone sidewalks, the slope of the hill as it eases up toward Prospect Park, the Norwegian maples, which in summer are so thick the rain doesn't come through. And the houses, a soldierly sameness that can't help but please you, beginning to light now, with tables being set for dinner, mail being read. Every house on the block was built in 1886, by the same builder. On the north side of the street they are three-storied. On the south side, four. Symmetry a hundred times over, and yet, inside, there is no symmetry at all. The O'Neill teenagers are at war in 664. Darlene Kilkenny Sheehan's long-awaited new baby cries out in 621, and Darlene also cries as she rocks him, because her husband, Donald, is getting drunk down at the Lucky. Old Mrs. Reilly watches you from her window in 621. Somehow their lives fit into these narrow houses: seventeen feet wide, clad in brownstone, and each lit window marks a history of birth, love, and death. Row after row of brownstone stoops line up, row after row of wrought-iron gates mark the entrances with fleurs-de-lis. You could easily walk by your own house and not know it. People do every day. Even though they know their own gardens or garbage cans or trees, the sameness of the gates and houses is a lulling, sweet drug.

You can catch glimpses of the interior detail: floral medallions on the ceilings, etched-glass doors. So beautiful for houses that have long been working class, affordable. Read the names on the mailboxes. Names that have been on these mailboxes for decades. Ryan, O'Connor, Kilkenny, O'Shea. Some since 1917, 1911.

And the new names: Hartman, Jarvis, Epstein, DeLee. No Irish ring to these names. No long Brooklyn history here. People whose cars are new, whose jobs are unstable but even in a bad economy pay shockingly well. People who buy and sell in a day, who worry about preschool, install soaking tubs, own Volvos, have tax shelters. People who five years ago wouldn't have been caught dead in Brooklyn.

In 645, while the movers clatter and jostle and hoist around her, Zosia Finney stands straight and silent, thrilled by the view of her new backyard. The real cause of her elation could not be more mundane: laundry. Festoons of laundry wreathe the backyards surrounding hers, strings of color, like Grand Opening flags. Orange boxer shorts and blue jeans, crimson T-shirts, amethyst sheets. They make crisp smacking noises in the spring wind. They catch the last of the sun in their billows.

Who would have thought that anyone still hung laundry out to dry, let alone in the city? Even her immigrant parents could not have guessed this. When Zoe bought the house, she wondered at the narrow iron ladders that rose four stories straight up from the fences of every yard on the street behind hers. Back in February, not a single line of laundry was out there—it was cold, and wet sheets would have gone stiff as papier-mâché. Against the grey sky, the empty ladders were eerie monoliths, promising a direct ascent to the clouds. Now they sway with the weight of laundry lines hooked to their rungs. Wheels and cranks outside apartment windows stand ready to draw the laundry in.

Once, Jamie would have loved the scene. He would have shared her surprise and elation. Not anymore. He is upstairs already, asleep on the floor, his head on his jacket. That's where she left him, since their bed hasn't been unloaded yet. It may be months until he comes down again. Lately, she is grateful for the smallest things: this morning, she actually managed to get him dressed for the move (she feared she'd have to settle for his coming out to the taxi in a limp bathrobe). She was grateful she got him into the cab at all. His hands were shaking and his lips were narrow with concentration as he folded his tall,

patrician body into the cab. He didn't look around or focus
on anything but the ground. In the sunlight, she was
shocked to see how grey his skin had become. His muteness seemed even more intense out in the world, with the
roar of Manhattan around them; and his vulnerability more
palpable. Later, as the taxi darted down Second Avenue,
he held her hand with the white, gripping panic of a roller
coaster rider, and she was appalled to find herself desperate to shake him loose. Mortified that the clawing of his
fingers made her remember a friend's puppy that, after
being introduced to her, bit right into her hand and, as she
drew her arm up, clung, spinning, from the fulcrum of his
teeth. "Isn't he funny?" her friend had said in all
sincerity.

Zoe can't, as with that plump, presumptuous puppy,
shake her husband off.

So she's moved to Brooklyn.

"Brooklyn?" Stuart, her assistant, asked her, with a
frown. "What good is that going to do?"

"I just like the way it feels there," Zoe told him. "Real
people live in Brooklyn."

"Check out the subways," Stuart said. "There are actually large amounts of real people living right in Manhattan.
And as a matter of fact, there's quite a dashing one right
here in this office with you." He did a runway turn—he
was always trying to get Zoe to pay attention to him—but
she only smiled and turned back to her editing screen,
where she was working on a commercial for baby food.

"Well, there isn't a single real person in our apartment
building," Zoe said. "Except maybe the doormen."

"And you," Stuart said dutifully.

Now that fussy, elegant Sutton Place apartment she and
Jamie inherited is behind them forever. This morning,
Aunt Delia's old-lady French Provincial gold-and-white
dressers, whose top drawers smelled of face powder and
pills, her purple velvet wool chairs and white bedside
lamps inscribed with bubbles, were carted away by sweating Salvation Army men. "Shit, this stuff is heavy," one

proclaimed with a moan. The best-made, the most solid furniture in all the world, it seemed, made to last two lifetimes. But not hers. Not anymore. Now only a few select things are being delivered to this house in Brooklyn. Zoe will have to furnish it with her taste, which even now, although she is thirty-five, seems uncertain. After all, she's had no practice. Last week she bought a sofa at Blooming-dale's: a subtle pink. After she went home and thought about it, she hated it. But it will fill a space until she finds something that suits her better.

There is so much in her life, she has realized lately, that needs filling. Since Jamie has become the way he is, since she has had to become a mother to him as much as to their daughter, Rose, her own sexuality has become a painful thing, out of place in her life. She looks at men on the street, behind store counters, looks at their hands and lips and imagines how they would feel on her own mouth, on the crook of her neck. How their fingers would feel defining the curve of her hip, the swell of a breast. She sometimes laughs at herself, to see how hungry she's become—horny as a seventeen-year-old boy. And then, also, there is her ''urge,'' her most shameful secret. She's had no luck keeping her urge away lately, God knows. When her life is the least bit empty, it comes upon her like water seeping into an empty, sinking ship.

Standing in her new house now, she shivers away the memory of her secret's last ugly episode and tries to think of other things, to concentrate on the purposeful ballet of the movers around her, creating the new landscape where her life will be played. If she cannot have a husband who is her lover, if she cannot have a simple, ordinary marriage, at least she can have a house that is truly her own, a place to wait until something changes.

Jim O'Connor is coming home late from the office, walking up Eighth Street from the subway, trying to hold his body so it won't tell on him, won't betray how weak with contentment he feels. He doubts Patty will notice anyway. She doesn't notice much about him, never did, really. The fact is, he was in the Village all afternoon, at Kim D'Amico's apartment, up to no good. Up to no good means drinking vodka tonics and sliding into sweet young Kim with abandon. Pretty good for a thirty-seven-year-old, to attract a girl like that. And to be able to do her three times in one afternoon. He can feel himself swagger as he walks up the dusky street, thinking about it, wanting Kim still. And, God, she feels the same about him, can't get enough. He told the people in his office he was going to a client. Kim came along to take notes. To take notes! He chuckles now, walking up the hill, thinking about it.

The rain's washed away the snow. Soon the spring flowers will be coming up in the front gardens on the south side, though they've been up for almost two weeks on the north. Patty made him plant hyacinths six years ago, and they still come up hardy as ever. He can't figure it. You're supposed to refresh bulbs every few years. He's just lucky all around.

Up the street he sees a moving van, and in a few more steps he knows it's the new people moving into the Dunbars' house, next door to his. He has lived on this street his entire life, seen so many people come and go it means very little to him now. His best friends are still around: Hal Shea across the street. Corey Costello, his brother-in-law, just down the block. What does he care if some new people come in? Patty foams at the mouth about it. Squawk, squawk on the telephone all day with Donna Shea about how the yuppies are ruining the street. He doesn't see it. What does he care if they're not all Irish Catholic or aren't members of Saint Agnes, or if they put in fancy bathrooms? What does he care if the wives work or the men carry five-hundred-dollar briefcases. He was never one for class distinctions. He never let anybody intimidate him. He went to college because he wanted to, even though lots of the other guys on the block didn't go. And he became interested in selling insurance because it was something that fit his personality, not because it was a common thing to do. Hal Shea's a plumber. Corey works for the MTA. That doesn't make them part of a different class. He just doesn't think that way. Lately, he's thought about hardly anything but Kim D'Amico. Wherever he goes, she comes along with him, in his head. He remembers her look, the sleek twist of her hip when she walks, the ticking of her high heels on the street as they sneak off to her apartment. Hal and Corey have been teasing him, calling him "spaceman" because he's always dreaming in the middle of poker games. He's just savoring his luck, like a hard candy, something meant to last a long time, delicious, solid. It's too good to be true, but he can taste it.

As he comes up to his own house, he sees the new people's furniture being carried up their stoop: a brand-new sofa the color of cotton candy—they must be childless; who could have such a thing with children around?—and a mahogany side table, gleaming in the dusky light. Rich too. Very chi-chi. He doesn't know squat about style, but he can identify expensive when he sees it. Patty doesn't have a lick of style. If an old brown chair is comfortable and it's cheap, it's Patty's style. The fact is, Patty has no play in her, no joy. She's rigid as a flag-pole. He wonders exactly what he's loved about her since the age of ten. Her straight back, her unforgiving way that made her seem like a prize?

She's in the kitchen when he comes in. They live in the bottom two floors of the narrow brownstone where he's lived all his life. His brother, Keevan, lives upstairs. It's not much space, but it's enough. Patty says that even if they could afford to buy Keevan out, she wouldn't want to clean all four stories. The kitchen smells of short ribs, or something long cooked. Patty's a great cook, but she always cooks the same five or six things. For hours.

"Hello," he says.

"Hello."

"I see the new people are moving in. Did you get a look at them?"

Michelle is sitting at the kitchen table in her plaid school uniform, her braids. She stands up to kiss him.

"They have a little girl. Like around my age."

"Her age, really?" he asks Patty. She turns and looks at him, as if she can see right through him. Can she smell Kim on him? Can she detect his guilt, the way a dog sniffs out fear?

"I didn't see the girl," Patty says. "Did you tell me you'd be late?"

"No. The train was rerouted. We took the A line and then sat at Jay Street forever. Some smoke in the tunnel."

"Did you actually see the smoke, Daddy?" Michelle asks.

"No, sweet. . . . Where's John?"

"In his room, doing homework. I did plan to feed us a half hour ago," Patty says, her voice sour.

"So is the food ruined?" he asks.

"No. It's not ruined. You just should have told me."

Jim's looking at the mail, but he's thinking of Kim. He wonders what she's doing now. Eating Chunky soup and watching the news, probably, in that silky floral robe that opens at the thigh when she sits down. He sighs.

"Well, you can't expect me to serve you whenever you just happen to show up."

"Excuse me," he says to her. "Take it up with your brother. He works for the MTA."

Patty fills the serving plates, yells for John to come downstairs. Jim looks at her. She once was pretty enough. Eyes watery grey like the thick, bubbly drinking glasses his grandmother used to set on this table. Now she just looks pinched. He can't bear to look at her, and turns to Michelle, who seems stalk-like and full of light.

"We had a math quiz today," Michelle says. "I got every one right."

"Great going. You're a whiz, honey. But I didn't need math scores to know that."

"I talked to my mother today," Patty says.

"Yeah?"

"She loves New Jersey. She can't believe she didn't leave Brooklyn sooner. She says Michelle and John would just love the town, and the schools are great."

"What? Does she want us to leave Brooklyn, move there?"

"It was just a suggestion."

"We live in Brooklyn," Jim says, opening a telephone bill and clucking his tongue at the cost. Christ. How did Patty manage to make so many phone calls?

"So what if we've lived here all our lives? It doesn't mean we have to live here forever," Patty says hoarsely. "My mother lived here all her life, and she left. Besides, I don't like what's happening to the neighborhood. Yuppies, Jews, Italians . . . It's like there's no one we know left."

"There's always been Italians. The Canellis are Italian. We like them fine. And you shop at Cordeiro's."

"The Cordeiros are Portuguese."

"So what?"

"I just don't like it. We could have a lawn. Real grass."

"Great, so I can mow it."

John drags in, head down. What a sad-sack kid he is, always was. Michelle is Jim's kind of kid, perky, plucky. John is like Patty in every way. A complaining, judgmental, low-energy kid.

"Hey, sport," he says, smacking John lightly on the shoulder, hoping to feel what he should feel for his own boy.

John looks up with a sneer. "What?"

"I just wanted to say hey."

"Will you pass the meat around," Patty says. "Let's just shut up and eat dinner."


Rose Finney comes down the steps in her new house. Slender and lithe, dragging a droopy dog named Homer behind her. Rose is the perfect image of her father, Jamie: straight eyebrows, caramel-colored hair, a pointed, exasperated chin. Even Rose herself, at the age of six and a half, can see the resemblance when she looks in a mirror.

She doesn't want to look like Jamie, who lies in bed all day and doesn't speak to her, won't look at her, even when she speaks to him. She cannot remember ever being touched by him. Her mother, Zoe, says it's because of what happened to her sister, that it really has nothing to do with her at all. But Rose already knows that there are things parents don't tell you. Her mother didn't tell her until just a week ago that she was going to have to leave the apartment where she was born in Manhattan, with her pretty room and with Fred and Walter, the doormen. She didn't tell her that they were going to move all the way over the bridge to Brooklyn and that for the rest of the year she would have to ride the subway with Teresa to her old school. She's heard from her friends at school that the subway is dangerous. Full of bad guys with guns. Her mother says there are only two and half months until school is over. Doesn't she know that two and a half months is a very long time?

Rose Finney worries about her mother. She's always biting her lip and making it sore-looking, and her eyes are sad, the color of the clear pale marbles Rose got last week from Mary Ellen Axner by trading her headband. Rose knows that her mother would like a husband who would spin her in her arms and dip her like Mary Ellen Axner's father did after dinner one night when Rose was over there. Everyone was giggling, and the dog was barking, and Mary Ellen Axner's father kissed both Mary Ellen and her mother on the forehead with big loud smacks, each kiss like a big slap across Rose's heart, until, leaning over, seeing the look in Rose's eyes, Mary Ellen's father gave her a smack on the forehead too. When she grows up, Rose wants to marry a man like Mary Ellen Axner's father. Or Mary Ellen Axner's father himself, if Mary Ellen's mother dies or something.

Just a few minutes ago, Rose's mother helped put Jamie to bed, after Teresa put sheets and blankets on it. Rose stood inside the room, near the door. She watched him rise up white and stooped and pale from the floor, then fold back into the fresh linens. Like an old man. The movers walked right past as her mother and Teresa helped Jamie. They carried in tables, tall cartons. As they left the room, each glanced over at Jamie, then looked away. Like he had cooties. That's the way Jamie looks at her, when he does. Although lately, he doesn't look at anything.

Now, downstairs, one of the movers is standing frowning at a clipboard with papers on it. Another is sitting on the floor by the front door, looking bored. He looks up at Rose. "Hello," he says.

"Are you done?" she asks him.

"Looks like it. Looks like you're in for good."

"Yuck," Rose says.

"Don't you like being here? Great house. You came from a nice place too."

"A much better place," Rose says, sighing.

"Your daddy's pretty sick, huh? What's the matter with him?"

"We're not supposed to talk about it," Rose says. "I don't think."

Zoe comes from the back of the house. "Is that it?" she asks.

"Just sign these three papers," the man says, handing her the clipboard.

Rose sees that her mother is smiling as she signs, that her eyes have more color than usual, are almost swimming-pool blue. She comes up to Zoe and puts her arms around her hips. Her mother is skinny and not so cuddly as some mothers, she knows. But she smells good. Like warm blankets. She nuzzles her nose into her mother's hip. Zoe's hands are full of clipboard and pen, and she doesn't run her hand along Rose's neck the way she usually does, until she passes the clipboard over to the man; and then she caresses Rose just below her hairline, in a way that makes her skin feel like it's sparkling.

When the men are gone, Zoe takes Rose upon her knee on the sofa. They sit in silence for a long time in the near dark, Rose resting her ear against Zoe's skinny chest.

"This is going to be our home," Zoe says.

Rose's eyes take in the empty bookshelves and mantel, the unadorned tables, the half-dark.

"It's spooky," she says.

"We'll make it our home. Once I unpack the lamps and lightbulbs, that will make a big difference. We're going to do everything just our way in this house. Not Grandma Finney's way."

Rose knows that the apartment in Sutton Place, the only one she's ever known, was given to them by Grandma Finney. And that her mother always hated the furniture there. Rose, on the other hand, already misses it. There were lots of curlicues to feel, gold-painted edges, ruffles.

"We'll put out all the things we love," her mother says, staring into this new dark room. "And the paintings we like."

"It won't be the same," Rose says. "It won't be ours."

"Oh, it will. We'll put the portrait of Aunt Delia there," Zoe says, pointing to the wall above the marble mantel. "And in your room you can set up all the dolls, make a new doghouse for Homer—"

"I already did that. I folded those two blankets that were mine when I was a baby, and I put in a baby bottle. Homer's going to try to get used to it."

"Is Homer still drinking from a bottle?"

"Of course. He's still a baby dog, isn't he?" Rose raises Homer's droopy, understuffed, overloved head and kisses the dirty plush of his nose, then turns it toward Zoe so she can kiss him too.

"Poor, dirty old Homer," Zoe says. "He needs a bath in dry-cleaning fluid."

"That isn't very nice, Mama. Don't hurt his feelings."

"Sorry."

"Will you lie down in my bed with me until I fall asleep tonight, Mama?"

"You never ask me to do that."

"But I don't like it here. It's spooky. You always lie down with Jamie until he's asleep. And he's a grown-up."

Zoe gives Rose a funny look for a moment, then smiles slightly. "Okay, ducky," she says. "If Homer doesn't object. I'm kind of taking his job away, aren't I?"

"Oh, he won't mind. We'll pretend you're his grandmother."

"Come on. Let's go downstairs to the kitchen, and I'll give you a snack before we go up. Teresa went out earlier to get you some milk and fudge stick cookies."

Rose loves the way her mother's hand feels in hers. She is sorry when Zoe lets go to hold on to the banister. Rose slides her hand along the banister behind her mother's, expecting it to be warm. Instead it is smooth and cool, like the back of the wooden horse Grandma Finney gave her last Christmas. Nice. Still, Rose doesn't like this house, with so many floors, so many stairs. The apartment in Sutton Place was all on one floor, so she could be near Zoe wherever she was.

Coming into the kitchen, Rose blinks in the sharp light. Their housekeeper, Teresa, is at the sink, scrubbing pots. The room is overflowing with open packing boxes full of pots and pans and glasses; and the crushed and twisted newspaper Teresa's pulled from them. Rose kicks a piece of newspaper, and it flies up, then flutters back into the pile.

"I wash tonight," Teresa tells Zoe. "Too much to do. I don't wait."

"Yes," Zoe says. "Thank you."

"Are there fudge stick cookies, Teresa?" Rose asks, coming up near her. Teresa always smells like cherry cough drops, though she's never seen her eating one. Rose has discovered it's from the gooey gel she smooths on her grey-black hair when she puts it in a bun. Rose has watched Teresa dress. Mornings when she was little, she would come into Teresa's room and talk and watch her. Teresa always put on a white silky slip before she put on her clothes. The silk would cover up the nice soft rolls of her belly, the ugly stitched-up cotton bra she wore. Rose liked the way the pale silky slip straps looked against her round, dark-skinned shoulders, and sometimes Teresa would let Rose pet her shoulders. Rose's mother once told her that Teresa had beautiful olive-colored skin, and Rose would always imagine Teresa's shoulders as two smooth green olives.

Always before she finished dressing, Teresa would put on her only piece of jewelry: a gold cross engraved with the word "Jesus." Rose sometimes would ask if she could put it on just for a minute, but Teresa never let her. It was a gift from her daughter in Guatemala, she said, and it was too special for a little girl to wear.

Now Rose looks beyond the cluttered kitchen to the tiny pale-blue room where Teresa will sleep. Rose can see the bed is already made and that Teresa's already hung her big wooden cross with the droopy-looking Jesus. Teresa has told her all about Jesus, but Rose has never understood why Teresa'd want to have him hanging over her bed all limp and dead.

"Teresa," Rose says again, louder, figuring she can't be heard over the running water. "Mama says you got fudge stick cookies." She takes hold of Teresa's skirt, then lets go. Teresa hates it when she pulls on her.

"No. They no have fudge stick. I bought others."

"They don't have fudge sticks in Brooklyn?" Rose says, feeling the disappointment like a thump in the chest. "I knew it."

"I'm sure they do," Zoe says. "We'll just have to find out where."

Rose sits down heavily on her favorite kitchen chair, the one with the seat stuffed fatter than the rest. At least the chairs are familiar.

Teresa shuts off the water. The silence makes Rose's ears ring. "I bought these," Teresa says, bringing over a bag of Oreos.

Rose looks in horror at the Oreos and starts to cry. She can't help it. "I don't like Oreos," she says. "I never eat Oreos." Her mouth fills with salty disappointment.

Zoe shakes her head at her. "You ate them last week."

"I don't like them anymore," she says. "Mama . . . I want to go home."

Zoe sits down next to her and kisses her forehead. "This is our home now, lovey," she says. "It takes time to get used to new things. We'll find you fudge sticks at another store. Tomorrow. I promise."

"I buy fudge sticks . . . somewhere," Teresa says.

Rose crosses her arms and lays her head down on the table. She thinks about earlier in the day, when she waved goodbye to Fred and Walter. How lucky it was, her mother said, that the family was leaving right when the doorman shift was changing, so Rose could see both of them one last time. They stood there side by side in their blue uniforms: Fred all tall and skinny and funny. And Walter with his wrinkly face and saggy eyes. She let them each say goodbye to Homer, holding him up to their faces, waving his limp paw. Walter even kissed him. "Goodbye, old man," he said.

"No," Rose said. "Homer's just a baby."

"Goodbye, old baby, then," Walter said, laughing, his face drooping just like Homer's.

Now Rose will never see Fred and Walter again. Or Sutton Place, or the play park, or Mary Ellen, even if Zoe says she will. It's a fact. Rose is stuck here forever in a place that has no doormen and no fudge sticks, no Mary Ellen, no elevator, and—she sighs just thinking about it— way too many stairs.

Long past midnight, Patty O'Connor looks over at her husband. For hours, she has listened to Jim sleep, snoring faintly, the alarm clock ticking in time with his whistling breath. Unable to sleep herself, she is thinking about the new family next door. Yuppies. Another family of yuppies, even though Jim said hardly any more would move in after the stock market nose-dived. But here's another one. She can tell already. Jim says she shouldn't call them yuppies; it's a stupid expression. But Patty suspects that Jim wants to be one himself. Besides, if she feels like calling them yuppies, what right does he have to tell her not to? This is her neighborhood.

She was born across and just up the street from here. In 720. The one with the blue curtains and the stained-glass cross. Since her mother moved to New Jersey, her brother, Corey, and his family have lived on the top two floors, her aunt Siobhan has kept the parlor floor, and Patty's old math teacher, Sister Mary Paul, rents the ground floor, because she's too old now to climb the steps of Saint Agnes convent. It's Sister Mary Paul's cross in the window. It does Patty's heart good every day to see it, catching the light when the sun rises high enough over the houses on Patty's side of the street, and sending off a faint blush of a rainbow on the window itself.

It's never occurred to Patty until now to leave this street. Except for a few family vacations to Niagara Falls, except for the two summers her friend Donna's parents bought a beach club membership on Breezy Point and let her come along, everything that's ever happened to Patty has happened here on Eighth Street. When she married Jim up the street at Saint Agnes, her family brought her things down the street that afternoon in a wheelbarrow: her suitcases, her old stuffed animals and spelling trophies, her wedding pillow, embroidered by her mother. Half the block came out to wish them well. The Shaughnessys brought a bottle of wine; the McNamaras a casserole in a heavy cast-iron pot, which they insisted that Patty keep. It was used, but it was still a nice present. A pot well seasoned, a pot well loved. She used it tonight. Uses it practically every night. And that is what this neighborhood has been for her until now: a pot well seasoned. Reliable. Broken in, in a good, comfortable way.

Her family's been here in some form since 1931, and Jim's family has lived in 643 since 1917. When his grandparents bought the place, the tree in the backyard must have been half its present size. It covers six backyards now, and nobody knows what kind of tree it is. It drops soft strings of seeds, yellow as bananas. All the neighborhood gang used to play under it as kids, pretending the seeds were money. The palms of their hands were yellow as buttercups when the game was over. How she remembers! Lisa and Brian O'Shea. The older Kilkenny twins, with their hair the color of pennies. Her brother, Corey, and of course Jim, the boy who would someday become her husband, his brother Keevan, and their brother, Ralph.

Patty still feels the sadness grip her when she thinks of Ralph. She loved him more than the other two O'Connor brothers once, though he always treated her like a little sister. How gentle he was, how funny. When Ralph was killed in Vietnam, half the street draped their houses with flags. Father Joe came down the street from Saint Agnes and sat with the O'Connors three days running. Come Veterans Day, the flags still go up on the houses of the people who are left, who remember.

And it was the week of Ralph's death that she discovered her feelings for Keevan. She remembers coming into his bedroom the night of Ralph's funeral. He was sixteen then, a slender, fragile version of his present self. His reddish hair was longer than that of any of the other boys on the street. Almost like a hippie's hair. And she remembers how slender and white his wrists were. He was sprawled on his bed, weeping loudly, his hands covering his eyes, his white wrists exposed. While, downstairs, Jim was saying, "The stupid bastard. I hate him for dying," Keevan was weeping for the loss of him. That should have told her something right there. She sat down on the corded blue bedspread beside Keevan and, in the dusky light, rubbed his slender back, played with the long strands of his red-gold hair. He turned his tear-stained face to her. "Patty, I don't know how I'm ever going to wake up tomorrow morning. I don't know how we can go on eating and breathing and sleeping when he's dead." She put her arms around Keevan and held him for an hour, cradling his head like a baby. She remembers the temptation to kiss him. She could feel it in her lips, like a buzz, a thrill of desire. How it embarrassed her: here they were mourn-

ing Ralph, just having buried Ralph, and she, at the age
of twenty, was longing to kiss a weeping sixteen-year-old.

For weeks after that, the neighbors visited the O'Connors daily. Bringing food for the old couple, spending time
cheering up the boys. Five or six people would crowd
the parlor every night, and she'd often be among them.
Gossiping, sharing, remembering.

That's what's gone now. The certainty of it. Knowing
your neighbors. Knowing they know you. That they worry
if you've had too many colds, that they gossip if you step
out of line. She never even minded the scrutiny. Everybody's always known that her husband, Jim, is selfish and
preoccupied. Everybody's always known her feelings for
her brother-in-law. "How's Keevan?" those who are still
around ask, with glittering eyes. She doesn't mind. It
makes her feel important. They care about her welfare.
They care about her soul. But more and more people are
moving out, or dying out. And selling their houses for
hundreds of thousands of dollars to Wall Streeters and
Madison Avenue advertising types.

Simply, Patty O'Connor feels a sense of loss as clear
as she felt when they buried Ralph. Maybe Jim will never
understand, though he grew up here too.

She used to think Jim was fascinating; different from
Ralph and Keevan, not as kind or as full of fun, not as
much of a dreamer, but special in his own way. He was
more serious, more likely to succeed, than his friends. He
took books about everything out of the Brooklyn Public
Library: aeronautical engineering, genetics, fly fishing,
even literature, like Hemingway. Patty never thought she
wanted more than to be a housewife; still, she'd always
wanted a husband who was successful, steady. And Jim
has been that. But something hurts her: something is missing. He never looks at her with any interest. He never
shows her real respect anymore. He never thanks her for
the things she cooks him. When she was a new bride, she
bought a whole shelf of recipe books and tried everything

that seemed vaguely interesting, but Jim never seemed to like anything unfamiliar or new.

"What is this?" he'd ask, his lip curling just slightly. So what's the point of trying?

Whenever she goes to confession, she talks about her feelings of disloyalty to her husband, and Monsignor O'Hardy asks her in what way she's sinned. "I had four angry thoughts against my husband," she says. "Three Hail Marys," Monsignor O'Hardy says. But she can't tell him that once, in a fit of pique, when Jim forgot their seventeenth anniversary, she thought of poisoning him with d-Con. And then there's last New Year's Eve, when she let Hal Shea press up against her in the kitchen, kiss her with his tongue and put his hand in her blouse. She was a little drunk, but she hoped he meant something by it, even though Donna Shea is just about her best friend. But nothing has happened since. She's thought about herself more since then, though. She put on lipstick for a few weeks after that and put combs in her brown hair when Hal came to play poker, but he looked at her the same as always, with basic disinterest, and she has begun to wonder if he even remembers.

And she could never tell the monsignor about her feelings for Keevan. Keevan lives upstairs now, on the top two floors of the house, and she can't help it, how she still feels about him, the daydreams she has. She seeks out things to do for Keevan. Her family uses only the downstairs door, but she always salts the front stoop when it's icy, so Keevan won't slip when he climbs the stoop to his door. She leaves slices of roast beef in his refrigerator, plastic-wrapped on a plate, or a piece of pie. He loves her apple pie. Tonight she left him some short ribs, some cottage potatoes. She knows he never heats the food. Just unwraps it and eats it cold, alone at his kitchen table. Today, when she left the food, she wandered around his apartment. For a man, he keeps it neat, though not as clean as she would. Still, his living room is the prettiest room in the house, the way he's painted the walls maple syrup brown, has so many shelves of books, some of them his grandfather's, old and bound in leather. The masculinity of the room always excites her. She likes to touch everything that belongs to Keevan. To imagine he's there with her. This afternoon, she climbed up to his bedroom, on the fourth floor, and made the bed. A piece of his pretty red-gold hair still clung to the pillow, and she wrapped it around her finger. She pulled his pillow to her face and breathed in the scent of him. Human, warm. She lay down and pressed her body into his bed, imagined what it would feel like to have him beside her.

My God, she thinks, as she lies beside her husband now. I am in love with my brother-in-law. If that isn't the most terrible sin of all!

To shut out the feeling she has for Keevan and the guilt about it that seems to push the very breath out of her chest, she begins to think about New Jersey. Every time she drives the children out to her mother's new town house, there Patty feels released, younger. It's something she could never explain to Jim, wouldn't even try. Last summer, when her mother first moved out there, Patty, on her first visit, kicked off her shoes and walked barefoot in the stiff, dark-green grass. Michelle joined her, and before Patty knew it, they were running, all along the continuous lawns in back of the houses, down to the little stream that separated the town house properties from the corporate park behind it. The stream was clear as tap water, smelled sweet, and they dipped their toes in it. Icy even in July, it made them giggle and lean against each other with shared joy, like two schoolgirls playing hooky. Michelle kicked her feet in the water, got her pink shorts soaked, but Patty didn't reprimand her. The sky was so open and softly blue, the air so fresh, the stream so tingly, she couldn't even find the central wick of anger that so often seemed to ignite in her. She couldn't find the need to control Michelle, to teach her. She felt lazy and young and without any responsibility at all.

Jim didn't come with them that day, has never yet to

come to her mother's house. He always has paperwork to do, or bills. She's thought of asking Keevan to come see it. He would appreciate the grass, the stream, the clear air. But part of the draw of moving out there is escaping Keevan, escaping the impossibility of caring for him. She gets up from her bed now, and feeling a heat about her ears, a muffler of shame, she goes out into the hall, propelled, unstoppable, and climbs two stories, up to his bedroom. She always waits until she feels safe to do this. There hasn't been a footstep for hours up there; it's well past midnight, and Keevan, like Jim, sleeps like the dead. She has an excuse ready too: Did I leave my watch up here? I washed a dish or two. I always take it off . . .

This is worse than nail biting, worse than eavesdropping or prying. What absolution would absolve this?

She silently, slowly opens the door to his room. Her eyes, already used to the low light, can see him clearly. He is sleeping naked, half on top of the covers. Her heart pounds. At least once a week she comes up here and stares at his sleek body, the covers caught and twisted between his long legs, his beautiful, angelic face, the dark, soft curl of his penis. She dreams of him waking up, inviting her into his bed. "Patricia," he would whisper. Like one of those romance books she likes to borrow from Donna. She closes her eyes, clenches her fists. She runs her closed fist down the length of her nightgown. Forgive me, Father, for I have sinned and sinned and sinned. Keevan. Who could resist his laughing golden eyes, his broad chest, his capable hands? God has set temptation in my way, and I have failed the test. "I will try not to want him. I will try," she whispers, like a prayer, before she goes downstairs to bed.

At nearly 3:00 A.M., the night is punctuated by a car hurtling down Eighth Street, streaming rock music and laughter; high-school kids out for late-night fun. In her bed, asleep for two hours now, Patty turns fitfully and makes it part of her dream. But upstairs, anticipating his alarm clock, set for this unlikely hour, Keevan O'Connor wakes and listens to the Doppler effect of wild fun, and for a moment, even half asleep, he is washed in exuberance. Moments like this remind him: once, he was king of John Jay High School. He sang in a rock band called Dare Me. Girls hung on him. Boys imitated him. He drove a turquoise Ford, which he packed with his friends. The music on the radio called the neighborhood to run to their windows and see the fun. At night, in bed, his body would tingle with possibility. He could almost see electricity jumping branched and blue from his skin.

Keevan is thirty-four now, a high-school teacher himself, and that zest for life still seems to arc around him. He feels ageless, ready for anything. Simple things still please him utterly. Like the bright-blue plastic they wrap around *The New York Times* before they throw it on his stoop: the color reminds him of his old Ford. If he tears the film off the newspaper and holds it up to his eyes, the whole world is a great, glorious swimming blue. And the Norwegian maple in front of his house. The maples on the block were planted when he was four or five. Now they line the street with their shock of leaves, stretch higher than the houses, and he can hardly remember, except to hear Jim tell it, when the street was nearly bare and they could play baseball smack in the middle of the road in summer and not have to worry about the obstruction of the branches. His students who read books far more complex than he'd expect them to read, and really understand and enjoy them, thrill him. And then there are his nights in the park, like the one he's planning tonight.

Keevan can clearly remember the first time it happened. He was restless one night in August two years ago. It was just after his divorce, and the apartment seemed to echo without Helayne. It still smelled of her hair spray and perfume, the powder she doused herself with—under her breasts, between her legs—leaving a cloud of it on the hardwood floor. She was long gone, yet her powder still lined the cracks of the floor that night. The hangers in the closet jangled, creaked in unison, without her clothes. The empty spaces where the bed table, the comfortable chair, the dresser, had been seemed to laugh at Keevan. In bed, the sheets were cold and sweaty, though Keevan himself was sure he was burning up. Not knowing what had awakened him, he got up and stumbled to the window. How disoriented he felt! How lackluster! As though, in leaving, Helayne had taken not just half the furniture and all the wedding gifts but his zest for life, the one thing that made him most himself. Staring out into the empty street that night, he knew what had brought him out of his sleep: in the Norwegian maple, a mad, crazy bird was singing its heart out. Not one song but a hundred different songs, repeating nothing, one melody after another, and loud! So loud it seemed to rattle the windows. Could a mockingbird have strayed too far north? What made it sing so loud, so well, so thrillingly at two in the morning? He strained to see the valiant little bird, but could see nothing in the thicket of green leaves. And then it began to do the oddest thing. It began to imitate a car alarm, the kind that has four different warnings. First the *whoopwhoopwhoop* of an ambulance, then the old-fashioned spinning sound of the twelve-o'clock whistle, then the blare of a modern fire truck, and last, the terrifying bray of a Gestapo wagon: *heehawheehaw*. It was mimicking them all, and on pitch. Laughing, recovering his joy for life with the suddenness of a cold shower, Keevan shivered with pleasure. In imitating the overwrought alarm, the bird was mocking all of Brooklyn. But also celebrating its passion, its uncertainty, its absurdity, together in one song.

That night, tingling, thrilled, Keevan pulled on his clothes. He knew he couldn't sleep with the bird making its exultant racket. He simply had to go out. The air felt odd and wonderful and soft as he came out the door and strode shyly down the steps. He felt so excited. Why? Why did the night feel like such a challenge? Out on Eighth Street, he was suddenly struck with the exhilarating certainty that he was the only one enjoying this, seeing this. He stood under the tree awhile, searching for the bird, then, giving up, he walked up the street toward the park, marveling at how his footsteps made the most extraordinarily loud sound, how even his breathing seemed notable in the lamplit silence. He began to smell the wet trees, the newly mown grass, their sharp aromas waking him even more. Helayne would never have gone out this late. And, especially, never have gone into Prospect Park! Two miles wide and dark, punctuated by lakes and woods and ravines—the dangers in a place like that! Helayne spoke of dangers all the time. She liked the safe, the tried and true. She refused even to taste an artichoke, for fear of pricking her finger on the leaf tips.

It was thinking of what Helayne wouldn't do that made him long to go into the park. Keevan knew it was dangerous. He knew it wasn't unlikely he might run into a street gang, a psycho, a mugger, or a cop who might mistake him for any of the above. But he was enticed by the smell, the danger. Other men climb mountains, he thought to himself, or raft through rapids. Why not explore Prospect Park at night, grab the risk by the throat and own it? Suddenly he was walking past the monument of Lafayette that he used to climb when he was a kid, the brass of Lafayette's sword polished pink by millions of sticky little hands using it as a handhold. He was passing the playground, with its swings creaking in the breeze, the hot wind whipping at the slide, making weird bonging sounds like an African drum. He was running into the hollow of the Sheep Meadow, thrilled at how the grass squeaked beneath his sneakers, how it tickled and drenched his bare ankles.

Everything seemed to sparkle and sing around him. Standing in the middle of the Sheep Meadow, tinted an eerie, exquisite green by the lamplight, he wondered if he was dreaming. He couldn't see a single high-rise behind the trees. He could have been in Maine or Pennsylvania. All around him, the trees waved, their long branches graceful as ballerinas' arms. At the edge of the ravine on the

far side of the meadow, he could just make out two raccoons pawing playfully at each other.

Keevan felt a charge of joy through his heart, so sweet
and explosive it weakened his knees. God had done all
right by man. After Ralph was killed in Vietnam, Father
Joe tried to tell him: See the joy the world has to offer.
It's not just in the obvious. Thank God for each moment,
each subtle, remarkable moment.

And then Keevan heard a noise, a human invasive
sound, rowdy laughter, war whoops. Feeling his heart fold
up, tuck itself away, and harden with fear, he moved to
the edge of the ravine, not far from the raccoons, which,
completely ignoring him, continued their play. He heard
the silken shuffle of clothing. He heard language,
challenges.

"Get out, mother, you lie."

"Shut the fuck up, Davon. Shut the fuck up."

"No, man, it's true."

Keevan was embarrassed to be skulking in the woods,
watching. Three black teenage boys, laughing, shoving
each other, rose from the dark of the ravine and began to
traverse the Sheep Meadow. Boys the age of his own
students.

"Hey," Keevan called out, surprising himself. It was
almost involuntary. He wanted to share this moment with
them, not have it spoiled by fear. I'm out of my mind,
he thought.

"Hey," he called again. What on earth was making him
do this?

But the boys' bodies stiffened. He could see it even
from across the meadow.

"Oh, shit, let's get the fuck out of here," one called
out, and then they were running, all long legs and panic,
cutting a swath through the wet emerald grass and up the
embankment Keevan had just come down. They were as
scared of Keevan as he was of them! Keevan began to
laugh, so hard it hurt his belly. His laughter magnified
itself in the wet air. And that was his mistake, for up on

the ridge one teenager turned around, and Keevan could
see him, as though in slow motion, extend his arm. And
like a circus trick, for an instant, fire splashed from the
end of his arm. It seemed a long time afterward that Keevan heard the crack of that gunshot, longer still that he
heard the bullet whispering past his ear. He ran to the edge
of the thicket and, squeezing between the sharp branches,
crouched there, his heart chugging wildly. I might die, he
thought. They might come after me now. Childhood pray-
ers came to his lips. "O Lord, this day please protect
me . . ." He squeezed his eyes shut. When he opened
them, the teenagers were gone.

Standing up, his shirt wet, his legs weak with fear, he
felt more utterly alive than he could remember ever being.
And he felt oddly purified, in a way he hadn't since before
things went bad with Helayne.

He did not go back to the park at night right away. A
month passed, and he felt his energy ebbing, and he woke
one night with a restlessness that propelled him. That first
night in the park had been an epiphany, a rebirth, and he
had a need now for its transfusive qualities. With a gang
of six or seven rats galloping past him, and a schizophrenic
screaming at him to get off his "property," his second
sojourn once again mixed fear and pleasure.

He isn't sure why he needs this test, this cleansing, but
now it draws him at least once a week. It excites him to
know that lurking among the trees there are bums, gang
members, murderers. They add the fear, the edge that
makes the beauty even more sharp, even more seductive.

The alarm clock jangles now, sending an electric jolt to
the tips of his fingers. He gets out of bed stretching to
ease the ache in his muscles. Nothing else could get him
up out of bed at this hour. Nothing else makes him feel
quite so hopeful. But lately, even the park is not enough
to distract him from the fact that his heart is bruised and
hollow. He was seeing a woman for a while, Tina Block,
a fellow teacher, the first person he even considered being
serious about since Helayne, but in the end he pushed her

away too. Oh, there were reasons to turn from her. He discovered, for instance, that Tina, like Helayne, had no sense of adventure. Both of them had had everything given to them since they were born. Both disliked change or surprise. Was it her similarity to Helayne that made him shut Tina out? When he told her about the park, she railed at him, called him a lunatic. "Great, get yourself killed. I always wanted to have a dead boyfriend."

Easing into his jacket, he tries to put Tina out of his mind, to focus only on the park, the dark surprises he may find there. All day, he has spoken to no one. He read, he walked to the grocery store, he napped. When Tina was around, he yearned for that kind of silence. She never stopped talking. Never stopped trying to make him admit things he didn't feel, feel things he couldn't. Wasn't it better this way?

Stepping out the door, he is startled by the cooling night air and breathes it in with thirst. He feels he owns all the night air of Brooklyn. Stopping for a moment to zip his jacket, he notices the packing cartons at the house next door, six or seven wardrobe boxes set out on the curb. The dew forming on them sends off the scent of wet cardboard and reminds him of the night Helayne moved in with him, bringing along a wardrobe that shoved his clothes right out of the closet and on their way to Goodwill. He kicks one of the boxes as he passes it, and the boom seems to echo all the way up the street.

# TWO

———————◆———————

Monday at 7:00 A.M., the sun spills through the trees of Prospect Park and cuts into the windows on the south side of Eighth Street. Shutters open. Employees from Methodist Hospital, on Seventh Street, walk wearily from the night shift and start their cars, waking up the children too young to need to wake up for school. Darlene Kilkenny's new baby cries out so loudly you can hear him on the street. Her husband, Donald, is asleep on the couch with all his clothes on. So drunk last night, it's amazing he came home at all. The street's older children, the ones who do need to wake up, like the O'Neill teenagers, lie submerged beneath warm covers, shaking their heads. No. Not another school day.

Like them, Keevan O'Connor has never outgrown the response to burrow, to procrastinate. Despite a good full night of sleep, he is exhausted, probably because he was up half of Saturday night in Prospect Park: it usually takes two days to hit him. Oh, but what a night it was! He stayed in the park until nearly dawn, walking its perimeter, mapping the ravines, the meadow, smelling spring rise up from the oozing paths. God, he must be getting old. Yesterday he was a total zombie. And now he can't help tunneling deeper under his quilt, hoping that the time before his snooze alarm goes off again will seem much longer than it really is. He's been late to work three times in the last two weeks, and he knows he needs to get a move on, take his shower and bolt for the school. But ever since he broke up with Tina, he's found it hard to face the other teachers. Everyone's taken sides regarding them. "She's a bitch," some people have told him. "You bastard!" others say. Why does it matter to them?

Now he struggles out of bed and wraps his old terry bathrobe around his slender frame. The robe is far too short. He feels like a fool in it. Tina bought him the perfect bathrobe: red and black buffalo checked, flannel, generously long. But when they broke up, she took it back. "I can use this," she said, bundling it into her angry little arms. He tells himself that he misses the robe far more than he misses Tina.

But as he dresses he thinks of her, how she would call him "Keeeevan" and talk in a baby voice. How when he made love to Tina, she cooed and thrilled at his hands on her, at the initial delicious shock of their coupling. And afterward she would stroke his hair and whisper to him, but he would lie there empty and angry, feeling somehow that she'd drained him of his very blood. Later, he would feel guilty for how coolly he treated her, how remote he'd become. How wrong it had seemed from the start.

He sighs and grabs a piece of bread, doesn't have time to toast it but smears it with margarine and the dregs of some apricot jam, folds it in half, and, carrying it with one hand, goes down the stairs past Patty and Jim's, hoping Patty doesn't come out and try to talk to him. Patty's another one. He likes her okay. He feels sorry for her mostly, married to his coldhearted bastard of a brother. But the fact that she's set her heart on Keevan shocks him. She doesn't try to hide it at all. Keevan wonders why Jim doesn't seem to notice. Sometimes Keevan thinks he should tell him, "Jim, your wife needs some attention." But Jim wouldn't hear him anyway. The jerk. Keevan gets past their door without detection, steps out on the stoop, and locks the door safely behind him. Thank God.

And then he sees her: his new neighbor, standing right

next to him, in the doorway at the top of her stoop. Wearing a watermelon-colored robe awash with big cabbagy flowers, she is looking in the other direction, up the street. Her hair is the color of ginger ale and equally alive, fizzy with light. Her skin—what he can see of her smooth cheekbone—looks fresh-washed and rosy.

"Hello," he says.

The woman starts, turns to him. There is something touchingly awkward about her, self-conscious. And she is painfully thin. But delicate, with clear eyes like a child's. She draws her robe about her neck.

"You're my new neighbor," Keevan says.

"I guess so."

"I'm Keevan O'Connor."

"I'm Zosia Finney," she says. Her voice is powdery, deep. She stretches out her hand and then laughs. They are too far away to reach each other.

"Where'd you move from?"

"Manhattan," she tells him. Her lips are the color of those fake pink pearls his grandmother used to wear when he was a kid, and equally luminous, yet it doesn't look as if she's wearing lipstick. How could a woman who looked like this be so self-conscious? All the beautiful women he's known have had a certain chilling ruthlessness.

"Zosia. I've never heard that name before," he tells her.

"It's Polish."

"Zosia . . ."

"My parents were from Poland. Most people call me Zoe. Zosia is distracting to people somehow."

"I like it. It's beautiful, really. Zo-o-osia. Welcome to Park Slope, Zosia."

"Thank you." Zosia looks down at her hands and smiles. "In Manhattan, no one says welcome at all, or knows each other's names."

"It's nothing like Manhattan here," Keevan says.

"I think I saw your wife out in your yard yesterday. I was going to come out and talk to her, but . . . well, I guess I felt shy."

"You must mean my sister-in-law, Patty. Believe me, I don't have a wife." He raises his hands like a teller in a bank robbery.

"Do you have something against wives?" she asks wryly, but cautiously, like someone about to dip a toe in a possibly cold pool. She looks up at him through her lashes. Her eyes are amazing. Pale, but almost turquoise.

"No. I had one once. Wives are just fine," he says, "but maybe not . . . not for me."

Even though he's embarrassed at how he's stumbling over his words, Keevan can't stop looking at her. It's impossible that someone this lovely could live in the house next door to him. He supposes she's married. No one who isn't married buys a whole house. Too bad. But she certainly is an improvement over grouchy Nora Dunbar.

"Do you live with your sister-in-law and brother?" she asks him.

"The house is kind of divided up," he says. He realizes that he is not far from Patty and Jim's bedroom window, that they can probably hear every word he is telling their pretty new neighbor. "It works out fine," he says, though recently, with Patty mooning over him, he has his doubts. Once, he even dreamed she came into his room while he was sleeping.

"That's nice," Zosia says. "I mean, to be surrounded by extended family and all."

"Sure," Keevan says. "Well"—he shrugs—"gotta get to work."

"See you," she says.

"I hope so," Keevan says. "I really really hope so." He walks down the block. Christ, he thinks, taking a bite of his bread and jam. I have just spoken to the most amazing woman I've ever met, and I sounded like a fourteen-year-old.

Zoe stands awhile more on the stoop, watching Keevan O'Connor walk down the street toward the subway. He has a nice loping gait, rangy and confident like a cowboy's. Though he is turned away from her now, she can still envision his face clearly: its windburned ruddiness, which avoids the crinkles at the corner of his eyes (they are like white stars); the straight, masculine line of his lips; and his hair, which is the most remarkable feature of all—the color of polished bronze. She's never seen hair quite that color.

When the echo of Keevan's footsteps is gone, all is silent a few moments, but for the birds. They twitter and scatter and meet again inside and outside the gate of the house next door to Keevan's. She laughs at them, so insistent, so busy. Hearing a long, painful squeak, she looks the other way. Up the street, a ragged man is pushing a red cart. He stops at each gate, opens it, and rifles through the trash cans. There is a chuckling sound as he sifts through each blue recycling can, looking for returnables. Zoe sighs. As he comes closer, she sees he's wearing a dark-blue stocking cap and a ripped blue ski jacket—too warm for this spring morning. She has noticed that many homeless people seem to have lost their thermostats in some way. They wear only shirtsleeves in winter, all their clothing, layered, one over the other, in summer. The man comes to Zoe's gate, sees her at the top of the stoop, and goes on to the next house, resignedly, not wanting, she supposes, to tangle with her. Finishing an inspection of Keevan's garbage, he stretches in the morning sun and puts one hand flat against his back as though it pains him. A black man, he is very tall, rather elegant despite his shabbiness. But his face has a dry, gray sadness. Suddenly Zoe hears pounding. Keevan's sister-in-law is standing in the window next door, yelling: "Get out of here. I mean it. I'll call the police." Even through the glass, her voice is piercing.

The man, at his own pace, tamps down the few cans he's found at the O'Connors' into a bag in his cart and steers it out the gate and down the sidewalk to the next house, unfazed, probably used to the abuse. Keevan's sister-in law still stands by her window, her eyes squinted, her hands balled up with anger.

Zoe draws her robe close and shuts her door. The man's homelessness has touched her. She has known poverty, hungry, gnawing poverty, and yet it was never this hopeless: never like this.

As Zoe Finney climbs the stairs to wake Rose for school, she touches everything with delight. Mine, she thinks. Mine.

Always before, she has been a guest in her homes. And not always a welcome one. The Sutton Place apartment they left yesterday had been a wedding present from Jamie's parents, given to them along with the engagement party at the Pierre and a pair of hideous Foo dogs. "Of course, the newlyweds will live at Aunt Delia's. It's been empty for months," her mother-in-law-to-be declared to the entire engagement mob. Neither Zoe nor Jamie, each twenty-one and unsure of everything, had had the personal strength to speak up. To say, "Let us at least be the ones to decide." Besides, who could turn down an absolutely free river-view co-op with three bedrooms? Zoe, who hadn't had a penny all her life and had bad nights wondering if somehow, unbeknownst to her, she was marrying Jamie for his money, was thrilled with the thought of a beautiful place to live. Even with the ugly Foo dogs on the mantel. After growing up over a dry-cleaning store she could not easily turn her back on a Sutton Place apartment. But sometimes, late at night, sitting on late great Aunt Delia's gold brocade sofa, she sobbed, because she felt like a stranger in her own home.

Now she sits down on the step and looks below her into the hallway at the front parlor, bathed in buttery morning light. It is mostly empty, waiting for her taste, her choices. For now, she can't envision a single thing she might put in it. A soft, cushiony sofa fuller than the pink one in the back parlor but what color, dark or light? A round table with a beautiful lamp. But what sort of wood, what kind of lamp? For a while, she thinks, this house will echo, until she learns what pleases her. She will be patient, though. Patience is the one thing at which she's always excelled. Climbing the steps to wake Rose, she thinks: I will climb these stairs every morning. I will hear the same steps creak. This house is mine, and I will know it the way I've never known a house before.

When Zoe silently eases open the door to her daughter's room, she finds Rose asleep on top of the covers, naked except for a baggy pair of striped underpants. Her skinniness breaks Zoe's heart. How beautiful she is! Such a miracle! She touches Rose's cool back.

"Rosie," she whispers. "Morning. Rosie . . . come on, lovey."

Rose groans and rolls over, but her eyes are still shut. Her upper lip protrudes over her lower one. Her eyeballs move frantically beneath their lids, caught in a dream.

"Ring around the Rosie. Pockets full of posies. Ashes, ashes, it's time to go to school."

"No," Rose says suddenly.

"Come on. Teresa's going to take you on the subway." Already Zoe can smell Teresa making cinnamon toast downstairs.

"I hate the subway."

"Sorry, pal."

"Are we going to live here forever?" Rose asks, suddenly, miraculously wide awake. This is how she always wakes, with no warning, no reentry. She sits up, waits for an answer to her question.

"Maybe," Zoe says. "Come on, let's get up and go into the bathroom." Rose is standing in an instant, holding Homer by the neck, trotting, not walking, to the bathroom. She is never the sort of child who drags or stalls; all suggestions of movement propel her. Zoe loads her toothbrush while Rose pees.

Rose laughs. "Noisy pee," she says. "The world's noisiest pee." Zoe always marvels at how she narrates her life. Rose flushes the toilet, washes her hands. Zoe gives her the toothbrush.

"I don't want to live here forever," Rose says. "Homer already hates it."

"Why?"

Rose brushes and brushes. Zoe can tell she's thinking by the way she knits her brows. "Well . . ." Rose spits and licks a foamy wave of toothpaste from her lower lip. "He says it doesn't feel like home. And I . . . I want adventure in my life," she says.

Zoe shakes her head with wonder. "Where'd you hear that?"

"Nowhere. I just think it."

"You're only six and a half. You're supposed to want . . . security!"

"What's that?" Rose says. Zoe runs a warm washcloth over Rose's delicate face, aware of her tiny ears, the perfect upturned nose, the slender neck. How fragile she seems to Zoe. When you've lost one child, you never take your next for granted. Not even for a moment. Zoe smiles at her, feeling so tenderly toward her that she experiences it in her mouth. Only a parent could know this: to love a child so much your very saliva flows at the sweetness of her.

"Security means knowing that things will always be safe, always be as you know them to be."

"Oh." Rose shakes her head.

"What?"

"That sounds boring."

Zoe laughs. "Does it?"

"It does to me."

What Zoe wouldn't have given as a child to have had security, to have a house like this. To be one of the Finneys. The Baltimore Finneys, as Rose will always be.

Zoe's own family was one of the poorest in a rich town: Highland Park, Illinois. All around Zoe as she grew up, people lived in mansions. Lawns were putting-green emerald. Faces were smug with money. Zoe's house was the ugly exception, situated on treeless land that was now more commercial than residential. The other houses in the row had become a car wash, an auto body shop, a vacuum repair store. The air smelled of machine oil, and twice every hour it filled with the clip and roar of the nearby Northwestern commuter train, rushing businessmen in either direction. Long after it was gone, the tracks would still rattle.

The house was a scar. Asphalt shingles, dun brown, peeled at the corners. A cement stoop threatened injury, its edges cracking and pebbling. At the bottom of the house was her parents' dry-cleaning shop, its own plant at the rear.

Zoe used to think the smell of sleep was the sharp, musty scent of dry-cleaning fluid. That's when she smelled it most strongly: at night, in the dark, when there was nothing else to distract her. The odor would seep up through the floorboards from the plant below, fill the room, fill her lungs, sometimes even her dreams. Morning was the sound of the steamers hissing, dragon-like, groaning as they were raised, and the squeak of the automated racks sending clothes to their fate. Her mother used to come in at ten minutes to seven, flush-faced, her apron already catching perspiration at the neck in its neat little row of rickrack, and say, in her thick accent, "Now you get up, Zosia." Her voice was as metal dull as her hair. She'd been pressed flat over the years, as a pair of thin grey flannel pants.

And her father, standing before the giant steam presses day and night, clocking down the bars with his beefy arms, anger curving his back, filling his face with ugly intensity . . . What use had he for a little girl who loved dolls and drew pictures of suns and flowers?

Zoe's parents never talked about the war. She was twelve before her mother answered the question Zoe had asked her since she was four years old: Why do you have numbers on your arm? Is that your phone number? Is that your address? And the question was answered only because Zoe already knew the answer: she'd seen a film about concentration camps. Survivors turned their forearms toward the camera, and there were the ugly numbers, marking their flesh forever, just like her mother's. Just like her father's.

"Is that what's on your arm, Mama?" Zoe asked. "Is it because you were there?"

"Yes, I was there," her mother told her, with no apparent feeling.

"Why didn't you ever tell me?"

"What good is it to think about what was before?" her mother asked her. "I can't change what happened to me."

Zoe knelt by her mother—by all standards a cold, impatient mother—and laid her head in her lap.

"I'm sorry you had to be there, Mama. I'm sorry if they hurt you." She felt a pain and bewilderment that she would never experience anything that reached the depth of what her parents had experienced.

"You will never know," her mother said. She touched Zoe's hair tentatively, then took her hand away.

It wasn't until she was fourteen that Zoe discovered her parents had had two children before her, both dead of starvation behind the barbed wire of Auschwitz. Zoe found a small, worn picture in a hatbox in her mother's closet. It was of her parents, posing proudly behind two children who looked frighteningly like Zoe but were dark-haired. A boy and a girl, with laughing lips and eyes, and surprised, arched eyebrows just like her own.

"What were their names?" Zoe asked. Her mother only shook her head. "Can't I know their names?"

Her mother shook her head again.

Her father was angry when she asked him.

"How did you find out?"

"I found their picture in Mother's closet." Would they hide Zoe's picture if she died?

"Their names were Ana and Frederik," her father told her. "Your mother wore that picture in her shoe, in the lining, the whole time in the camps. I never want you to speak their names to your mother. I never want you to ask more questions about them."

"Why can't I know? They were my brother and my sister. Why can't I know? Was Ana as pretty as she looked in the picture? Was she prettier than me? Did she like dolls?"

"You ask too many questions. You always ask too many questions."

Zoe was the Kazmaraks' only child after their move to America, and they let her know often that they were sorry they'd conceived her. A mistake, a regret. Who could bring children into such a world? Later in life, Zoe met the children of other Holocaust survivors, and they told her that their parents felt it was their duty to have as many children as possible, to repopulate the world with Jews. But Zoe's parents no longer chose to be Jews, did not even raise her as a Jew. (Entirely without religion, she would go with her friends to church or synagogue when she was eight or ten, to try it out, wondering "What am I?") And her parents felt no interest in repopulating the world, chose merely to survive until they died, broken-spirited, mean-hearted. How could they tolerate Zoe? Untouched, full of life, complacent with her freedom?

Discovering her parents had suffered in the war was a key for Zoe, explained things she had never been able to explain. Like why her parents never left their shop/home at the same time. If Esta went to the grocery store, Stash stayed home. If Stash went to pick up new drums of dry-cleaning chemicals, Esta remained behind. They did not go to restaurants, on vacation, or to school functions together. They had no friends, no outside interests.

"Please both come to my Winter Sing," Zoe begged them.

"And leave the shop alone?"

"What could happen to the shop? You don't open until eleven o'clock on Fridays anyway."

"Plenty could happen to the shop. Plenty."

The shop could be stolen from them, burned, looted, lost forever, they said. Little girls couldn't possibly know.

Now she understood. They had been robbed of all their possessions: everything. They could not risk it again.

The war explained Zoe's mother's ill health, her inability to eat much: she was so thin and weak it was painful to watch her, and she had an odd stoop to her posture, always said her back hurt. Later, Zoe discovered she'd been beaten after trying to steal a leftover crust of bread from an SS officer's snack plate, to give to her starving little girl, Ana. While she recovered from the beating, in a separate place of punishment, Ana died.

The war explained why both her parents called her "ungrateful child," why her mother taught her not to cry. She can remember it as clearly as if it were happening now: her mother slapping her because she cried when her favorite doll lost its arm. She had been hit many times by her mother, and sometimes for what seemed to Zoe no reason at all. But this time the slap was particularly vicious. Zoe can still feel the sting on her cheek, the shock. "You have no right to cry," her mother said. "You have everything you need: enough food, a roof over your head, heat. You think you have a right to cry because you break a doll, a stupid toy? Do you know how others have suffered? Do you know?" Others meant her brother and sister, dead long before her, but Zoe didn't know anything about them then.

She remembers, in slow motion, her mother grabbing the doll, Junie, from her and pulling the other arm off. Zoe can remember how the arm looked, the rubber bands that held it to the body snapping, the frightening rounded joint with its deformed flesh-colored button that was never meant to be seen. Then her mother went on ripping the doll apart, the legs, the head. Zoe can see now just as clearly, as she did then, the mechanism that made the eyes open and close, open and close, rolling back and forth in the hollow head. Junie! She reached for the pieces, her friend lost forever, dismantled. Junie! But her mother dropped all the pieces on the floor and crushed them beneath her dark, ugly shoe. Zoe saw Junie's delicate smiling

face, which had comforted her through so many bleak
moments, caving in, transforming, becoming monstrous. A
single eye dislodged. Zoe's tears were desert dry now, but
her throat twisted with pain, was on fire. "There," her
mother said at last, kicking the shards with her toe. The
small blue eyeball rolled across the floor and disappeared
beneath the sofa skirt. "The next time you cry for no
reason"—she looked into Zoe's eyes, her own soulless
eyes green and flat—"the next time, perhaps I do this
to you. . . ."

After making Zoe clean up the remains, her mother left
the room, and Zoe got down on her stomach to find the
single saved eye. Taking the tiny glass bead into her hand,
she brought it to the rocking chair and rocked it for an
hour, maybe more, just the way she used to rock Junie,
cooing to it, whispering to it. She has it still, keeps it in
her jewelry box, along with the deco diamond ring, the
antique gold chain, the pearl earrings Jamie gave her in
the beginning of their romance. When Charlotte died, at
the age of two, their baby, their firstborn, Zoe, blinded
with shock, took the eyeball from the satin box and would
not let go of it, through the night, through the funeral,
through the next month. Its little metal clip dug into her
palm. She pressed it until her hand stung, even bled. But
she did not cry for Charlotte; she could not. Her throat
closed and spasmed, her heart felt like it was torn from
her chest. The glass eye looked up at her from her palm
when she opened her hand to see if it was still there. It
knew her pain, it absorbed it. And not once since that day
has she cried tears, no matter what pain she's faced. Even
if she wishes it, she simply can no longer cry.

The war explains it all and has colored every aspect of
Zoe's life. How can she complain about *her* life? How
can she even call what she feels disappointment or pain?
She's lost one child. Yes. But they lost two. And lost
everything besides: their families and their fortunes, their
hopes, their health. In a world of tragedy, Zoe simply will

never be able to compete. The best thing she can do is be a different kind of mother to Rose.

She now steers Rose to her bedroom to dress and watches her patiently as she rifles through her drawer and picks out a wonderfully absurd pairing of a red polka-dot shirt and a green-striped skirt. Usually Zoe tries to direct her in her choices, but today she shrugs and helps her put it on. It looks quirky and perfect somehow. Rose admires the combination in the mirror.

"Stylish," she says.

"You're the very best girl in the whole world," Zoe tells her. "Do you know that?"

Rose considers for a moment. "Jamie doesn't think so."

"Sure, darling, sure he does."

"He won't even talk to me," she says.

Zoe swallows down the pain. "He won't talk to me either, or anyone. Not right now. He's sick. But being in Brooklyn's going to make him better. It will make everything better. I know it."

Rose nods her head solemnly and says, "Mama, didn't you hear Homer?"

Lately, Zoe's noticed how Rose will bring Jamie up but never let the conversation run for long, as though it hurts too much to talk about him. Zoe knows just how she feels.

"I guess I wasn't listening hard enough," Zoe says. "What did Homer say?"

"He says he wants cinnamon toast immediately."

"Well, Homer, you certainly are demanding," Zoe says.

"Yes," Rose says in a squeaky voice, nodding Homer's head. "I'm a champion baby dog, and I deserve the best."

"I'm trying to teach him manners," Rose says in her own voice, shaking her head, lifting her hands in exasperation. "But what can I do? Homer's not interested in manners. He's only interested in telling the truth."

# THREE

◆

Keevan O'Connor walks through the doors of John Jay
High School briskly and full of purpose. No one else
seems to do anything at John Jay with a sense of purpose,
and Keevan always feels someone needs to set an example.
One of his students, Marquita Dominguez, sidles up to
him.

"Mr. O'Connor . . ."

"Marquita."

Always, even in the dead of winter, Marquita has tor-
mented Keevan with her neat, swirly little navel, pierced
with a silver ring. He spies it now, the ring glistening
above her jeans.

"My sister took my *Grapes of Wrath*."

"Can you get it back?"

Marquita scrunches up her sharp-chinned little face.
"She used it to start her boyfriend's motorcycle. It's all
torn up."

Keevan shakes his head. The lives of his students are a
constant source of wonder for him. How would one use a
book to start a motorcycle anyway? "Get it at the library,"
Keevan says. "Okay, Marquita?"

"What library?"

"The one at Grand Army Plaza. The Brooklyn Public."

"I don't know where it is."

"Oh, come on. You really don't? Well, it's the perfect

time to discover it. Ask someone how to get there and go after school. You'll like *Grapes of Wrath,* I guarantee it. Or ask Alice German. She finished it. She told me.''

"She don't like me."

"All right. Then the library. I'm sure it's out at the school library, so you've got to try the Public.''

"I'll never find the library," Marquita says, with the sort of defeat in her voice that rallies all Keevan's energies.

"Look," he says. "Let me draw you a map. Okay? Put out your hand." Marquita, already interested, beaming, unfurls her hand. Keevan takes a ballpoint from his shirt pocket and begins to draw on Marquita's bronze-skinned palm. The high school, Seventh Avenue, Union Street. Grand Army Plaza. He can tell that Marquita loves having a handful of his efforts, his interest in her. He thinks she probably even loves the feel of the smooth ballpoint making celebrity of her skin. Keevan draws the library as a cartoon. Faces, buildings, lightbulbs—he cartoons everything he hands back to his students, and they love it. Keevan writes along her wrist: "Marquita's Map."

"Okay?" he asks.

"Thanks." She's truly pleased. She's beaming. She'll go to the library. She'll find *The Grapes of Wrath.* He sighs with pleasure. His day's already made.

Keevan knows most of his students like him, because he doesn't scream at them, doesn't pander to them. He treats them as if he expects good things from them.

Now he pushes his way into the faculty lounge. Tina is there with Lucy Jackson, the typing teacher (since last year, when the school received two used computers, she's called herself the "keyboarding" teacher), drinking coffee. When Keevan comes in, Tina leans forward and whispers something to Lucy. Their laughter tightens the muscles in the back of Keevan's neck.

"Hello," he says, hoping that being direct will break through the childish war that's gone on too long.

"Hello," Tina says sullenly, reminding Keevan of his

students. He grabs his mail, mostly teachers' junk mail,
and leaves the lounge. They titter behind him, like the
teenagers they teach. He hears Tina saying, "God, I hate
him."

But he tries not to let it affect him. Each day when he
walks into this building, Keevan hopes that he will make a
difference in someone's life. This is not a romantic notion.
Keevan O'Connor not only believes it possible; he believes that most days he succeeds. Tina used to call him
Don Quixote. But Keevan thinks that's just because she's
jealous that somehow kids walk out of his classes better
off than when they walked in.

The thing is, he's tough with the kids. He uses their
language. Someday it will probably get him fired. He calls
assholes assholes. He makes the class laugh at the pupils
who are disruptive. He uses the power of the peer group
to keep his students in line. It isn't cool to disrupt Mr.
O'Connor's class. The whole school knows it.

As Keevan climbs the stairs to his classroom, he sees
Marquita Dominguez by the water fountain, holding up
her hand to a circle of friends. He wishes for a minute
that his neighbor Zosia could see Marquita boasting, could
know that what he does in his life carries as much weight
as a lawyer's work, or a doctor's. Perhaps someday, he
thinks, I will tell her.


On the subway, Zoe Finney watches the people around
her as though she is watching a movie. She hasn't taken
a subway in years. A few times in the early part of her
marriage, she did out of curiosity. But Jamie always dis-
couraged it, and Lois, his mother, told her there was no
way a Finney should *ever* be caught dead on public trans-
poration. "You could get killed," she told Zoe, "or at
best lose your jewelry."

In those days, the subway was hard to even see beneath
its mask of graffiti. The old maroon cars were shabby, and
no air moved inside them unless the train was moving
sixty miles an hour and all the windows were cranked

open. Zoe, new to New York and easily intimidated by everything, wasn't sorry to be told not to ride the subway.

But the Park Slope real estate agent told her that even if she could afford to hire a car to take her to Manhattan every day, the subway would be much faster. "It's really not so bad," she said. "Everybody just likes to complain." God knows, with Jamie's money, Zoe could afford a private car. But looking around, she thinks now that the real estate agent was right. The F train she rides is silver on the outside, graffiti-free everywhere, and the ventilation system is pumping air so well its breath is fluttering her skirt. The rest of the people in the car are well-dressed, reading, sleeping. She watches two Chinese women with string shopping bags, talking nonstop and gesturing in a nervous, staccato way. She also spends some time on a girl with hair that is too dark not to be dyed, and coral colored false nails, who, while sitting between two annoyed business types, is applying eye makeup, a long and complicated ritual, swinging her elbows in the process as though she thinks she is the only person on the train.

Mostly Zoe focuses on the few Hasidic Jews who sit together at the end of the car, with their long curls and their yarmulkes with wide-brimmed hats set over them. Zoe can't relate to these Jews or any Jews. But she longs to feel a kinship and watches them with interest as they read their books backward, moving their lips inside their full beards. She has seen their wives too, in Manhattan, with their wigs, their pillbox hats and their unstylishly long dresses. Could her ancestors ever have been as deliberately separate as they are? Her parents never told her where they lived in Poland. But even those who lived in nice neighborhoods were herded to the ghetto in time, she's read. She remembers the picture her mother carried in her shoe. In it, the family looked well-dressed, stylish. And her mother once spoke of the silver flatware she owned, with vines so thick they ridged your fingers when you held them. So perhaps that was part of her parents' anger, that they were not separate, yet had been separated out.

So what is the point of the Hasidim choosing separateness? Walking hunched in their crowlike iridescent coats, men in pairs, turning their backs to the world. Their choices must be narrow, Zoe reflects. But perhaps, she thinks, in those narrow choices there is also a kind of freedom.

Zoe sighs and looks around. This is the beginning of her new life. She wonders what choices she will make. And if they will prove to be better ones than the pale-pink sofa she can't wait to replace.

At least I've taken a step, she thinks. Maybe I will come to know these faces, their habits—their favorite cars, their favorite seats—and they'll smile at me, and I'll feel like I belong. The notion comforts her, and she finds herself smiling, lighthearted.

Zoe knows she'll be late to work this morning. It will be nearly eleven o'clock before she gets there. But last week she informed everyone she would be moving, and she's been doing her job well enough, hasn't she?

Zoe gets off at the last stop in Manhattan, Fifty-third Street, and walks down Third Avenue to her office. Things are not so bad, she thinks. I'm still young. I have a good job. I own a house in Brooklyn.

The truth is, she hasn't been very happy with her job lately, and she can't figure out why. Film has always been her passion. As a child, she saved every penny of her baby-sitting and chore money to spend at the movies. On Saturday afternoons, when her work at the dry-cleaning shop was finished, she would sneak out to the Alcyon Theater, where for fifty cents she could sit in the cool dark and see a movie and have free popcorn and soda. Because the Alcyon's Saturday matinees were geared to children, all the movies ended happily. And the heroes and heroines had pluck that Zoe's parents never had: the conviction that no matter how bad things got, they would keep on trying. Zoe imagined herself as every one of those characters. She came out of the dark, butter-smelling movie house speaking like them, moving like them. After

*Mary Poppins,* she had an English accent. After a Doris Day movie, she smiled so much her cheeks ached.

And when she went to UCLA entirely on scholarship, majoring in film, she found that what she loved most was editing. The head of the film department said he'd never seen a student so natural in her cutting style, so able to "squeeze the essence out of a filmmaker's intention." He even asked her to help him edit his own movie, a low-budget story about a boy who follows a glamorous movie star around and discover that she's really a man. It played in art houses along both coasts, and Zoe would duck into a theater just to sit through it and see her name on the credits.

But when she came out of school and moved with Jamie to New York, her options were narrower, and she could only find a job cutting commercials. Commercial cutting was a challenge in its own right. And in some ways, an editor could be more experimental and instrumental in a commercial than a movie. But after twelve years of editing commercials for salad dressing, feminine hygiene products, telephone companies, fast food, the work has become painfully rote and no longer very appealing. Everything nowadays is done on an Avid computer system. She misses the tactile pleasure of handling the curls of film, the splicing, the wonderful chuffing sound of the clear sprocketed tape being pulled from its roll and the precision with which she had to lay it down across the two pieces to marry them. Now she presses a button. Now she doesn't touch the film at all. Lately, she has wondered what it would take to get back into editing real films, in editing rooms that still smell of developer and where, as an editor searches for the perfect cutting point, the film runs backward, making the actors sound Swedish or Russian.

And she has also wondered what it would be like to leave film editing altogether, to simply stay home. With Jamie's money, she certainly doesn't need to work. There are plenty of people who tell her she's crazy to keep working, sometimes putting up with late hours, difficult clients.

She could probably be more helpful to Jamie if she were around all day. Talking to him, sitting with him, trying to stimulate him, maybe she could pull him out of his depression more quickly, get him to speak. And wouldn't Rose love it if Zoe were there when she came home with her book bag and her half-eaten lunch and stories of her school day?

But still, the thought of life without her own work frightens Zoe. Work is the only place these days where she can be social. And though, since Jamie's illness, she hasn't had the time for the sort of friendships she once had, she enjoys the laughter, the camaraderie, of the dark editing room. She enjoys sharing her efforts with others. And having this skill, this ability with film, is the thing that kept her afloat after Charlotte's death, during Jamie's depression. It's something her parents never had: a job that occasionally gives her happiness.

Nevertheless, arriving at Editor's Fair now, she finds she'd rather be in her new house, admiring its details, unpacking her boxes. She takes a deep breath and steps from the elevator into the hot-pink reception area, where some decorator thought it was a fine idea to place three six-foot neon-green blow-up palm trees.

"We thought you'd been killed by a bus," the receptionist says. Her name is Nancy, and her hair is the color of beets.

"Is someone looking for me?" Zoe asks.

"It's eleven o'clock," the receptionist says.

"Oh, well, you know, I'm still moving in." She doesn't wait for an answer.

In her office, Stuart, her assistant, is working at Zoe's computer, waiting for her. Stuart is only twenty-three. The one thing she does enjoy at her job is teaching him. He is eager to learn, adoring. Once, he invited her to come for a drink after work. "What for?" she asked him. "Just to spend time talking," he said, blushing. They talked for hours, and it was remarkably warm, intimate. Woozy from their drinks, they went outside to find taxis in the light rain. While the lights changed, he kissed her on the lips softly, then passionately, exploring her mouth with his tongue. She found herself moaning, pulling him into the kiss, then pushing him away. What was she doing? He whispered, "Oh, God," and blushed crimson.

"Too much to drink," she said clumsily. That night, after tossing and turning beside Jamie, she leaned over his cold sleeping body and tried to kiss his lips, but they barely seemed to be there. They were dry and papery and nonresponsive. It's not his fault, she told herself again and again, not sleeping all night.

She found herself the next day, the next week, hoping Stuart would ask her for drinks, or kiss her again, or that an opportunity might arise to help them talk about it. But it never did. Still, she's seen the way he looks at her. And she feels certain his desire for her is still there. She finds him attractive too, his curly dark hair, his long, slender fingers. And admonishes herself often for how easy it is to dwell on that desire.

"I'm setting this all up for you, this soup spot. You know, since you were late," he says. He has a nice voice. Deep and full.

"The film's in already?" she asks, hanging up her coat.

"The client will be here in an hour. I've got it all downloaded."

"Thanks."

"How's your new house?" he asks.

"Beautiful."

"Brooklyn," Stuart says thoughtfully. "I can't quite wrap my head around that."

"Do you think I'm going to start talking funny. Saying stuff like 'Where's da film?' "

Stuart shrugs. "I'm afraid you'll start teasing your hair."

"Where's da hair spray?" Zoe asks. "I might as well rat it up now. You know, to go wit' the accent."

Stuart stares at Zoe in a way that makes her uncomfortable. As though he's imagining her with souffléed hair and likes the idea. She turns toward the screen.

"Soup, huh? How's the film?"

"Fair. Kind of a stupid concept. Olympic skier tells us how soup warms her bones after hours on the slopes. How's Jamie taking the move?"

Zoe bites her lip. She regrets that once, feeling sorry for herself, she told Stuart about Jamie, how he no longer speaks. How he fears leaving his room. How sad it makes her.

"He jumped out of the taxi in Brooklyn and started talking right away. 'What a to-tally cool neighborhood!' he said. 'Is dis our house?' And he greased his hair up and felt right at home. He looked exactly like John Travolta in *Saturday Night Fever*. And he's thinking of buying a powder-blue suit and taking up dancing."

Stuart looks annoyed.

"Okay, I lied," she says. "But I just . . . just feel things are going to get better. You know, in Brooklyn. It's quiet. And the house is so serene. He was very alert this morning, looking around, and he ate more than usual." Again it's a lie, but Zoe wants to be cheerful today, wants to extend the way she felt in her house this morning, the way she felt on the subway.

Stuart gets up from her chair and Zoe sits down. Standing behind her, Stuart reaches over to point to something on the screen, and she feels the pressure of his body against her back.

"See, I put all the tabletop stuff together, starting with the pot shot, then the bowl," he says.

Zoe drinks in how the touch of him makes her body tingle. Nearly every day, they touch like this. Sometimes he does it. Sometimes she does.

Once I've unpacked the house, she thinks, I'll ask him for a drink. I'll be brave, for a change. Though she has dreamed a great deal about kissing him again, she can't imagine ever being serious about him in any way. But her physical loneliness is so overwhelming sometimes that it gnaws at her energy level, her desire to do anything.

"Okay, Stuart, my dear," she says, trying to rev herself up. "Let's jump into this soup." She turns to take in his soft, hopeful smile.

After the clients come and choose their favorite takes, Zoe leaves her monitor, her keyboard, the seventy-five shots of vegetable soup being ladled into a white bowl, and walks along Madison Avenue. It's warmer today. A tease of spring. Zoe is somehow not surprised to find, without even realizing what she's doing, that she's opening the door to Woolworth's.

She knows instantly what's going to happen. The urge. It always starts somehow with heat. And a tightening in the back of her neck. Shame already, and nothing has happened yet. The aisles are particularly colorful and well stocked, decked out for Easter. Purple and yellow and pink and blue boxes hold every possible type of Easter candy. Chocolate bunnies with hard sugar eyes and fat bodies, with names on the boxes like "Pete!" and "Augustus!" Yellow marshmallow chicks. Packets of malted-milk eggs. Down at the end of the candy aisle a little girl stands— she can't be more than seven—biting her knuckle, looking from bunny to bunny, trying to choose. How troubled she looks, touching the cellophane of the boxes tentatively with the fingers of the hand she isn't chewing. She pokes at one package, then the other. Zoe watches her, wonders if she should buy the little girl the rabbit, if that act alone might free her from doing what will inevitably happen.

As she walks toward the girl, to offer the cash to buy the chocolate bunny of choice, or two if she wants, the girl's mother, in a dirty white sweater and some kind of thick, dark support hose, grabs her daughter by the wrist.

"Let's go," the mother says. "You're not eating no candy. Your teeth are falling out."

"I'm supposed to lose my teeth," the girl says in a remarkably husky voice.

"Shut up. Don't sass," the mother says. She drags the little girl by the wrist. Zoe watches as the child tries to shake off her mother's hand, whipping it with a downward motion as though trying to rid herself of a clinging mosquito. God, the hatred Zoe feels suddenly for the mother! The rage boils up inside her, effervesces to her fingertips.

Now there's no avoiding the inevitable. Her heart is beating hard. Slamming. Her blood sings with its treason. The old voice tells her that if she doesn't take something, she will never have anything. Not anything. Maybe she will starve. Maybe she will die. And there is an emptiness that gnaws inside her. Her stomach feels as though it's tearing, the desire is so keen. If she doesn't take this chance, if she doesn't break all the rules right now, she will be crushed by them and left with nothing. And if she does act, she will win, she will thrive: a gambler galvanized by even the smallest stake. Her hand reaches out and palms a packet of speckle-coated eggs. How right it feels in her hand. I deserve this. It was meant to be mine. The cellophane kisses and crackles in her fingers. Her mouth floods with saliva. She looks to either side of her, then slides the packet into her coat pocket. Yes, she's got it! It burns there, heats her hip. Hot merchandise. Hot. Her heart is still pounding as she walks past the cashier, crackling with each step; it's still slamming long after she is out on the street. A wave of joy sweeps her. She feels perversely, thrillingly alive. She's done it! Two blocks away, Zoe pulls the candy from her pocket and squeezes the package. Its crackle is deafening. The spongy, crunchy candy is shamefully sweet when it hits her mouth: the thin candy shell, the deep lining of chocolate, and then the rich malted burst. She is walking down Madison Avenue laughing.

Then it sours. She had promised herself she wouldn't do this anymore. She had vowed. Squeezing the package, with its picture of a nest and a bird, and the word "Easter" in purple, she pitches it into a wire trash can. As the package hits bottom, the eggs shoot from the cellophane and spill out through the wire onto the sidewalk. A few people turn to look at her, standing there, candy eggs at her feet. I deserve to have them stare at me, she thinks. Go ahead, stare at me. I am a thief.

The first time Zoe took something that wasn't hers, she was spending the night at her friend Emily's house. She was nine years old, and Emily had asked her, as she did at least once every other week, to giggle long into the night, eat homemade pancakes for breakfast, torment Emily's brother and sister, and have the luxury of pretending to be part of the Macomber family.

Of all her friends, Emily Macomber was her favorite.

"You're my best friend," Emily told her again and again, in her fairy-tale bedroom. The ceiling was blue and had clouds painted on it. The carpet was a velvety rich violet. Emily's house had fourteen rooms (not including servants' quarters) and two staircases, and was literally filled to the brim with little things: crystal clocks and silver candy dishes, flowered guest towels and soaps shaped like strawberries.

Emily's mother, Leslie, was like the mothers of all her rich friends, in their mansions just blocks from Zoe's tumbledown house. She wore tennis dresses, bought paintings, served sandwiches on green-and-white china plates that had always been in the family, and called Emily and her friends "ladies." "Anything else you want, ladies?" "What are you ladies doing this afternoon?"

Emily's mother never bought anything. She "picked things up," as though she didn't have to pay for them. "Can I pick something up for you ladies?" "I just picked this blouse up yesterday, and it didn't fit Emily. Would you like it, Zoe?" "Emily already has three watches, and since I picked up a new one yesterday, would you like this one?"

Zoe was in love with her. In love with Leslie's silky dark hair, pulled back cleanly from her head like a ballerina's, her beautiful face with its flare of raw cheekbones

and dark mascaraed eyes. Leslie was the woman Zoe
wanted to grow up to be. How chic she was, how understanding. Her voice was like cobwebs, dusty and soft.

Zoe brought her flowers she'd gather by the railroad
tracks. "Aren't these wild things the sweetest!" Leslie
would exclaim in that soft, seductive rasp, making great
ceremony out of finding just the right crystal vase in which
to display them. Zoe made her a vinyl mosaic trivet in art
class (all the other students made them for their own mothers), blue and white to match Leslie's dining room. Leslie
insisted the cook use the trivet when she set out hot dishes.
It was on the Macomber table nearly every night. Emily's
never was. Zoe made Leslie a valentine encrusted with
lace, seed pearls, and drawings of birds. Leslie displayed
it for months on her night table, Zoe's seemingly the only
valentine Leslie saved. She must love me, Zoe thought.
She must really care about me.

Zoe would wait for Emily to be in the bathroom, or on
the phone, and then would happily wander into Leslie's
bedroom, where Leslie often spent time, asprawl in the
chaise longue reading a book, or writing something at her
desk—Zoe never knew what and longed to see it: a journal, a letter? Leslie's bedroom was painted the colors of
opals: the milks of greens and pinks and lavender blues.
Her bed was bigger than any bed Zoe had ever seen. Entire
families could sleep there. And since Bruce had his own
bedroom, on the other side of the bathroom, Zoe wasn't
even sure whether Leslie shared it.

"Hi, Zo," Leslie would say. "Sit down. How's my
favorite kid?"

Love would well up in Zoe, so it was hard to contain
the feeling to not reach out and touch Leslie's peachy-
pink ankle or her slender wrists, moving freely in their
cage of golden bangles.

"Is that a good book?" Zoe would ask. Leslie's reading
tastes tended toward gothic romances, their covers embla-
zoned with escaping maidens in the foreground, brooding
castles in the background.

"In this one, I'm really wondering if the husband is actually the bad guy. They want you to think he's a sweetheart, ready to protect her, but I just have a feeling . . ." Leslie's eyes would sparkle.

"Tell me how it turns out," Zoe would say. "Tell me if you were right. I bet you're right."

One afternoon, Zoe pointed to the cover of one of Leslie's books, leaning ostensibly to touch the illustration but longing just to be near Leslie, to breathe in her cool green perfume.

"If I had a house like that, I'd paint it white or light blue or something, so it wouldn't look so haunted. And plant some flowers."

Leslie laughed, displaying her impressive pearly teeth, the eyeteeth so long and elegant they alone seemed to acknowledge her breeding.

"Yes," she said. "You'd think any woman would realize a man with a haunted-looking house like that is not a wise choice." She leaned back in her chaise and took a sip of her soda. "I should have known that too, I suppose," she added, her dark eyes suddenly distant. She took such a deep breath it hurt Zoe's lungs to hear her sigh it out.

Zoe didn't know what to say. Wasn't Leslie happy, after all? No one deserved happiness more or had more reason to be happy than Leslie.

"Oh, this house isn't at all haunted-looking," Zoe exclaimed firmly. "It's beautiful!" But she knew her words were inappropriate and lame.

"I used to be beautiful," Leslie said, talking not to Zoe, really, but to herself. "Bruce used to say it burned his eyes to look at me." Her own eyes looked wet and miserable now, but somehow, as if by magic, her nose didn't redden or run, her face lost none of its elegance.

"Oh, but you are. Still beautiful. You're the most beautiful mother I know," Zoe said. "Everyone says so. I wish I could be so beautiful. Truly."

Leslie took Zoe's face in her hands and kissed her

squarely on the top of her head. "You are really the sweetest child. Really, the very sweetest."

"I wish you were my mother," Zoe said.

"Do you?" Leslie said, distracted now, picking up her
book once again. "Aren't you darling!"

"I wish you could adopt me," Zoe said, hoping that
Leslie would hear her, before she was lost once again to
the brooding mansion, the imperiled heroine.

"That's nice," Leslie said. "Very sweet." But she was
gone, into her world of jeopardy and love.

And then, not long after, it seemed there were whole
days when Leslie would stay in her room, weeping. Emily
would warn her, "My mom's having one of her crying
jags." And Zoe would hear through the door unladylike
whoops of distress that chilled her.

"Shouldn't we see if she's all right?" Zoe would ask.

"Nope. It's a lot better to leave her alone when she's
like that."

"What's wrong? What's she so upset about?"

Emily would shrug as though it didn't matter at all, but
Zoe could see in the set of her mouth how it disturbed
her too.

Then Zoe started to notice all the bottles of pills by
Emily's mother's bed. Half open. Zoe would snap them
shut if she noticed, worried about Emily's little sister getting into them.

"Is she sick?" Zoe would ask.

"I don't know. It seems like she's always going to
doctors," Emily said, sighing. "She says my father is
making her sick."

If Leslie was unhappy with her husband, Zoe couldn't
understand it. Bruce was so crisp and handsome. Everything about him reminded her of a freshly ironed shirt. He
even smelled like laundry starch. And he was so boyish.
Until Zoe met him, she never imagined fathers could be
so breezy or agreeable. Zoe loved it when he touched her,
as he often did. Encouraging little squeezes and pats on
the head, which he also gave to Emily, and her sister,

Molly, and her brother, Peter. Her whole body tingled just to be touched.

He laughed easily. He was interested in her, so caring. "I hear you're the spelling whiz of the whole school," he said, in his rich, accent-free voice. He didn't smell like her father, sweaty, chemical. He smiled. He had all his teeth.

But when she thought about Bruce with Leslie, she could see no picture at all. She couldn't remember if he kissed Leslie on the lips when he came home from his office. Though he brought presents for the children often, she couldn't recall his bringing any to Leslie. At nearly every dinner, though (and Zoe attended many), he would raise his glass and say, "To the family who, just by sharing dinner with me, makes me the luckiest man in Highland Park." To Zoe, the toast seemed wonderfully generous and grand—this was what families were supposed to be—but it made Molly and Emily and Peter groan with impatience. How could they not appreciate all this? she wondered. She would trade places with any of them.

The truth was, for all she had, Emily never seemed quite happy. She didn't like the beautiful things her mother bought her. She thought her mother was nosy or loved her sister more. She thought her father was a "fathead," a "tightwad," and her little sister, who was enchantingly beautiful, with long, wavy hair and a voice full of air, like Leslie's, was a "fuckface." Because she never liked what she had, she gave things to Zoe constantly. But then, later, she would say, loudly and in public, "When are you going to give me back that green sweater? It looked better on me. It's falling off you. My mother bought it for me, after all."

And she was the one of all Zoe's friends who reminded her constantly about her weight, how if only she weighed more, boys might notice she was a girl, or how it might be nice if she could fill out her clothes better than a clothes hanger for a change. It was rare that Zoe would acknowledge how cruel Emily was. Somehow she could never get enough of Emily's company.

Often, Zoe played a game: that she was Emily. That her hair was chestnut and glossy. That her skirt pleats danced when she walked, the product of many years of ballet and social dancing. That if she opened her eyes, her room would be Emily's room. It would all be there: the royal bed, the dresser with its creamy white paint, its golden edges, the carpet the color of crushed violets, which would feel like petals on your bare feet.

When she visited Emily's house she made every attempt to know what it was like to be Emily. Zoe would put on Emily's Tabu perfume and big, smoky powder puffs of her Friendship Garden talc. She'd apply her Yardley lipstick, even slip her feet into Emily's loafers and feel the buttery softness of the leather. Her own shoes said "man-made material" on the bottom; basically cardboard, they didn't stand up well to the rain.

Dressed in Emily's cast-off clothes, smelling like Emily, Zoe tried to ignore that Leslie was growing increasingly miserable and hollow-eyed, was paying less and less attention to Zoe, even when she walked into her room and talked to her, and would sometimes fail to show up at the dinner table or come in with her buttons buttoned wrong or smoke all through dinner with glassy eyes, not saying a word. Zoe tried to ignore the even more disturbing fact that Bruce seemed just as charming and happy as ever, as though he noticed nothing unusual about Leslie.

And then, one day, Leslie wasn't there. "She's in the hospital," Emily said, white-lipped and distant. "She'll be there for a while."

"What's wrong with her?"

"I'm not allowed to say." But Peter told her that one night, right in the middle of dinner, his mother had grabbed a steak knife, got up from the table, and tried to stab Bruce.

Zoe was stunned, didn't believe Peter at first. "It's not nice to make fun of your mother."

He shook his head at her. "I'm just telling you what happened," he said. "You asked. I'm telling you."

That night at dinner, Leslie absent, Bruce was his usual cheerful self. A man whose wife tried to stab him. What had he done that was so awful? Zoe felt a twisting in her stomach that made it hard to eat.

"I guess you're not a big fan of meat loaf," Bruce said.

"Oh, no. It's very good," Zoe said. "I'm just not very hungry." She loved Bruce. But she didn't want to look at him.

"That's why she looks like a skeleton." Emily laughed. "She's never very hungry."

"Well, we're going to work on her. We're going to fatten her up," Bruce said.

Emily became more the Indian giver than before, one day offering Zoe a nightgown she hated, insisting on having it back the next day. She never talked about Leslie, though Zoe often asked how she was.

"Does your dad visit her in the hospital?" Zoe asked.

"Oh, sure, sometimes. Mostly, these days, he's out of town or on the phone."

"Do you visit her?"

"They won't let me."

"Why not?"

"How should I know? I don't want to go to that stinking hospital anyway."

Then Leslie came back, and was the same as she had been, doe-eyed and quiet and caught up in her romance books. Except that she seemed much less patient with all the children and with Bruce, but especially with Zoe.

"Why is she always here?" Zoe once heard Leslie whispering to Emily. "Can't we have time to ourselves as a family?" Though crushed, still Zoe came to the Macombers' as often as she was invited, hoping that maybe it was Leslie who suggested the visit to Emily, that she felt about Zoe the way she used to. For even with all the tension, it was better to be at the Macombers' than at home. No one spoke at home. No one laughed or played. And no one wanted her around at home either. Besides, the Macomber house was much more beautiful.

Once, spending the night at Emily's as she had so many times, she woke from a nightmare before dawn. The dream was about her sister, Ana. Ana had somehow been found alive and was living with them in America. Zoe's parents were loving and affectionate with Ana in a way they'd never been to Zoe. Even Leslie fell in love with her, telling Zoe, "Only Ana can come into my room. We're reading together." "Have you ever seen a girl so lovely?" Zoe's father said. He sat her on his knee, as he never had Zoe, and Ana laughed in a disinterested way. Ana, who in the one picture left of her was mild and kind-looking, was in real life cold and demanding. She was undeniably beautiful, in a lusty, full-bodied way, as Emily was. But she had cruel eyes. And a voice that could cut paper when she was alone with Zoe. It was Zoe's job to show Ana around the school, and she was surprised to discover that Ana was in her very class. Her teacher said, "We've all been waiting for you, Ana." And then she turned to Zoe and laughed. "It really was Ana all along who was supposed to be in this class. Not you."

Zoe woke in a sweat. Her mouth was dry and her fists were balled up in anger. Why had she dreamed such a stupid dream? Why had she dreamed of Ana at all? She felt intensely bereft. She had lost her parents to this apparition, even lost her teacher. She tried to go back to sleep, to dispel the sense of mourning the dream had left her with, but it was getting light, and she could not shut the dawn from her eyes. Besides, the room smelled of all the perfumes and powders Emily displayed on a mirror tray on her dresser. They called for Zoe to put them on: Friendship Garden talc, Little Lady toilet water, real White Shoulders perfume, Tabu, and the Violet Violet creme sachet that Emily had offered to Zoe the night before and then snatched back. Along the window seat, Emily's beautiful dolls sat silhouetted by the streetlight, primly waiting to be played with again—Emily had nearly outgrown them, had never really been devoted to them in the first place.

Collections. Emily's room was filled with collections.

Not one but many examples of everything a girl could want. Not one pair of shoes but eight. An entire drawer of hair ribbons, in every color. One shot with gold. One edged in silver. Seven made of silk. Six of velvet. Zoe got up and wandered about the room. She touched the dolls' silky heads, she opened the ribbon drawer and pulled out the tangle of rainbowed ribbons, spread them on the window seat. She sorted them by fabric, then by color. There was just enough light to see them. When she put them back, they were in much better order than before, straightened and sorted and laid delicately in the drawer. Now Zoe opened the jewelry drawer. She and Emily had often played with Emily's jewelry, dressing up, pretending to be sophisticated. Emily had drawers full of jewelry: costume pins with dogs on them, ballerinas, Pierrot faces. She had ropes of beads, bangle bracelets of plastic in many colors, rings that glistened and clanked in their boxes: none of them real or valuable. Not much of it meant anything to Emily.

But this morning Zoe saw something in the drawer that made her heart pound. It wasn't even something she liked, but the least pretty ballerina pin, the one with the green glass-chip eyes and the badly gilded lace skirt and the legs oddly akimbo. What drew her was the face. She couldn't say why, but it reminded her of her sister Ana. It wasn't very finely rendered. And the green glass eyes made it cartoony and eerie. But the sharp, certain set of the chin reminded her chillingly of the Ana in her dream. Her fingers almost bled, holding it so tightly. She didn't know why she had to have it, but suddenly there was no choice. She had to own this ballerina. She couldn't even risk asking Emily, because if she knew Zoe truly wanted it, she might suddenly find it impossible to give away or, even worse, offer it to her, then ask for it back. It seemed she was truly generous only when Zoe didn't care. Glancing nervously over at Emily, sleeping like a princess in her fancy bed, Zoe slipped the pin into her little overnight bag. Hers, forever.

What made her do it? All her life, she'd been so good, following every rule, hoping it would make her parents love her. Why that pin? Why risk anything for that ugly pin, which reminded her of something upsetting? The guilt was new and oddly delicious and made her see herself in a new way. Underneath everything she was truly bad, and oddly enough, it was a relief.

For months after, Zoe treated the pin like a favored doll, sleeping with it every night under her pillow, talking to it. Years later, she threw it out, couldn't stand the sight of it: but that one early-morning theft, that one ugly ballerina pin, started an obsession that has lasted all her life since: wanting things that it made no sense to want. Having them by stealing.

How often it comes on her now: this need for a fix, no less powerful than a drug addict's. Her adrenaline flows, her hands sweat, and her heart drums in warning. And she can never stop herself. She talks to the cashier on the way out, she chats with the store manager at the door, her heart thudding. On the sidewalk, her body thrills to the end of every nerve, throbs as sweetly as an orgasm, sometimes so intensely she must lean against a shop window a block up the street, every fiber pulsing with victory.

Later, she is soaked in shame. Later, she can barely face herself in the mirror, can barely hold her daughter in her arms for the disgrace of it. Once, she asked a doctor who was treating Jamie about it. She said she had a friend who got a nearly sexual thrill from stealing. That it was a compulsive act, unstoppable. "Yes," said the doctor. "The way you describe it is more than shoplifting and relatively rare. Sounds like kleptomania." She merely nodded, because she had already diagnosed herself. She had written it in her diary, gotten books out of the library about it. Kleptomania. She keeps thinking that one day it will leave her. Something, someone, will fill her emptiness enough so she won't need to steal anymore, won't even have to worry about it. Jamie's money didn't do it. Neither did the birth of Charlotte, or of Rose. What would it be like never to have the urge again? To no longer know to her core that she is bad?

That evening, still mortified about stealing the candy eggs, Zoe leaves work feeling miserable and worn. The symmetry of Eighth Street's houses doesn't soothe her, nor does the laughter of little girls chalking the sidewalk across the way. Not even the sight of her own house, lit like a Chinese lantern (a house all her own!), manages to cheer her. She can only note the curtainless windows and their bald display of stacked boxes and empty walls.

"Jamie's sister, Alicia, call from Manhattan," Teresa tells Zoe as she closes the front door. "She come tonight to see the house, if you say okay."

"Tonight? Not tonight."

"She's probably coming soon now. Too late to say no. I no can find the number to call your office."

"Oh. I guess we'll have to find the old telephone sheet and put it on the wall by the telephone," Zoe says. She raises her hands in exasperation. Alicia is one of the people Zoe loves most and is almost always pleased to see. But feeling defeated and blue, even about Brooklyn, Zoe wishes she didn't have to greet her or tour her through the house, which at any other time would be a pleasure to show. Still, when Alicia shows up, just moments after they've begun their dinner, wearing boots that come up to the top of her thighs and carrying a huge wrapped present, Zoe finds herself softening, not sorry to usher her in.

"Look at you. Look at you. A Brooklynite," Alicia says, hugging Zoe with that girlish excitement that marks everything she does. "Hey, Miss Rosie, take this, ducky. It's a housewarming gift for you and your mom."

Rose takes the outsize gift and rips into it without concern for the slippery pastel ribbons, the expensive paper in which it is wrapped.

"Save the paper, Rosie," Zoe says.

"Oh, no, Zo—let her rip into it. That's the whole point

of wrapping packages. To let us be animals and rip it apart. Very satisfying.''

"Aunt Alicia!'' Rose pulls from the torn paper a plastic-topped box displaying a huge slab of chocolate in the shape of a brownstone, with details and a stoop and all. "It's this house.''

"Not bad, huh, Zo?'' Alicia asks as Zoe helps Rose remove the top. "It's actually pretty close to the way this place looks, isn't it? Of course, I just guessed.''

"It's uncanny,'' Zoe says, trying to sound enthused. "And nearly as big.''

The scent of chocolate blooms in the room, sickening Zoe with its reminder of this afternoon's episode with the malted-milk eggs.

Rose insists on breaking off a piece of the cornice right away and eating it, despite Zoe's reminder that they have barely begun their supper.

"Kind of like Hansel and Gretel, eh?'' Alicia says to Rose, breaking off a piece for herself. "There's something indescribably good about eating a house.''

Rose laughs and pokes at Alicia, hoping for a "tickle fest,'' as Alicia calls it. In a moment, they're on the floor, rolling around like two puppies. When it's over, Rose curls up next to Alicia and rests her head on her aunt's arm.

Something about Alicia makes Zoe forget all bad things, makes her feel hopeful. Soon they are having dinner together, laughing and talking, though Zoe still can't bear the thought of tasting the chocolate brownstone.

"This place is gorgeous, Zo,'' Alicia says, looking around. "And of course, the best part is that Mother will never visit it, way out here. Or hardly ever. I hope you sold most of Aunt Delia's froufrou furniture.''

"Most of it I gave away,'' Zoe tells her. "To my assistant and to the Salvation Army. I asked your mother if she wanted it. She said she didn't have a single place to put it. That I should absolutely keep it. It was mine. But she didn't want it, so I gave it away. I didn't know what else to do.''

"Bravo. Defying her *with* her permission—it's positively passive aggressive. You must get her to come out."

"I'd rather not," Zoe says, laughing.

In fact, she shivers just thinking of her mother-in-law. Escaping Lois Finney was one of the chief reasons she moved to Brooklyn. And since they've moved, she's had only one phone call from her, to ask if they've settled in. Zoe is intensely relieved. In Sutton Place, Lois would show up at any hour to see them. Without warning, she'd walk in, set down her eight-hundred-dollar Mark Cross handbag, and tell Zoe all the things she was doing wrong with the apartment. She would move furniture. She would tell Zoe to put certain photographs in drawers. She would shake her head and say, "You don't seem to have any sense of how to do this apartment the way it's *meant* to be done."

When Zoe first met Jamie's parents, she instantly realized she'd never encountered people like them before. They believed there were two classes in America: "us" and "them." And Zoe was clearly "them." Because she was from a poor family—of Jews, no less, and concentration-camp Jews, worst of all—Lois let her know that she simply considered Zoe inferior. It didn't make a bit of difference that Zoe graduated third in her college class of thousands, or that she'd practically lived with Emily's wealthy family, who were not as wealthy as the Finneys, certainly, but just as cultured. Zoe tried to tell her; she dropped experiences as others might drop famous names. She was ashamed at how defensive the Finneys made her. But she couldn't help her horrible behavior, until the day Lois Finney told her:

"Zoe, I've already heard about your year in Paris, your magna cum whatever. I have heard your entire résumé. You have made it all painfully clear. Do you think that matters to me? I will do everything in my power to keep you and Jamie apart." Zoe was glad at the time that Jamie wasn't there to hear what his mother told her. Later, she was sorry he hadn't been there to defend her. But then, he might not have defended her at all. That's what the

Finneys did to people. They reduced them. They put them in their place. And Jamie, being the brunt of much of their reduction, was used to it.

Alicia is different. Her own person. She fights back. Maybe that's why Zoe loves her so much.

The truth is, Alicia could not be more different from Jamie if she tried. While Jamie's response to his parents' coldness, their self-centeredness, is to fold up, Alicia is so outgoing it's offputting at first. She is addicted to rebelliousness, and it's apparent in all she does. She loves to wear extreme clothes, and she can afford couture things that shock. Clothes that models parade down the runway, the outrageous ones that Zoe used to see in the newspaper, and think no one would ever wear, are the staples of Alicia's wardrobe. And at forty-six, she is willowy and girlish enough to wear all or any of them. She's even had her breasts lifted and slightly augmented so that she can go braless under her clothes. She smokes constantly, catching ashes in her hand, never wincing at the heat, a feat that astonishes Zoe. The only part of Alicia's life that she hasn't triumphed at is her relationship to her own face.

"It's completely unfair," she's told Zoe far too many times. "Jamie got all the looks, and I got the dregs. Well, you know. You've seen pictures when we were little. I think my parents would purposely stick me behind fat Aunt Celeste. There's hardly a picture of me without Aunt Celeste's elbow covering my nose."

Zoe has seen pictures of Alicia without Aunt Celeste blocking her, black-and-white photos from fifth grade, sixth grade, seventh, eighth.

"You probably won't recognize her," Jamie warned Zoe, pulling the yearbooks off a shelf in Aunt Delia's closet, shortly after they moved in. Delia had saved the annuals from the trash after Alicia had thrown them out so no one could see how she used to look, Jamie explained. For years, it was a secret only he and Delia shared. "Aunt Delia said someday Alicia will want to know what God intended her to look like. He wouldn't recognize her now, believe me.''

She hadn't been pretty, it was true. She had a Roman nose, eyes set too close to its bridge, straight, certain brows, not unlike Rose's, an overly sharp chin, and generous, horselike teeth that might have marked her as a member of the British royal family. But it wasn't a homely face either. It had character. It was unique. It was a kind face, with a genuine smile. At least in the early photos she smiled, but with each year she grew more and more scowly. Her face, more and more sour.

By the time Alicia was in high school, her teeth were fenced in by braces; her sophomore-year picture shows her nose completely different, though still swollen after surgery. And since she turned twenty-one, hardly a year has passed that she hasn't used her face as a canvas for a plastic surgeon's whims. Her chin has been diminished, her cheekbones accentuated, her under-chin vacuumed, her eyes widened so that whiteness at both top and bottom gives her a look of perpetual overexcitement.

The effect is unsettling. No matter how long Zoe sits with her, she can never get a fix on Alicia's face. It is a jigsaw puzzle badly put together, a cubist travesty. Her eyes never seem to be really seeing you. Her smile is a gash, stiff and unfeeling and slightly off center.

This face holds Alicia's secret. It is a secret that Jamie's whole being holds: their parents are perfectionists, and no matter how they try, the children can never live up to their parents' expectations.

To the outside world, no one can doubt that Alicia enjoys life. She takes big bites of it and never worries about whether she'll be able to chew it all. She goes on trips to Nepal and Zimbabwe. She throws lavish, orgy-like parties for charity. She loves to give gifts and has made an art of finding just the right thing for everyone. Her generosity is even more potent because it's so honest, so from the heart. She loves to see everyone as happy as she appears to be. But she is not essentially happy, Zoe thinks. She merely acts as happy as possible to spite her mother. To say, Though I'm not beautiful, I'm as happy as you.

Once, a few years after Zoe married Jamie, Alicia found a man who truly loved her. His name was Manny, and he was a Mexican painter. He begged her not to have any more plastic surgery. He painted her nude portrait a hundred times over. He brought her presents. He was the only one of Alicia's lovers Zoe really liked. And for a while, Alicia was softened, deepened, by his love for her. She even put on some weight, which made her look lush and almost exotic. But in time she couldn't bear to be with him. He persisted in the ultimate faux pas. He liked her just as she was.

"I got a letter from Manny," Alicia says now as they clear away the dishes.

"Really?" Zoe says. "I didn't know you've been staying in touch."

"Well, not really," she says wistfully. "This is the first letter I've gotten in a long time. Do you think I should see him again?"

"Yes. I loved Manny. He was such a nice guy."

"I don't know if I could. He's the only man I've ever been with that made me feel like a nasty bitch. Nice guys do that, you know. You compare how nice you are to how nice they are, and you can't measure up."

Zoe wonders what it would be like to have a man fawn over you. She imagines it would be just as uncomfortable for her as it is for Alicia.

"I doubt Manny saw being nice as a competition," Zoe says. "Write him."

Alicia smiles slightly in that disturbing lopsided way she now smiles.

"Maybe I will. He was awfully good in bed."

After the last dish is in the dishwasher, Alicia helps get Rose into her nightgown and, tucking her between the sheets, reads her a book she's brought, *Bedtime Stories to Help Raise the Perfect Child,* hysterical tales about incredibly bratty children. Rose laughs all through it, and when it's over, she insists that Alicia hold her hand while she falls asleep.

Zoe leaves them alone together, and later she hears Alicia climb the stairs up to the top floor, where Jamie is. Zoe thinks about joining her but then decides not to. Maybe it's best if Alicia sees him alone.

When she comes down to the kitchen, she's shaking her head. "He's worse, Zo."

"Do you think so?"

"He's definitely worse."

Zoe shrugs. "It's hard for me to tell anymore if he's worse, if he's better."

"He should be in a hospital. Mother's been saying it for weeks. Well, now I'm saying it."

"You know how I feel about that. How *he* feels about that."

"Zoe. You're such a martyr. It's really very unbecoming." She lights a cigarette and drops the match in the sink. "Come on, puss. How long are you going to put up with this? Him not talking?"

"I just will. Until he talks."

"I'm not going to lecture, I am not going to lecture you," she chants. "*But* I'm going to be on your case."

They are silent for a while. Zoe offers Alicia fruit, a soda, and she says no, but in a few minutes Alicia rifles through the refrigerator as though she's at home, finally pulling out a package of smoked turkey from the deli and picking at it like a woman who missed dinner.

"Rose is wonderful," Alicia says, chewing thoughtfully on the turkey. "And you get all the credit. My selfish brother turned his back on her."

"You're too hard on him, Alicia. He's sick."

"He's self-indulgent. I'm not saying he's not sick, but how could he turn his back on Rose? How could anyone not love a darling like our Rosie? She even makes Mother crack a smile now and then. Neither you nor I can do that. Mother still tells everyone the story of how Rose said, 'Grandma, don't your friends get lost in this apart-

ment? You need street signs!' And the time she was flying
with Rose to Florida, and Rose turned to her as they were
taking off and said, 'So, I'm ready. When do we get little?'
I love that. It's so logical. And so perfectly childlike.''

''Rose is my miracle,'' Zoe says. ''She's what makes
me survive not having Charlotte.''

''Charlotte. God,'' Alicia says. ''I hear her name and I
want to cry. She'd be what? Eight now?''

Zoe nods.

''You should remarry. Have another,'' Alicia says.

''Will you stop saying things like that?'' Zoe pleads.
''I'm happy with Jamie. I love Jamie. All right, he's sick
right now. Is that a good reason to abandon him?'' Zoe
is surprised at how loud and insistent her voice is. So,
apparently, is Alicia. She holds her hands up as if to protect herself.

''Okay. Okay. I won't say another word. But if you
ever do have real honest human emotions of anger, frustration, and the desire to murder Jamie, call. I'm here to
listen and possibly to help.''

Zoe shakes her head at her.

''Don't you love him?'' she asks. ''Don't you love
Jamie at all?''

''Of course I do, lovey. But Christ. I don't think it's
okay for the half-dead to suck the life out of the living.
It's not fair to you or Rose. Personally, I think it's great
you've moved here. Done something to make yourself
happy, at least. Gotten away from Mother. It is lovely
here. This house feels like you.''

''Thank you.''

''Aunt Delia's apartment never did.''

''I know. Do you think Jamie will like it?'' Zoe asks.

Alicia chucks her cheek tenderly. ''I hope so, dolly.
Really I do. I hope so.'' But then she shakes her head,
gathers her purse and jacket. ''I just don't have the patience to wait around and find out.''

# FOUR

On Friday night, at eight o'clock by the church chimes, Keevan O'Connor comes down the outside steps at 643 and looks around at the street. Up at 652, Maggie and Jack Kilkenny are sitting on the stoop, drinking beers in tall glasses, and raise them to salute Keevan.

"Lovely night," Maggie says, waving, enthroned on her familiar plaid seat cushion. It recalls to Keevan the cold march Sunday when he was a child and Maggie Ryan was the Saint Patrick's Day queen, laced up in a kelly-green tight-busted, full-skirted costume, waving from a float in the shape of a top hat that the Lucky Pub sponsored. Keevan stood on Seventh Avenue, vying for space with Jim and Ralph to see the vision of her flower-pink skin and black hair, contrasting exquisitely with the vegetable green.

"Good enough to eat," his grandmother said of her, and she did look like a cake decoration, high above the flowered float. Hard, sweet sugar.

Now, as Maggie Kilkenny, mother of four, she's too large to be called voluptuous. Her hair, which was so black it made him understand the blue undercoloring in comic books, is turning an iron color. She and Jack—also large now, with too much beer, too much of Maggie's good cooking—are always out on the stoop on mild nights, keeping watch on the street. Jack's red hair is turning grey

too. He works up at the church as a custodian. The kids
at the church school love him. He is as much a popular
character as old Douggie McCue was when Keevan was
a boy, pushing his broom around, trying to tell all the
Catholic children that there was a just fine church over on
Seventh Avenue, which they would like maybe even better: Presbyterian, with beautiful bells that made a much
lovelier sound. Like angels, he said. Maybe it was Douggie's missionary zeal that persuaded them to hire Jack
Kilkenny when Douggie retired, since Jack has been a
member of Saint Agnes all his life.

From the moment all her kids were in school, Maggie
Kilkenny became Monsignor Patrick's personal secretary.
She deposed old Mrs. Fitzgerald, with the wart, who
moved to the Madonna Residence on Prospect Park West,
to terrify the other old ladies. Maggie's a popular character
too. And she knows everything. If your kids act up in
school, Patty's told Keevan, all you have to do is ask
Maggie for the real story. She can tell you that it was
Sister Joan who started the whole thing by not allowing
your eight-year-old to have his recess, or tell you that
your child is a juvenile delinquent and you had better pay
attention. Or that your little Mary is hanging out with the
one kid at Saint Agnes who is definitely selling illegal
substances. As far as Keevan can see, Maggie and Jack
Kilkenny are the deans of the neighborhood.

Tonight, as Keevan sits down on the stoop with them,
he can't help thinking of his new neighbor, Zoe. All week
he has envisioned her long silver-gold braid, the delicacy
of her throat, her fingers. Keevan can't remember the last
time he was so struck with anyone. The astonishing thing
is, he hasn't seen a man come out of the house, not even
once. He has seen a Hispanic-looking maid, but not a
single man. If she had a husband, wouldn't he show up
at some point? No man goes out of town the second his
family moves into a house. Not even a selfish one. Or is
he wrong?

"You're certainly deep into it, Keevan."

"Just thinking."

"What?"

"Don't torment him, Maggie. If he wants to tell us anything, he will."

Maggie shoots Jack a dirty glance but changes the subject anyway.

"Darlene had such a row with Donald last night she came right home with the baby. She's upstairs napping right now. The baby cried all night. I never thought Donald was much of a choice for her; now I'm certain of it. She's tuckered out with that baby, and he doesn't lift a loving finger. He's drinking his life away." Maggie folds her large arms and shakes her head. "You'd think a girl with a fine father like Jackie here would have the sense to marry an equally fine man, wouldn't you?

"Donna Shea's trying to get pregnant," Maggie continues, changing the subject without skipping a beat. "But we all wonder whether Hal has it in him, if you know what I mean. I used to think Hal was going to grow up as one of those sissy boys. He was always hanging around with that boy who did go that way—what was his name?—David McGill. I thought they were in love or something. I was the most surprised on the block when Hal married Donna."

"Don't bore him with silly gossip like that," Jack says, sipping his beer. "You want beer, Keevan?"

"Yeah. I'd love one."

As soon as Jack's gone, Maggie leans toward Keevan conspiratorially. "Patty's in love with you, you know," she says. "And you've got a responsibility to set her straight."

"What, Maggie? Do you think I encourage her?"

"For all I know, you're monkeying with her every night, and I *don't want to know*. I'm just saying—"

"I've never touched her in my life. I don't like it at all that she's acting this way. She's nice to me, I try to be nice to her."

"You're obviously giving her the wrong message."

"Have you met the new people in 645 yet?" Keevan asks, desperate to change the line of questioning, and thinking that Maggie, in her reign of all knowingness might actually have news about Zoe.

"He's one of the Finneys," Maggie states, with clear pride that she has the scoop. "*The* Finneys. You know, I had a great-aunt once who worked for them. The stories I could tell . . ."

"Her husband's really one of *the* Finneys? I mean, I knew that was her name."

"Oh, yes, absolutely. The mover told me. He said you wouldn't believe where they moved from, this unbelievably fancy place, and there were pictures of the Finney family everywhere. Senator Finney. The whole lot. And the husband, he's like crazy or very sick or something."

"What do you mean?"

"The mover said he came in the house and went upstairs and lay down on the floor until his bed came. He said he might have AIDS or something really awful. Of course, the mover wasn't sure."

"AIDS? Jeez, Maggie. And the wife? What's her story?"

"I wouldn't know."

"Nothing?"

"Why are you so interested?"

"I met her. I liked her. She's beautiful. Have you seen her?"

"Well, she's married to one of the richest men you'll ever meet, sick or not, so if I were you, I'd look elsewhere. And set Patty straight. It's unkind to let it drag on."

"Here's your beer." Jack comes out with a frosty glass of dark ale. "Guinness."

"Great." Keevan gulps a mouthful of the rich stuff, sighs.

"So what's Maggie been gossiping your ear off about?" Jack asks.

"The people in 645."

"Oh, yeah. I saw the lady. She's a looker, isn't she?"

"Too skinny, if you ask me," Maggie says. "Did you know, Jack, they're the Finneys, the Baltimore Finneys?"

"Sure, darlin'," Jack says, lifting his glass to her. "And I'm John D. Rockefeller."

Watching Keevan walk away, Maggie Kilkenny sees him as a little boy: the same thatch of red-brown hair, so thick and glossy it invited your fingers to lose themselves in it; the confident, boyish walk. Too pretty, Keevan O'Connor, Maggie always thought. All the O'Connor boys were way too pretty. It got them in trouble.

Jim, of course, is a whole 'nother league of trouble. Ever since Maggie discovered what was happening between him and her Darlene five years ago, she hasn't been able to stand the sight of him. Three of her closest friends stumbled over themselves to tell Maggie that her own precious Darlene, nineteen years old and still living at home, was meeting Jim O'Connor all over town for one of the most public displays of adultery Park Slope had ever seen.

"He loves me, Ma," Darlene told her. "He can hardly stand Patty anymore. Don't I deserve some happiness?"

"If you think Jim O'Connor can give you happiness, Darlene, you need a brain transplant, I swear," Maggie told her. "He's a snake, a real snake. And if I ever see you going round with him again, I'll kick you out of this house so fast you'll land before you know what hit you."

The next thing she did was go down to Jim O'Connor's house and tell him she needed him to come right over to the church and talk with Monsignor Patrick about a problem with the building improvement fund—Jim was in charge of the books. He walked up Eighth Street, protesting. "Those books are in perfect order. Do we need to do this now?"

Once in the church, she grabbed him by the ear, pressed his lobe between her thumb and forefinger, and twisted it until he gasped.

"If you ever—*ever*—so much as speak to Darlene again, I shall not only tell Patty, Monsignor Patrick, and

everyone you've ever met; I will personally call Met Life
and tell them they are employing an adulterer.''

"Maggie, calm down," Jim told her. "I kissed her,
big deal.''

"I know everything, buster. Everything." The cool,
dark church echoed with Maggie's angry voice. She knew
that soon the good monsignor or one of the nuns or Mrs.
Clark, who did the church sewing at night, would be coming down to see what was going on, but it was no skin
off her nose.

"I won't see her again. I swear it," he said. Jim's
handsome face seemed to shrink before her gaze. "I swear
it." Maggie let go of his ear.

"Break your promise, and you won't have the equip-
ment to repeat your mistake," she said, her words and
voice so fierce she almost laughed. When Sister Edwin
came in to see where the noise was coming from, Maggie
smiled at her.

"Is there a problem, Mrs. Kilkenny?" Sister Edwin
asked.

"Not any longer," Maggie replied, and that, as far as
she knows, was the case.

As she watches Keevan open his garden gate, she thinks
about the O'Connors and the terrible childhood they had,
losing their parents when they were hardly more than babies, raised by grandparents who were really too old for
the task. For a crystalline moment, she remembers the
night Keevan's parents, Brian and Violet O'Connor, had
their accident. Maggie remembers the dress she was wearing when she found out—scratchy gray wool, a hand-me-
down from her sister Marie—and the root beer float she
was drinking, with double the ice cream. When the news
was relayed to them by Alda Draper, the street's gossip,
the root beer refused to go down her throat. She finally
managed to swallow, and it burned and choked her.

Her mother went down the block to be helpful to Brian's parents, and she ended up bringing four-year-old Jim
home with her to spend the night. He had no idea what

was going on. He drove his toy truck back and forth across the kitchen linoleum, making accelerating noises until Maggie wanted to throttle him. She was eighteen. And everything seemed indelible to her then. She couldn't imagine that anyone on Eighth Street would ever feel the same again.

That night, Maggie cried for Keevan's father, Brian O'Connor, as you might cry for a lover, for once, at age seven, she had loved him desperately. Brian O'Connor was maybe the handsomest boy Maggie'd ever seen. His face was honest, his features were clean. He was hard-working. His father owned an auto body shop on Fourth Avenue. It was clear Brian was someday going to take over. He worked at the job as though it were far more than a living, and went to church regularly. Girls vied for his attention, but he always traveled in groups, never singling out one girl over another. Maggie thought he was a god. She used to tell him, "Someday I'm going to marry you," and he'd blush, though she was only seven years old, and say, "You bet, kiddo," just like it was a real deal.

Then like so many other boys, he enlisted and went off to war. Within a year of shipping out, Brian lost an arm. Ripped clean off at the shoulder. Should have killed him, people said. He came back quiet and pale. And after that, his face was always hateful. Unquenchably angry. He'd get drunk on rum and urinate right in front of Mrs. Reilly's house, just past the Lucky Pub. Sometimes he got violent, swinging at other fellows with his left arm. He couldn't do what he did before at the auto body shop. His left arm didn't have the strength to pound out dents or the dexterity to fine-tune with heavy tools. He even stopped caring about running the shop. Everyone felt sorry for him, so they made excuses and covered up for his slack.

He was such a hateful man, no women so much as looked at him anymore, and it wasn't because of his arm. Or if women did approach him, after church or on the street when he occasionally sat out on the stoop, Brian was rude to them, cutting. He mocked their questions.

Then he met Violet Moore in the park, the story went. Head bent, she was crying because she'd just broken up with some guy. She was sitting on the stone steps of the boathouse by the Lullwater, sticking a big long stick into the pond, stirring it around and around, weeping. Brian sat down next to her and asked her her troubles. She questioned him about his arm, not at all shy to touch where it should have been. Her very presence found the kindly side of him, lost since the war. They went out together on a paddleboat all afternoon.

Violet was just nineteen, but in a matter of months they married. Maggie went to the wedding, stood in the last row, and cried right along with her mother. She's never seen such a beautiful bride since. Violet seemed to float down the aisle. Maggie was jealous. She was just ten, but she knew she would never be dainty and feminine and delicate like Violet. She would never have Brian O'Connor now.

The newlyweds moved into the upstairs apartment where Keevan now lives, and Maggie would visit them sometimes, sit on their old horsehair couch and talk to Violet about Jesus. Violet was very interested in religion. She told Maggie she'd once wanted to be a nun. Violet would serve Maggie pineapple hard candies from a crystal dish she'd gotten for her wedding. The candies smelled so perfumy, tasted so fruity, Maggie's salivary glands would ache as she sat there, trying to sit straight and sound older than she was, talking about "Jesus' expectations of us." Sometimes Brian would come in, not so angry now, his prettiness more seductive somehow than ever. Even at ten, Maggie longed to kiss him. She dreamed of it sometimes, what his straight, handsome lips would feel like on hers. She imagined that his mouth would taste of pineapple candy.

But Brian only had eyes for Violet. When she was pregnant, he bought her a big, comfy chair she could hardly get out of. She'd sit there eating her hard candies, holding court, getting bigger by the day. Ralph was born just a year after the wedding, and instantly Violet was slender and beautiful again, showing her baby all around the neighborhood. Three years later, Jimmy was born, then Keevan. Brian should have been the happiest man in the world. Even the job had worked out: he'd learned to handle all the books, all the business arrangements for the shop, and he was good at it. Only one thing troubled him: his jealousy. Violet was a beautiful woman, delicate and feminine and fragrant. And Brian thought every man who saw her wanted her. He wasn't a drinking man anymore, but he acted like one when he got jealous. A dry drunk, they called it. He punched people. He even roughed up Violet on occasion. Nothing serious, just some shaking. But people who witnessed it talked, and worried.

One day, the O'Connors asked Maggie if she wanted to come with them to Coney Island for the day, to help with the boys and get a free day of entertainment. In the Ford station wagon, they sang songs: "By the Sea" and "Que Sera, Sera" and "Rock Around the Clock." Keevan was just a baby. Maggie held him while the others went on the Wonder Wheel and the Log Flume. He was the calmest baby she'd ever seen. Pretty and happy, with eyelashes like a giraffe. The sea air was bracing. The carnival music excited her. Little Keevan grabbed a lock of her hair and wouldn't let go, but he didn't pull it, just smiled at her and was happy to be in her arms.

Ralph and Jimmy were hopping up and down like Mexican jumping beans, pulling them all one way or the other, to whatever rides caught their eyes. Ralph wanted to play bean bag toss—bean bags tossed at bowling pins on different levels. Knock over three and win a stuffed dog. Knock over four and win a stuffed rabbit. Knock over five and win the biggest, ugliest stuffed toy Maggie had ever seen: a raccoon with huge, mean teeth. Brian said he needed to find the men's room. Ralph did too. But Violet said she thought she'd be good at the bean bag toss and wanted to win prizes for her sons.

"And the beautiful little lady's going to play," the barker shouted. "The very beautiful lady."

"Thank you," Violet whispered softly. The man did indeed seem to leer at her; even Maggie noticed it.

Well, Violet knocked over six pins.

"Holy Mac. That's the best a woman's ever done," the man said, his eyes wide.

"Do you think," Violet asked in that whispery contralto of hers, "that we might be able to get some of the little toys, instead of that big one?"

"Well, for you, maybe. Which ones do you want?"

Violet pointed to a stuffed Rin-Tin-Tin, a fat white rabbit, and pale-blue rabbit with pink ears. "I've got three boys," she said, gesturing. "Three boys, three toys."

"And I'll bet they're all just as pretty as you, darling," the man said. "Say"—he leaned toward her with as much sense of conspiracy as can be mustered at a carnival—"you don't happen to be a single woman now, do you? 'Cause if you're a free woman, I'm a free man."

Maggie didn't realize that Brian was back, standing right behind her. Maybe Violet didn't either. What happened next happened so quickly there was no warning at all. With his one good arm, Brian punched the guy out cold. The booth attendant keeled over behind the counter of the game booth like one of his bowling pins.

Violet was crying. Brian's face was crimson. He hissed to Violet, "You brought this on. You were flirting with him."

"I wasn't. Why would I be interested in a carnival barker?"

"Because he has two arms." He grabbed her elbow and began to pull her away.

"We can't just leave him there, unconscious," Violet said. There was no one else around. The punch had happened so cleanly, so fast, with nary a scuffle, that none of the other barkers had noticed.

"We should go," Brian insisted.

"No," Violet said. Her own face was red now, and her

eyes were swollen. She went to the booth next door. "I'm afraid there's been an accident," she told the attendant.

"What kind of accident?"

"I hit the man with a bean bag," Violet said.

Maggie's mouth fell open. She could never have imagined that Violet was capable of lying. It was not something Jesus would have expected of us.

"*You* did this?" the other attendant said, finding his neighbor on the ground.

"Yes, sir. I'm terribly sorry."

The bean bag man was waking up now, moaning.

"I'm afraid we have to go," Violet said. "I certainly hope he'll be all right."

The other attendant paid no attention. He was busy taking care of his downed neighbor, while the family skulked away.

"Let's go to the sideshow up on the boardwalk," Brian said. "The kids will like the snake lady."

But Violet didn't answer. She just walked along beside him, holding Ralph's hand, white-lipped and miserable. They did go to the sideshow. Brian insisted they sit in the first row. They saw a brave, slender lady dance with a boa constrictor and eat fire. Jimmy cried when they sawed her in half. The MC did amazing card tricks. One man showed off his tattoos and demonstrated the hole in his tongue by nailing his tongue to a board. Keevan, sitting on Maggie's lap, kept reaching out for his tattoos as though he could pull them right off.

But Violet sat there with glassy eyes. Maggie had never seen her so miserable. Later, when they ate hot dogs at Nathan's and played on the beach, Violet didn't say one word to Brian, and Brian didn't say a single thing to her.

That night, Maggie couldn't sleep. All her fantasies about Brian and Violet had been shattered. Their life was misery. Their happiness was a sham.

Brian's jealousy got worse. Maggie heard about incidents all the time. Even the boys seemed a little afraid of him. Sometimes on humid summer nights, when sound

carried in an eerie sort of way, she would hear Brian's
voice raised. She could never hear Violet's meek one.

Violet and Brian died that winter. No one knows the
whole story. Just that they went to a movie in Bay Ridge,
and there was an incident with the manager, something to
do with Violet. And the manager socked Brian right in
the jaw. Some people said that Brian might have had a
concussion, and that's why he lost control of the car, that
he might have been going blind from the trauma to his
head. Other people said he was so upset, or fed up, or
miserable with his whole life, that he did it on purpose,
but his car—that 1952 red Ford station wagon—flew right
off Bay Shore Parkway and turned over twice before it
landed in a pile of rocks below. Brian died in seconds,
they said. Violet lived for a day, but she never opened her
eyes again.

After that, the boys' grandparents, who lived downstairs,
raised their grandsons as best they could. In time the boys
grew up, Ralph got himself killed in Vietnam, Jim married
Patty and cheated on her with Maggie's own Darlene, and
Keevan, beautiful Keevan, married and divorced a sharp,
nasty little girl, and walks around these days pretty as
Brian before the war, like a trap baited with honey for
any girl to fall into and drown herself.

Isn't it astonishing, Maggie thinks, how we all start out
at square one? How we never seem to evolve somehow.
Wouldn't it have been more efficient for God to have
allowed us to pass down our knowledge in our genes?
Wouldn't it have been better if lessons learned could send
the next generation forward. Instead we stumble each time
anew. Each man a clean slate prepared to make the
same mistakes.

Zoe climbs the steps in her new house, bringing a dinner
tray to Jamie. She always adds a linen napkin to his tray,
a flower in a tiny crystal vase. Still, he only picks. It
seems to pain him to eat, and he avoids the foods that

take any effort. So she cuts his steak in little pieces just as she does Rose's. She butters his roll.

Even in the apartment, when they had a full-time cook, Zoe brought Jamie all his food. He eats more when she's there. Her chatter seems to soothe him. And sometimes, when she reminds him of their first years together, at the University of Southern California, stealing oranges from the dean of students' prize tree, slow dancing naked on the dorm roof; or their married years before Charlotte was born, when they made love in a bistro bathroom in Paris, bought matching robes in Marrakech, she can even bring a sad smile to his lips.

In those rare moments, she sees Jamie as he was when she met him, the gentle boy with the limp who had already suffered the unthinkable, whose voice was so soft and manner so kind he instantly rose above all the other, brash boys she knew. He didn't talk about his accident. He didn't tell her who his family was. She simply sensed that his sadness lifted when she neared, that his love for her made him newly open to life. And the pleasure she gave him was all the pleasure she needed.

Recalling those happier times, Zoe finds it easier to bear the silence now.

The room is dark, but Jamie is sitting up.

"Hi, baby," she says.

He looks at her. It's been so long since he's spoken. She wonders if his vocal cords are as atrophied as his legs.

"How are you feeling?"

He raises his hands, palm upward.

"I've got steak, a potato . . ." she offers, smiling.

He looks like a little boy, in his saggy pajamas. His hair needs cutting; she's been doing it herself. She looks down to see his nails: long and horny, yellowed, thick. Unhealthy. It reminds her that he is sick. "Hungry?"

He shrugs.

"This room is nice, don't you think?" she asks him. "Every time I come here, I think how nice it is. The fireplace, the bed alcove. It would be nicer if you'd let me open the shutters now and then, though.''

He shakes his head. He lies down. The sheets smell of him: a damp ground-cover smell, not unpleasant, but strange.

"It's going to be over soon. You'll be feeling so much better. In just a week or two, maybe. I know it," she croons, setting down his tray. He once told her these were the only words that made him feel better during the last depression. But it's been three months since he took to his bed this time, except for the recent cab ride from Manhattan to Brooklyn, and now, in light of his silence, she has begun to lose hope that the words are true.

When Zoe knew the depression was starting again, when she first spotted those subtle signs of anxiety in the morning, woke to the first night thrashing, she tried to get him to see a new psychiatrist.

"Stop it before it starts," she said. "Maybe before you're actually in it, the drugs will work."

But he refused. "I can't bear even trying this time," he said. "I can't face the disappointment again."

During the last depression, the psychopharmacologist gave him a cornucopia of drugs; Jamie's medicine chest overflowed with them. First the doctor prescribed an anti-anxiety drug, which didn't quell Jamie's anxiety. And then a stronger one, and a stronger one. But the anxiety attacks grew worse, not better, and were horrifying to witness. She hadn't known that people who were capable of seeming normal could ever act this way. He'd hyperventilate, wring his hands, pull at his hair. He would sit on his knees, doubled over like a man with stomach cramps. He was in pain, a pain she couldn't reach or reason with. He told her he was dangerous, that she shouldn't get too near him, that everything he touched went bad, broke, died. "If I had the strength, I'd leave you," he'd say. "I'd leave you just to protect you." But sometimes, after a particularly bad attack would pass, he would lie weak, in a sweat, whispering, "I couldn't live through this without you,

Zoe.'' And she would feel miserably guilty that being with him had become unbearable, that she counted the minutes until she could escape to Editor's Fair.

Along with the anxiety drugs, the doctor tried every new antidepressant available on him. Each time, she would be hopeful. These were the new miracle drugs, which seemed to help everybody at some dosage level. Zoloft was the first, and she was especially hopeful because Jamie exhibited none of the side effects the doctor warned him about: nausea, grogginess, confusion, exhaustion. But weeks passed, and the drug did nothing for him. After three months, the doctor gave him Paxil, and again there was no effect, though the dosage was elevated slowly to its maximum level. Then came the Prozac, which jacked up his anxiety level alarmingly. Jamie told Zoe he felt as though he were jumping out of his skin. He actually began to tear at himself with his nails, made his arms and chest bleed. The lithium the doctor added had the opposite effect: made him groggy, weepy, miserable. As the parade of drugs went on, the depression became more and more acute; he became unwilling to leave his bed; a stony look masked his face. His whole body was transformed by the weight of his misery.

Zoe began to understand the eighteenth-century notion of possession. Was this her tall, lithe husband, this gaunt figure with the hunched back, the one who shuffled like an old man?

And much of his pain focused on Rose. ''She's going to die,'' he'd say.

''No,'' Zoe'd say as soothingly as possible. ''She's fine. Just fine.''

''Don't let her play on the playground.''

''She's a healthy little girl. She needs to play.''

''Don't let her eat strawberries.''

''We had her tested. You know we did. She's not allergic.'' And then he would spin down into the weeping.

''She was so beautiful,'' he'd whisper. ''She was so beautiful.''

And Zoe knew he meant Charlotte, their first child, who had died of anaphylactic shock from eating a single strawberry. Zoe flinched, remembering. The pain for her, too, even after all this time, was exquisite. But she went on. There were times when she forgot entirely.

Jamie got worse and worse. At his mother's insistence, they took him to the hospital, one Lois said they *must* go to because one of the doctors there had been highly recommended. Now Zoe suspects this hospital was chosen for its remote location—a place where no society friend or reporter could find him. In this cold, sterile environment, Jamie wouldn't eat at all, so they insisted on feeding him intravenously. And then they suggested the shock treatments.

"It's not like the old days, Mrs. Finney," the doctor told her. "They're much milder doses now. And we don't tie people down as they used to. People would react so violently to those old treatments, patients would sometimes break their arms or legs with the intensity of their muscle flailings during the treatments." Zoe winced. Felt ill.

"It's not so barbaric now, I assure you. It's very controlled. And frankly, very effective. It's all we have left. And he's suffering so."

The doctors told Jamie, and his moaning, sulky misery turned to pleading.

"Don't let them do it to me," he begged. "Zoe, don't."

"They say it's all you have left. That it's not so bad. And if it would make you better, wouldn't it be worth it?" she asked him. She'd been driving to the hospital to see him as often as she could. Three times a week at least, though the drive was grueling, and the visits miserable.

"Please don't let them do it," he still insisted. "I'd rather die."

She signed the sheet for the shock treatments, the taste of ashes in her mouth.

"When he's better because of this, you won't mind so much you did it," the nurse told her.

Looking back, Zoe thinks it was the worst thing she's

ever done. After the treatments, he became so disoriented it terrified her. He didn't recognize her. He could barely speak.

"Usually the disorientation eases after a day or two," the doctor told her. "Don't be alarmed. It's to be expected."

But by the end of the first week, the doctor himself was alarmed. Oddly enough, he recommended yet another shock treatment, saying it would help. Zoe no longer trusted him. But she was frightened, and tired. She would look in the mirror in the mornings and not recognize herself. The strain was killing her. She agreed to the second shock treatment.

Now she can't stand to recall one moment of those months. Can't even bear to remember the doctor's apologies, his own confusion over what had gone wrong. It took Jamie months to clear his mind again, to think in a straight, useful manner. It was as though they had taken a large stick and stirred his brain. Everyone at the hospital stopped her to say it was an anomaly. It was unheard of.

"It's terribly rare," they'd say. "He's wired differently, in effect, than most people. No one could have predicted."

When Jamie was more himself, though still depressed, Zoe took him home. He was instantly happier. He clung to her, squeezed her hand so tight sometimes it frightened her.

"I love you, Zoe. I love you," he would whisper.

A month after his return home, the depression lifted as mysteriously as it had come. But she knew he felt she'd betrayed him by agreeing to the shock treatments. And the truth was, it changed him. Weakened him, aged him. There was something essential missing in him: his sense of humor, his tolerance, were gone. No matter what she did, she could not stir them. She would never forgive herself for what she had permitted.

So hospitalization terrifies her more than she can say. And there is nothing left to do, it seems, but to be kind to him and share his suffering. He touches her hand now, as if to say he's sorry. She knows that even in the depths of his sadness he loves her desperately. The way a child loves a mother. Her presence is all he has.

Zoe has a sheaf of doctors' numbers. More to try. She always asks if there is a new drug. She brought in an acupuncturist for a while. Spoke to a herbalist. She keeps hoping to find someone with a simpler solution. A recipe that allows Jamie to stay home, where she can protect him. In her arms at night, sometimes, she feels him relax.

Zoe finds her cheerful voice. "Maybe after dinner tonight you might want to come down? To see the rooms downstairs. I've hung Aunt Delia's portrait. It's just meant for the room it's in. You could sit with me while we eat, Jamie. Join us."

He looks at her, startled, worried. How could she ask him? his eyes implore. Zoe's throat tightens, fills with pain.

"Well," she says, "I'll sit with you. Rose is downstairs, watching television. She said she wasn't very hungry yet anyway."

He struggles to sit up. He sighs. She watches him push the steak around the plate, listlessly eat a bite. He looks up at her every few moments, even smiles very briefly once.

For a long time after he finally lies down and turns out the bedside light, Zoe watches him. She isn't sure what she is wishing to see, to know. But her longing is monumental. She is astonished it doesn't wake him.

She thinks of what Alicia told her last week when she came to their apartment in the city to see it one last time. Alicia stood looking out over the East River, her arms crossed, "Christ. I'll miss this view," she said, "Aunt Delia sure knew how to live." Alicia blew out a plume of smoke and stubbed her cigarette into her hand, as she always does. "Listen, baby," she said, in that cool, jivey way that was hers alone, and she turned and looked Zoe clear in the eye, as clear as she could with her mismatched face. "Stop punishing yourself, Zoe, and take Jamie to a hospital. He's become an invalid. Maybe if you found him a doctor whom he could respond to, a man with just the right personality . . . it's real psychotherapy he needs, not medicines or cures.''

Zoe gazed at the river and wistfully remembered *Now, Voyager,* a movie she'd once loved for its editing, not its story. But that day last week, she remembered how Bette Davis was transformed by psychiatrist Claude Rains's fatherly belief in her. How she turned from an anxious, depressed spinster into an exquisitely dressed, sophisticated traveler, simply because she responded to her kind-voiced psychiatrist. If only that could happen to Jamie. If only he could rise from his misery like a phoenix, could become a charming, witty scion in flannel pants and a cashmere sweater, a male version of the Bette Davis transformation. If only.

"I hear of good doctors all the time," Alicia said. "Miracle workers, they say. With good hospitals."

"He'll die in the hospital," Zoe said.

"No, Zo. He didn't die last time. Even with those shock treatments. You wouldn't agree to them this time, okay. But it's *like* he's dead now. How can you live any kind of life, with him needing so much attention? I know you love him, but you're a zombie lately. Look at you. You weigh ten pounds less than the last time I saw you, and you needed to gain weight then."

Zoe thinks about Alicia's words: "Stop punishing yourself." She looks across the room at a mirror and sees that she has indeed become too thin, too sharp-edged, and then she looks at Jamie, sleeping, and wonders how the man she once loved so much could have become her punishment.

Her hand caressing the soft, worn mahogany rail, Zoe goes downstairs to spend time with Rose. Her little girl is curled up on the couch, in the very corner—her spot already, though they haven't been in the house a week yet—watching "Looney Tunes." In the TV light, her face is delicate and serious. She does everything with intensity and, it sometimes seems to Zoe, little delight.

"Mama, I'm hungry," Rose whines. She is rubbing her eyes, and she yawns with a stretch of her neck, like a cat.

Zoe shouldn't have stayed upstairs with Jamie so long. It's really too late to be feeding a six-year-old dinner. Teresa should have checked on her. Should have fed her. But then, Zoe was neglectful. Teresa's supposed to be off in the evenings. Zoe should never have let it happen.

"I'll bring it up in a flash," Zoe tells her, feeling guilty. "Sorry, dolly. I lost track of the time."

"Were you up there with Jamie?"

"Yes."

"Why do you sit with him? He never talks to you."

"I just like to sit with him. I talk to him. I think it makes him feel better."

"I went up there yesterday, and he was sleeping. He was snoring." She turns her head back to the television. Zoe aches at the sight of her neck, exposed by her ponytail. So slender, so reedlike, so fragile. Charlotte never grew old enough to have a neck like this. She had a baby neck, tucked with baby fat, a catchall for crumbs.

In the kitchen, it takes Zoe a while to remember where she unpacked the TV trays, the canned soup. To the mumble of Teresa's Spanish television program, Zoe heats up a bowl of Chickarina, Rose's favorite, gives her crackers, carrots, celery, a glass of milk. It's a feeble supper, but the kind of supper Zoe would have preferred when she was a child. Her father demanded that her mother make heavy pot roasts and gristly stewed meats. They would spank her sometimes if she wouldn't clean her plate. To waste food was a sin.

Now, when Zoe climbs the steps to the living room, she finds Rose asleep. How astonishing that children can drop from being awake to sleep with no transition at all. Just as easily as Rose goes from sleep to being awake. Zoe sets the tray on the table and takes Rose's chin in her hand.

"C'mon, baby. Supper's here."

Rose frowns, murmurs, and turns her slender little body

toward the couch. Moving the TV table away, sighing, Zoe lifts Rose, fifty pounds of endless legs, sharp chin, delicate hands, and cradling her against her own body, feeling guilty for neglecting her, she climbs the steps to put her unfed child to bed.

# FIVE

◆

That night, late, as Keevan is getting ready for bed, he hears a clanking on the sidewalk and goes to the window. She's out there in her bathrobe, Zoe Finney, dragging garbage cans out to the curb. Even from up here on the third floor, he can see her regal bearing. And yet she has an oddly self-conscious way about her: like one of his students, she's a tad clumsy, as though she has yet to come to terms with the size of her body. Her ginger-ale-colored hair is braided in the same Chinese plait down her back. Her watermelon bathrobe seems to blaze in the streetlight. What's she doing out there at one o'clock in the morning? In the dark, the whole street asleep, who will defend her, if need be? But Keevan's watching. If anybody so much as gets near her, he'll pull on his pants and get out there in a single breath. His body tenses at the thought.

Now, as she turns back to the house, sweeping her braid over her shoulder, he does put on his clothes, rushing, breathing hard. Suddenly it is the most important thing in his life. He *must* speak to her again. Running down the stairs, he shoots out the front door like cannon fire and then, embarrassed, wonders how he can explain it.

"Hello," she says. Her voice is soft as a whisper. A little dusky, womanly.

"Oh," he says. "I thought I heard my car alarm." Zoe

stares at him, her eyes glistening in the streetlight. Is she laughing at him?

"I didn't hear an alarm," she says.

"Maybe I heard it through the back window. On Ninth Street. You didn't hear an alarm at all?"

"No."

"I'm probably hearing things. Isn't it late for you to be playing garbage man?"

"Someone has to do it. Don't the trucks come at the crack of dawn? The woman who owned my house before said they did."

"Earlier sometimes. And they make the most god-awful squeaking. Someday I'm going to donate oil for those brakes. I'll be the hero of the neighborhood." Keevan stops, embarrassed: he's been babbling. "Don't you have a husband or someone to take out the garbage?" Keevan is proud of himself for having formulated so effortlessly a question that will get at the truth of what he's wanted to know.

"The housekeeper's asleep. And my husband can't."

"Can't what?"

Zoe bites her lip, baring her pearly upper teeth. "Can't take garbage out."

"Oh," Keevan says.

"He's sick."

"I'm sorry. Flu? Cold?"

Zoe shrugs and struggles for words.

"I'm sorry," Keevan says. "Is it something I shouldn't ask about?"

"Yes. I mean . . . yes." She smiles at him, looks relieved that he's given her an out.

"I'm sorry," Keevan says. What an idiot! Why did he make it so easy for her not to answer his question? She was about to explain, about to tell him everything.

"You've said you're sorry three times, I think. You don't have to be sorry. Really. I'm used to it. I'm just not used to explaining to people . . ."

"That he's sick?"

"That he's . . . well, he's depressed."

"Depressed." Of course. Rich guys. That's the common illness, isn't it. "I'm sorry. That's rough. But it's a lot better than the rumor I heard."

"You heard rumors? People are talking about us?" Keevan notices how she seems to stiffen, how her lips tense with worry. Beautiful lips, full and soft.

"No. I just heard that the moving man told someone on the street that your husband . . . well, there's no point in telling you."

"Yes, tell me, please."

"I think it might offend you."

"I'd rather know what people are saying." She looks so worried he has the greatest urge to cradle her, to say everything will be all right.

"Please." Zoe comes up to him. "Tell me."

"I don't know why I brought this up . . . really. He said your husband might have AIDS or something."

"What!" Even in the streetlight, he can see her cheeks are suddenly aflame. "You've got to tell everyone on the street that isn't so. That it's a terrible, vicious rumor."

"Of course I will. I'm sorry I told you. I should never have mentioned the rumor at all."

"Look," Zoe says, touching him. It is so tentative, the way she touches, so innocent somehow, and yet it sends a wave through his heart. "I want you to tell me everything the moving man said. Please. Damage control, my mother-in-law calls it. Family damage control."

"He just said your husband lay down on the floor as soon as he arrived, because the bed wasn't there yet, that he seemed very ill and it might be AIDS. He shouldn't have said that. I don't know why he'd leap to a conclusion like that. And here I am repeating it. But I wouldn't have repeated that to anyone else. An unsubstantiated rumor like that . . ."

"I don't know why people need to talk about us."

"He said your husband is a Finney . . . I mean, one of *the* Finneys."

"That moving man certainly had a lot to say." Zoe is crossing her arms now, folding in on herself.

"We're not all gossips and busybodies here in the Slope," Keevan says. "There are occasional nice guys. Sometimes I'm even one of them." He sits down on his steps now, feeling dispirited. To his surprise, Zoe comes cautiously through the front gate. Her robe is inflated momentarily by a gust of wind, revealing one long, slender leg. Tucking the rich pink fabric around her legs, she sits down on the stoop next to him. His heart feels as if it might burst.

"I just think everyone is too curious," she says. "We're a really private family. We've had to be."

"I guess."

"We're a family that's had a lot of success and a lot of tragedy. . . . I don't know why I'm telling you this."

"Because I asked."

"How long have you lived here . . . in the Slope?" she asks him.

"All my life."

"Really?"

"My great-grandparents bought this house in 1917. From the original owners."

"There's just you and your brother now? In the house?"

"I had another brother. He died in Vietnam. I guess that's *my* family tragedy."

"Were you close to him?"

"He was my hero."

Zoe looks at Keevan as though seeing him for the first time. Her eyes are eerily clear in the low light. She smells like the guest soap his grandmother used to put in a seashell when there was company. Clovelike, sweet.

"How old were you when he died?"

"Sixteen. He was twenty-two. I think sometimes about what it would have been like if he'd lived. We couldn't have divided this house into three. Not really. I guess I wouldn't be living here at all. It would be Jim and Ralph.

I could never afford to live in a place this nice on a schoolteacher's salary. Not since the prices have gone up.''

"You teach school?''

"High-school English.''

"That's great. I loved my high-school English teacher. I loved the English books we read in high school.''

"You like books?''

"I love books. Jamie—my husband—he used to love books too.''

"You talk about him in the past tense.''

Zoe shrugs. "Did I?'' she says, and begins to bite her hand. How vulnerable her knuckle looks beneath the assault of her beautiful teeth. Without thinking, Keevan takes her wrist and draws her hand away from her mouth. He has never felt skin so silky, so fine. He holds on to her wrist for a moment, loath to let it go.

"Bad habit,'' she says sheepishly.

"You have a lot to worry over, don't you?''

"I feel lucky,'' she tells him.

"Lucky?''

"My parents consider the life I live obscenely lucky. I send them money sometimes, but they never accept it.''

Zoe gets up suddenly, drawing her robe more tightly around her. "I'm chilly, and it's late.''

A breeze is blowing, and Keevan can hear the melody of someone's backyard wind chimes. "I wish you'd stay. Talk a little more. I could go get a blanket to sit on.''

"Another time.''

"Okay. Thanks for talking to me as long as you did.''

"You're welcome,'' Zoe says with almost childish politeness.

"Maybe sometime . . . Maybe you would be willing to have a drink with me?'' he ventures.

"I'm married,'' she says.

"Yes, of course, I didn't mean . . .''

"Good night, Keevan.'' He watches her go into her house, a flash of hot pink and flowers. The night feels empty without her, full of mourning. This is not at all how the night usually feels to Keevan: flooded with possibility, thrilling. He gets up. His knees hurt from the cold. He stands for a moment before going in, staring at her house, vainly searching for her movements through the open slats in her shutters.

Zoe Finney leans against the door she's just closed as though she's holding the outside out. She shivers and draws her robe around her. How could she have sat there with her new neighbor so long, showing such interest? There's no denying that Keevan O'Connor is one of the most appealing men she's met in a long time. She can't get the sound of his deep voice out of her ears. It is so sympathetic, and somehow full of life. And interest. He was truly interested in her.

He has just the sort of personality she's bound to be vulnerable to right now, she tells herself. Lively, available, charming. And then there's the virility that emanates from him. She feels invigorated and full of feeling for him, the way she used to when she would go to the movies and fall in love with the leading man. How odd it is to feel so stimulated, so buoyant. How disturbing.

Later, as she lies next to Jamie, hand-tinted pictures of Keevan O'Connor tease her. The subtle natural pink of his cheeks, the rich cognac color of his hair. The way he laughs, his teeth as even as ivory keys. It's only the circular song of her fingers, and the swirling climax they conjure, that allows her entrance into her dreams.

It was long after Zoe had fallen in love with Jamie that she discovered who he was. They met in the college library. Their assigned study carrels were next to each other. Jamie had come to UCLA to get away from his family, who, since his accident, worried and fretted about him constantly. He was happy to have a continent between them, at least for a while. Zoe and Jamie started to date, and for a long time, though she was very drawn to him, he seemed like a total stranger. He never said anything about his family. In fact, he never started a conversation. It was up to her to set the topic, to direct the talk. Mostly they talked about their classes, the people they knew in common. She knew he was from Baltimore, his family now lived in New York, but who would have imagined he was so wealthy, so well known? He wore blue jeans, like everybody else, and faded flannel shirts. He was just a shy boy with a limp and a soft voice. The vulnerability he displayed drew her closer to him: the way he could never get through a joke without apologizing for telling it wrong; the sadness in his eyes; the regretful sound of his Baltimore accent. Something terrible must have happened to him, but she didn't press him to tell her; he would explain everything when the time was right. She simply noted that he didn't own a car and hated even getting into one, that he covered his glass when anyone tried to pour wine into it. His sadness was the most attractive thing about him, in an odd way. It was cozy and familiar. She spent a great deal of time trying to cheer him up with jokes and information and bubbly talk, just as she had with her parents.

When she found out who he really was, she was stunned, and thrilled to think of him as a member of not just a family but a clan. A group of people famous for their supposed closeness. Everything about the Finney family thrilled her. She was happy just to be in the presence of his parents at first. What fascinating figures they cut: financier Paul Finney and his wife, Lois, so different from Zoe's Eastern European parents with their unhealthy, sad faces, their memories of the death camps dictating everything they did. The Finneys, with their elegant, upright backs, their ruddy liquor-blushed faces, seemed to have invented joie de vivre. It was as though the whole world belonged to them, and knew it, and paid obeisance. Who didn't read ten articles a year about Senator Abbott Finney, Jamie's uncle, the most charismatic politician of the decade? Or Jamie's eldest sister, Felicia Finney Rockefeller? Her Georgetown apartment was featured in *Architectural Digest*. As was her summer home, and her "cute" little farmhouse in Provence. Or his other sister, Alicia, with her wild parties for charity?

And then Jamie told her about the other side of his life: about his accident. She has often imagined it: the night that Jamie, wild and handsome at sixteen, drove his racing-green MG down Maryville Street, having just left a party where he'd kissed at least three different girls. He'd had eight, maybe ten beers, and whiskey chasers, but was too drunk to know he was drunk. He said he thought he was just straightening the wheel; instead he swerved into the opposite lane, hitting a motorcycle with two people on board. The man died instantly. The woman lingered for a week, a leg torn off, both lungs collapsed, a gash in her chest the size of a fist from the cycle's handlebars.

Witnesses reported that by the time the police came, he was sitting with the wounded woman, acting stone sober and crying. His own leg was badly injured, but he hadn't even realized it. He knew that what had happened to the motorcycle riders was irreversible. Despite his clarity when the police arrived, his blood test revealed enough alcohol to kill a smaller man.

The papers put him on page one. This is what happens when you are raised with too much wealth, too little care, they said. You kill and maim and walk away scot-free. But Jamie hasn't known freedom since.

He sees himself as a bad-luck carrier, as virulent as Typhoid Mary. Wherever he goes, he's sure people catch it. This is the context in which he views the world. Coincidence takes on a menacing certainty. Men he's walking with lose their wallets to even bumbling pickpockets. Old women he passes fall down in the street. Secretaries spill stacks of delicately categorized files or entire boxes of paper clips whenever he is near.

And to prove it, the final proof, there was Charlotte. When Charlotte, their firstborn, came into the world healthy, clear-skinned, all her perfect little organs in the

right places, her fingers and toes correctly numbered fluttering digits—she snapped her toes back and forth from
the day she was born—he thought maybe the bad luck
was over. Charlotte with her pouffy lips so like Zoe's, her
slate-blue eyes, her hair like spun gold in the light.

Jamie has told Zoe over and over that he should have
known. He says he should never have attempted to father
a child. One day when she was two, while she was in his
charge, he fed Charlotte a strawberry, and without even
the allergic response of an anaphylactic reaction—asthma-
like wheezing, or closing of the throat—Charlotte went
into a coma. She was limp as he held her in the taxi on
the way to the hospital. In the emergency room, they
shocked her tiny chest, as Jamie stared. They forced their
breath into her rosebud mouth. But she never moved those
tiny fluttering toes again. He had killed her as surely as if
he had shot her full of bullets. She had caught his bad
luck and simply died of it.

Zoe mourned too. She felt as though all her teeth were
pulled from her mouth. That her head was filled with
scalding oil. Pain beyond words. Loss beyond description.
The silence in the apartment was deafening. The crib still
wore the same sheets. The changing table still valleyed
where she'd laid Charlotte to receive her last fresh diaper.
Her room gave off the warm breath of powder and milk
for days. Moments of panic would wash over Zoe. Where
was Charlotte? Where had she left her? Like a purse left
under a table. Where? My God, where was she? And the
answer was more painful than the question. She had left
Charlotte with Jamie so that she could shop for a new
coat. *She* could easily have fed Charlotte the strawberry.
She could have carried the horror of this guilt.

But it hadn't happened that way. And now Jamie's life
is strangled, stunted, because he could not see it as simple
terrible fate. What he saw was a pattern. A pattern he had
for a moment ignored.

When Zoe discovered she was pregnant with Rose,
Jamie wouldn't acknowledge the pregnancy. If she spoke

about it, he pretended he didn't hear her. When she gave birth to Rose, he would not come into the birthing room, did not come to see her afterward. Once she brought Rose home, he wouldn't change a diaper, he wouldn't even hold her. "Keep her away from me," he told Zoe. "If you love her, keep her away from me."

A few months after that, Jamie stopped going to his law office. He lay down in bed and became as needy as a baby himself. That was his first breakdown. After many months, it passed, and there were a few years when he was functional at least, though he never did go back to work. There have been six episodes in all now, but these last months have been the worst. In the past, he would at least speak to her, and now there is only this chilling silence.

But even after all these years of trouble and pain, she can still remember how clearly she once felt about him, how lucky she thought herself to have found him. How they decided that even with Jamie's fear of his parents' disdain, they had to be together always. For once, Jamie stood up to his parents, told them in her presence he would give up anything—even his inheritance—to be with the woman he loved. Just like the Duke of Windsor, she'd told him later, proud of him, heady with her love for him. After that, like pinching herself during a dream, she would repeat: I am married to Jamie Finney. Jamie *Finney*. The name, the wealth, thrilled her. But there was more: the pleasure of bringing someone so sad forward into the light. How healing it had been for her, to make him so happy. To do for him what she could never do for her parents. That's gone now. Forever.

# SIX

———————◆———————

Rose Finney wakes to the sound of her mother singing. She sits up slowly in the streaming sunshine, in the yellow glow of her new room, feeling she must be dreaming. The gentle, sweet sound reminds her of the baby years when her mother would rock and sing to her. Rose still climbs into her mother's arms sometimes, but her legs have nowhere to go, and her elbows get in the way, and it's hard to feel really safe anymore. Safe the way she felt only in her mother's arms.

Still, Rose doesn't think she's ever heard her mother sing in the morning. And so joyfully.

"Somebody loves me . . . I wonder whooo . . ." Rose pulls in her toes, leans her head on her knee, and listens.

When the singing stops, Rose gets up to find her. She's in the laundry room, doing a load before work. Rose has never seen her mother do laundry before. Other people did that for them in the old apartment. Rose wonders why Teresa isn't doing it.

"Hi, baby," she says.

"How come you're doing the laundry?"

"I used to like doing laundry. I just thought I would."

"Why?"

"It's like getting a fresh start, doing laundry. A clean slate. You ever hear that expression?"

Rose shrugs. "I guess. You were singing."

"Yup."

"I liked it."

"Good. Want some breakfast?"

"How come you were singing? Because you like doing laundry?"

"I don't know. I just woke up happy." Zoe measures the laundry detergent in its cap and pours it on the wash. Even though her mother never ever did the laundry before, the smell of the laundry room—even in the old apartment—always reminded Rose of burrowing her face in her mother's clothes and finding safety in her warm, scented comfort. Zoe takes down the giant bottle of fabric softener with the picture of the baby on it.

"Can I measure it?" Rose asks.

"Okay." Rose lifts the heavy bottle from her, unscrews the giant cap (thinking how it would make a wonderful tub for her littlest dolls), and begins to tilt the bottle into it. Zoe quietly puts her hand underneath the bottle to steady it but doesn't interfere with Rose's efforts. That's why Rose thinks her mother's the best. Other mothers, her friends' mothers, do things like snatch bottles away from their daughters. They don't let their kids do anything. They're always expecting the worst things to happen. But Rose's mom even lets her dial long-distance numbers for her. She lets her fill the bathtub by herself. She lets her pick her own clothes in the morning. Even when Rose picked the tie-dyed shirt to go with the printed pants (and she knew it was kind of a messy combination), her mom didn't say anything except, "You sure must be feeling colorful today," which she was. Rose thinks she must have the best mother in the world. But her father . . .

Zoe says it has nothing to do with her, that Jamie's just sick, sick with sadness because her sister died. Rose hates her sister for that. It would have been nice to have a sister. If her sister hadn't died, Jamie might be holding Rose on his knee, smiling, liking her even better than he liked her sister. She's seen pictures of him with Charlotte sitting on his knee. She hates those pictures. Charlotte ruined everything by dying.

"Breakfast?" Zoe asks again, touching the button that turns the washer on.

"No. I just want to stay with you, Mama," Rose says.

"You have to eat breakfast sometime."

"When you eat," Rose says. "I just want to stay right with you."


Patty O'Connor sits on the stoop, waiting for her new neighbor to come out. She knows she works full time and has to come out at some point to go to work. She's seen her leave other mornings this week in her fancy clothes and a purse in the shape of an envelope, like some mom in those TV commercials Patty hates, who works and raises kids and never breaks a sweat or a nail. Patty's not sure what she's going to do when she sees her. Talk to her? Ask her what the hell she and Keevan were doing, talking to each other on the stoop in the middle of the night? They must have talked twenty minutes. Patty saw her standing out there in her robe. She was so slender. Maybe she's one of those people who eat and put their finger down their throat to make themselves throw up. She looks like someone who would do that.

Patty lights a cigarette. Jim left at seven like usual, the kids left shortly after, and Keevan had some early teachers' meeting. With all of them gone, who's going to give her a hard time about smoking? She exhales, enjoying the spicy burn of the cigarette on her tongue. She looks down at her own outfit—the too-often-washed baggy shirt, the cranberry-colored jeans. Hardly sophisticated. But she's more or less kept her figure. She used to think she was pretty, back in high school. A lot of people thought she was pretty. Jim doesn't think so anymore, obviously. The funny thing is, the way he shows it is by treating her too respectfully. When they were first married, he wanted her every night, and he would talk dirty to her.

"I want to fuck you, baby," he used to say, just like

he was some guy from a street gang. "You want me to fuck your pussy, sugar?" It always made her tense up. Who the hell did he think he was, talking to her like that? But it also excited her, no denying it. Now he says, "Are you in the mood?" and he only asks her once a month, it seems; less lately. Now she's in the mood almost every day. She wishes he was interested in her. She's tried a few times lately to tell him she wanted to make love. But he pretended he didn't get what she was trying to tell him, or that he was asleep. He is instantly asleep a lot. So maybe it's just in her head.

Finally, two cigarettes into her vigil, Patty hears the door open next door and sees Zoe step out on the stoop. Her silk suit is long and slender, the color blue of children's finger paints. The kind of blue so intense it makes your eyes ache.

"Hello," Patty says, inhaling deeply afterward so she doesn't have to look at Zoe.

"Hi," Zoe says.

"What do you do?" Patty asks.

"Do?"

"I see you going off to work every day. . . ."

"I edit TV commercials."

"Oh." She almost laughs aloud. Wasn't Patty just thinking how she looked like a TV commercial?

"What do *you* do?" Zoe asks.

"I sit out on the stoop and smoke cigarettes," Patty says, "and clean house and feed my family."

"Oh." Zoe smiles one of those nervous, condescending smiles Patty's always hated. "I have a six-year-old. How old are yours?"

"Seven and twelve."

"Good ages," Zoe says, shifting her purse to her other arm, looking uncomfortable, Patty thinks.

"There are no good ages," Patty says. "So I noticed last night you were talking to Keevan."

"Yes. It was late. Were you up too? He's very nice. He's your brother-in-law, right?"

"We're very close," Patty says.

"Uh-huh . . . I hope we didn't disturb you, talking out there."

"No. But I could hear you." The truth is, Patty was lying awake, hoping that Keevan would stop making noise upstairs and go to sleep. She's restless when she knows he's up. She can't even close her eyes when she's thinking she might miss something—a sound, a movement, that would reveal him in some way. So she lay there in the dark, watching shadows on the ceiling, listening with rapt attention the way she used to listen to top forty hits on the transistor radio under her pillow.

Just as she was giving in, drifting off, she heard footsteps running down the stairs, and then his voice outside, and a woman's voice, and she felt a grip and a chill that made it hard for her to swallow.

She went to the window woozily, sleep making her dizzy, and she saw them out by the gate, Zoe in that fancy robe, Keevan leaning toward her like a dog sniffing a beloved scent. It made Patty sick.

"Well, I'm late for work," Zoe says.

"I'm not going to stop you," Patty says. She stands up and stretches her legs, gripping the cigarette neatly between her teeth. She suddenly feels she could bite right through it. She watches Zoe Finney, all lanky sophistication, glide down the street. Definitely everything handed to her from the day she was born.

Friday night is the second garbage night on Eighth Street. The Kilkennys have put out their garbage—extra full, with diapers from Darlene's baby, now that she seems permanently camped out with them. In front of the Fitzgeralds', bags are bursting with toy boxes from Abby's sixth-birthday party: Baby Surprise, Chuckie the Strolling Pup, Cool Kitty (batteries not included). There are also wads of wrapping paper, that, with the wind picking up, are beginning to blow out of the cans and skitter down toward Seventh Avenue like colorful tumbleweeds.

From his window, Keevan watches them, one after the other, spin comically down the hill. Then he glances back at the empty place where the Finneys' garbage should be. Surely she won't forget to put it out . . . ? If she does, she'll have to wait for next Tuesday. Maybe she doesn't know Friday is garbage day. Or she's forgotten. He takes a deep breath, closes the shutter, and goes back to his book: Jack London. He's having his students read *White Fang*. He has always loved it, lost himself in it as a kid, wants them to lose themselves, transport themselves from Brooklyn to Alaska and return forever changed.

Tonight he'll go to the park. Later, when the dew's on the grass, he'll walk by the tennis house, where the pigeons sleep among the eaves like grey fists. Down into the wet meadow. He'll think about Zoe Finney.

Now he hears the squeak of a gate and hurries to open his shutters. She's dressed in jeans and a pretty T-shirt, the color of—what?—violets?

He gets up, barely shuts his apartment door—he doesn't want to alert Patty—and goes down the steps, leaning hard on the railing, trying to rush but not make too much noise. "Zoe," he calls softly from the top of the stoop.

"Hi, Keevan." She looks up immediately, almost as though she were expecting him. His name sounds sweetly foreign emanating from her mouth. She is dragging huge packing boxes toward the curb, tripping over them in that surprisingly clumsy way that only endears her to him.

"Let me help you," he tells her.

"Oh, please do. These are the last ones left. The movers took most of them. Do you think the garbage men will take these?"

"Sure. They're not heavy."

"When these are out on the curb, I can say I'm all moved in."

"Here. Let me take that." Near her, he can smell her scent again: expensive, it seems, and complex. Cinnamon? Grapefruit? Clove? His arm brushes hers as he lifts the box, and it sends a charge through his body that weakens him. "You had to do all the unpacking by yourself, didn't you?"

She shrugs. "Our housekeeper helped me. And besides, I didn't mind. I love the house. Rose doesn't like it yet, but she'll get used to it, I'm sure."

"Who's Rose?"

"Oh . . . my daughter. She's six and a half."

"I didn't know you had children." He feels a curious stinging in his heart. If she has a child, she is more tied into her marriage than he imagined. "Do you have more than one?"

"Well, now there's just Rose."

He looks at her, understanding what she's telling him. "You had another child?"

"She died."

"I'm sorry. Recently?"

"Before Rose was born. . . . Jamie hasn't gotten past it, that's why he's . . ."

"Your husband?"

She nods. "It's when everything started, really. When it all went wrong."

"Sometimes I feel, with you . . ." He pauses and hitches his fingers into his jeans pockets. "Not that we've talked that much—well, hardly at all—but I feel like . . . you know . . . that we could talk more. Zoe, look, it's terribly late, but I mean, you wouldn't want to . . . just take a glass of wine with me . . . ? Believe me, I know you're married, and I respect that, really. I—"

"Yes."

"Yes?"

"Yes, anything to make you end this sentence."

Keevan laughs. "Cool." He rues his choice of words. He hangs around teenagers too much, he thinks. "I'm glad," he adds, in a lower register.

Zoe follows him up his front stoop, silently up the steps to his part of the house. He wonders if Patty is awake, if she's been watching him. It gives him a shiver.

"Oh," Zoe says, as she enters his living room. "This is so nice."

"Thank you. You didn't think it would be."

"No, it's just . . . there are so many books. And it feels so sophisticated."

"Does it?" Keevan asks, truly pleased. No compliment could have warmed him more.

"I like the color of the walls. Just about the color of your hair, actually."

He realizes he is blushing. "I didn't realize that when I picked it."

"You should stay here all the time, like a portrait in a setting. It flatters you."

Keevan feels a fullness in his chest, and even his fingertips seem aroused.

"In our house, this is Rose's room," Zoe goes on. "A room full of stuffed animals. I like what you have. It doesn't seem like a place where a bachelor lives."

"Well, it is. There's hardly anything left from my marriage. My ex took it all. Most of this furniture was my grandparents' or my parents'. That desk was where my grandfather used to pay the bills. That table is where my grandmother used to put her sewing machine. She never bought a dress in her life. She made them all. Right up to the time she died. They weren't too attractive, but . . ." He shrugs. "Anyway, she made them. Sit. My grandmother always loved that chair. I've got some white wine in the refrigerator."

"You don't seem like the white wine type," Zoe says.

"You think I drink beer, right?"

"You look like someone who would."

"I'll pretend I'm not insulted." He smiles at her, noting that she looks beautiful and fragile sitting on his couch, her pale hair set off by the cordovan leather, her hands folded nervously in her lap. Her nervousness translates to him, and as he takes out the balloon-shaped glasses he bought at the Pottery Barn when he was wooing Tina and wipes the dust off them with a dish towel, he finds that his hands are unsteady and his head feels light.

"I like people," Keevan says. "But I hate getting to know them. I suppose that sounds uncharitable. But I want to be past the getting-to-know-you part."

"Socks in your laundry," Zoe says.

"What?"

"I used to have a friend who would say she didn't want to have to get to know anyone she dated. She just wanted to get to the point where their socks were already in her laundry. . . . She was shy. Getting to know people was excruciating for her. Are you shy?" Zoe asks.

"No, it's not shyness. That's not it. Maybe it's having to justify what you're already comfortable with yourself."

"Like?"

"Well, like defending my job. I love my job, but the people I went to college with, some of them think it's beneath me. I started off in prelaw. You know, all those poli-sci classes, worrying about getting into law school. Most of my friends from those days make way over six figures in law firms now, but they're totally miserable. They have no lives. And yet they sneer when they talk about my teaching.

"I actually applied and got into University of Virginia law school. I was all ready to go. But that whole summer I couldn't sleep. Law and rules and all that prescribed stuff isn't what matters to me. It's books that always thrilled me. The only classes in college that had any impact on me at all were English lit. So I'm really doing what I like now.

"I mean, okay, it's a city high school; it's not glamorous . . . but I love it. And I think I can affect my students' lives. In this neighborhood, I was one of the few guys who went to college. Sometimes I think that's why I stay here. Because here, who I am, who I've become, has more weight. God. I'm talking way too much about myself."

Keevan feels hot, ashamed. Helayne always said he was self-centered. Why is it that when he's attracted to someone, this side of him comes out? But Zoe doesn't seem bored. She looks up through her pale lashes and smiles sympathetically.

"You shouldn't care what other people think if it makes you happy. I think what you do is great."

"I try not to let it bother me. But the world revolves around status, you know. If I told my old classmates I had become a college professor, for instance, think how differently they'd treat me, and it would essentially be the same job, maybe even less challenging. And I wouldn't be making any more money. I mean, look at you. When I heard that you're married to a Finney—you're one of the Finneys—I didn't want it to, but it changed what I thought of you."

"Yes . . ." Zoe seems to grow smaller as she speaks. She sips her wine with a regalness that's merely a front, a facade, he sees. It draws Keevan to her even more.

"I bet it's rough being in a family like that. So visible."

"It comes with a duty. Something I never imagined. You're always being photographed, observed, criticized. The press put Jamie through hell when he was a teenager. They love to zero in on the failures of the rich. They portrayed Jamie as a prototypical rich spoiled brat."

"He wasn't?"

"Oh, no. He's nothing like that. At least not since I've known him."

Keevan looks at Zoe's mouth, her soft, pearly lips, and his longing to kiss her nearly closes his throat. He takes a deep breath that comes out as a sigh, then leans over and fills her glass again.

"This all bores you," Zoe says.

"Oh, believe me—the last thing I am is bored. And I totally talked your ear off. I want to hear more about Jamie." He doesn't, he thinks, as soon as he says it. Jamie is the last thing he wants to hear about.

"Well, I don't know if I can really explain it, but ever had a day when your hair stood straight up, or you felt ugly or fat? Maybe men don't feel that way—"

"Sure they do."

"Imagine it gets commented on in the press. That's what Jamie had to put up with all his life. And when he got in trouble for anything . . . the press was there."

"He's the one who had the car accident, wasn't he?" Keevan suddenly recalls the headlines.

"How can you remember that? You're too young."

"I was fourteen. My grandmother cut out the newspaper article for me. 'That's why you won't drive a car until you're twenty,' she told me. And I didn't. I read every detail."

"I can't believe you know about it."

"Is Jamie an alcoholic? That's how they portrayed him, I remember. A teenage alcoholic. A joyride . . ."

"No. He's not an alcoholic. He hasn't touched a drop since." Keevan is shocked by how fiercely protective she seems. "He can barely make himself get into a car. I had to literally push him to get into the cab to move here. He shakes in a car. He won't drive. At UCLA he practically never left the campus." Zoe is biting her knuckle again. Her pale, freckled skin dents beneath her white teeth.

"You knew this about him when you married him?"

"Haven't you ever loved someone who's flawed or helpless in some way? It makes them easier to love, in a way. Safer. They need you more."

Keevan tastes the wine and closes his eyes. "That's the thing," he says. "I never fell in love with a single person who wasn't a perfect little dumpling . . . and here I am alone."

"Oh," Zoe says, her voice disappointed.

"Do you still love Jamie?"

"Of course." Zoe's lips draw into a slender white line. "I should be going," she says.

"So soon?"

"I should." She stands, and Keevan sees the iciness even in her stance.

"I shouldn't have asked. I shouldn't have brought him up."

"Oh, no," Zoe says. "I brought him up, didn't I? It's

not that. It's just time for me to go. Our housekeeper might not hear Rose call out, if she's afraid or has a bad dream. Teresa's on the first floor, Rose is on the third.''

"Okay. I'll walk you to your door." Keevan is astonished by how disappointed he is to see her go.

At her door, she turns to him. He again has an urge to kiss her, as though they've been on a date. It is so strong he finally leans forward and kisses her cheek.

"Zoe," he whispers, overcome by her scent, the creamy velvet of her cheek.

"Good night, Keevan," she says. Her voice has turned to Freon. She shuts the door definitively behind her.

# SEVEN

There is one hour of the day when Eighth Street is completely silent, when the littlest babies nap and their mothers snooze beside them, when the older children are still in school, when the mailman has made his rounds and the squeaking D'Agostino carts have delivered all their groceries. Hardly a car whooshes down the street. Hardly a footstep makes its chalky sound on the bluestone. The silence starts at two and ends at three, when the schoolchildren stream down from Saint Agnes with their backpacks and their taunts.

Maggie Kilkenny works on a different schedule. She leaves school at one, naps until two, and usually spends the afternoon in her garden, or writing letters, or reading the Bible, an activity that refreshes her as much as a nap. But this afternoon, eight minutes after two, Maggie Kilkenny is putting on a fresh blouse and skirt. Her round figure still has its assets, she thinks as she looks into the mirror on her bedroom door. Still hourglassed, bosomy, feminine. God knows, Jack never complains, desires her as much as he did when they were first married. Ah, but she will be fifty-two in August. And age is as much a feature on her face now as her nose or eyes. Maggie applies her lipstick and smacks her slender pink lips together. Are they thinner than they used to be? Certainly the parentheses of lines that run from her nose to her mouth are more pronounced, perhaps more pronounced than her lips themselves. To once have been pretty is a curse, really, for prettiness opens doors, makes you think those doors will always be open. Well, she looks good enough for her mission. She closes her bedroom door quietly behind her, so as not to wake Darlene and the baby, who are napping in the guest room.

Out in the street, even the birds seem respectfully quiet. The breeze makes a lovely hush through the maple leaves. Maggie takes a deep breath before she turns in at the O'Connor's gate. It squeaks with warning and relatches with a clatter. Before she can ring Patty's bell, Patty is at the door.

"Hello, Maggie," she says. "What's up?"

"Can I come in, do you think?" Maggie asks.

"Well, sure. There, take the couch. I was just sitting, trying to figure what to make for dinner. Do you like pot roast? You know, I make it maybe twice a week, and I just realized I hate it. I can't stand the sight of it anymore."

Maggie looks at Patty in her blue jeans, her faded T-shirt. In Maggie's eyes, Patty was never a pretty girl. She was plain and angry-looking and pinched even as a child.

"The thing is," Patty goes on, "I want to eat things I've never tasted. Ever try Thai coconut-milk soup?"

"No." Maggie smiles at her and shakes her head.

"It's called *tom ka gai*. And duck-breast confit. You ever tried that?"

"What?"

"I don't know. See here? Duck-breast confit. It sounds so good." Patty holds out a magazine to Maggie, and she takes it.

*"Bon Appétit?"* Maggie asks her.

"I bought it at Key Food. I was standing in line with the same meat, the same potatoes, the same spaghetti, that I've bought for ten years. And I saw this magazine, and I don't know what possessed me, but I threw it on the counter. Jim will probably kill me when he sees it cost three dollars. But wouldn't you think he'd be tired of the same old food? He never wants me to experiment. Do you want something to drink?''

"No," Maggie says. "I came down to talk to you."

"About what? Not about *Bon Appétit,* I guess."

"Well, I guess you could call me a busybody, but it's about you, really."

"What about me?"

"Well, I noticed you don't seem very happy lately. And then there's you and Keevan." After that conversation with Keevan, how could Maggie keep her nose out of the matter?

Patty opens her mouth to speak, but nothing comes out. New color seeps into her face.

"It's just that it isn't right, you doting on him the way you do and Jim paying you no attention at all."

"Is it that obvious?" Patty says.

"Well, you know everyone knows how you feel about Keevan."

"I mean that Jim ignores me. Is it that obvious?"

Maggie nods gravely. For years, everyone but Patty has known about Jim's infidelities. Somehow there wasn't one woman in the neighborhood noisy enough or nosy enough to let Patty know.

"Here's what I was thinking," Maggie says. "You could do something about Jim. I mean, you love him still, don't you?"

"Well, I'm stuck with him. I guess I love him, all right."

"You could fix yourself up is what I was thinking. I've known you for your entire life, so I hope you won't take offense, but you could be a stunner, Patty, if you put your mind to it." Maggie reviews the word "stunner." It's a lie, of course. Patty could never be a stunner.

Patty just stares.

"I've offended you," Maggie says. She wonders if Patty thinks she already is stunning.

"No. I was just realizing I didn't have a clue about how to fix myself up. What would I do?"

"We're not talking drastic here. I don't mean breast implants. Get a hairdo, for one."

Patty touches her ponytail. "What sort of hairdo?"

"A haircut; a perm, maybe. And sexier clothes. Men don't like ripped T-shirts. Okay, so you don't have much of a bosom." Patty looks down at her breasts as though she's never seen them before. "But you could play it up by wearing something tight. You're still slender. The right bra . . ."

"For Jim?"

"Why not? He's your guy, isn't he?"

"He always complains about my jeans. . . ."

"Men do."

"I don't think he's once said a single word about my hair. . . ."

"A makeover," Maggie says. "Makeup too. You could be sexy. You could have Jim in the palm of your hand. Darlene could help. She's very good at things like that."

"Wear as much makeup as Darlene?"

"She looks good. Most men think so anyway." Jim thinks so anyway, Maggie thinks to herself. Of course, Darlene has breasts like Dolly Parton. Maggie stares at Patty's chest and tries to imagine real breasts, at Patty's plain face and tries to envision Darlene's makeup adorning it. She can't make the image stick.

"Most men think she looks good, except maybe her own husband?" Patty asks.

"Darlene left *him*, not the other way around. He comes nosing around every night, begging her to come back. 'Pahleeze, Darlene! I love you,' as though he thinks that should do the trick."

"If I left Jim he'd shrug his shoulders. Oh, well. Big deal. There are prettier fish in the sea." Patty's voice is joking and cool, but Maggie can see she's close to tears.

"You could be as pretty a fish."

"Oh, what's the use? He won't notice."

"It's worth a try. Seems like it's so easy to get into the

sloppy mode. And whining for what you want, for what they don't do."

"I don't whine," Patty says haughtily. "I don't think—"

"Men are babies. They need constant bolstering, stroking."

"So do women."

"Yes. But somehow we're taught to fend for ourselves, to not expect much." Maggie leans back on the ugly brown couch. It's not only ugly; it's not even comfortable. It seems just like everything in Patty's life. Ugly and un-easy. Maybe she could get her to change her furniture too. A nice floral sofa with big cushions, or at least a slipcover . . . Maggie feels a sudden flush to her cheeks, realizing once again how she's plotting, just like the busy-body she's heard other people call her.

"Maybe at least *Keevan* will notice if I change," Patty says.

"That's not the point, darling. He's not yours, and you're fooling yourself if you think he ever will be."

"You don't know how he feels," Patty says, pushing out her lower lip.

"I know enough."

"Keevan hasn't spoken to you, has he?" Patty's voice rises with each word.

Maggie bites her lip. "Well . . ."

"Has he?"

"He's said . . . he's said he's uncomfortable how obvi-ous you are about the way you feel for him."

"But he didn't say he didn't *like* the way I feel about him."

"What?"

"He doesn't like that I'm being *obvious* about the way I feel. But maybe he's glad I feel that way because he returns the feeling. I know he cares for me."

"Like a sister, Patty. Like a sister."

Patty is silent.

"Well," Maggie says, getting up. "I've said too much,

I'm sure." Patty clears her throat. Suddenly Maggie wants to leave so badly it hurts. Why did she even start this? She goes for the door, finds relief in the click of the door handle.

"Wait. If I wanted to do what you said, fix myself up, would you help me?"

"Sure." Maggie feels her back straighten, her face brighten. "We could make an appointment for your hair at New World."

"I'm free just about all the time."

"Let's see if we can get you in tomorrow afternoon."

"Okay," Patty says. "Will you go with me?"

"Well, sure."

"Would you?"

"Yes. I said so. You know, Patty, what you probably really need to get Jim to pay attention is something that would make you feel good about yourself. Like a job."

"Oh, come on. What would I do?"

"Anything. You're perfectly capable."

"I have no training. Nothing."

"If you wanted to perk up your life, it's what would really make a difference. You'd be much happier. Donna Shea's got that job in a real estate office."

"Donna was born confident. It used to be okay not to be confident. As long as you were 'nice.' 'Be a nice girl, Patty,' my mother used to say. It's all she expected of me."

"Things have changed," Maggie says, surprised by the clarity of what Patty is saying. Truthfully, she didn't know the girl *had* opinions.

"Lord," Patty says, sighing. "It seems like everything's changing."

"How so?"

"Well, if you want to know part of why I'm not happy, it's the neighborhood. All these Jews and blacks and whatevers coming in and mucking it up. Mucking up everything we had. The Jews have money. Too much. And fancy things they shouldn't. And the blacks come in to steal it. Suddenly everybody's got burglar alarms and can't walk down the street, and it's all *their* fault.''

"Patty! To point to Jews and blacks . . . It's so . . . racist.''

"It's true, isn't it? So why not? People used to say it, and no one called them racist or anything. Sensible, I think. My mother called them kikes and niggers. You've probably used those words yourself.''

"I don't know that I have,'' Maggie says, but she's disturbed at the thought. "It's just not acceptable anymore, in any case. You wouldn't want to be called a dumb mick.''

"I wouldn't care if anyone called me a mick. It's the 'dumb' that's the problem.''

Maggie smiles. "Yes. I see your point. But then, it doesn't seem like the Irish have to band together anymore like we used to. Nobody's keeping us out of things, like they did in our parents' day, just because we're Irish. There's not the same prejudice anymore. We had a President in the White House, for land's sake. But the blacks . . . even the Jews . . .''

"Why don't they live in their own neighborhood, then?'' Patty says, squinting her eyes and widening her nostrils as if she smelled something rotten. Maggie looks at Patty's sad grey eyes.

"My father once said, 'If you don't accept change, it destroys you.' ''

"My father said, 'To hell with anyone else but me and mine.' ''

"Yes, I rather imagine he did,'' Maggie says, remembering Patty's father, a mean drunk who used to sit on the stoop and snarl at neighbors who didn't agree with him. "Well, let's start with a haircut,'' she says crisply. "We'll worry about that first. World change can come later.''

"Sometimes I think we all should only live until thirty,'' Patty says, standing, walking Maggie to the door. "Seems like most people are happy up until then.''

"I don't know,'' Maggie says. "You've just had a bit

of a hard time lately. Things will change for the better soon, I think.''

Coming home from the high school, Keevan sees a little girl on the sidewalk in front of Zoe's house. Her hair is darker than Zoe's, a golden brown, and pulled tight into a ponytail. But her cheekbones are just as fine, and her eyes are the same eerie, clear blue. Rose. It must be. He cannot stop watching her as she crouches in a navy sweatshirt and red corduroy jeans, drawing a crooked hop-scotch grid with chalk on the bluestone. Already up and down the bluestone she has drawn the sun, a bird, and a fat man with a beard. The Hispanic housekeeper is sitting on the third step, legs wide apart, eyes half closed, a dish towel in her hand, impatiently being patient.

"Is that Santa Claus?" Keevan asks the little girl, pointing to the man with the beard.

"I dunno," she says. She squints up at him. She has a comic little face, an upswept little nose.

"Looks like Santa to me. I once heard he watches all children, and the ones who draw him often get extra-nice toys for Christmas. . . . Hello," Keevan says to Teresa.

"Hullo," she says dully. She is looking from the little girl to him and back.

"You know, I'm kind of magic myself. I bet, for instance, I can figure out your name."

"No you can't. No one can do that."

"I can."

"Okay." She sets down her chalk and stands up. "Do it." She has the same determined, graceful/clumsy stance that attracts him to Zoe.

"I know it's not Ethel or Peter."

She laughs. "Of course not. I'd change it if it was."

"Or Desdemona or Cordelia."

"Uh-uh."

"And you look like a nice pink flower, so it must be . . . Wait, I'm getting it. Daisy. No. Rose."

"I'm not supposed to talk to strangers," Rose says suddenly, her face closing up with worry.

"I'm not a stranger. I know her name too," Keevan says, pointing to Teresa. "Teresa." He remembers how Zoe pronounced her housekeeper's name last night: Teray-sa.

"How did you know our names?"

"Do you believe in magic?"

"Sometimes."

"Well, then, okay."

"He must know your mama," Teresa interjects.

"Don't spoil the magic, Teresa," Keevan entreats.

"You a friend of my mom's?" Rose asks him.

"Certainly am. I live right here. Right next door to you. I met your mommy one night when she was carrying out the garbage. Sometimes I can actually hear you sleeping."

"How can you hear me sleeping?"

"Your room is right next to my living room. Third floor, right? And you wozzle in your sleep."

"I what?" She jams a fist into her waist, leans on one leg, and frowns at him with amusement and challenge.

"Wozzle. Like this." He makes a funny whistling noise and a snort. "It's backward snoring. Only very special people are capable of wozzling."

"I don't wozzle."

"Oh, yes. Someday I'll tape it. 'Rose wozzles,' I'll tell the whole neighborhood. I'll play them the wozzling tape for evidence."

Rose blushes and laughs, and her whole face seems to light. He hasn't realized, until that moment, how truly closed up she's been. But her sparkle warms him like brandy.

"We must go in, Rosa," Teresa says. "I start dinner." She gets up from the stoop, groaning, wipes her forehead with the dish towel.

"What's your name?" Rose asks Keevan, gathering up her chalk and clearly not happy to leave.

"Keevan."

"It is not."

"It is so. That's my name. Keevan O'Connor. You could ask anyone. See that lady walking across the street? You could ask her."

"You must mean Kevin. Like in *Home Alone*."

"Uh-uh. My mother named me Keevan. It's an Irish name. I like it."

"I don't."

"Rosa!" Teresa calls, unlatching the gate.

"You know my mom. Do you know my dad too?"

"I never met your dad, but I'm sure I would like to," Keevan says.

"Uh-uh. You wouldn't want to meet him," Rose tells him, as she walks toward the gate. "He sleeps all day. He would bore your pants off."

Keevan, surprised, shakes his head as she disappears behind the closing door.


Some days, when the weather is warm, Zoe chooses to take the D train home and walk along Seventh Avenue. Today, she thinks of Keevan O'Connor. She has an indelible vision of him in his soft wrinkled oxford shirt, his grey sweater, his jeans. How she would like to touch his thighs through his jeans, feel the muscles. He would have hard, long muscles; just the way he walks tells her. God, she wishes she could get him off her mind.

She stops at The Dragon Seed, a New Age shop, with its incense and decks of tarot cards and books about life essence, the Tao, eternity. She has come here twice since she moved to Park Slope. To smell the incense and see the pretty dishes of tumbled stones, with their descriptions hand-lettered behind them. She loves to sift the stones through her fingers. They are cool as water. She can imagine slipping one in her mouth, feeling its glassiness on her tongue. Instead, now, she takes one from each dish and gracefully slides them into her jacket pocket. They weigh down her pocket as seashells did when she was a child, on a beach vacation with Emily's family. How wonderful they sound, chirping in her pocket as she walks past the counter and out the door. Her heart is pounding, her blood feels molten in her veins, and for a moment she feels truly alive. Later, she'll rue it. But for now, her pockets are singing with healing stones.

The entire walk home, she imagines the stones nestled in the dark cloth of her skirt, waiting for light to reinvent them. Coming into her house, she calls, "Hello," then, finding no one on the bottom floor, begins to take the stones out and arrange them on the dining room sideboard. She startles when she hears above her, on the second floor, a far too familiar voice: Lois Finney. She is asking Rose the same rote questions she always asks, using her perfectly modulated, though gravelly, upper-crust voice. Generally, Grandma Finney bores Rose to death. "She bores my pants off" are the words Rose used. Zoe hears: "And what is your teacher's name again, darling?"

Zoe imagines putting her jacket back on and slipping out like the thief she is. She even wonders what it would be like to wait in the cellar until Lois is gone. But Teresa, carrying down a pile of fresh linens, gives her away.

"Oh," she says, far too loudly. "Mrs. Finney is upstairs. She wait for you."

Annoyed, Zoe finds herself smoothing her hair back, tucking in her shirt, and going up to face her mother-in-law.

Lois is sitting on the couch, her neck stretched up, looking around the room like a giraffe foraging for leaves. "I understand you got rid of Delia's burlwood commode. You know, it might be priceless. I never got around to having it appraised. It's not pretty, but I'm quite sure it is worth quite a lot. Maybe Alicia would have liked it. And the chinoiserie desk. You didn't give *that* to the Salvation Army? And the Foo dogs? Teresa said they took it all away."

Zoe feels herself blushing. She has almost never defied Lois before. She is astonished she ever had the courage to get rid of all the things she's hated.

"You'd think a poor girl like you would have respect for expensive things," Lois sniffs, and Zoe could swear she mutters the word "trash" under her breath.

"I gave both the commode and the desk to my assistant," Zoe tries to say evenly. "He barely has any furniture. The Foo dogs are wrapped in the cellar, if you'd like them. And if you'd like me to ask for the commode back for you . . ."

"Well, I don't know where I'd put it. But that's not the point. Delia's things came into your hands. You were lucky."

"I've kept some. The things Jamie and I liked," Zoe says. For years, she has allowed Jamie's mother to intimidate her, bully her. Not anymore. That's why she moved. It was not just to help make Jamie better but to move away from Lois Finney and her bible of Finney rules and values.

"Why don't you take me around," Lois says, rising. "I'd like to see it all. See what you've given away. Of course, I've already seen Jamie. He looks terrible." She takes Zoe's elbow and propels her toward the stairs.

"I know," Zoe says.

"He's never been this thin before. And this business of not talking . . . He needs professional care." Lois shakes her head. Why does Zoe always feel Lois thinks it's all her fault, what's happened to Jamie. She never says it aloud, and yet the implication is there.

"I'm not taking him to the hospital this time," she says. "Not after what happened last time."

"Well, at least get a full-time nurse, for heaven's sake."

"What would a nurse do for him? Read to him. Play cards with him? There's nothing to do, Lois. Nothing. Teresa bathes him. We feed him. Here he has his own bed, at least."

"Which you so kindly moved to a completely strange location for him. Without his consent. Without his input . . . You might as well have put him right in the hospital. I frankly don't see the difference."

"Here," Zoe says icily, "he has me."

"You could have afforded a house on Sutton Place, if you were so keen on a house. Madge Mitchell would have been happy to show you a dozen choices right in the neighborhood. What you see in being over here, I really don't know." Zoe notes that Lois's hands are shaking. Zoe knows she probably wants a cigarette. Lois thinks she's a secret smoker, but her clothes smell charred and stale, no matter how expensive they are. And sometimes she has even greeted Jamie and Zoe at her apartment door with smoke coming from between her teeth.

"I'm happy here. Rose is learning to like it too," Zoe says. "And when Jamie's better, I'm sure he'll be happy we made the move. It will be better for him: it's quieter here, less crowded than Manhattan. And the neighbors make you feel welcome." Zoe thinks of Keevan and finds herself smiling.

"What happened to the milk-glass lamp and the Royal Doulton statuettes? And the carved jade wall hangings? You didn't get rid of those too, did you?" Lois charges forward from room to room, frustrated and wild. Perhaps, Zoe thinks, it's because she knows that Zoe is no longer under her thumb.

"I asked if you wanted them."

"Where would I put them?" Lois huffs. "*You* were supposed to have them."

"You said they were mine. I assumed that meant I should do as I pleased with them." Zoe does feel guilty under Lois's stare. But she hated those ugly china statues of mustachioed men kneeling before maidens, of women in ball gowns, with blank Snow White faces. Statuettes that caught dust and cluttered tables and glared from their niches with the admonition: "You'll never become a real member of the Finney family. Real Finneys appreciate us." One night, miserable, before she decided to move to Brooklyn, Zoe took one, a haughty lady in a green gown, and smashed it. Right afterward it felt wonderful; her arm actually tingled with the intensity with which she flung it at the floor. But then guilt took over as she swept up the pieces, embarrassed to call a maid to help.

"The carved jade is in the cellar if you want it back," Zoe says. "With the Foo dogs. Lots of things. I'd be happy to bring them up for you."

"You're a very selfish girl. Ungrateful. And stupid to think only of yourself in this situation. Leaving Manhattan without even consulting with me. Moving so far away. And frankly, I really blame you for letting it get this bad with Jamie."

"There's nothing I wouldn't do for him," Zoe says. "I've tried so many things. The best we can do, it seems, is wait it out."

"Until what? Until he dies of starvation?"

Zoe feels her teeth clenching. Lois is the only person who can really bring out her venom. "Perhaps, if you're so worried about him, you should come and see him a few times a week," Zoe says, as warmly as possible, though beneath it all, she's snickering. "You know, you could sit with him during the day. Or you could move in with us for a while. There's an extra bedroom. Seeing you so often, he might wake up."

"Oh." Lois takes a few deep breaths. For one terrifying moment, Zoe fears she might actually take her up on it. "That's nice that you asked. But you know I've never been any good at that sort of thing." When Zoe can no longer contain her smile, Lois sends her a withering look. She knows she's been had, and not long after, she goes out on the stoop and waves her hand to summon her car, parked across the street.

"I'll visit again soon," she says coldly.

We won't see her for a while, Zoe thinks with relief.

On Eighth Street, the commuters come home for dinner. Inside the houses, a murmuring tide of dinner table conversations: teenagers daring each other, mothers scolding, fathers giving ultimatums, and hundreds of requests for food to be passed. But you will hear hardly anything from the

O'Connor house tonight. Patty is staring out the kitchen window at the backyard, just having finished the dishes. John and Michelle are sullenly completing their homework before they can watch "Nick at Night." They don't notice their father going past, and up the steps to Uncle Keevan's.

Keevan is reading the last pages of *White Fang* when Jim bangs noisily on his door and walks right in.

"Great," Keevan says. "Don't you wait for 'come in'? What if I had someone here?"

"Like who, Keevan? You been fucking Marilyn Monroe?"

"Asshole."

"Can I use your phone?"

"Did your phone go dead or something?"

"It's a private call. The bedroom?" He heads upstairs before he finishes his sentence.

"Private from whom? Patty?"

" 'Whom.' God, you really are an English teacher." Keevan hears the bedroom door slam upstairs.

Keevan stares, hears murmuring through the ceiling. The ending of *White Fang,* and he can't even read the words. What is it about Jim that sets his hackles right up? His arrogance, his condescending tone?

He was never close to Jim, the way he was to Ralph. Even as a boy, Jim was a bully. Terrorizing the Kilkenny twins. Breaking Corey's arm after he told Father Joe that it was Jim who was supplying the eighth graders with cigarettes. And in middle age, he is blustery, insensitive. His jokes are cruel, his opinions narrow. By all rights, he should have been Keevan's role model. He was the first one in the family to put himself through college, but it was somehow never for the right reasons. He once boasted that he cheated on every math final he took; he was sleeping with the daughter of the chairman of the math department, and she stole the test keys for him. "I had to make some mistakes," he told Keevan, puffed up with his cleverness, "or they would have caught me. So I made exactly five mistakes."

What Jim really cared about was the degree—to get rich, to "get the hell out of Brooklyn," though somehow he never did get out. He married Patty and dug himself in deeper, because with Ralph dead, it was easy to keep the house divided in two, to share it, to go on as the family had always gone on.

Keevan would gladly have given up his share of the house to Ralph. There is nothing Keevan wouldn't have done for Ralph. It's hard to say what Ralph would have become if he'd lived. Even without schooling, he had the makings of a philosopher. And his philosophy of life became the template for Keevan's own.

"This is the way I see it, Keev," he said, the last time Keevan saw him, before he went to Vietnam. They were out in the backyard. Ralph had a beer in his hand, his uniform crisp as a new dollar bill. Keevan clinked the ice in his lemonade, and he pulled his chair close to Ralph. He could smell his brother's aftershave and the starch of his uniform. Though only fifteen, Keevan knew Ralph was worth listening to, always. "The way I see it is to take life as it comes, no matter what comes, and just appreciate the hell out of it. See, it works for me, thinking like that. I don't feel bad I got drafted. Other guys, they say, Why me? They struggle and moan. I figure it's just what's meant for me. Far as I'm concerned, life is to be stunned. Life is to be knocked right the hell off your chair with surprise and be grateful for it. Good or bad, Jesus, you're alive."

Five months later, he bit it by stepping on a land mine. Jim called him an asshole. Ralph should have become a conscientious objector. Or run to Canada. No one smart went to Vietnam. No one with the least bit of smarts. But Keevan still gets tremendous satisfaction from the last thing he remembers Ralph saying: "Life is to be stunned." Somewhere in the jungles of Vietnam, Keevan knows, Ralph was thrilled and stunned by the variety, the surprise, of life.

"Because I can't come tonight, Kim," Keevan hears

though the ceiling. "Don't turn on the waterfall; I can't fucking stand it." Jim isn't even trying to keep his voice low. He's probably proud of the fact that he's cheating on Patty, is flaunting it in front of Keevan. What would Ralph have thought of Jim? Would Jim have turned out differently if Ralph had lived?

When Jim comes downstairs, he takes a beer from Keevan's refrigerator and settles into the couch.

"I don't want to go back down there until I have to," he says.

"Why not?"

"Because Patty is such a pain in the ass, that's why."

"She'd probably say the same about you."

"Who cares. You know who I was calling?"

"I don't want to know."

"Kim D'Amico. She's a secretary at Met. With a body from a centerfold."

"Am I supposed to applaud?" Keevan says, suddenly thirsty for a beer himself. Or does he want to get up just so he doesn't have to look at Jim's smug face.

"When I do her, she begs me: 'Fuck me, fuck me, Jimbo. Harder, baby. Deeper, baby.' She says I'm the best she's ever had."

"Do I have to hear this? What are you going to do? Leave Patty?"

"Are you kidding?"

"Well, what's the point?"

"What's the point? Getting laid. Having someone appreciate what I have to offer."

Keevan takes a swig of beer. "I think Patty appreciates it too. It's you who don't appreciate her."

"Who cares? I don't care what she thinks."

"She's your wife."

"She's a bitch. Nothing I do pleases her at all. She's a fucking bitch, or haven't you noticed? I think she'd rather get into your pants than mine."

"You're right," Keevan says. "She makes that clear."

"Does she?" Jim looks up suddenly.

"Yeah. You're neglecting the hell out of her. Give her the attention a wife deserves." Keevan can't believe how mad he feels.

"What the fuck do you know about what a wife deserves? You did a great job on your own wife, didn't you?"

"Shut up."

"You want to pay attention to her, Keev? *You* can have her. When you fuck her, she'll screw up her face like a lemon. Like she's just tolerating it." Jim demonstrates.

"Do you ever try to talk to her? Do you ever try to make it romantic for her?"

Jim shakes his head. "I just close my eyes and try to pretend it's someone else. I try to imagine it's Kim, calling, 'Fuck me, fuck me, Jimbo!' "

"That's lovely," Keevan says, already feeling his beer, realizing he's forgotten to eat dinner tonight. The plate that Patty made for him is still in the refrigerator. His stomach aches.

"Well, where do you get off being so high-and-mighty, dickhead?" Jim says. "It's not like you've got Madonna lying on your bed, waiting for you."

"Right," Keevan says.

"Or anyone."

"Right," Keevan says.

"I've got two women fighting for me, and Mr. Right over here's working his hand overtime every night."

"Get the fuck out of here."

"Fine. I'll send you a quarter, Ma Bell." Jim trudges out, leaving Keevan furious.

This is exactly what it was like when he and Jim were kids. Jim would bait and bait until Keevan got really mad and a fight ensued. Keevan closes his eyes now, trying to pretend Jim never came tonight. He tries to shrug off what Jim said, that he has nobody. He evokes Zoe Finney, her scent, a mix of grapefruit and cinnamon and clove, her pale-pink lips, her airy voice. Last night, masturbating after she left, he was finally sent over the edge by the thought of giving her an orgasm. How long has it been since she's arched her back, opened her mouth in surprise, and let that sacred pleasure roil and splash under her skin? To give her pleasure would be better than any pleasure she might give him. There's no question in Keevan's mind that Zoe is sexually starved, needy, dying. And her lonely little girl. He thinks about what she said about her father. If ever there was a child who needed time and attention from a man . . .

Someone once told Keevan that when the row of houses was built, there used to be a passageway, from the houses at the top of the hill all the way through to the houses at the bottom. Each house was built with an archway somewhere, where the woodwork, plaster medallions, and doors could be carried down from the "lead house" (where the craftsmen poured the medallions, milled the wooden moldings) without interference from the weather. Somewhere in his house is a boarded-up tunnel to Zoe's house. Somewhere there is only a thin patch that prevents him from walking into her life.

In the morning, Keevan writes Zoe a note:

*It's Tuesday. When you put the garbage out tonight, will you come for wine? Could you come over at ten, by any chance, or anytime earlier than usual? Just ring the bell marked K. O'Connor. I hope you won't think this is too forward.*

Then, having signed the note, he erases the last sentence, glad he's written it in pencil, and draws one of his cartoons, a caricature of Zoe ringing a huge church bell by swinging on its cord like Quasimodo. Her braid is akimbo, her long, slender legs wrap themselves around the cord. He puts the note in an envelope in her mailbox, not at all sure it is the right thing to do.

That night, pleased with Keevan's funny little drawing, Zoe dresses for taking out the garbage almost as carefully as for a charity ball or a black-tie opening. People have told Zoe that she's beautiful, but she doesn't think of herself that way or comport herself like a beautiful woman.

It wasn't until she was twenty, looking through a book about Dante Gabriel Rossetti, that she began to see herself differently. The subject of the painting was a girl with a lantern, whose light splashed upon her face, lit her hair, delineated the velvet folds of her heavy dress, and in this Pre-Raphaelite image Zoe saw her own long, kinked blond hair, glorious and unashamed, hair she had ironed, straightened, and tortured all through her teen years. She saw the pale face and wide-set eyes she had so long despised in her own mirror, a face on which makeup looked superfluous and no makeup seemed neglectful. She saw, in the slide of the artist's brush, her own slender wrists which she had tried to fill out by drinking cans of soy supplement, eating bread, sweets, just so there could be a sense of flesh and not just bone. And there was her own reedlike neck, exposed above the tight bodice, almost delicious in the lantern light, the neck that she had wrapped in turtlenecks and scarves since puberty. Here, it was offered up as fruit. Delectable. For the first time, she saw herself as acceptable, desirable even. She tore the page from the book with a guilt-provoking rip, though it belonged to the college art library. It was an act of passion, much deeper, more indelible, than her petty stealing. For this, unlike all the things she stole, was something she truly needed. She has the picture still, lining the lingerie drawer of her dresser.

She goes to her drawer now and takes it out. The edges of the paper have yellowed, and it gives off the smell of old magazines: slightly burned and dusty. The odor mingles with the laundry soap from her lingerie. She breathes in the odor, looks into the face of the lamplit girl, and finds courage: she could be beautiful too. If only she could feel so lit, so pure.

Opening the door from the dressing room to the bedroom, she sees that Jamie is asleep, his mouth open. How innocent he looks! She lies down on the bed and nuzzles him, kisses his cheek, which is bearded with neglect, hollow with illness. What a fraud she is to say she loves him and want another man.

And yet the desire lingers, propels her from the bed to the bathroom. The one room in the house that doesn't quite fit, it is too modern, too fancy. A huge soaking tub with a waterfall faucet. Pink marble tile, the hue of the interior of conch shells, lining the floor and walls. Before she moved in, Zoe didn't like the room and thought she might change it. It was tasteful enough, but it reminded her of Sutton Place and all she was leaving behind. Living here, she's discovered that the pink tiles make her skin look rosy, the tub allows her to sit in water up to her chin, and every morning she notes how the marble feels cool and surprisingly soft on her feet. Perhaps she is not so ready to give up the pleasures of her wealthier life.

Taking her hairbrush, she draws it through her long hair. The strands are straightened by the big silver-backed brush, then ripple back into waves the color of straw. As a teen, how she wanted dark hair, like her sister and brother in the photo she found. How is it she came to have such light hair? It made her question whether she was her parents' child at all. But she is glad for her blond hair tonight, she is glad for her face, for it has seemed to attract Keevan.

She finds her prettiest lingerie, her softest clothes, a loose blue top that drapes low on her neck, a skirt of rayon painted with flowers and birds. When she steps outside, dragging the big garbage can behind her, she feels like a fool, dressed for a date. Then she looks up and sees Keevan pulling aside his shutter. She puts her hand up to wave, but feels self-conscious. He looks embarrassed too: she's caught him watching her, worrying whether or not she'll ring his bell.

The sound of the bell startles her when she rings it, and the steps to his apartment seem steeper than her own. Or is it her fear that makes them loom in the low light?

Keevan is at the top of the stairs, and coming close to him, she finds instant pleasure in his face, his mildness. She wears her desire for him, a hoop skirt, an encumbrance. Surely he can see it, or smell it like perfume. It must fill the air.

"Zoe," he says softly. "You came."

Zoe is surprised once again by the warmth of Keevan's room. The lamps with their parchment shades glow mellow. The golden light strikes the walls, painting them exactly the color of sherry. The books filling the bookcases, stacked upon each other in every possible inch of space, all work to make the room seem well loved and of another era. And the room smells of what? Aftershave, mothballs? Something else, stimulating and spicy.

"Are you always so neat?" she asks him.

"I'm cyclically neat," he tells her. "One month on. One month off."

"You do your own cleaning?"

"Usually. Except . . . well . . ."

She smiles. "Except what?"

"Except my sister-in-law comes up and cleans sometimes."

"Your sister-in-law? Really? Why?"

He wipes his mouth thoughtfully with his thumb and forefinger. "She wants to improve my life, I guess."

"Nice sister-in-law."

"She leaves me dinner practically every night. I don't know what to do about it."

"Eat it."

"It obligates me."

"Is she in love with you or something?"

"So it appears." He looks so sheepish about it it makes Zoe smile. She sits down on the leather sofa and feels foolish, down so low, trapped in its pillows. But instead of sitting in the chair perpendicular to her, as he did last time, he lowers himself onto the couch beside her. The spicy odor emanates from him, reminds her of the bay rum Emily's father used to wear. She once asked Emily's father why he smelled so good, and he showed her the bottle he'd bought in Jamaica. He uncorked it for her and let her breathe in the sweet lime/ginger fragrance. She wishes she could rest her face against Keevan's skin now, drink in the scent. The desire is unnerving and strong.

"She's got it rough, Patty," Keevan says. "My brother is an animal. Totally self-centered. She tries to get too involved in my life, but I can never really get mad at her, I guess, because I feel sorry for her."

"I met her. She was . . ." Zoe hesitates, trying to find a not-too-damning word.

"Crabby," he offers, smiling.

"Yes." She laughs.

"You'd be too. He cheats on her all the time. Although she might not even know it."

"Did you cheat when you were married?"

"No."

"Somehow I didn't think you would. What happened?"

"To my marriage? I can't even piece it together any-more." She sees him closing up and is embarrassed that she asked.

Over on the bookcases, resting on top of a row of books, she sees a familiar box.

"Clue," she says, standing, something difficult to do gracefully from the low couch. She goes toward the box. "Do you like Clue?"

"It's my favorite game," he says.

"Mine too."

"Really? I use it with my classes sometimes. When we're discussing plotting. To show them all the elements that go into a plot. They like that lesson."

"You must be a good teacher."

"I'm not boring," he says.

Zoe takes the box in her hands, sets it down, and opens it. How familiar it all is. So many afternoons of her child-hood were spent playing Clue with Emily, letting Emily win half the time, though Zoe knew the answer long be-fore, just so that Emily would be willing to play it again.

Zoe didn't have games like this at her house. And if she had they would have been useless to her: board games were for at least two people to play, and she never once brought a friend over, never could have asked her parents to play. At Emily's, there was Life and Risk and Parcheesi, the Barbie Dating Game and Monopoly. But given the choice, she always chose Clue. Maybe because it took place in a grand mansion, with a "conservatory" and a "hall." There was the elegance of Miss Scarlet, the lovely stuffiness of saying "Professor Plum."

And the tiny instruments of death, how they thrilled her! The lead pipe that was really made of lead, and bent. The ivory plastic noose with its knotted shape that teased her fingers. Opening the game board now, she remembers the rooms with her fingers.

"Want to play?" he asks.

"Yes. Let's! Do you want to? You don't mind?"

He laughs. "I have a feeling you're going to cream me!"

She sits down on the floor by the coffee table, sorting out the playing pieces, the cards, the murder weapons. He's watching her; she can feel it.

While they play, she wears his observance of her like a crown on her head. Something shining and anointing, which makes her feel proud. He can see her. Really see her, the way Jamie once could. She takes a deep breath and closes her eyes for a moment, inhaling the sweetness of the feeling. Absorbing the moment so later she can reclaim it.

"Colonel Mustard did it in the conservatory with a knife," she says.

For a moment, accidentally, their fingers brush. Neither looks up, or acknowledges the touch, but Zoe feels electricity that makes her once again take a deep breath.

"You always seem so sad," Keevan says.

"I don't think of myself that way." She can't tell him that her deep breath wasn't a sigh, that she breathed with effort because it was the only way she could make herself breathe, with him so close. For a change, she doesn't feel sad at all.

"You must be, though," he says.

"Must I?"

"How could you not be sad, with your husband ill as he is. It must be lonely." Zoe is touched that Keevan is interested in her. It is odd to be asked questions, drawn out. All her life, she has been the expert at drawing out, at winning over. It is uncomfortable for her to be focused on.

"Sometimes it's worse than being alone," she tells him. She hears the tears in her voice. She is glad for once that they won't, can't, come to the surface.

She looks at his face, so squared and masculine and sympathetic, at his narrow cheekbones and rusty hair and golden feline eyes. The kindness in his eyes does something odd and wrenching to her heart.

"Miss Scarlet did it in the conservatory with a rope," he says, never taking his eyes from her. She has no rope.

She changes her tone, doesn't want Keevan's pity. "Well, pal. No rope."

Keevan raises one of his pale eyebrows. "No rope," he repeats.

"You must be terrible at poker," she tells him.

"My brother won't even play with me."

"He should. Your face would give him an edge," she says, laughing. In a very short time, Zoe wins.

"I hate losing," he tells her, sporting a fake sulk. His face is lionlike, she thinks, and his narrow golden eyes make it more so. He looks up, and because she is watching him, for a moment they are in a battle to see whose eyes will lower first. She tries to be stalwart but can't maintain the contact. He sees her too intimately. Her cheeks must be red.

"I wish I could kiss you," he whispers. "I want to kiss you."

Zoe feels the heat bloom now, rise up her back and cover her ears like a cloak.

"No, please."

"You want me to kiss you. I know it."

"I should go."

She stands up, hoping he'll stop her, put his arms around her. She thinks of the kiss Stuart gave her. What a delicious pang she felt then, wishes she could feel now. Caught in her feelings, she trips over the board, sending game pieces and cards flying.

"Oh, God. I'm sorry. I'm so clumsy." She gets down on her knees, trying to gather the pieces, dropping them in her nervousness. She knows she is blushing, can't look up at him. Still, she feels him watching her, sees out of the corner of her eye that he is smiling slightly. He kneels down beside her. But his movements, unlike hers, are solid and steady, sweeping pieces and cards into a pile, counting the cards, putting them into the cardboard space meant for them.

"There. All set," he says.

She can barely swallow as she puts on her jacket.

"You want to play Clue tomorrow?" he asks, in a charming, self-deprecating tone that eases her discomfort.

"You have nothing better to do with your nights?"

"What could be better than playing Clue?"

"You'd better play better than you played tonight," she scolds.

"I yam who I yam, Olive," he says.

If only she could feel that way.

"Will you come and play with me anyway?"

She stops and focuses on the floor, smiling to herself.

"How could I refuse to play my favorite game with someone who lets me win so easily?"

Before she goes down the stairs, she leans over impulsively and kisses his cheek, just to be near him. Just to smell him. She can feel the day's stubble on her lips, his prominent cheekbone through his skin. For a moment, she is wrought with a desire to taste his cheek and throat and neck with her lips and tongue, to take the lobe of his ear gently between her teeth. She backs off quickly, nearly losing her balance, and, overcompensating, steps forward onto his foot.

"God . . . I'm so sorry," she says. She feels miserable, overcome by the thought: Why is this man interested in me anyway? "I'm so, so sorry."

"Shh," he says. "It doesn't matter."

"Is your foot all right?"

"You can step on my foot anytime. You must weigh— what?—a pound and a half? C'mon. I'll walk you home."

"No. Please." She sees that he looks puzzled. But she can't bear to be with him another moment, to ruin what has been so memorable, so sweet. And she feels sure she will say something wrong, do something even more clumsy or embarrassing, if she doesn't get away from him.

"Good night, Zoe," he says softly, just touching the top of her head with his fingers as she turns from him.

All the way down the stairs, feeling too self-conscious to turn back, unsteady, knowing he is watching, she feels a liquid pull toward him like a tide to shore.

# EIGHT

◆

The next morning, no sun hits Eighth Street. The sky is silvery, as it often is for days in the winter. But today the spring air is heavy like a sigh, too warm. Clotted with rain, yet no rain falls.

Darlene Kilkenny wheels the baby down to her own house, to pick up the extra box of diapers she has stashed there. She figures Don will be passed out and senseless this early, so no words need to come between them.

Old Mrs. Reilly's been awake for hours, stiff and impatient for the day to begin. Each day, she thinks about dying. Each day, she walks in pain up to Saint Agnes and prays death will come soon. She is tired, and it is as though she has allotted nothing in her old age to look forward to. There is no joy in yet another grey day. And even the sound of the children, when they finally come out on the street to walk to school, even their conspiratorial laughter breaks her heart instead of uplifting her. She would be glad to go with Jesus now, to be his lamb and follow dumbly toward his golden heaven. Is that not what she has planned her whole life? Holding off doing so many things she longed to do, so that there would be no outsize obstacles at the gates of heaven?

Mrs. Reilly senses someone coming up behind her, but it is hard to turn and not lose her balance these days, even in these old-lady shoes she despises. Still, she slows down.

Dangerous, her daughter tells her. Someone could mug her so easily. She would like to die, yes, but she doesn't want to die in pain, or fear, or surprise. Yet she doesn't want to go to that nursing home in New Jersey her daughter's so set on. She wants to die here in the place that's nearly all her life meant home.

"Mrs. Reilly. It's Patty."

"Oh, Patty, dear. Take my arm. The street's especially bad today."

"Bad?"

"Hard to walk on. Haven't you noticed? I don't know why they don't replace this bluestone with concrete. Especially after this winter. It's all haphazard."

"But it's so pretty, the bluestone. And it's been here ever since the houses."

"The concrete seems so much more modern. The bluestone gets all tipped up with tree roots . . . dangerous," Mrs. Reilly says. "My daughter used to draw on the stone with chalk, though, when she was a child. Did you ever do that?"

"Hopscotch . . ."

"Oh, everything. It showed up so well on the stone. I didn't mind it so much then. But it jags up and catches my shoes now. And it seems worse today, just ready to trip us, Patty, don't you think?"

"It certainly seems that way," Patty says.

"I'm going to the church," Mrs. Reilly says.

"I'm going too."

"Do you find it comforts you?" Mrs. Reilly says.

"Sometimes."

"If only we could stay in church all day," Mrs. Reilly says. "That would have been the life for me. Nothing to do. Nobody to worry about. Nobody breaking your heart by making decisions without consulting you."

"Yes," Patty says. "Just stay in church all day." Mrs. Reilly hears the quiver in Patty's voice, as though she's going to cry, but she doesn't ask. Once, she might have. But now she's too old, and worn out, and it seems so tiresome to hear about someone else's problems. Let Jesus handle them. Surely he can do a better job than she can anyway.

Walking into his classroom ten minutes early, to give himself time to sort his papers, Keevan has an odd feeling, as though yesterday he took in too much sun. His skin is so tender, even his clothes seem to directly touch his nerves. And there is the blush of a headache behind his eyes, as though they'd seen something so painfully bright yesterday they ache with the burn of it.

Because of what? Because she kissed his cheek, because in that moment he felt the tenderness of her lips? No, it was something beneath that, an intensity, a passion, that made her draw away so quickly, trip over herself. How clumsy she is for a beautiful woman. Why does that make him want her more? Perhaps it is her only sign of vulnerability. On the surface, she is amiable, perfect, delicate. But underneath is pain.

Standing at his desk, staring blindly at his papers, he is caught up in his thoughts of Zoe. He doesn't see Marquita Dominguez come in early and seat herself in the first row, the row that almost no one uses in any of the classrooms. It is only when she opens her can of Coca-Cola with a *zshoop* that he looks up, to see her watching him.

"Mr. O'Connor, I got it."

"Got what?"

"See." She holds up a Brooklyn Public Library copy of *The Grapes of Wrath,* bound in thick purple, the page edges burned with age.

"You found the library!" he says. "Great."

"I read a whole chapter last night. It was pretty good."

"There you go. Books can be better than anything. Movies, parties—"

"Sex?" Marquita says slyly, sipping her Coke.

Keevan is grateful that Lonette Dennis is slogging into the classroom, dragging her oversize backpack.

"Hey there, Lonette," he says.

"What?"

"I'm just saying hello."

"Oh." She sits down with a thud. Lonette is a hundred pounds overweight and hates herself more than any of the teenagers Keevan's ever worked with. There is something in Zoe like that. It's strange for him to think it, but it's true. Something that is as self-loathing as in Lonette.

Behind her, others come in. Scott Johnson, one of his favorite kids, a black man-child with a tiny birdlike build and an incredibly deep voice, and Asha Pahdi, and Indian girl who yesterday wore a plaid miniskirt and today is wearing a sari.

Keevan opens up the grammar textbook and smooths it flat at today's lesson.

"Did you hear, Mr. O'Connor?" Scott says. "Davis Crosby got arrested last night."

"No. For what?"

Scott laughs. His baritone laugh sends a shiver up Keevan's spine sometimes, like the voice of a fine orator.

"For stealing cars. Bad stuff. Sixteen cars he stole. Everyone here knew he was stealing cars."

"Eighteen," Lonette says.

"With a bunch of kids?" Keevan asks.

"With his two brothers."

"He drove a new car to school almost every day," LaShana Boxford says from the door. "Yesterday he drove a BMW."

"He made a big mistake last night," Scott adds. "He stole a police car."

"On a dare," Lonette says.

"That was pretty stupid," Asha says.

Keevan shakes his head. "Maybe he wanted to get caught."

"Why would he do that?" they all seem to chatter at once.

"Maybe he wanted to stop."

"Nobody's that stupid," Lonette says.

Keevan takes a deep breath. Davis Crosby is not Keevan's favorite kid. He does the homework about every other time and has been known to fall asleep in class, his head down on the desk. But he is also not one of the show-offy kids, with their initials carved in the back of their hair and gold knuckle rings so thick and gaudy that it's nearly impossible for them to hold a pen. Davis doesn't talk back, cause a ruckus, confront others, or get stopped at the metal detector, a knife in his pocket. He's quiet, and appears poorer than some of the others. His clothes are used, old, and not well cared for. His skin is ashy. Keevan has wondered if he does drugs. Downers that make him fall asleep in class, or pot. No. Just stealing cars all night.

But even if he were all those things—gaudy, difficult, brash, mean—Keevan would still hate to hear he'd been arrested. It sickens him whenever a kid gets swallowed up in the urban quicksand that drags so many of his kids down. It's not entirely unusual to start a class with an announcement that someone's been arrested, gotten in trouble, or even been shot. That is the reality of most of these kids, who don't live in sheltered Park Slope but Bed-Stuy and Crown Heights, on streets where gang trouble, drug houses, and aimless violence abound.

"Well, how many of you have started *The Grapes of Wrath*?" he says, clearing his throat.

About half raise their hands.

"I want you all to read this," he says. "This is a book about oppressed people. About anger. About hope."

"What did Steinbeck know about that?" Scott says.

"If you read it, you'll see he knew a lot. Give it a chance."

He looks out at their bright eyes. This is a senior English class. The ones that make it to senior year are the best of the lot, the kids who have persevered. They stare at him hopefully. It buoys him to think how oddly optimistic they are in the midst of their difficult lives. How invincible they feel, though life challenges them daily.

"And there's some sexy stuff in this book," he added.

He sees John Evers write "Grapes of Wrath" in his note-book. Suddenly Keevan remembers Zoe telling him he must be a good teacher. He recalls perfectly how her eyes looked, how her mouth looked when she said it, and he has to pause for a moment before he can go on.

Zoe starts to edit a commercial for the U.S. Postal Service, about a postman who risks his life to deliver groceries, tools, and whatever else comes through the mail in Alaska. The footage, of Arctic landscapes and snowmobiles, makes her chilly. She shivers at her monitor and feels hands on her bare arms.

"Are you cold?" Stuart asks in his deep voice.

"I think it's the footage."

He rubs her arms like a mother warming a child's hands. Zoe feels her nipples blooming like fast-motion photography in science class. She imagines that at any moment, Stuart may plant his face in the crook of her neck and kiss her, and the very thought makes her stand up and turn to him, to break the spell. She realizes instantly that it was a mistake. Stuart stares with hunger at her chest.

"You gave me the chills," she says, embarrassed, crossing her arms.

He smiles. He's so young, so eager. "Is there anything else I can do for you?" he asks, a twinkle in his eye.

Zoe bites her lip. She thinks of Keevan O'Connor. Will she simply give in to one of them in time, like a dam that has held one too many drops of water?

"I'll let you know," she says softly.

Later, when the spot is cut and the client announces they can't come to see it until the next morning, she leaves the office early and goes to the movies. In the dark movie house, she becomes the leading lady and lets all her pent-up desire flow out on the dark-haired leading man. She kisses him passionately. She wakes up in bed with him, the spaghetti strap of her silk nightgown slipped down her shoulder. They will face life together forever. She steps out into the weak late-day sun, drained and happy.

On the way to the subway, she stops by a lingerie store. In the window are gowns similar to the one in the old movie, lace and silk, with thin tubular straps of knotted silk. She ducks into the dressing room with two, though she already knows which one she will steal: the deep-pink one, so thin and silky it could slip through a ring. She tries on neither, just shoves the pink gown into her purse. Hers. It will be hers. She feels her heart chug. That odd thrilling sensation of breaking the rules. She leaves the dressing room.

"Sorry," she calls out to the saleslady. "Didn't fit." Then stops for a moment by the door, to touch an embroidered set of bra and panties, savoring her excitement, prolonging the risk.

"Wait," the saleswoman calls out, stepping from the dressing room. "Where's the pink one? I gave you two."

"Two?" Zoe says, feeling the heat of shame swell inside her. "No you didn't." She stayed too long this time, too long.

"You took in two," the woman says, coming up to her, standing right in front of her. "Open your purse."

"What are you talking about?" Zoe says. But her mouth is dry. She can barely speak; she feels nauseated.

"Open your purse!" Zoe's eyes note her escape route. She braces to run, but the saleslady grabs her arm. She's much more solid than Zoe, much stronger.

"Give me the fucking nightgown," the woman says.

"Let go of me. I'll sue you."

"Give me the fucking nightgown. *I'm* not going to pay for it. And that's what they'll make me do. They'll make *me* pay for it." She pulls on the latch of Zoe's purse. Zoe tries to pull the purse back. A new customer comes in the door.

"Call the police," the saleslady says. "This woman is a thief. Call the police!" Her voice is as shrill as fingernails on slate.

The customer looks at Zoe, her eyes growing wide, then turns and goes out the door.

"You're dead," the saleslady says. "You're dead." She holds Zoe's purse so solidly there's no way she can grab it back. From it the woman pulls the deep-pink nightgown. "Fucking thief," she says. "You fucking thief." Still, she won't let go of the purse. Zoe's stomach twists, and the taste of garbage rises into her mouth before the vomit comes up in a flood. Bits of popcorn pour out onto the saleslady's hands, onto the nightgown. The woman jumps back, releasing her hold on Zoe's purse. Half covered in vomit, weak and sweating, Zoe runs. She cannot swallow for the taste of bile. Her head is swimming, the bridge of her nose is numb. In the subway station her hands are shaking violently as she buys a newspaper and wipes her raincoat and purse with the pages, shoving the soiled sheets into a nearby trash can, praying a train will come soon.

Patty's hair appointment is at four, and she walks slowly down Eighth Street, dragging along her umbrella, expecting rain. She's left the kids at Bonnie Bowen's for dinner. John and Michelle seemed perfectly happy about it. Maybe they're sick of her pot roast too.

Maggie's agreed to join her at the beauty shop. Patty's glad. She's never been comfortable with change. And it seems especially frightening today. She's exhausted. She knows she looks like hell. She didn't sleep a wink after she heard a woman's voice upstairs at Keevan's. She had to know who was up there with him, and she waited, hiding behind the shutters, hoping to catch a glance at the interloper. She was upset to discover it was that woman, Zoe, again. And unnerved to see her turn back and stare at the house, once she was outside the garden gate. The woman's married! How dare she spend a moment of time with Keevan!

In church this morning, Patty prayed that Zoe will be punished for her sins. She prayed she would go to hell for them. This was not exactly an appropriate prayer, but she didn't care. If Zoe's committing adultery, hell is inevitable anyway. She also prayed that Keevan would see the light and not partake in something so blatantly sinful again, that he might be redeemed. Of course, there is the fact that if he wanted Patty, if he reached out to her and told her he'd always loved her, secretly loved her from the time she held him in her arms the night Ralph died, she wouldn't hesitate, not for a minute. But how, in a matter of a week or two, could he even know this woman well enough to take her to bed? And if that isn't what happened, what did happen? And how could this woman, with her husband on the other side of the wall, make love to Keevan? It's inconceivable.

The fact is, Patty's never slept with anyone but Jim. She regrets that now. And damn the church. It would be nice, in the night, to have other memories than Jim holding her elbows down and forcing himself on her the way he does, when he does. It would be nice to have a past of gentle kisses and hopeful suitors. Guys with roses. Nights out at Breezy Point. Her friends had that. Romance in family cabanas at Breezy Point Beach Club, opened with stolen keys from their fathers' dresser drawers. Sex in changing rooms, with bathing suits smelling of seawater, sand on the floor under bare feet. Her friend Donna had that once. She said Hal made love to her right against the wall in that tiny changing room Donna's family rented for years. The one with the big sun hat on the shelf that belonged to her Aunt Nancy, and Chris's blue flippers hanging from a peg on the wall, and the blow-up dinosaur that Diane named Winky. It was so dark it was like being blind, Donna said. All she could sense was Hal's body and the way he felt as he touched her so softly, so slowly. And what he was saying, how much he loved her, would always love her. And how, in the midst of it, they were so weak with passion they almost fell to the floor. Patty grew faint with the description, tried to imagine it was she and Hal instead, gentle Hal, closeted in that little white room, their bodies soft and slick with suntan lotion. Sometimes with Jim she would squeeze her eyes shut and imagine that changing room.

There were no changing rooms with Jim. When they were dating, he was always studying or playing poker with his friends. He never much liked the beach. Neither of them belonged to a beach club. Mostly they took the subway to Coney Island to the amusement park, or they went to Giants games, or to the corner, where they persuaded Paddy Dunfey to slip them a beer, or they drank bourbon in Jim's cellar, with his grandmother cooking right above them in the kitchen, until he got so drunk one night he insisted on putting his penis in her mouth and almost made her gag. "I don't ever want to do that again," she cried pushing him away, horrified that even for a minute she'd agreed. Above them, his grandmother's footsteps made the basement ceiling creak. Later, upstairs in the bathroom, having passed his grandmother, scrupulously avoiding her eyes, she washed out her mouth. She scrubbed her tongue with her fingers, still tasting what she imagined was urine on her tongue. And she cried. How innocent and afraid she was. Why didn't he see that in her and guide her, act tender with her?

So much should have told her he was the wrong person to marry. He said in front of half his friends that her breasts were like pancakes. He told her before a party that her hair looked like a bush, that it always did. One Christmas when they were dating, he gave her a cheese slicer. "Why'd you give me this?" she asked him. It wasn't even a pretty one. It was lumpy and stainless steel. "I thought you liked cheese," he said. These are not memories that comfort a woman.

Stepping into New World beauty parlor now, she is assaulted with alternating whiffs of sweet hair spray and rotten-egg permanents. She is so tired and anxious she considers leaving, and she stands in the doorway, letting in the cool spring air.

"Can I help you?" the receptionist asks, clearly annoyed. Feeling trapped, Patty comes in, gives her name, and, picking up a magazine, sits where she's been told to sit. "What Married Women Long For," it says on the cover. She realizes she is on the verge of crying and knows suddenly that she doesn't care at all if Jim notices her new haircut. She only cares if Keevan likes it. But she feels angry at Keevan right now. It makes her clench her fists. How could he have done that: been with a total stranger? Every time she thinks of it, her heart feels bruised, as if she'd been punched in the chest. All these years, she's thought of him as so considerate, so moral, so kind, so entirely unlike his brother. In the end, isn't he precisely like Jim?

Halfway into the article, which tells her that what married women want most is to be "seen" and acknowledged, the receptionist clears her throat.

"Mrs. O'Connor. Danni's ready."

"Danni?"

Danni steps before Patty with a flourish, chewing on a hair clip. She's one of those petite women with tremendous breasts that make you wonder if they've had surgery. Her tight stretch top makes it immediately apparent that she's not wearing a bra, yet nothing is sagging whatsoever. Danni's hair, however, is a bleached-out disaster. Fluffy as a dandelion gone to seed. A beauty parlor victim. She can't be more than twenty-one. Patty sits reluctantly in her chair, feeling more apprehensive than she does at the dentist.

"What d'ya have in mind?" Danni asks.

"I don't know. I was hoping my friend might be here by now. She was going to join me."

" 'Fraid I have to take you. To stay on schedule. Well, what about the color? The log said you might want color."

"Maybe."

"Your hair's pretty dull. That happens when you get older. See, it's mousy. No color at all, really." Patty looks at her hair in the big mirror. It is dull. Everything about her looks dull.

"What do you think? Julia Roberts red. A mix of 'Ti-

tian' and 'Burgundy.' It will be perfect on you. I've done it many times.''

"Will it be bright red?"

"Absolutely not. I wouldn't do that to you. No one comes out of this shop looking like Bozo."

Patty glances around nervously at the other women in the shop, with their plastic capes and Saran wrap caps, the bullet dryers on their heads.

"And a cut, of course," Danni says. "Very short. To show off your bone structure."

"I don't have good bone structure."

"That's because your hair isn't complementing it."

Patty just wishes Maggie would show up. Not that she's so expert at all this, but another opinion would certainly help.

"I don't know," Patty says.

"We'll start with the cut."

"I'm not sure about short." Patty thinks of Keevan. That Zoe woman has hair to her butt. Ashy blond.

"What about blond?" Patty asks.

"Yeah? You interested in blond?"

"Maybe."

"You'd be hot as a blond. You'd be chasing the guys off ya."

"Blond," Patty says with determination. "I was blond when I was a baby."

Danni hands her a chart. "You pick it. I'll tell you if it suits you."

Patty sees a swatch of ash blond. She fingers the hair, like doll's hair; it glistens in the light. Come to think of it, she did have a Barbie doll with hair just this color, and a short bubble haircut like Marilyn Monroe's.

"This one," she says. "But it would look shiny, wouldn't it? It wouldn't look too bleached out?"

"Nah. I know what I'm doing. This will be great for you. I like big changes. You still got to start with the cut. So what will it be?"

"Sexy," Patty says. "Not too short. Fluffy. Like this." She holds her hands out around her head. "Like a halo."

"An angel, you want to be?" Danni says snippily.

Patty presses her lips together. "I can think of worse things."

Danni takes the hair clip she's been chewing and pins up a hank of Patty's hair, then takes another clip out of the waistband of her jeans. The bell at the front of the shop jingles, and Patty turns her head, to see Maggie bustling in, out of breath, slapping her chest.

"Sister Mary Elizabeth collapsed right outside the door of my office, and I had to stay until the ambulance came, of course."

"My God!" Patty says. "Will she be all right?"

"Keep your head straight," Danni says.

"Hard to say. They think it might be a stroke. So what are they going to do to you? Did you decide?"

"How can you even talk about my hair when you just went through what you went through?"

Maggie shrugs. "Life goes on," she says. "If I've learned anything, I've learned that. Is there coffee in the back?"

"I'll be happy to get you a cup, Mrs. Kilkenny," Danni says.

"How's she know you?" Patty asks when Danni's gone.

"She went to Saint Agnes."

"Everyone knows you."

"That's because I have a job. Something that makes me somebody. I still say that's what you need. But a haircut's good too."

"I'm going to be a blonde."

"A blonde? You're teasing me."

"No. I decided. Why not. If that's what I want."

"Well. We really are going to have a transformation here," Maggie says. "Did you know Sister Mary Elizabeth is only forty-five? I thought she was in her sixties, honestly."

"She's only forty-five? I didn't think people had strokes at forty-five."

Maggie shrugs.

"What happened?"

"She wasn't feeling so well, she told her class. She was on her way to the bathroom when she passed my office. I heard her go down with a thud."

"She wasn't a very happy person, was she?"

"Don't you think so?"

"No. She was always so glum."

"Yup," Maggie says. "You gotta live your life while you got it. I never did subscribe to the idea of saving it all for heaven. Not that I don't thoroughly believe in heaven. But I figure God puts us on this earth for a reason and doesn't send us chasing after happiness just on a whim. You sure you want to be blonde, Pat? I figured you for a redhead."

"I've got to be a blonde."

"What does that mean?"

"I've got to be. That Zoe Finney is a blonde."

"What's that got to do with anything?"

"She went up to Keevan's last night. She was up there a long time. Keevan slept with her last night, Maggie. I'm sure of it," Patty says suddenly, finding herself choking back a sob.

"Oh, dear, I saw that coming."

"How could he do that?"

"Fast worker," Maggie says.

"She's married."

"He was talking and talking about her. I saw it coming. I warned him. I said, 'You get your mind off her. She's married.' You know, she's one of the Finneys. The Baltimore Finneys, I mean."

"Oh, great," Patty says, putting her face in her hands. "She's loaded, too."

"But the woman's husband's seriously ill. The mover told me he came right into the house and laid down on the floor in the bedroom. The mover said"—Maggie low-

ers her voice now and leans in toward Patty—"that he
might have AIDS."

"Oh, my God, why didn't you warn him? Keevan could
get AIDS!"

"Hush," Maggie says. "You want the whole neighborhood to know?"

"Oh my God," Patty moans. She feels as if she's been
shot in the stomach. Now she'll never be able to sleep
with him.

"Anyway, I did warn him. I mean, I told him what the
moving man said about her husband. Those O'Connors.
They head right for trouble. Always have."

"No—wait. I bet he *didn't* do it with her last night. I
mean, Keevan's not so stupid, is he? He wouldn't risk
AIDS. No way. He's not pigheaded, like Jimmy."

"What? Now you're changing your story?"

"That Zoe, she's so snooty. She barely talks to you
when you try to talk to her. . . ."

Danni is back now, starting to snip at Patty's hair with
her long scissors. Patty wipes an errant tear from her
cheek.

"I *hope* he's not that stupid anyway. I hate him," she
says, "but I don't want him to die."

"You hate him? Ha. You got a funny way of showing
it," Maggie says, folding her arms across her ample chest.

Patty watches her thoughtfully in the mirror, then she
asks, "How much do you think it costs to have breast
implants?"

"Patty!"

"It ranges from three thousand to fifteen thousand, de-
pending on the doctor," Danni says with authority.

"What do you want with breast implants?" Maggie
says.

"I don't know. I just thought they would go nicely with
my new blond hair."

"Just keep your mind on the haircut for now, Patty.
That Zoe Finney doesn't have half the breasts you have.
She's bony as a skeleton."

"I don't have breasts at all."

"Hers are concave."

Patty laughs, but the laughter dies quickly. "I guess breasts aren't what Keevan's looking for."

"You should be glad for what God gives you," Maggie says gently. "Besides, it's not Keevan you're improving yourself for, remember? Look, if you want, wc can stop by at Lace Lovelies afterwards. We will. Okay? Haven't you ever heard of padded bras? Or those new push-up bras. They make skinny models look like me."

"Yeah. I've seen those bras. I know. I'll get one. Hey!" Patty leans suddenly toward the mirror. "I think that's too short."

"Just trust Danni," Danni says, waving her scissors menacingly by her own ruined hair. "Believe me. You'll be deliciously surprised."

Stepping out of Kim's apartment house, Jim O'Connor is in a foul mood. Imagine, telling him he wasn't giving her enough. What does she want? His blood? In the last six weeks, he's given her roses, chocolates, lingerie, including edible panties, a dirty novel, and tickets to a Silk Stockings concert that she insisted they both go to and which he instantly hated. He's also taken her to dinner four times at ridiculously expensive restaurants and given her an orgasm in an elevator, which is something she said she always wanted to try. She almost teetered off her high heels.

But he is *not* going to marry her. It's never even been an option. He told her that from the start. Not that Patty has such a grip on his heart, but good God, he has his priorities. He's hardly going to break up his family for Kimberly D'Amico. He's hardly going to see his kids just on weekends and have to live in some crummy five-hun-dred-dollar-a-month apartment just for lust. It almost feels good to be on his way home to Patty, to the certainty of her, away from Kim and her scheming. On Kim's kitchen counter, he saw a piece of paper scribbled all over in childish script: "Kim and Jim," "Kim and Jim," maybe seven times in all, the dots on the *i*'s like big fat open circles. Sitting out for anyone to see. Like the girls in high school, embarrassing him by writing "Mrs. Jim O'Connor." Thank God for Patty. She never did that. Maybe that was one of the reasons he always liked her: she wasn't into all that crap. Jim sighs as he puts the key in his lock, just glad to be safely home.

He knows something's wrong right away. There isn't a light on in the whole house. And clearly, nothing's been cooked for dinner at all.

"Patty?"

The house echoes with his call. "John, Michelle?"

There isn't a soul home. Well, this is fine indeed. Patty never even told him. At least she should have warned him—unless there's something wrong. Unless something's happened to one of them. Jim feels the back of his neck tightening up, as though his skin is shrinking. The shrinking feeling crawls right up to the top of his head. He picks up the phone and dials Donna's number, but before he enters the last digit, he hears the door.

"Patty, for God's sake, I was worried. You didn't say a word about being late. What are we going to have for dinner? Where are the kids?"

Patty just stands before him, staring.

"What is it?" She's smiling. "What? Is it your birthday or something?"

"No. It's not my birthday. Are you blind?"

Now Patty's acting up too. What's she pulling? Oh . . .

"Your hair. What'd you spend on that?"

"Do you like it?"

"It's fine. What'd you spend on it?"

"Is that all you care about?"

"Don't start on me. Do you have any idea what kind of day I had? And you waking me up half the night. 'Someone's up there with Keevan.' As though we should care. Where are you going? What is your problem?"

Patty is running up the stairs, sobbing, kicking at the railing on the way up. Her shoe makes a clattering sound

on the old wood. Oh, God, Jim thinks as he sits down in
one of the kitchen chairs. Some days, it's just not worth
getting out of bed.

Keevan finds Patty at his door, red-eyed, her hair shockingly bleached and short, reminding him of old movies.
*South Pacific.* What was that actress's name with the cap
of blond hair—Mitzi Gaynor? Patty lets out a long, piti-
ful sob.

"What's wrong?"

"Can I come in?" She's so choked up her voice is a
full octave higher than usual, like a little girl's. It makes
him want to put his arm around her.

"You want a beer?"

"Yes."

"Did you just have your hair done?"

"Yes. Do you . . . do you like it?"

"It's really different. I guess I have to get used to it,"
he says, fishing for a glass that isn't in the dishwasher.

"Oh."

Keevan opens a can of beer for her, goes to pour it into
his one clean glass, then decides just to hand her the can.
She takes it, sets it down on his coffee table, and then
sinks into his couch, hands folded into her lap, her body
doubled over.

"You want to talk about it—whatever's bothering
you?"

"Jim didn't even notice my hair."

"He's a pig."

"He doesn't know I'm alive."

"He should. You're real sweet to him, Patty. The hair's
very nice," he says. "I'm getting used to it now." Somehow Patty always brings this out in him, a desire to protect
her from Jim, a wish to make her happier. Even if it means
lying to her. She looks terrible. Anachronistic. Silly, even.
But she tries so damn hard. How can he slap her in the
face? She gets that every day from Jim.

"Why'd you sleep with her last night?" Patty asks suddenly.

"What?" Keevan looks her in the eye

"She was here for hours."

"Who?"

"That woman. Zoe."

"Oh."

"What kind of name is that anyway—Zoe?"

"Polish."

"Polish?"

"Her name is Zosia, really. . . . The name Zoe itself is actually the Greek word for 'life.' "

"I don't care what it is. Did you sleep with her last night?"

Keevan stares at Patty, at her fierce look, her silly dyed hair, and he debates. Should he tell her he didn't sleep with Zoe, that they played Clue instead? Or should he let her think they did make love? Maybe it would force Patty to give him some space.

"I'm sorry. But I don't think it's something I really want to discuss with you," he says finally.

"Because you're ashamed. She's married."

Keevan feels an iodine-like heat rise to his face. "How do you even know Zoe was up here?"

She doesn't answer him at first. He can see she's embarrassed. "I just happened to look out when she was leaving."

"Could you please just keep your nose out of this, Patty?" He hears how arctic his voice sounds. But what does she expect from him?

"Her husband has AIDS, Keevan. You would risk your life for a quickie?"

"He doesn't have AIDS. That's a total lie.'

"Maggie says—'

"That was hearsay Patty. He's depressed, not sick."

"He's what?"

Keevan just shakes his head. "Just trust me. He doesn't have AIDS." Telling her more would feel like betrayal.

"You should talk to Monsignor O'Hardy," Patty says very evenly now, patting his hand with magnified concern. "He might help you. I know you can't feel good about what you did."

"How do you know how I feel? Or what I did?" He says to her, feels defensive now. "What are you?" he says. "The morality police? Christ! You come up here, and you start ranting—"

Suddenly Patty is weeping, pressing her lips into the back of her closed fist. Her whole body shakes.

"Everyone hates me. I don't know why. I don't try to do things that make people hate me—"

"Come on, Patty, stop it. There, come on. I'm sorry I made you cry." He pulls her to him. She's light in his arms. He feels brotherly toward her, kisses the top of her head. "Let's just not talk about this, okay?"

"Keevan," she whispers.

"What?" She looks up at him. Her nondescript grey eyes are rimmed in red. Mascara is coursing down her face, leaving a streak by her nose. He wipes it away with his finger.

"I think you're the sweetest person I've ever met," she says.

"Come on, pal. I just made you cry." He remembers last evening Zoe called him "pal." How that simple word reverberated in his head all night!

"You *cared* that you made me cry. That's what's so special about you," Patty says.

The worshipful quality of her voice makes him shiver. His mouth tastes bitter. "That's what people are supposed to do," he says. "You live with the biggest jerk in the world. You're not used to simple human kindness."

"I just love you," Patty says. "Really, I do."

"Sure," Keevan says, so uncomfortable his clothes feel tight. To get up, he has to push Patty aside. He pours himself another glass of beer, though his is still half full, and doesn't offer her another can of beer though she has set hers down on the coffee table with a hollow clunk.

"So why don't you just go down there and tell Jim he's an asshole. It will do your heart good," Keevan says. "It will do mine immense good."

Patty gets up, straightening her clothes primly. Her shirt is parted at the bustline. Is she sticking out her chest? She is. How pathetic she looks, with the overbleached hair, the—what is it?—falsies? She looks like a demented Marilyn Monroe.

"Well," she says. "I'll let you have some privacy. Thank you. I feel much better."

"Okay."

"I'm sorry I didn't cook you anything tonight. I didn't cook anyone anything tonight."

"You don't have to cook for me ever, you know. I'm very happy with canned soup."

"Don't you like my cooking?"

"Sure. It's terrific. You just shouldn't do it for me all the time. It makes me feel guilty."

"It makes me feel wonderful."

Patty closes the door behind her, and Keevan sighs with relief.

Zoe is devoting all her energy to trying not to think of what happened this afternoon in the lingerie shop. The shame of it has made her quiet and numb all night. When she got home, she gave Teresa her coat to send off to the cleaners. But the odor of her vomit haunts her. What would have happened if she'd been caught? What would Jamie think if he ever knew such a thing? If he woke from his depression to discover his wife was in jail? What would happen to Rose? Would they jail a person for stealing a nightgown these days? Didn't much worse offenses fill the prisons? The questions make Zoe dizzy. She shivers. And Keevan, he wouldn't want anything to do with her if he knew.

How long she has nursed this shame, so terrible, shared it with no one. Not even Jamie. Now she wishes she had shared it. Like having cancer and not being able to tell anyone, it eats away at her, and no one will know until it's too late.

Rubbing Rose's back to help her sleep, she thinks now of the one time she tried to tell Jamie. Just once.

"Have you ever had a desire to do something that you just know is bad for you, but you can't help it?" she asked him. It was early in their relationship, they were in bed, and she felt closer to him than she ever had before. "You know. Something wrong or shameful . . ."

"Yes. Drinking, when I was a teenager."

"But you stopped. I've never seen you take a drink."

"Yeah," he said sadly. "I stopped because it stopped me." And when he began to talk about the accident again, Zoe knew she could never bring up her stealing. How petty it seemed against his tragedy, against his pain.

Zoe sets Rose in her bed now, kisses her smooth forehead. Her chance to go on with life. That's what Rose is to her. She quietly goes down the steps and knocks softly on Teresa's door, to tell her she's going out. If Rose wakes up crying with a nightmare, she knows Jamie is incapable of responding. It's comforting that Teresa's there. She has hooked up Rose's old baby monitor. She hands the receiver to Teresa.

"You go out *now*? So late?" Teresa asks.

"Just for a while."

"Where you go?"

Zoe hesitates. "To a neighbor's. I was asked for a drink."

Teresa looks surprised, but she shrugs.

"Well, I listen. Okay. I listen." She goes back to her knitting and her Spanish-language television show, indicating with her shoulders that she can't figure out Zoe at all.

Zoe finds that her hands are shaking as she puts on her jacket. Clue. She's just going to play Clue. "Stop," she says out loud to her hands.

She rings Keevan's bell, and when she climbs the inside staircase of his apartment, she notices how handsome and happy he looks, standing on the landing. He's wearing a charcoal-grey sweatshirt, with a torn neck, exposing his own strong, ruddy neck; tight jeans; cowboy boots. The cowboy boots suit him most of all.

"I've been practicing all evening not to show victory on my face. Do you think this is the proper poker face?" He pulls his eyebrows up, his chin down, makes himself look dowager-like, stiff.

"You're a total cipher," she says, shaking her head, smiling. She sits right down on the floor by the coffee table, where the Clue game is already waiting.

"I've thought of you coming here all day," he tells her, sitting across from her. "It's all I could think about. . . ."

She looks up at his face, which moves her so, his odd-colored eyes and rosy skin, and softens the tone that she was going to use.

"Please. You scare me when you say things like that."

"Aren't you glad I want to see you, think of you?"

"Yes," she says. "But I'm married. I know it doesn't seem that way, to anyone but me . . ."

"You're like Mr. Rochester," he tells her.

"Who?" She thinks of Jack Benny's black sidekick, looks at him, confused.

"Mr. Rochester in *Jane Eyre*. With his mad wife up in the attic."

"Jamie isn't very likely to burn my house down," she says dryly. "I don't really appreciate that."

"Sorry. You're right. That was insensitive. Let's play," Keevan says. She regrets the tone she used on him: self-righteous, cold. He sounds so deflated. That was never her intention, but for so long she has had to be defensive about Jamie, since he can't speak for himself.

"I'm sorry," she says, touching his sleeve.

"Me too."

He says nothing while they play except what is required in the game. It hurts her that she's done this to him.

"Keevan," she says after a while, trying desperately to form what she will say, how she can say it.

"Yes?"

"I . . ."

He waits patiently for the rest of the sentence, then must see that it isn't coming. She can't find what she needs to say. She can't seem to tell him.

"Tell me," he coaxes softly. "Anything. Tell me."

"I know why you say the things you say to me," she says, finally. "About wanting to kiss me. About waiting all day for this. Because it's how I feel."

His eyes brighten perceptibly. She instantly feels a pang beneath her throat. Pleasure and confusion and desire.

She braces herself, expects him to come around the table, make a move. She realizes that she's terribly afraid he will. But he just sits across from her, nodding his head, smiling.

"I know," he says.

"But see, I don't want anything to happen with us," she tells him. "I value my marriage to Jamie, as ruined as it is. I value that he once loved me the way he did and now needs me. I can't ever turn away from that. He'd die if I left him."

"Is that what you think I want from you?"

"I'm not certain what you want from me."

"I'm not asking you to turn your back on Jamie. But where does that leave you? Is he even there for you at all?"

The tears are closing her throat again, acid pellets that burn, shutting off her ability to swallow. How much less painful it would be if she could only cry.

"I'm at your house playing Clue. Can't we just play Clue? Can't we just be friends and get together sometimes?" she asks.

"Is that what you want?"

"Yes."

"Really?"

Somehow she can't lie to his face. It is so open, so vulnerable. "No."

"There could be something else," he says. "An alternative."

"Is there an alternative?" she asks.

He takes her wrist now. She sees it is a tender gesture, gentle and purposely not too invasive. He strokes her blue veins, turns her hand over in his hand. The tips of his fingers scout her palm, lightly enough to arouse her skin, not so soft it tickles.

"Couldn't we just be together, in whatever way we can, and not think about the future, or commitment, or change? I would understand. I would know how you felt, and not press you, not pressure you. . . . Whatever happens happens. Whatever doesn't doesn't."

"What would be in it for you?"

"You."

"That would be enough?"

"It's all I want," he says. "Should we just play Clue now?" he asks gently. "Should we not talk about this anymore tonight?"

"Yes. Thank you."

"Because I want you to know, I want to show you, that I could be patient. That all I want is to be with you in whatever way you want to be with me."

"Why me?" Zoe asks suddenly.

"Who can explain love or chemistry?"

She cannot speak after that, except to play the game. She thinks about his word choices: love and chemistry. Which one is it? Chemistry, she guesses. Doesn't love take much longer? She doesn't know. These feelings he arouses in her are so rusty and disquieting. As they play, she finds her hands are trembling. The more she concentrates on stilling them, the more clumsy they seem. She nearly tips over her wineglass, and twice knocks cards off the top of the pile. Still, she beats Keevan in no time.

"I suppose next time I should let you win," she tells him.

"I don't care if I win or lose, as long as there will be a next time."

At the stairs, she once again kisses his cheek, then briefly, cautiously, kisses his lips. He draws her to him.

She is instantly lost in the pleasure of his mouth, cool and wet and inviting. The rest of her body drops away: she can't even feel his hands on her back, in her hair. All she can sense is his mouth, his lips.

"Good night," she says, pulling away.

He lets her go with a smile. "When?" he asks.

"When?"

"When are you going to come over and beat me again?"

"I don't know."

"Garbage night is Tuesday."

"All right," she says. "I'll be here garbage night. I'll be your garbage girl."

# NINE

◆

The gardens have come to life on Eighth Street. Early roses have already unfurled, with their dizzying scent; salvia and violas, pansies and petunias, sprout in neat fenced squares in the front gardens, in wild, spreading patches in back, in cheerful window boxes on the parlor floors. In Zoe's garden, once the magnolia has dropped its thousand slippery tulips, hot-pink azaleas hold their color for weeks, followed by rhododendron the hue of Christmas bows, satiny and red. Forget-me-nots bloom around an old stone urn. Zoe finds their pictures, their names, in a garden catalog. She wants to learn them all. To choose new ones and grow them. She orders sweet williams to grow in a sunny patch. Clematis to wind themselves on a wooden trellis she hammers to the fence. And violas as tartly colored as lemons to sprout beneath the azaleas.

Rose chalks a hopscotch grid on the sidewalk and, throwing a small rock, starts to hop it. She's more used to Brooklyn now. She likes coming outside and playing. She never could do that in Manhattan, except when Teresa took her to the playground. It's nice to know that this sidewalk is hers to chalk. That these trees are her trees. She likes the way the air smells under the big maples. Sweet. Like watermelon. But still, it doesn't feel like home.

Today is the first weekday of Rose's summer. School
was over Friday, and she had to say goodbye to the classroom, to her friends. She'll probably never see her school
or her friends again. She tries not to think about it. She
hates the word "never." She's surprised that other kids
aren't out playing too. Then at three-thirty, she sees kids
coming down from the top of the street, still in school
uniforms: the boys in dark jackets and grey plaid pants,
too hot for the weather, the girls in pleated plaid jumpers.
She wishes she knew them. She wishes she had a uniform
like those girls, with a pleated skirt that swings back and
forth when you walk.

One of the girls peels off from a group of four girls
and a mother, opens the gate to the house next door. Rose
has seen her before and always wanted to talk to her.

"Hello," she says.

"Hello," the girl says. It's easier to be forward without
Teresa there. Teresa hates sitting outside with Rose, so
lately she's gone inside to cook or clean or do whatever
she does, and she just checks every now and then to see
that Rose is still there. Good thing Rose's mom doesn't
know. She'd probably be mad. But Rose likes the freedom
of being outside alone. It makes her feel grown up.

"My name's Rose," she says. The girl in the uniform
comes up to the low wrought-iron fence between their
front yards and smiles.

"My name's Michelle. I saw you when you moved in.
How old are you?"

"Six," Rose says.

"I'm older. I'm seven," Michelle tells her.

"You want to play hopscotch?" Rose asks.

"I've got to go ask my mom. She'll say yes. Wait
for me."

Rose watches the girl go inside. She's pretty. Rose
thinks she's going to like her. In a moment, she's out
again. She does a cartwheel to show Rose how she wears
shorts under her skirt. She takes a cootie catcher out of
her shorts pocket and tells Rose's fortune.

"Is that your father? Tall, with red hair?" Rose asks.

"No."

"But he lives at your house," Rose says.

"Oh, that's my uncle Keevan. He's cool. Did you meet him?"

"Yeah. Is his name really Keevan? I thought he was just kidding."

"Nope. It's really Keevan."

"When's your school out for good?" Rose asks.

"Friday," Michelle says.

"You want to have a play date Friday?" Rose asks.

"Sure."

"And maybe some next week?"

"Sure," Michelle says.

Maybe it won't be such a boring summer, Rose thinks, as she and Michelle play hopscotch, tell stories, and hide in Rose's backyard shed, whispering jump-rope rhymes until it's time for dinner. That night in bed, she tells her mother, "I kind of like Brooklyn. But I still miss Sutton Place. I miss Fred. He always made me laugh. And Walter. And I miss the playground. I miss the noise. Michelle's nice. But I wish she was Mary Ellen."

"It takes time," Zoe says. "Change is hard, but then, often, you're glad you made it. Later. In time you'll be glad."

"I don't know," Rose says. She turns away from Zoe, closes her eyes, and thinks of the playground swing with the special squeak, of the way the river smelled some mornings when she and Teresa went marketing, of the oceanlike sound of the cars below their window in dear old Sutton Place.

The next afternoon, Patty O'Connor looks listlessly out her kitchen window, pausing in her ironing. She takes in the huge nameless tree that is already dropping its stringy yellow seeds, the squares of slate put in years ago by Keevan's parents. It is a grey garden. Nobody's bothered planting anything in it for years. If the bulbs didn't come

up in front, there'd be no colors around the house. This
summer, she's going to change things, she thinks. Pull up
a few squares of slate along the edges. Plant things that
will color the view from her kitchen window. She wishes
the color were there now. The somber tones of the garden
suit the way she feels: she's had a bad feeling all day.
She woke with it this Tuesday morning, a day way too
warm for the season. It haunted her through breakfast,
through her lonely lunch at the kitchen table, with a paper-
back about Jackie O. At first she thought the bad feeling
was because Keevan's been clearly ignoring her. The
thought of him with that Zoe woman makes her skin crawl,
like the time the Kilkenny twins got the head lice and
described them to her. She knows Zoe's been up there
two or three times, for two or three hours at a time, but
she has heard nothing definitive, except, once, laughter.
Still, it's something else telling her it's a bad day. Or why
would she be feeling suddenly even worse about something she already feels bad about?

Then she thinks the feeling is about how Jim hasn't
said another word about her hair, or her push-up bra. Patty's thrilled with the bra. It does give her a miraculous
new cleavage, which she can't help admiring in the mirror.
She wishes she felt surer about the hair. The blond curls
in her mirror remind her of how she looked dressing up
as a child. Mommy's high heels, her lipstick, so potent
and red it clung to her lips for hours after she applied it,
raggedly, making her mouth clownlike. And Aunt Kathleen's wig. Just as blond as this, and curly too. Funny
how Kathleen became a nun . . .

But this feeling isn't about Jim not noticing her. It is
one of dread. Her mother sometimes got feelings before
something big happened. She had a bad feeling the day
Ralph died. A nervous feeling the day Patty announced
her engagement to Jim.

The premonition stays with Patty throughout her conversation with Donna when she calls from her real estate
office. It stays with her during the few minutes she spends

snooping in Keevan's apartment, sifting through the change on his desk, looking through the notes and doodles by his phone. And she can't shake it now as she irons Jim's handkerchiefs, mopping the perspiration from her forehead—how she hates to iron in the late spring and the summer—and wearily climbs the stairs to put the crisp white squares in his drawer, just as she does every Tuesday. And then, as she reaches into his drawer to straighten the still clean handkerchiefs from last week, she finds it. The packet. She holds it in her fingers, turning it over and over. Red. The color of a child's balloon. Patty feels a cold sweat creep up her neck, cover her forehead. It's all come to this. To this. She was only putting his handkerchiefs away in his drawer. Freshly ironed. Just the way he likes them, with the edges perfectly matched. He can't accuse her of snooping. Funny. It was Keevan's apartment where she was snooping. She was far more concerned about what she would find in Keevan's room than in her husband's things. She closes the little packet in her palm, then opens her hand again with curiosity.

The red condom has the translucence of jelly. The packet crackles prettily. This is the first time she has ever seen one, and yet she knew immediately what it was. Even when they were first married and didn't want to have children right away, she and Jim didn't use these. Jim made her go to the doctor to get the pill. And it angered her so much, because she was much more religious than he and *she* had to be the one to get and use the birth control. It never crossed his mind to use these. Now she's choked by the feeling of his betrayal. Who's the woman?

She opens the packet—how easily it rips, like old-fashioned brittle cellophane—and unrolls the rubber ring. It looks translucent, limp, ridiculous. Like a balloon before it's blown up. She laughs out loud. And suddenly she feels better. She starts to think about how she now has a hold over Jim, how she can now demand something from him. She stretches the condom and holds it up to her eyes. Through the red rubber, the whole world looks rosy. She hasn't felt

so powerful in regard to him in ages. Not since they were
first seeing each other and she wasn't even sure she liked
him. But this could be useful. Really useful. If she can
just swallow down this feeling of hurt. Just think, New
Jersey! She can demand that they at least consider moving.
She thinks of the grass behind her mother's town house.
Of running. Of laughing. She can have that. She can demand that. Or maybe she can have it all without him.
Wouldn't that be even better? To have everything she
wants and not have to put up with Jim ever again? To not
have to make the same old food because he won't try
anything new. To not have to wash and iron his clothes,
to not have to hear him snore? She closes her eyes and
feels a moment of thrill that makes her ears tingle. She
blows into the condom until it fills like a balloon. Bigger
and bigger. Astonishing how much it stretches! Then she
ties it off and leaves it on his pillow.

When Keevan gets home from work, he finds a small
blue envelope on his bureau, where Patty puts his mail.
There's no address on it, just his first name. He rips it
open and uncurls the prissy blue paper painted with faint
flowers, stationery like a teenage girl's. He reads:

> *Keevan, I would appreciate it very much if you could*
> *come down to our house for dinner tonight, if it*
> *wouldn't be too much trouble. It would be very help-*
> *ful to me. I really need you to be there.*
> *Love, Patty*

He's painfully tired. The school day was rougher than
ever: two boys had a fistfight over a girl, right in his
classroom, and he had to call the security guard to come
and subdue them, take them away. He always hated to
call the authorities in any way. It undermined his own
authority. But he wasn't about to get between these murderous two. There was hate in their eyes. He imagined
that together they'd beat up anyone who got between them,

for one moment united against a single target: him. With him powerless to stop them, they both soon had blood under their noses, swelling lips, cuts near their eyes. And then the guard came in, brandishing a gun. That upset Keevan even more. A gun was a bad example to the kids: wasn't the message they shouldn't carry, use, or threaten with weapons. Seeing the gun didn't even stop these two at first. So the guard knocked each of them on the back with the butt and then cocked his gun right at them, nervously alternating between their heads. They went with him, bloody and still wanting to murder each other.

The rest of the students seemed disappointed that the fight was over. They were restless until the end of class and didn't accomplish much. The whole thing left Keevan unnerved and dispirited.

Now he's being summoned to Patty and Jim's. It's the last thing he wants to do. But somehow he sees that this is different, this formal summons. There is something oddly urgent about it.

He takes a moment to wash his face, comb back his hair. All right, he tells himself, I can put up with Patty for a night, if she needs me. She leaves me food practically every night. Another voice says, See, she did obligate you to her. See.

When he knocks on the door, Patty ushers him in, dressed more formally than usual, a skirt and shirt, an apron to cover it.

"Jim's not here," she says. "But he should be soon."

Michelle comes over, and as soon as Keevan sits down, she sits on his lap.

"I sold one hundred and fifty-two boxes of Girl Scout cookies, Uncle Keevan. The most in my whole Brownie troop."

"A born saleswoman," he says. "Doesn't surprise me a bit. When do I get my Samoas?"

"You remembered the name! Not until a week from Friday. Right, Mommy? A week from Friday?" Patty nods, clearly distracted. "We're the only troop that delivers cookies after the school year's over. I think it's cool we're the only ones. Know what else?'' she asks. What a little pistol she is, so full of life. ''All month I've been reading the third-grade reader. I'm the only one in second grade they gave it to.''

''Wow,'' he tells her. ''You are something. What's the good word with you, buddy?'' he asks John.

Keevan loves his niece, her exuberance and sweetness, loves children altogether. But his heart especially goes out to his nephew, who is always sad-mouthed and silent, unable or unwilling to extend himself. Whenever he's with him, Keevan makes a deliberate effort to draw him out.

''Nothing,'' John says.

''C'mon. You playing any sports these days? You were doing great at baseball last time we talked.''

''I did okay last year. We're just starting this year.'' It seems like an effort for John to even open his mouth.

Michelle tugs on the back of Keevan's hair. ''I got an A on my math quiz four times in a row.''

''Terrific! How 'bout you, John. How's school?''

''All right, I guess.''

Keevan wonders if at any point in his life he was as sulky, reticent, and miserable as John has been from birth. It pains him that he can't do anything about it, that neither Patty nor Jim has been able to draw him out.

Jim comes through the door, pale and looking irritated.

''What are you doing here?'' he asks.

''That's very nice, Jim,'' Patty says. ''Nice of you to welcome your brother. I invited him.''

''Me too,'' Michelle says. ''I never get to see Uncle Keevan.''

''Sport,'' Jim says, slapping John on the back. John seems to cower away from the slap. This is Jim's idea of drawing John out. ''Hi, baby,'' he tells Michelle, kissing her cheek. ''What's to eat tonight?'' he says, turning to Patty.

''Chicken française,'' Patty says triumphantly.

''What the hell's that?'' he asks.

"Something delicious," she says. "If you'll just give it a chance."

"I'll give it a chance, if it doesn't rise from the plate and eat me alive."

"Oh, thanks a lot, asshole," Patty says. "That's very big of you."

"What's gotten into *you*?" he asks her. Then, under his breath, he says, "Don't say that in front of the kids."

She shrugs. But Keevan sees that something is going on with Patty. She's smiling like the cat that ate the canary. "You'd better change your clothes," she tells Jim. "Dinner's ready, and this kind of food doesn't wait."

"Don't rush me," he says.

Keevan hears him climbing the stairs to the bedroom. His feet are loud and oafish on the steps. And he seems to be walking purposely slow. How he despises his brother. Odd to feel that way about your own flesh.

"You'll like the chicken," Patty tells Keevan.

"Sure," he says. "Sounds good."

From upstairs he hears, "What the hell!"

Keevan looks over at Patty, who is crossing her arms with satisfaction.

"What's going on?" he asks.

"You'll find out. Eventually."

The room is silent while they wait for Jim. Even the children are silent, looking at each other with worry.

Jim comes down in his jeans, red-faced. He doesn't say anything at all.

"Sit down, dear," Patty says, pulling out the dining room chair for him. Jim sits with the misery of a captive.

God, Keevan thinks. This is some kind of trap. He wishes desperately he could go upstairs and lie down on his bed with a worn copy of *An American Tragedy*. Or at least go up to the silence of his apartment and think about Zoe and what's going to happen tonight when she comes.

"Keevan, you sit here," Patty says. "Sit down, everybody." The children come to the table. He can see that they're reluctant too. They glance at each other warily, then at Keevan.

Patty passes out the plates of food, piled high with chicken, mashed potatoes, brussels sprouts, cranberry sauce. No one speaks for a while. They hide their faces in the job of eating. Then finally Jim sets down his fork.

"Why the hell d'you do that?" he says in a low voice, his mouth half closed over his words.

"Thought it would be fun," she says cockily. The blond hair doesn't look nearly so wrong on her, Keevan thinks, now that she's sporting this new sassy attitude.

"Well, it wasn't funny."

"I didn't think it was funny when I found it," she says. "I didn't laugh one bit."

"What are you guys talking about?" Michelle asks, mouth full of mashed potatoes.

"Don't talk with food in your mouth," Jim snaps. Michelle sits back in her chair, her eyes wide, as though she's been slapped.

"The chicken's delicious," Keevan says, hoping in vain to clear the air. He can hardly swallow.

Patty smiles at him, looking triumphant.

"It's not what you think," Jim says. "It was a joke."

"Like I said, I'm not laughing."

"This chicken's gross," John says.

"Leave it and eat the rest," Patty tells him. She's flying high. Her pale-grey eyes are bright as stars.

"We'll discuss this later," Jim says. Still flushed, he's barely eating.

Keevan wonders why Patty insisted on involving him in this. To shield her, to show off to him, to make a public statement? God knows what it's all about. Keevan supposes that Patty has discovered something about Jim's infidelities.

There is little talk for the rest of the meal. Though the chicken is good, Keevan merely cuts it and pushes it around his plate: under the mashed potatoes, under the brussels sprouts and cranberry sauce.

"Well," Keevan says. "I'll be going." When he gets up from the table, the tension in the room is so strangling, he's stiff from the strain.

"Stick around," Patty says.

"No. I have lots of papers to grade." It's a lie. He doesn't have a single one. But he can't imagine why Patty forced him to come, or what's brewing between her and his brother.

"I love you, Uncle Keevan," Michelle says, reaching for him to bend down and kiss her cheek. He hugs her skinny body to him.

"Want me to take the kids upstairs, Patty?" he asks, feeling sorry that sunny little Michelle should have to weather whatever storm is forming.

"No," Patty says. "They have homework to do. No reason to take them upstairs."

"You sure?"

"I'm perfectly sure," Patty says.

He's never seen her so lit up. Dangerous, he thinks. He lightly tousles John's hair.

"Come on up some other time, Johnny. We could hang out and watch a baseball game."

"I don't like watching baseball on TV," he says.

"I do," Michelle says. "Can I come up with you sometime, Uncle Keevan?"

"Sure, darlin'. Fabulous meal, Patty."

Keevan has never been so thrilled to close a door behind him. He senses that later he'll be hearing arguments through the floorboards, that he can't entirely escape what's going to happen, but at least he won't have to witness it.

Jim hears Patty come into the bedroom. He's been hoping that somehow they won't have to talk anymore about the condom, that Patty will miraculously forget. So he's busying himself looking through his closet, for nothing in particular. What should he tell Patty if she asks what he's looking for? Those grey slacks she gave to the church clothes drive?

"Okay, so give me your song and dance," Patty says.

"No song and dance," he says.

"So then, give me whatever lie you've been cooking up." How cool she looks, almost unconcerned. It shakes him, seeing her so in control.

"Someone gave the condom to me. A joke. You think if I really *had* bought this for myself I would have left it in the drawer for you to find? I'd hide it in a sock or something. And I wouldn't have bought red, believe me."

Patty stands with a hand on one hip. She isn't buying any of it. The funny thing is, it's true. He doesn't use condoms with Kim. They both hate the things. He got this condom from Zack Borris at the office Christmas party, months ago. It's been sitting in that drawer ever since, so there's no reason Patty shouldn't have found it earlier. He even intended to show it to her one night when he first got it, but she was on the phone with Donna, and after an hour he gave up waiting. Zack handed them out as a joke. "Have a safe Christmas," he was saying to everybody. He had red ones and green ones. "Here, O'Connor," he said. "The red is really you." Jim tells all this to Patty, but she shakes her head.

"You want me to have him call you?" he asks Patty. "He'll tell you it's true."

"Like you wouldn't set this up with him first, I suppose."

"He's my boss."

"You're both men. It's not impossible that you'll stand by each other." She sighs the sigh of a martyr. The same one her mother used to sigh at Thanksgiving when she carried in the turkey and said, "Do any of you men want to eat?"

"I'm being unjustly accused," Jim says, moving forward to take her elbows, to draw her to him. But she backs away.

"Are you saying you're not having an affair?"

"Well, of course I'm saying that." The lie feels odd in his throat, tastes bitter. He finds his heart is pounding just as it did when he was ten and he and Corey lied to Father Joe about not eating all the cookies Mrs. Carragan made for the bake sale. Corey's face was smooth and pleasant as glass, but Jim's heart was chugging, nudging his chin. He wondered then, as he wonders now, how much it shows. Father Joe knew he was lying. "I think there's something you want to tell me, Jimmy. I think Jesus is asking you to speak the truth." Corey laid into him later for getting them both caught. And they had to spend the whole summer helping Father Joe around the church, cleaning the bathrooms, sweeping up, while Douggie was on vacation in Ireland. Remembering, Jim can smell the Bab-O. Patty eyes him carefully.

"You've been late a lot lately. I'm sure it wasn't always the subway—"

"When was the last time you took the subway?" he says.

"When I went to Macy's."

"When was that?"

"I don't know. Three weeks ago, maybe."

"Right. And did you know they're working on the F train these days? Laying new track. Just in the last two weeks."

"Yeah? I'll call Corey to verify that."

Her brother . . . Oh, God. How stupid. Jim sits down. He made the lie too detailed, and now it's going to bite him back.

"Go ahead," he says. "Call Corey." She never does what he dares her to do. And she never talks to her brother on the phone. Hardly ever. Usually she just crosses the street, uses her own key.

She picks up the phone.

"If you're going to call someone, call Zack. He'll tell you about the condoms. A joke. I didn't ask for it." He can hear the desperation in his voice, the quaking.

"So why did you keep it?" Patty asks, dialing. She

would make a fine police interrogator. "Most people who don't want something just throw it away. . . . Corey. Hi. . . . Tell me, they working on the F train right now? Replacing the tracks or something that would cause a lot of delays?"

Just like her not to ask about Kathy or the kids. Just like her to launch right into the business, then hang up. No give in her. No give at all.

"Yeah. . . . I don't know. Someone who obviously didn't know what they were talking about. Thanks." She hangs up and stares at Jim.

"I'm not afraid of kicking you out," she says. "But I don't believe in divorce." Jim swallows. Nights with Kim. All night with Kim with no interruptions. But maybe it isn't so good. He remembers the hearts he found on her kitchen counter. Doodles. Kim and Jim. Kim and Jim. With the *i*'s dotted as fat and round as polka dots. Living with her every day would definitely be cloying. It's nice to have a piece of cake for dessert, but for a steady diet? And he wouldn't get to see Michelle every day—her sweet little face. What would Patty tell her about him? That Daddy was a cheat? John, on the other hand, he might be glad to avoid for a while.

"It's a mistake," he says feebly. "You're making a mistake, Patty."

She shakes her head. She looks remarkably pretty right now. Young. Blond. Her eyes are glowing.

"Why don't you pack," she says.

"I can't believe this."

"Go ahead. If you think I'm going to let you sleep here, you're wrong."

"I'll sleep on the sofa."

"Out."

"Really, Patty. You're being totally ridiculous. Totally. I'll call Zack—Oh, God, he's out of town right now. In Atlanta, I think."

"Right."

"As soon as he's back, I'll have him call you."

"Pack. Now. Get out. I'm getting a Coke. You want something?"

It's so weird. She doesn't sound angry, or shaky, or anything. She's transformed, like a different person. Invasion of the body snatchers.

"A Sprite," he says weakly.

"Okay." She leaves him. As she goes out of the room, she looks back at him. Her eyes can only be described one way: merry.

When Zoe comes up the stairs, Keevan has his coat on.

"Do you mind if we don't play Clue tonight?"

"No. Why? Do you have to go out?" She feels stricken, shocked by her own disappointment.

"No. I just wondered if you'd take a walk with me. Patty and Jim have a fight brewing, and I don't want to hear it. Anyway, it's a soft night. . . ."

She smiles at him and repeats the words. "Soft night."

She turns and goes down the steps, Keevan following her. The night *is* soft. She failed to notice it before, rushing to take out the garbage so she could climb the stairs to Keevan's. But the temperature is neither warm nor cold. Only half the houses are still lit, but their lights are haloed and magical in the moist air. It has rained since noon and only an hour or two ago stopped. The streets are dry now, but the bluestone is dark as obsidian.

"Your dogwood tree is still blooming at the top," Keevan points out to her as they pass her house.

"Is it dogwood?"

"I'm surprised the Dunbars didn't tell you. They bought it half grown. Incredibly expensive. The old-timers on the street hated them for it."

"Why?"

"Jealousy. When you don't have much money, you hate people who do. They hate your marble bathroom too."

"My marble bathroom?" She feels a guilty pang, thinking how she's grown to enjoy it.

"Everyone was gossiping when the Dunbars brought in all that pink marble."

"You make everybody here sound like busybodies."

"People watch. They see what goes on in every house."

"Makes me wonder if I should be out here walking with you," she says.

Up until now, she has walked close to him, brushing shoulders, feeling his warmth through her thin jacket. But now each lit window represents a pair of eyes to her. The sound of their footsteps magnifies with her concern. She finds herself walking farther from him, her arm no longer brushing his.

"What's wrong?" he asks after a moment. Keevan reaches for her hand. His is pleasantly rough and warm.

"I don't think that's a good idea," she says softly, pulling her hand away before she can own the feel of his skin on hers. She hears her voice husky with—what? Regret? Desire?

"No one will see us. No one will look out at this hour."

"Please."

A dog is barking down the street. In the distance, a garbage truck squeals, doing late rounds.

"Will you go in here with me?" he says when they reach the top of the street. "Into the park? There's a boathouse by a little lake called the Lullwater. Will you come and sit there with me? We can talk. I want to share it with you."

"Should we go in there at night?"

"I often do."

"Isn't it dangerous?"

He turns to her and shrugs, then smiles. She hesitates, leaning all her weight on one leg. His strong face, his long, delicate fingers combing his hair back, arouse her again. Her body rebels at the insistent intrusion of him.

"I won't make you do it, of course," he says. "I'm not saying it isn't dangerous. It definitely could be."

"You do this often? Why?"

"It's beautiful at night. Magical."

"And you find risks seductive."

"Don't you?"

She thinks briefly of the wooden comb she stole from the Seventh Avenue Pharmacy on her way home from the subway tonight, its edges so smooth and sanded; her fingers caressed it all the way home. She remembers the thrill that risk gave her. She feels him move toward her. His lips are suddenly on her lips, parting them slightly, as they close on her lower lip, her upper lip. She is lost for a moment in the cool draw of his tongue on the rim of her gums. She pulls away suddenly. The wetness of the kiss turns cool in the moderate night air.

"I'm scared," she says.

"Of the park?"

"And you."

"I'll take you home." He starts to turn.

She stops him. "No. I want to go." She's sensed his dare, wants to go.

He takes her hand again. "Okay, if you're sure."

Venturing under the canopy of trees, she feels weak and shaky. It makes her lean close to him. The park is lit with old gaslights, pretty but dim among the dark branches, the meadow.

"It doesn't feel like New York," she says.

"It isn't New York. It's Brooklyn." The echo of his voice is eerie.

Except for the brooming of the trees against the sky, all is still and dark, thick as chocolate, Zoe thinks. She feels she is in a movie, on a stage set. Nothing seems entirely real. Especially Keevan. The smell of him beside her—mothballs and soap and something indefinably personal and sweet—is more seductive than any cologne. The sound of his breathing, the warmth of his hand, his palm, slightly roughened, his fingers, so long and encompassing, quicken her as nothing has in a long time. In his apartment playing Clue, the mundanity of the game, the sound of their glasses being picked up and set down, the murmuring of the television in his brother and sister-in-law's apart-

ment below, helped to ground her somehow. But out here,
where she can't see a building, a single city light, where
the grass is wet on her ankles and the clouds are drifting
so fast they dizzy her when she looks up, she is lost and
alive as she can barely remember being. A virgin, she
thinks. I am a virgin to all this.

"There's the boathouse," Keevan says.

Across a small lake, like a castle out of "The Twelve
Dancing Princesses," a white building shimmers in a slash
of moonlight. Ornate as a wedding cake, it duplicates itself
in the still water, its arched French doors repeated exactly.
The white beaded columns lose none of their brightness
in reflection. On the far end of the pond, a bridge is barely
visible, grey or green it must be, nearly the color of the
water. Together Zoe and Keevan walk around the lake.
The sound of lapping water mingles with an owl's call.

"I didn't know there are owls in Brooklyn," she says.

"There are here."

"It's a sad sound."

He leans over and kisses the top of her head. A charge
runs down her spine like cold water, raises every hair on
her body. Her nipples rise and press against her shirt.

When they reach the boathouse, smaller somehow than
it appeared across the lake, they sit on the wooden slats
that slant from the boathouse steps down into the Lullwater. Behind them are the dark gated doors, the old ceramic building pristine as a bride. At their feet, the water
splashes and sings. Out of the corner of her eyes, she sees
Keevan start.

"What is it?" He shrugs. She follows his line of vision
and thinks she sees a rat scurrying into the bushes. She
shivers. He puts his arm around her shoulder and pulls
her close.

"I'm a risk for you too," she says after a while.
"That's it, isn't it?"

"What's it?"

"The reason you're with me. I'm a challenge. Like the

park. But I'm not sure you should find this risk so seductive." She feels the hold of his eyes on her.

"I can't help it," he tells her. "I do."

"I'm in love with Jamie," she says.

"Shh," he says. "I told you I'm not taking that away from you."

"He and Rose are all I have," she says.

He smooths her hair. "Now you have me," he whispers.

She doesn't say anything. She merely feels his words inside her, filling her slowly like warm water, easing the ache, the emptiness.

"Come here," he tells her. His voice is tolerant and soothing. She wants to hate his voice, the feel of his strong arm around her, but she can't. "At night," he says, stroking the fine hairs at the base of her neck, "every night, if I can't sleep, I feel you in the room next to mine."

"Oh . . ."

"Don't you think of that? How our rooms touch?"

"Keevan . . ."

"Don't you?"

"Do you feel Jamie in the room next to yours? Because he's there too," she says. She is sorry when she sees him wince.

"Do you still sleep with him?"

"I keep hoping . . . ," she begins.

"What?"

"No, never mind."

"Tell me."

She sighs. She feels bone-tired, weak. "I keep hoping that my being near him will make him feel safe, will soothe him, maybe even wake him."

"You must be lonely. I know you are. . . ."

"I'm all right," she says, but her voice belies her uncertainty.

"At night, I think about you. About . . ." Keevan strokes her cheek. "Let me make love to you, Zoe. I know you've thought of it too."

"Please, I—" But she is interrupted by the sensation

of his lips finding her neck and shoulders, by the pleasure
of his warm breath brushing her hairline.

"Let me," he whispers.

"Don't," she says. Beneath the elastic edge of her peas-
ant shirt, his fingers find her bare shoulders, then her
breasts. She is chaos, the sensations colliding beneath
her skin.

"You said you wouldn't push me," she says.

"I'm not trying to push you. I wasn't planning this,
really. But I'm human," he says.

His fingers make her skin burn. She has no control over
the intake of her lungs, her head, which falls back in a
gasp of skin hunger and delight.

"I don't want this," she says, but there is still no certainty in her voice.

"Tell me you don't want this."

"I don't."

"Tell me to stop."

"Stop."

He pulls away suddenly, and she finds herself shaken
by the pause.

"Keevan . . ."

"I stopped," he says. He sits back, leaning on his arms,
turning his face from her. The night air is mild. But the
chill he gives off is palpable. She, however, is throbbing.
Her desire for him is almost painful.

"Keevan?"

"We'll go. We should go. I guess I was being selfish."

"No, I . . ." By pulling away, he has unlocked the
door to her. "I want . . . I want you to." She reaches for
his arm. Slowly and with a gentle smile, he turns to her.

"You sure?"

She nods. Tenderly, he lays her back on the warm
wooden slats, and the weight of his body against hers
gives her the oddest sense of safety. Solidity. A man who
has his own heft, his own reality, who owns the space in
which he moves.

"Zosia," he whispers. His fingers are everywhere,

arousing her nipples, pulling her tight to him, cupping her thighs in the tender place just below her buttocks. Then his lips are warm on one nipple, his fingers brush and play the other. There must be effort in his tenderness, she knows. She thinks that beneath it is the same impatient wildness that rocks her.

She reaches for him to kiss her again. She can tell he thinks her return to kissing is an indication that she wants to stop, or at least slow down. But as he lies atop her, kissing her, her hand finds the shape of his penis arching against the cloth of his jeans.

Clumsily she unzips him, frees him, so that his penis is thick between them. She presses it to her belly and begins to stroke it, moving her hips at the same time. There is an unreal quality to the softness of the skin. It is difficult to determine where her hand stops and he begins. Like baby flesh. She is stunned by the roaring desire she feels. Like electricity, it courses through her.

He lifts her skirt and pulls down her panties so swiftly they slip from his fingers, into the water.

"Leave them," she whispers. "Leave them." She cannot wait any longer. She takes his penis and presses it to her, guides him in. They are both loud and lost now, and when they join, his swollen penis opens her as though it is the first time she's ever made love. The pain radiates. She feels she could bleed from it, it is so keen, so wounding a sensation. But her hips buck up to meet his and her hands lock him to her and her whole body is suddenly awash in a long unfamiliar pleasure. Keevan is spinning a rhythm much wilder than she's ever known, insistent, enveloping, hypnotic. Like the wheels of a rushing train. Her whole body sings in the embrace of this rhythm, clutching and straining and thrilling to keep up. "Keevan!"

Suddenly all is explosive, endless. Lost in the vortex of her climax, she is hardly aware of him at all. "I feel you. I feel you coming all around me," she hears him say, thrusting more wildly, galvanized by her pleasure.

But the moment after her orgasm, in the middle of their bucking and coupling, she steps out of herself and watches. What is she doing, lying by this polluted pool? On this dirty wood. Rats could be running over her hair, which has fanned out behind her head. People could come by and see them, kill them for all she knows. Keevan is still lost to the pleasure. Why doesn't he stop? His wildness suddenly embarrasses her. The frenzy to push him away, run away, overtakes her. She's got to pull away from under him. She's got to get away. As her body strains to do so, maybe his body reads the movement as desire, for he comes finally with a long cry and then her name, whispered in a hiss. Zosia.

She cannot wait for him to get off her, but he settles down on top of her, loose-limbed.

"Keevan?"

"Shh," he says softly.

But the desire to escape won't let her be silent.

"I want to get out of here. Please," she says.

He rubs his face, a perplexed dip in his pale brows. He moves off her, pulls up his underwear and jeans.

"You okay?" he asks her.

"I need to go," she says. With his withdrawal, she feels the cooling liquid of his semen pouring from her. Her underwear is lost in the Lullwater. She feels exposed and filthy.

"Do you have a handkerchief?" she asks. He pulls a clean one from his jeans, watching her steadily, worried. She uses the handkerchief to clean herself. "I'll wash it," she says, as she stands.

"No, give it to me," he says. But she won't let him have it. She holds it tight in her hand.

They are silent for a long time as they leave the boathouse and cross the meadow. He does not touch her, but she feels his longing to. If he touches her, she thinks she'll just start running. It can't be changed now. She's done it. She's as bad as her parents always told her she was. As bad as she always feared. The liar, the thief, the adulteress.

Finally Keevan says, "Are you angry? Zoe, tell me."

"I just want to go home," she says.

"You wanted me."

"That doesn't make it right."

"Feeling guilty about it doesn't make it right either," he says.

She wants to tell him she's sorry, but no words come. Mostly, she just wants to pretend this never happened, to be in her own house, separate and safe, washing Keevan and the memory of him from her, out of her. Then, scrubbed clean, she wants to lie down close to Jamie and breathe in that odd odor he emits lately of singed leaves, to get drunk on it until she is numb again.

Suddenly they hear voices from behind them, on the other side of the Lullwater. Keevan puts his finger to his lips to hush her. The fingers of his other hand dig into her shoulder. She wonders if it's fear she sees in his searching eyes.

"Lovebirds," the voice calls to them. Then another. "Lovebirds." Raucous laughter fills the woods, grips Zoe's spine. But the laughter goes off toward the road behind the boathouse, leaving only its chill behind.


Jim sits on the bed at the New York Hilton and stares at his socks. Kim isn't answering, her machine is unplugged, and he's angry. What the hell is she up to anyway, at 1:00 A.M.? He has a dark vision of Kim in bed with some young stranger, who is dancing beneath her like an untamed bronco.

He moans aloud. He's always made it a point not to ask who she's seeing besides him. He knows she's single, she's free. But the vision of her with someone else creates a twinge in his stomach, even more upsetting than the fact that he's here at the Hilton, instead of home. He can't believe how much this place costs. Or that no one's going to pick up the tab for him. All those business trips he's taken, never thinking of the cost of his room. Sometimes he's actually gotten to bring Kim along. Mother Mary, those nights were sweet. Kim on her knees, growing him hard with her insistent lips and tongue, hard as he's ever known. Long, hot fucks and room service champagne.

He doesn't know what to do with himself. Packing in front of Patty, he could only concentrate enough to bring the necessities. He has nothing but a briefcase full of work and a few changes of underwear, some business suits and shirts and a pair of jeans. What he wouldn't give for John's Game Boy or a bottle of scotch. He thought he'd end up at Kim's, not here in this cold room with its orange bedspread and stained carpet. Listlessly, he picks up the TV remote control and flips through the channels. Pay cable has movies from six months ago and soft porn with all the good parts cut out, the kind of thing you fall for only once, on your first business trip, hoping the movie's title won't show up on your bill. That time, what did he pick? Something with a title that wasn't too damning, like *Kathy's Pals.* His boss, Zack, who got him into this mess in the first place with his stupid red and green condoms, once said in regard to a client who wouldn't buy any insurance but would always tease you into thinking he was close, "It's like sex without orgasm—just a skin irritation." These movies were skin irritations. His whole life feels like a skin irritation right now. He dials Kim again, but no answer at all. He wonders if he should go over there and sit on her stoop and wait for her. No, he isn't going to sit around there like a lost lamb, asking for her sympathy. Especially if she is with some cowboy.

Instead he does flip to a movie called *Slippery Satin* and pulls his limp cock out of his blue jeans. But after a half hour of licked lips and strummed nipples, it lies in his hand, sleeping. Leaving the TV on, with its sounds of unrequited desire, its silly high voices, he rolls into the bedspread, face down against the rough corded fabric, and imagines he's fucking Patty so hard she's crying out beneath him, sliding his suddenly hard cock in and out of her, shoving himself deep, making her moan like the girls on the screen, until his hand is sticky with streams of cum and he feels sick with exhaustion.

"Rose won't throw nothing away," Teresa is saying, very agitated, her mouth almost angry. She is practically up to her elbows in lettuce leaves, tearing them in wild jerks, as though she is wrestling.

"What do you mean?" Zoe asks. She is tired from her day, but mostly weak from the exhausting effort of trying to force from her mind the memory of last night in the park with Keevan. How could she have done it? She wants to peel her very skin off and put it in the washing machine. What games she's been playing with herself! It was juvenile to imagine that she could have a warm friendship, a high-school flirtation, with him and never make love.

"She save everything," Teresa says. "Her napkin. Her candy wrapper. Her food. She make me put her food in the refrigerator if she don't finish."

She'll never see him again. Never. No matter what he says. No matter how he feels about her.

"She save her dirty tissue too."

"When did you notice this?" she asks wearily. Teresa's always worrying about Rose.

"Three days now." Teresa gathers an armful of torn leaves from the chopping block and puts them in the bowl. Then she angrily shakes off the leaves that cling to her fingers and wrists. "She cry, 'Teresa, no! Save the napkin. Don't put that food in the garbage. Where will it go?'

" 'Why you want to save napkin?' I ask her. 'Is just a napkin. Paper. It go in garbage.' 'No! No!' She is all crazy and crying. 'Save it. Save it. Where will the garbage go?' So I say, 'Staten Island. It go to Staten Island.' 'No. It needs to stay here with the rest of the napkins,' she say. 'Here with its family.' 'The rest of the napkins go to Staten Island too,' I tell her, but she don't believe me."

Teresa thinks that Rose is made of glass. She never disciplines her enough, thinks she is seriously ill when she merely complains of a stomachache. And when Rose insists on candy, she usually gets candy.

"I'll talk to her," Zoe says. "Where is she?"

"In her room. With her napkin. She take her dirty napkin up to her room."

Zoe climbs the stairs, takes a deep breath. Why won't her head clear?

"Rosie?" Rose is sitting on her floor, surrounded by baby dolls. One has red hair in a big pink bow. One has a plump little thumb that, inserted in its mouth, triggers a mechanism that makes it suck like a real baby. Another is stark naked, its belly distended. Next to it are a crumpled napkin, a candy wrapper, a torn envelope.

"Mama!" Rose gets up and puts her arms around Zoe's hips. "You're home."

"Hi, baby. What did you do today?" Zoe asks.

"I played by myself. I pretended Homer and I were beggars on the street."

"That sounds depressing."

"Uh-uh. It was fun. We lived in a cardboard box with a television and a heater. Like that guy we once saw. I wish Michelle weren't still in school, though."

"It's nice you like her. Camp will start soon too."

"Uh-huh."

"Teresa told me she's worried about you. She says you saved your napkin and other things." Zoe stoops to pick up the crumpled napkin. "Was that part of your beggar game?"

"No."

"Well, I guess Teresa wondered why you wanted to save it."

"She didn't want it."

"But why did you?"

Rose's pointy little chin dimples. "I don't want to talk about it."

"Why not?"

"It's private." She pronounces this with certainty.

"Oh," Zoe says. "I see. Between Teresa and you—"

"No!" Rose sounds outraged. "Between the napkin and me."

"The napkin and you?"

"I don't want to talk about it." Rose pulls the thumb from her doll's mouth, saying, "That's enough, young lady. How many times have I told you what a dirty habit it is to suck your thumb?" She sets the doll down with a thump.

"It's rough being a mom, huh?" Zoe says.

"Yeah. She never listens to me."

"Look. You want to give me those things, I'll take them down to the kitchen with me."

"What things?"

"You know. The napkin. The wrapper—"

"No," Rose says.

Zoe shrugs. "Well, bring them down later, okay?"

"Why?"

"Because you don't want a dirty napkin in your room. I don't like food things in your room. They attract bugs. Mice, even. We don't want mice in the house."

"I like mice. And besides, don't call my napkin dirty."

"Isn't it?"

"It's a little curly. It is *not* dirty."

"Well, the wrapper, then. Bring it down when you're ready." Zoe sighs. What's the big deal? Let her keep them. Zoe feels uneasy, but as often as not, things seem to pass with Rose. A phase. A hiccup.

Rose turns back to her doll and shoves the tiny thumb into the mechanical mouth. "There she goes again," she says to no one in particular.


"Isn't Daddy coming home in time for dinner?" Michelle asks.

"Not tonight," Patty says. Not ever, if I can help it, she thinks. Today she is much angrier than she was last night. She hates that she ever loved Jim. Hates that she ever trusted him. And is surprised at how hurt she feels.

"How come he's not coming for dinner?"

"He's busy," Patty says. "Go do your homework or something. Don't stand on my heels. I've got a dinner to put on the table."

"I'm not standing on your heels. What are we having?"

"Meat loaf."

"Daddy loves meat loaf. Maybe if Daddy knew we were having meat loaf—"

"Go do your homework," Patty says.

"So where is he?" Michelle asks.

"What do you mean?"

"He didn't sleep here last night. John doesn't think he did either."

Patty turns to her daughter. All day she has been wondering what to tell the children. That he had to go out of town? That they had an argument?

"It's because of your stupid hair, isn't it?" Michelle says. She is squeezing up her little face with anger, distorting her mouth with clear distaste.

"It has nothing to do with my hair."

"It does so. He hates what you did to it. I hate what you did to it. Johnny hates it too. You look stupid. Like you're not even trying to be our mother."

Patty puts her hand to her hair, which feels unnaturally dry and stiff to her fingers. She begins to cry. The tears make a straight line from her eyes to the corners of her mouth. "It has nothing to do with my hair. Besides, Maggie says my hair looks good. And Uncle Keevan too." She expects Michelle to soften, seeing her cry, to ask forgiveness. Instead she hustles away, her little body rigid with anger and self-righteousness. She goes running up the stairs, the sound of her forced, angry retreat echoing throughout the house.

Keevan, grading papers, is still suffering over what happened with Zoe last night—how, standing at her door to say good night, the smell of the park still on her, high color from lovemaking staining her cheeks, she wouldn't agree to see him again. When he touched her hairline,

feeling the perspiration from their loving still damp, curling the fine blond hairs there, she recoiled as though he'd
burned her. She did not look back at him after she'd turned
to open her door.

Today he has barely eaten. His stomach feels raw and
hollow. He is startled to hear a knock, and disappointed
to find Michelle standing solemn and cross in baggy khaki
shorts, holding on to her elbows.

"Where's my father?" she asks.

"Your father? Is he missing?" Keevan asks.

"My mother says it's not because of her hair, but it is
because of her hair, I know it."

He takes Michelle by the shoulder and directs her in.
"Tell me," he says.

"He didn't come home last night."

"Hmm."

"Mama says he's not coming for dinner. I think they
had a fight."

"Sounds like it."

"It's her hair."

"I don't think it's her hair," Keevan says. "You want
a soda?"

"I hate her."

"Coke . . . 7UP . . . root beer . . . ?"

"It's dinnertime. Mommy doesn't let me have soda before supper."

"How's she going to find out?" He winks at her. Her
small face is flushed with worry.

"Well, okay. Coke."

Poor kid. Worrying about that idiot brother of his as if
he deserved it. He goes out to the kitchen and comes back
with her glass clinking with ice, frosty with the fresh-
poured soda. It still hisses.

"She looks dumb," Michelle says. "She doesn't look
like a mother at all. Like she's trying to be Madonna
or something."

"Or something," Keevan says, knowing it is inappropriate to be cruel about Patty right now but finding it irresist-

ible. All Patty ever wanted was attention. "Really, I don't
think you should be mad at her," he says. "I don't think
this is all your mother's fault. Maybe it's not her fault
at all."

"That's just because you're always mad at Daddy."

"Is that what you think?"

"Adults are always mad at each other, and then they
go around telling kids they should stop fighting," Michelle
says, taking a long, satisfied pull of Coke. "That's what
I think."

"Maybe you should ask your mother if there's a way
you can call him. Maybe if we go down together, we
can get her to tell us. Just so you can be relieved he's
all right."

"Johnny says he doesn't care. He says he would be
happy if he never talked to him again."

"They're not the best of pals, are they?" Keevan asks.
She shakes her head. "Come on. Let me run interference
for you." Together they descend the steps. Her hand in
his is strangely comforting. He loves this little girl, with
her sense of certainty, of justice. How sad that she should
have his asshole brother for a father. That she should love
her father despite his faults, as children do. Does Zoe's
Rose love her practically absent father?

Patty is chopping carrots with a vengeance.

"Pat?"

She turns. "Yes," she says with some annoyance. She
drops her gaze to Michelle. "Did you bring Uncle Keevan
down to attack me too?"

"I'm here to get at the truth," he tells her.

"About what? About how Jim must have left me because of my hair?"

"Apologize," Keevan tells Michelle.

"I'm sorry, Mommy."

"You like my hair, don't you, Keevan?"

"Yeah, sure," he says. "Michelle was just upset because she wants to talk to Jim. This has nothing to do

with your hair, and she's very sorry she made it sound like it did—right, Mich?''

Michelle nods.

"All right," Patty says. Keevan notices how pinched her face looks, not at all glowing and self-satisfied, as it did last night.

"He's at the New York Hilton. His secretary called today to tell me. Oh, and by the way, we're selling the house.''

Keevan feels as though an arrow has pierced his heart.

"What?" he asks, sure he's heard her wrong.

"We're selling the house. If Jim and I split up, I'm moving to New Jersey.''

"I own half this house.''

"Well, unless you want to buy out our half too, we're selling it. And even though the prices have dropped lately, I still doubt you can afford it.''

"You and Daddy are splitting up?" Michelle asks.

"It's not yours to sell. It's Jim's and mine. It's been in this family seventy years.''

"You and Daddy are getting a divorce?" Michelle says, louder this time.

"Could be. Keevan, discuss it with Jim. Ask him if he can afford to pay my rightful one quarter, pay alimony and child support, and maintain this house too.''

Keevan feels a tightening in his jaw that aches. Christ. He takes back everything he said about her being harmless.

"I hate you, Mommy," Michelle says. "You're dumb and stupid.'' She holds up her fists with menace.

"Don't you say that," Patty says, her voice sharp with rage. She raises her own hand as though to hit Michelle, but Keevan grabs her wrist, gives her a warning look.

"Come on, Michelle. We'll go upstairs and get your dad's number for you." He directs her back toward the stairs, but before he is safely out of the room, Patty grabs Keevan's elbow.

"Later tonight . . . can we talk?"

Keevan feels his nostrils flaring. He can barely stand

the degree of intimacy that modulates her voice to a hush,
the way she looks at him.

"Yeah, okay," he says. "Just keep your hands off the
kids. It's not their fault."

Walking up the steps behind Michelle, feeling protective
of both her and the house, he touches her delicate shoulder, then grasps the banister with a new sense of threatened ownership. Like Keevan, she has lived in this house
since the day she was born. This is mine, he thinks. This
is ours. No one can take this from us. This is ours.

Later, he can't read. He can't concentrate on anything.
The house has always been a given in his life. Except for
his share of taxes and the endless expenses of maintaining
it, he has always had free housing, free housing filled with
family and family history. Never once in his life has he
had to worry about where he should live, where his place
is in the world. He goes now to his bedroom, to the shelf
of books that used to be his grandfather's. Dickens, Thackeray, Balzac, and most of all his grandfather's beloved
Walt Whitman. His grandfather used to read Whitman
aloud. His favorite poem was "Crossing Brooklyn Ferry."
Keevan heard it for the first time when he was thirteen.
The words were lulling, especially coming from his grandfather's lips, graced with his Irish accent, but Keevan
didn't understand any of it.

"What does it mean?" he asked when the old man had
read all nine pages.

"What does it mean?" his grandfather said huffily.
"Exactly what it says. That a hundred years from the time
he wrote the poem, nothing will have changed. That people will have all the same feelings, do the same things as
then. They'll be caught in the flow of life, like the people
on the ferry. They'll commute home from Manhattan just
as then. They'll have all their yearnings and all their hopes
and all their greed just as then. People will be people.
That's all he is saying, really. Of course, he didn't predict
there'd be a bridge 'stead of a ferry; how could he? But

it makes no difference. Life goes on. That's all. Life goes on."

Keevan takes the book from his shelf and reads the poem now. The same book his grandfather read him, in the same chair, and it evokes his grandfather's voice, his manner. Born in Ireland, lucky to own an auto body shop by the time he was forty, he never went to college, was glad to have been able to finish high school. Yet he loved to read. He found solace in literature, in the majesty of words. All of which he passed on to Keevan.

"Now, isn't 'ebullient' a beautiful word?" he'd say. "It sounds like what it means. It makes you feel fine just to say it."

By the time Keevan was old enough to remember him, he was white-haired and lined, like Walt Whitman himself, and he groaned when he climbed the stairs. He smoked a pipe with cherry tobacco, and he snored so loud Keevan could hear it from two floors below his own bedroom. It was comforting knowing Grandpa was around, keeping things safe. He was that sort of man, competent and certain of himself and comforting.

Keevan puts *Leaves of Grass* back and goes to the mantel, where one of his grandfather's pipes still sits, the stem still wearing the indent of his teeth. Down in the basement is a box of newspapers Grandpa saved from important events in his life: Pearl Harbor, Roosevelt's death, D-day, the election of Eisenhower, of Kennedy. Also in the box are family pictures from the day Keevan's great-grandfather (his grandmother's father) bought this house in 1917. He could afford it because he'd been in a terrible train accident in Ireland in 1915 and had a gash on his head thick as two fingers. The money the train company paid him was his down payment, and ownership of the house made him proud all his life.

So how can Keevan allow his stupid brother's infidelity to take this away from him? To break this steady flow of history, to part it from Keevan's own future family. For surely there will be a future family?

If he moves, perhaps he will lose Zoe too. He thinks of how she's talked about her house, how much she loves it, as he loves his. He wonders often what hers is like inside. Does she step on a wood floor when she gets out of bed, or has she laid a silky Oriental rug against the old floorboards? From her room, does the maple tree that covers the front yards of both their houses block her view of Manhattan? Do the rooms of the house smell of her, a scent that marries grapefruit and clove and cinnamon?

Now maybe he will never know. Now the friendship that began so tentatively feels crushed beneath a too hasty step. Last night he felt she hated him. He picks up the phone and asks information for her number, then dials. It rings three times.

"Hello?" So tentative.

"Zoe. It's me," he says.

"I don't want to talk to you."

"Please. I think we need to discuss this," he says. "If now isn't convenient . . ." He wonders where she's standing, if she's upstairs with Jamie.

"Keevan. What I need right now is not to speak to you. Not to see you. I'm sorry."

"Zoe—" She hangs up. "Zoe," he says again, to nobody.

He feels sick to his stomach, like the time Jim and he were playing tackle football in the park and Jim accidentally on purpose kicked him in the balls. He puked so hard he thought his skin would turn inside out.

He hates himself for pushing her. For being so greedy. Maybe he will give her a day. A day to miss him. A day to get over whatever is fueling her anger, her withdrawal.

Around nine-thirty, when the voices of the children have quieted downstairs, Patty comes to his door.

"Can I come in?" she asks.

He opens the door for her, but with a sense of reluctance.

"I found a condom in Jim's drawer. He says he got it

from his boss at the company Christmas party, but I don't buy that at all.''

''I figured it was something like that. You never know, though,'' Keevan says, trying to avoid her eyes. ''He could be telling the truth. . . .''

''Please,'' she says. ''Don't treat me like I'm six years old.''

''I'm just raising the possibility.''

''He's cheated before, hasn't he?'' Her grey eyes are very wide, almost pleased. He can't figure out what she is feeling.

''I don't know.''

''I think you do.''

''This isn't my business,'' he says.

''You've made it your business before. You've always told me to leave him, to give up on him.''

Keevan shrugs.

''I've been thinking,'' Patty says, sitting down on the couch and crossing her legs. She has nice legs, slender ankles, with delicate, sail-like bones at each side. They are the one part of her, Keevan has often noted, which are graceful and vulnerable. ''I've been thinking about what it means not to live here anymore.''

A bitter taste comes into Keevan's mouth.

''I mean . . . I mean, then I won't be able to live near you. You know, all these years . . . well, I've just gotten so used to having you around.''

''I was here first,'' he says coolly.

''Well, you know what I mean. I mean it's almost like we've been living together for years and years.''

''Maybe you should patch things up with Jim.'' He thinks of the house being sold. He mustn't let her do this.

''I can't believe that you of all people would say that. You hate Jim's guts. You're always telling me to dump him. Well, now *I* think it's time I dump him.''

''But what are you going to do, Patty? You may not get alimony. They don't give alimony much anymore. Or they only give it for a few years, until you're on your feet.''

"Maybe I need to get on my feet. Do something. Get what I want for myself. No one else has ever gotten it for me." Keevan stares at her. He never dreamed she'd have the guts to chase any of her own dreams. He's never thought of Patty as having any dreams, as aspiring to have more in her life than romance novels and cigarettes and ironing.

She takes his arm lightly in her fingers and then leans forward and whispers, "I'm going to miss you." Before he can stop her, she's kissing him on the mouth. The feel of her lips on his, though it is only momentary, brings up a rage that is murderous and frightening. He pushes her firmly away, doesn't care what she feels. He swallows down the saliva in his mouth.

"Well, we'll always stay in touch," he says. He wants her gone.

"But I don't want to stop being close," she whispers. "I want to be more than close. . . ." She looks up at him with eyes as trusting as a puppy's.

"Well, sure, Patty, you'll always be like a sister to me."

He sees the words forming on her lips before she says them, and he knows he must stop her.

"I don't want to be like a sister to you. I want—"

"Was that Michelle?"

"Keevan . . ." Her body leans in toward him.

"Did I just hear Michelle call you?"

"What? . . . I think she's asleep."

"No, I'm sure . . ." He stands up. He has to get her out of here. "Why don't I go check."

But he sees she's realized his rebuff. Her eyes look haunted and miserable. Her face is blotchy.

"I'll check on her," she says.

When she is gone, Keevan knows she won't be back tonight. He feels glad about it, but sorry too. Later he thinks of phoning her. "Sorry our conversation was cut short. I'm sure we'll always be friends," he might say.

Or: "Did Michelle finally go to sleep?" But by the time he picks up the phone, he hates her again. Would kill her if he could.

Zoe decides to go to bed early, to lie next to Jamie for a while and talk to him. Teresa must have changed the sheets, today, which means that Jamie would have showered. Once a week, Teresa is somehow able to direct him into a shower. She isn't at all afraid of him, is less afraid of him, in a way, than Zoe is. She treats him like a child. She shampoos his hair, scrubs his armpits, his feet, and even his genitals with a washcloth, and lets him stand in the shower while she changes the sheets. Then she returns to dry him, to help him on with clean pajama bottoms, to settle him back in bed.

Teresa used to care for an autistic cousin. She says it's not so different.

"Now, though she lies near him, there is no scent to Jamie but deodorant soap.

"Do you remember the night before we got married," Zoe begins, trying to conjure up the vision in her own mind, "We made love on the grass outside your parents' boathouse. And even though I kept thinking I heard someone coming, you didn't want to stop. You were so excited. You said, 'Shh. It's just you and me. Just you and me.' We were so happy then, weren't we? We were defying your parents by getting married. And they were paying for the wedding! How many times did we make love out there that night?

"And at the wedding, I was sad because my parents wouldn't come, and you said, 'I'm your family now. For now and forever. And I'll always be there.' " God, how she does want him to be there! To come out of his funk, to hold her.

"Do you remember," she asks him, "how Charlotte always wanted you to sing that awful yodeling song to her. The one about the lonely goatherd from *The Sound of Music*? It made her laugh. And you would sing it over and over. She would laugh and laugh and clap her hands.''

Zoe smiles, remembering the sweetness of Jamie's tenor voice, free, innocent. His singing lulled Charlotte like nothing else. For her, he would clown, he would light up, he would put on a show. How Zoe loved him then. How proud she was to be married to him.

"We were so happy once, Jamie. Even if you feel only pain now, we were so happy once." His eyes are still open, though his hand is limp in hers. She raises it and kisses it. "We were happy. I want you to remember."

Long into the night, she recites her litany of the good and painful moments that have marked the path of their time together, describing them as a guide might to a blind man, so that they will be as vivid to him as they are to her. Once, he seems to smile slightly, when she reminds him of the time he was tickling Charlotte in her crib to wake her up, and though she was not quite two, she, suddenly awake, said to him in a voice as clear as an adult's, "Cut it out, Bozo."

In the end, she tires herself out and falls asleep, touching him, and dreams her brother and sister have come back from the dead and need a place to sleep. "This is the perfect place for you," she tells them in the dream. "Come and live with Jamie and me."

# TEN

◆

Summer grows hot and stale on Eighth Street. The hydrangeas droop. The impatiens spread and squeeze the other flowers away. Darlene Kilkenny is back with Donald, on the condition that he never again enters the Lucky Pub, and drinks no more than two beers a night. Maggie is relieved to be alone with Jack again, to make noise when they make love without curbing themselves, or to argue when they choose, without worrying about upsetting Darlene or waking the baby.

Zoe puts on the air-conditioning every night, shutting out the noise of the street so she can feel safe and closeted when she lies beside Jamie and talks to him. She spends hours now in the dark with him, talking. She read once about a woman in a coma whose sister visited her every day and told her news of the family, the world. The woman woke up ten years later and asked: was that the new mustard-colored suit that her sister had bought on sale last week? Very nice. She had heard everything! She had simply not been able to respond. He's hearing me, Zoe tells herself every night. All this care, all this attention, may bring him out of his pain and fury.

And during the day, she steals. More than ever. The close call at the lingerie shop seems only to have made it worse. The itch overtakes her, and she can't stop. She finds herself taking the oddest things, doesn't even know

what provokes her. Yesterday, at one of the millinery-
supply shops on Thirty-eighth Street, where she went to
get gold coins for a Gypsy outfit Rose wanted to wear to
a costume party, she stole a bridal veil that was sitting in
back as a display. She crammed the crunching endless
tulle into her backpack until the clasp could barely be
closed. Later, in her editing room, when Stuart went to
the men's room, she pulled it out, looked at the wrinkled,
soiled veil in horror. What could be possessing her? She
stuffed it in her desk drawer, and later, after everyone
had left, took it out to the compactor and threw it down
the chute.

Keevan keeps trying to see Zoe, to call her, but she
won't come to the door or the phone. Lately, Teresa's
been taking out the garbage. Teresa screens all the calls,
answers the door, looking as if she would just as soon
chop off his genitals with a carving knife.

"She does not want to see you," she says.

"Please. Tell her only for a moment."

"She does not want to see you." Teresa's nostrils flare
above her long lip, darkened with hair. She slams the door
closed. Keevan has never felt so foolish. Or angry. He
feels it in his spine. How could she be so unfair, to not
even let him have his say? To be so rude as to not end it
neatly, at least. And yet there would be no way to end it
neatly. He knows this. If only he could see her again.

Without that option, he bathes his wounds in books: all
of Jane Austen, Richard Russo, Thackeray, Alison Lurie.
Because he did not sign up to teach summer school this
year, he sits out in the backyard under the big tree, reading. Or at night, inside, by his window, hoping to catch
sight of her walking home from the subway.

He, himself, has barely walked, done anything physical
all summer. His whole body feels like someone's been
punching him. He hasn't gone back to the park. She has
spoiled it for him. Worst of all, he can't even delight in
the memory of their lovemaking. His sexuality, which

once was so easy for him, has become a burden. At night, he is ashamed to masturbate, finds it nearly impossible. He's even picked up a few pieces of pornography at a newsstand to help. In the anonymity of the women's faces, the slack mouths of their supposed desire, he finds a small safe place where he can be sexual. Sometimes he falls asleep afterward with his face on these pictures and feels sour in the morning, waking with them, these women with their huge breasts and welcoming pussies and lolling tongues. He folds up the books, hides them under his mattress like a sixteen-year-old, wonders if he will ever get past all this discomfort, which reminds him of how his early sexuality felt, out of place and laughable.

Since the summer began in earnest, he's barely seen anybody, except Patty. In the afternoons, Patty brings trays of sandwiches out to him, sits under the tree and talks. She has had her hair colored again, a softer color. Palest brown-blond, like a dried oak leaf. And her new tight jeans show off her small waist, her competent boylike hips. Things are easier between them suddenly. It feels again like the sister-brother connection they had long ago, when she was still in love with Jim. Keevan doesn't know why. Maybe it was his rejection of her when she tried to kiss him. They haven't talked about selling the house again. He hopes it was just momentary anger on her part, that she's forgotten.

Late in the afternoon, when she refills his glass of soda, bends to pick the dead heads off the geraniums and petunias which she's planted this summer for the first time, it distresses him that he finds himself actually drawn to her. In late-day shade, when she sits for a while, her hands filled with browned and blown petals, ready to throw them out, when she laughs at things he says and throws back her head, his heart strains to draw from her whatever seems to be healing her. She's so much freer now that Jim is gone. So much younger.

She tells him about the few times she's met with Jim. "We couldn't stand the sight of each other. Did you know he's taken an apartment across the Gowanus Canal, in Carroll Gardens?''

Keevan does know. "Small as a coat closet," Jim told Keevan when he called. "Not even enough room to fuck Kim on the floor. So we use the bed like an old married couple. Boring.''

Keevan once saw them walking down Seventh Avenue. Kim was dark-haired and busty, chewing gum.

"This is Kim," Jim said, quickly. "And this is my ugly little brother, Keevan.'' Kim, in her too snug tank top, looked Keevan over with what seemed to be far too much interest.

"Hello there, little brother," she said, with a studied cock of her head, a chomp of gum. He asked her a few questions, and she giggled. She called Jim "Jimmy-boy." She seemed no more accomplished mentally than Michelle. Or was Keevan being unfair? But then, anyone who was drawn to Jim or would fall for his bullshit couldn't be a rocket scientist, could she?

"I never expected it would be over when I kicked him out," Patty tells Keevan one afternoon. "I thought he'd be so guilt-ridden over my discovery, we'd move to New Jersey and he'd spend the rest of his life trying to make it up to me. But then I just felt so angry. I was so much angrier than I knew. And now that he's gone . . . It's kinda funny. I never thought I could be so happy without him. Even the kids seem happier. Do you miss him?" she asks Keevan.

"God no," he says, laughing. It is one thing that has bound them these last few years: their distaste for Jim. The truth is, when Jim calls Keevan, his neck instantly tightens, his mouth goes dry. He can't wait to get off the phone.

"Hey, Keev, how's Patty?" Jim always asks just before he says goodbye.

"She's doing great," Keevan reports gaily. "She never looked better. And she's cooking like a maniac."

In the evenings now, the scents from Patty's kitchen are

all new and rare: curry and lemongrass, basil and rose-mary, waft from the big breakfast room window out onto the backyard.

"Will you join us for lamb and couscous tonight?" she asks Keevan.

He won't. He always demurs. His new odd desire for her frightens him. More than ever, he needs to keep his distance in the evenings. Michelle comes up to his apart-ment and sits on his sofa and complains. "She's fixed something gross again for dinner. She sat there and said it's like totally delicious, and John and I just about threw up, smelling it. Then we had to make our own peanut butter and jelly sandwiches like always."

Keevan tastes the food eventually. She leaves it on wrapped plates in his refrigerator. It's remarkably delicious and delicate, with layers of flavor as thin as pastry leaves. He always lets her know how much he enjoys her dishes, aware of what it means to her. But no matter how she coaxes, he won't eat with her.

Then one day, Patty says, "Listen, I'm calling real es-tate agents. We've got to get going on selling this house." And he feels his whole body clutch.

"I thought maybe you'd changed your mind about it." He hears a waver in his voice.

"Are you kidding? It's all I'm going to get out of that marriage: the money from this place."

Keevan calls Jim, desperate, hoping that despite Patty's plans, his brother has no intention of selling. But Jim laughs. "What do you care? It's probably just as well. What good has the family ever come to in that house? Only problems, tragedies, as far as I'm concerned. Now we can all move to newer places, with less upkeep. The damn place needs so much fucking maintenance. And even though the economy sucks, people are still getting a ton of money for ones like ours." In a week, three different real estate agents sweep through Keevan's apartment with notepads and pencils and measuring tape. "Does the fireplace work?'' they ask. ''Are you leaving the air conditioner?''

Maggie is worried about Jack. He hasn't been himself lately. He seems particularly tired, and she's noticed his color isn't good.

''Maybe we should take a vacation, darlin','' she says.

''Ugh. You're always trying to drag me somewhere.''

''Europe. We've never been to Europe.''

''I'm happy here, Maggie. Perfectly happy here,'' he says.

But she begins to observe him more carefully. She notices he's often out of breath. And less patient with her. One night, up late and watching cable TV, she's drawn into an infomercial and orders him a cross-country ski machine.

''If you think I'm getting on that contraption, you're crazier than I already thought you were, Mags.''

''It looks easy,'' she tells him.

''Fine. You figure it out and let me know how you enjoy it,'' he says.

''It will do you good,'' she tells him.

''The only thing that will do me good is if you stop spending money on ridiculous things like that. Send it back.''

''How? We had to rip the box to get it out. And what will I tell them? You choose to be out of shape and flabby instead of taking a few minutes to learn how to use their machine?''

''Speak for yourself,'' Jack says, pinching her not very taut waist.

''You're impossible. I should have married Larry Flynn.''

''Maybe so. Then I could have married Margaret Dooner.''

''I hear she lost all her teeth and got fat as a boat.''

''There are benefits to women without teeth.'' He flashes an evil smile.

"Shut up, Jackie," she says, swatting him. He grabs her arm affectionately, then kisses her and draws her into the bedroom for one of the more invigorating sessions of lovemaking they've had lately. Arguments have always stimulated Jack's libido.

In a week, Darlene spies the unused cross-country machine, takes it down the street with her, and that's the end of Maggie's plan to improve Jack's health.

Zoe doesn't know what to do about Rose. She insists on saving everything: the sticks from Popsicles, the uneaten contents of her plate, the tags from new clothes. Her Kleenex, for God's sake. Used. And when Zoe cut Rose's toenails, she insisted on saving them too, in a paper cup. She'll cry for hours if something is lost or thrown out. Real weeping. And Zoe can't get to the bottom of it. Except that Rose will say, "The tags need to be near the clothes. They'll miss the clothes. They've been with the clothes so long." Or: "The Popsicle stick needs to be near the other Popsicle sticks. If it goes to the garbage alone, it will be so lonely."

"I told you," Teresa says smugly. "I see this is bad thing, this saving."

Zoe wonders if she should blame herself. When Rose was three or four, Zoe anthropomorphized everything, to move Rose along, to help her decide. If Rose didn't want to wear a brand-new dress, Zoe used to have the dress speak to her. "I moved into your house, hoping you needed me." She would sway the dress, wagging its shoulders on its hanger. "Now you don't even like me. I'm so sad."

"But I do like you." Rose would perk up. "Don't feel bad. I was just kidding about not wearing you."

And: "Your toothbrush feels neglected. It wants to feel useful. It wants to get in there and do its job, and you're not letting it."

"I'm sorry, Toothy," Rose would say in a forced cheerful voice. "Let's get to work."

Even as a baby, Zoe used to say, "One more green bean. It wants to go in there with its mommy. I'm coming, Mommy."

"This is not normal," Teresa says. "I try sometimes to throw things out. She cry and cry."

Then one day, Rose simply won't go to summer camp—a nice little program at the nearby school, where they swim and make puppets out of socks and put on skits. She has enjoyed it from the beginning and made lots of friends, who, along with Keevan's niece, spend time with her after school. But this one morning, she won't go because one of her slips is missing. It is recovered later, under the bed, wrapped around a baby doll. But until that moment, Rose cries so hard she simply stops breathing, her face turns completely blue, and she passes out.

Of course, once she does, she breathes again, wakes up, and is utterly silent. The silence somehow frightens Zoe even more.

The pediatrician says, "That sort of behavior isn't unusual in a two- or three-year-old, holding their breath till they pass out. But in a six-year-old . . ." She pauses. "Let me give you a name," she says. "A child therapist."

Just the word "therapist" makes Zoe shiver. Will her daughter someday be like Jamie? She can't even bear to think about it. Zoe writes down the therapist's name. Her hands are shaking.

"This is serious," the therapist tells her. She is a tall woman with large bones, blond hair, sucked-in cheeks. Though Zoe doesn't like her, she can't help but pay attention.

"We can start with play therapy. Twice a week, I think. Obsessive behavior such as this can be a sign of deeper problems, which may surface at a later age."

"Her father is a depressive. A serious depressive," Zoe says weakly.

"Ah," the woman says. "Yes. You said he has no involvement with the child. I see."

Zoe looks at her with hatred. Why does she feel this woman can't see anything at all?

"She will be all right, though, won't she?" Zoe asks.

"With a great deal of help," the woman says. "I think it can be overcome."

For a moment, Zoe closes her eyes. Her heart feels as if it's on fire; her head throbs.

"Thank you," Zoe says, getting up.

"Would you like to make an appointment for her to come see me?"

"No," Zoe says, looking at this woman, her haughty face, tasting her unrelenting negativity in the air, like metal on Zoe's tongue. "I'm sorry. She won't be seeing you."


In the night, Keevan wakes. It's his bell. What time is it? Only eleven-twenty. He never even managed to eat dinner, he'd had such a terrible headache. He'd fallen asleep on his bed with the lights on. His heart slamming in his chest, he pulls a pair of cut-off shorts over his bare skin and rushes down the stairs to find out who might be ringing at this hour. Through the vestibule glass, he sees her on his stoop. Zoe.

He opens the door and stands there, assessing her, wondering why she's here. Her eyes are glistening with determination. And though it's warm, she's shivering in the light gauzy shirt and slacks she's wearing.

"Come in." He wishes he could brush his teeth. His headache is gone, though he feels odd and light-headed. "Come upstairs," he says. He thinks for a moment that he's dreaming and tries to wipe the sleep from his face.

"I'm sorry if I woke you. I thought you'd still be up."

"No. No. I'm glad you came." He can't believe she's there, that she's come to him.

Upstairs, her hands cupping her own elbows, she sits in what was once his grandmother's chair. Is it her chin that makes her look so charmingly defiant? He thinks of his grandmother sitting in that chair, being forced to listen to

some of Grandpa's endless favorite poems. Grandma was
a highly practical woman, with no patience for poetry.
She, too, jutted out her chin on those occasions, shielded
herself with crossed arms. Like her, Zoe doesn't look entirely pleased to be here. He would like to touch her, to
comfort her. She looks in need of comforting, but he's
afraid if he so much as reaches out, she'll bolt from the
chair.

"I need your advice," she says.

"My advice?"

"You know about children. You teach them. I know
your students are much older . . . but . . . It's Rose," she
says. "I thought maybe you could help me."

"What's wrong?"

"It's not just because you're a teacher. I just feel so
alone in this," she says. "I didn't think there was anyone
who would understand . . . but you." He is flattered, and
stunned by her presence. As she tells him about Rose's
saving things, he watches her face lose its determination
in the telling, watches fear cloud her eyes.

"I went to see a therapist about it. A child therapist.
She said it would take years of therapy. Twice a week, she
wants to start with. If Rose is ill like Jamie . . . if she's
going to go through what he's gone through . . ." She closes
her eyes and shakes her head.

"No," Keevan says. "I don't believe that. I don't. You
should get another opinion, for one thing. Someone less
interested in making money on twice-weekly visits."

Zoe looks up with interest.

"Do you think she could be wrong?"

"Rose might not even need a therapist. In an adult, it
would be worrisome, her behavior. But in a child . . . I'm
not personally convinced it's so serious. Listen, if you
think about it, it sounds like she feels she's lost something,
and she's acting out to let you know it."

"Lost what?" Zoe asks.

"Well, her way of life, for one thing. Doesn't she miss
her friends from Manhattan?"

"Well, there's one friend, Mary Ellen, that she says she misses." Zoe looks up at him, hopeful. "But she's made friends here. Your niece and children at camp, and besides, the one time she and Mary Ellen got together for a play date, Rose cried the whole time."

"That sounds like evidence right there."

"Do you think?"

"She's lost the familiarity of the place where she grew up. All she's ever known, hasn't she? Weren't there doormen and neighbors she saw every day? The man at the deli? The car attendant?"

Zoe shrugs. "I never thought . . ."

"Children thrive on certainty and sameness. On routine. When they were small, Michelle and John used to watch videotapes twenty times and never tired of them, because they loved knowing what would happen before it happened. I figured that mastering the videotapes gave them . . . I don't know . . . some sense of safety."

"Rose loves routine, always has." Zoe's voice is picking up now, brightening.

"And you. Haven't you been sad lately? Maybe in a sense she feels she's lost you too."

"How do you know I've been sad?" she asks.

"Because I know how sad I've been for you."

Zoe searches his face. She nods. He feels more connected to her than he thought he ever would again.

"Children do amazing things to cope with their lives," he goes on. "Valiant things, really, though to us they may seem strange. Do you know what I did to cope when I was a kid? I drew thousands of pictures of my parents, whom I didn't even remember. But I needed to create them, so I drew these pictures. I was obsessed with it. And I drew myself into those pictures. Not Jimmy or Ralph. Just me.

"My parents were different in every picture. They had different faces, different attitudes. But I was the same in all of them. In every one, I had no arms. My grandmother told me that before she died. She said she used to worry that I drew myself with no arms because I somehow felt crippled by their death. And she said she wondered if there was something wrong with me that would never mend. She said it kept her up nights, wondering if she could do anything to make me whole somehow. And you know, what really haunted her is that my father's losing his arm in the war made him a tortured and bitter man, and she wondered if somehow I had absorbed that even as a one-year-old. That somehow I saw myself like him—with no arms.

"But the funny thing is, I sort of remember drawing myself that way, and you know the reason *I* think I did? What I remember, anyway, is that I drew myself without arms so that I would be more huggable. More able to be wrapped up by their arms. I don't know if it's true, but it's what I remember. That having arms would somehow make me less accessible to them. And so I simply left them off.

"So I figure that even though what Rose is doing frightens you, it's probably just her way of coping. Ingenious, really: insurance against losing anything ever again. I see it with my students. The weird things they do and wear and say, to put up with what's been dished out to them. And if what they do to cope just happens to annoy their parents or authority figures, the coping mechanism intensifies. They do it more. They do it harder. Drugs. That's one thing. Saving toenails. That's maybe another."

"Next stop drugs?" Zoe asks, arching her brows.

"No." He smiles at her. "What would happen, do you think, if you just accepted her saving things? If you told Rose that since she finds it so important to save, you want to help her. Get a box and mark it 'Used Kleenex.' Special places for toenails and Popsicle sticks. Bring home shoe boxes. Make it such a big deal, so important for everyone to follow, she tires of it. If it no longer annoys you, no longer worries Teresa, it just might go away."

"It sounds too easy," Zoe says.

"It just might work, though. Parents of teenagers can't

say, 'Go ahead and do drugs. Pierce every body part. Tattoo your face if you like. Stay out all night.' It might make teens lean toward the opposite and right choice, just to spite them, but it's too dangerous. The stakes are too high.

"But see, what Rose is doing isn't hurting you or her. This is a risk you *can* take. It might not work right away. Probably won't. But in a month or two she may not need to act out anymore, since you're giving her permission. If both you and Teresa go out of your way to help Rose, eventually it will just annoy the hell out of her. Tell her all you want is to help add to her collection."

Zoe shrugs. "You think?"

"It's sort of like reverse psychology. I use it all the time. She's little, but not too little for that. God. Kids are so amazing. Little coping machines."

"I'll try it. You don't think there's harm in waiting to see someone?"

"Get another opinion if you like. I'm not going to tell you I know best. It's only amateur advice."

"I like it, though, and I will try it. It makes sense to me." Zoe looks down at her hands and smiles to herself. "I've really missed you," she says. "More than I realized." When she looks up at him, her eyes are soft and loving. Her body has uncoiled. She's no longer holding her elbows.

"Zoe."

"I'm sorry about the way I've acted. I was afraid after the park. Afraid that you had too much power over me to make me do what I didn't think I should do."

"I know. It wasn't fair. I pushed you before you were ready." All summer he's wanted to say this, and she wouldn't let him. All summer he just wanted to speak this sentence. "Come on. I'll walk you home." He stands up and holds out his hand to her.

"Don't take me home," Zoe says softly, standing, pressing her face against his chest.

"Not yet?"

"Take me up to bed with you."

"Zoe . . ." He finds himself actually weak with her words.

"No," she says. "I don't want to make love with you. Not tonight anyway. I just want to put my arms around you, and lie there with you for a while, and kiss you, maybe. And since you *do* have arms, Keevan, please—God, please—put them around me."

Zoe tests out Keevan's theory. Rose looks at her suspiciously when she brings in a set of file boxes from the stationery store and labels them: "Used Kleenex," "Food Things, Save for Rose." But Rose, with some wonder at her own needs being so scrupulously met, goes along with the plan, depositing her ragged Kleenexes, gathering tags clipped from her new clothes in the box marked "Tags," never forgetting both the severed sides of the little plastic T-clamps.

"Don't worry," Zoe hears her telling the plastic clamps. "You're together again now." Rose in any case seems happier not to be fighting for every lock of hair or Popsicle stick.

And now, at least two nights a week, when Rose is clearly asleep, Zoe turns on the old baby monitor and brings the receiver down to Teresa, then goes out her own garden gate and through Keevan's. She cannot neatly justify why it is suddenly all right to do this, to find the comfort in Keevan that just a few months ago she so squarely rejected. But his enfolding of her stuns her deprived spirit, and she is renewed by him. She never knew how lightened she could feel by sharing her fears. She revels in his whispered confidences, in the memories he reveals with such storytelling ease in the dark of his room.

And she's the one who chooses to become sexual. It's something I must have, she tells herself. Too much like stealing, but just as inevitable. This time, she takes it slowly. Each night, after they have talked, and whispered, and swept the crumbs of the day from their minds, she offers herself up slowly, one part at a time. "Tonight let's just kiss. Only that," she tells him the first night. And he, rejected before so strongly, enjoys, it seems, the slow, long kisses, each different, each revealing. Two nights later, she opens her shirt for him and unhooks the flimsy bra that she wears simply because it's expected of her, not because she needs it. "I'm only ribs, no meat," she tells him sadly, but beneath the witchery of his fingers, her nipples rise, her breasts seem to become fuller in the cups of his palms, and he kisses them with reverence. One night, she tells him he cannot touch her; she only wants to touch him. She helps him out of his too-often-washed oxford shirt, his jeans and underwear. Before the underwear is off, already she sees his excitement.

"I can't help it," he apologizes to her.

"I'm glad," she says. She touches the velvet of his stiff member, its head, cool and large and smooth, the veins that twine the sides. She cradles his heavy testicles in her fingers, gently squeezing them until he just moans. And then she brings her lips down to his penis and takes him into her mouth. He cries out more loudly than she's expected. Jamie never liked this as much as she did. The taste of him is sweet, floods her with desire.

"You like this," she states softly, drawing her mouth away.

"Don't stop," he says. In giving him pleasure, her own sex aches like a muscle long unused. She sucks his swollen penis for a long time, slowing when she senses he's close to coming, wanting to prolong the pleasure of giving him pleasure. Jamie taught her how to suck a man's penis, to touch it, to please. But he would never come in her mouth, would never share himself that way, though often, in the beginning of their love affair, she was curious about what it would be like and begged him to. "I wouldn't do that to you," he said.

And Jamie didn't like it when she talked dirty to him. It made him uncomfortable, almost angry. Sometimes at night she imagined what she wished she could say to him.

Thinking of those words while he slept beside her, she would masturbate, pressing herself against his sleeping body while she came. Now she talks softly to Keevan as she strokes him with her hand. About his cock. About her desire. Words she's never been able to say to Jamie. And this is what finally makes Keevan come. Though he has held back much longer than she expected, knowing how much they've wanted each other, it is her words that capture him. About how much she wants him, how he'll feel when he finally slides inside her. About how much she wants him to come in her mouth.

"Oh, Mary. Oh, Jesus," he cries. She sees that his face is laced in perspiration, his copper hair soaked at the hairline, his mouth open with longing, and then she brings him over the edge, thrilled he hasn't drawn away from her. She drinks down the endless soapy ropes of his semen, excited to finally know the flavor, the sensation. To, for a brief moment, own him.

Afterward, she rests her head on his chest, listening to the drum of his now settling heart, feeling the closeness that she learned long ago can come only from giving. She breathes a sigh of pleasure. Then sits up.

"What's wrong?" she asks.

He just shakes his head.

"Something's wrong," she says. She feels his turning away. Anger is a palpable thing for her. In her childhood, she learned to read its subtlest signs.

He gets up and walks to the window. "It's late. I think you should go."

"What's wrong? What did I do?" she asks.

"I just think you should go."

She gets up, feeling as though she's been slapped, finds her hands shaking as she straps on her shoes. Not having allowed him to touch her, she is fully dressed. She can still taste his semen on her tongue and finds that in the face of his anger, she can barely swallow.

She is surprised by his anger. Frightened by it. At the

door, she asks him, "What did I do, Keevan? I thought I made you happy."

He looks at her a long time before he speaks, squinting with anger or upset, she isn't sure which.

"What?" she asks again.

"If you go," he says, "maybe I'll get past this. I'm sorry." He opens the door and steps back so she needn't brush him when she leaves. Her throat balloons with pain. Later, in bed, next to Jamie, she lets her throat spasm with tears that won't come, not understanding what's happened. And yet struck with the irony that at the very moment when she was finally able to open to him, Keevan slammed shut.

Keevan cannot understand his anger. It's happened every time. With every woman he's ever cared about. As soon as his feeling for her blossomed, and the desire owned him, as soon as he felt he was losing himself to Helayne or Tina, he felt absolutely murderous toward her. It rose in him as unexpectedly and violently as lava in a volcano.

With Helayne, it wasn't until they were living together, and she was forcing all her whims on him, that he first knew this feeling. He'd walked into the marriage like a sleepwalker. Just glad to be getting regular sex and so much attention. Maybe he didn't even love her until this time, three months after they were married, when he found he could hardly stand being away from her. He saw her coming out of the shower one morning, naked and without makeup. Her freckles were like a scattering of stars across her perfect, slender nose, and his feelings for her caused him so much pain he thought he'd choke. It was then that everything she did began to annoy him. She was buying things he didn't like for the apartment, too many things, insisting they go to parties every weekend with her friends, and interrupting his reading of *Great Expectations* or *Leaves of Grass* so she could sit on his knee and "play," as she called it. Kiss and tickle and waste time. And he

began to hate her. To push her away with every exchange
and to let her know everything she did disappointed him.
It was loving her that made him hate her. It was thinking
he would die without her. It was the same thing with Tina.
Only he never really loved her. Never let it get that far.
Just becoming slightly vulnerable to her did it. He wanted
her out of his life.

But to turn on Zoe, of all people, when she's just given
herself to him so happily. And after so long a fight to
have her. He can't believe he's done it. Tomorrow he'll
apologize, he tells himself, he'll make it up to her. He has
to. Still, he lies awake all night, desperate to fix everything
but wondering if he has the strength to fight his own insid-
ious feelings.

The next day, Zoe doesn't come to see him. And when
he calls her, her line is busy. After a while, he is certain
it must be off the hook. He goes to her door and rings
the bell. It's nearly 11:00 P.M., and when Teresa, with her
bulldog face, appears his heart sinks.

"I'm here to see Zoe," he says.

Teresa eyes him with suspicion. "She's busy," she
says.

"She was supposed to . . . we had an appointment."

"She no tell me," she says flatly. She blocks the doorway, her hands on either side of the jamb, a linebacker in
a green flannel robe.

"Please, Teresa," he says. "I have to see her. I want
to apologize to her for something I've done."

The oddest smile comes to her face. He does not know
whether using her name has softened her, or if she finally
understands his relationship with Zoe, but she shakes her
head and shrugs, then moves aside. He finds a surprising
tightness in his chest as he passes Teresa and steps in. He
has never been in Zoe's house before. He has imagined it
so often through the wall, the colors she might have, the
neatness he expects, the wealth of the furniture, the details.
Now he steps in, afraid that she will be angry that he's

come, and thrilled to finally get beyond the door. The foyer is cool and smells of something watery and pure, like lilies of the valley. An old wooden sideboard, the color of nutmeg, is stacked with mail. A glass vase holds wilted pink coneflowers; the flowers have grown in profusion in Zoe's back garden since long before she lived there.

"Come," Teresa says. She plods heavily before him up the narrow stairs, covered in petit point carpet, black and starry with flowers, similar to the footstools his grandmother used to stitch. In the parlor, she turns on the lights, a torchère that washes the room in soft light, a table lamp. She points to a pale-pink sofa and tells Keevan to sit. Still, in her eye, he sees something—is it amusement or damnation? After she leaves to climb the next flight of stairs, he sits down gingerly. The sofa is pristine and pale; it appears never to have been sat on. There isn't nearly enough furniture in the room. And the walls are mostly bare. But over the mantel is a portrait of a woman in a pale-green gown. About the era of John Singer Sargent, he thinks. Perhaps it is Jamie's grandmother. She is very beautiful, seems as long as a gladiola, and her fingers are like tendrils, glowing and curled in her lap, faintly green like her dress. He gets up to look closer at the painting. It is signed: John Singer Sargent. He shakes his head. This is what Zoe is married to: wealth beyond his imagining. What would Maggie Kilkenny say if she knew that on this very street, a museum painting adorns a wall.

Keevan sits back on the untouched sofa, and feeling like a boy left alone in the priest's study, he looks with awe around the large, softly lit room, the walls the color of a woman's blush. Next door, at his house, this room is Patty and Jim's bedroom, painted a dirty turquoise. Since it is the largest room in the house, it always seemed wasteful to Keevan that they should use it for sleeping and use the much smaller original dining room on the ground floor of the house as their living room. Zoe's parlor is the way it must have been originally, not with Patty and Jim's hollow-core closet doors and a bathroom jammed into the side of the room. There is an arched niche for a small sofa and table. And a wealth of plasterwork and molding, other arches, and bookcases, medallions, and Greek keys. How grandly people must once have lived! How much they expected! This is what he is thinking when Teresa marches past the parlor and heavily down the stairs toward her room, and then Zoe's light footsteps follow from upstairs. She comes no farther than the doorway of the parlor. Her slender body in its watermelon robe looks as fragile and beautiful as a flower in the frame of the ornate door. What would John Singer Sargent have done with Zoe? Made love to her, Keevan thinks.

"I don't know why Teresa let you in," she says curtly. "She usually acts as a better bodyguard." Her long fingers hold her arms close to her body.

He stands and walks toward her but is completely unsure how to win her back. Her stance is icy, and her pearly lips are pressed together until they are nearly white. As he moves forward, she steps back, but only a little. He can feel her wanting to be touched by him. And though he doesn't touch her, he is close enough to actually feel the heat of her skin.

"Forgive me. I don't know what happened to me," he says.

"I don't either." Her tone is now more bewildered than angry.

He reaches out and traces the line of her jaw with one finger.

"Do you want a drink?" she asks, stepping back again.

"No. I want you to forgive me."

"I want a drink," she says. She opens one of the little Victorian closets with hinges more ornate than jewelry. He touches one, and its engraving kisses his fingers. In his house, if these hinges remain, they're covered with paint. Taking a bottle of sherry from a shelf, she pours a small glass full and offers it to him, but he waves his hand.

"No?" she asks.

"No. Too sweet for me."

"I got to like it at Jamie's parents' house. It's what they always gave me before dinner. It's dry sherry, not sweet. Of course, Jamie didn't drink it. He hasn't drunk anything since the accident. So, unlike his parents, I thought it was cruel to have it in the house, with him there. Even when he was well, and we had friends over, we would just say, 'We only have soft drinks,' and everyone seemed just fine with that.

"But two weeks ago, I realized that he's never even set foot in this room, or any room but the bedroom, and I was so miserable . . . I bought all this." She gestures to the closet. Keevan sees bottles of gin, vodka, brandy, sherry.

"All for you?" he asks.

She shrugs. "No. I thought I'd have people over. I'd entertain again and have fun, call people I haven't spoken to in a long time and invite them over, even if Jamie can't join us. The night I bought it, I tried to get drunk, but after two drinks I just became sick. Do you ever drink too much?"

"Sometimes," Keevan says. He is surprised she is speaking so much, almost avoiding his confession to her, his begging for forgiveness. He wonders if she merely senses his discomfort and is trying to help him, or simply doesn't want to hear it.

He watches her stand by the closet, drinking the sherry. "Do you want anything?" she asks, gesturing to the full bottles.

"I want you to forgive me," he says again.

"I don't have a bottle of that in this cupboard. Sorry. I'll have to look in the kitchen."

"Zoe."

"What happened to you last night? I thought you were having a good time."

He raises his eyebrows, shrugs. "I thought *you* were having a good time in the park."

"Ah." He is surprised and relieved to see her smile.

"Parallel neuroses," she says. "You must have caught it from me."

"I think I've had it a long time, actually. Long before I met you. I love you, Zoe," he says. He's surprised to hear it come out of his mouth. The last time he said that to a woman for the first time, he and Helayne were engaged in a week. The thought makes him shiver.

"Now, don't go scaring me, Keevan."

"Okay. Scared me a little too," he says, laughing, relieved. "Well, since I got beyond the moat and the dragon here at 645, at least take me on a tour of the house."

"There's not much here yet."

"I've spent sleepless nights wondering about that pink marble bathroom. At least show me that. And start with the painting." He points to the portrait above the mantel, struck once again with its grace.

"It's Jamie's Aunt Delia. A lot of our things were hers. She was so beautiful she terrified every man who ever met her, and no one married her, so she lived alone with lots of pretty things and grew into this very sour, very unlikable person, apparently. She died before I met Jamie.

"Upstairs, there's a Corot she bought in Paris. And there's a little Matisse in the dining room. It's the littlest one he ever painted, I think. About the size of a fist. It's not a drawing or etching. It's a painting. And there's a Childe Hassam in the dining room, and a Lilla Cabot Perry in the bedroom, of a little girl in a nightgown, which I don't think you'd like because it's too feminine, too sweet, though I do. And I have lots of diamonds in a vault at the bank, inherited from all sorts of Finneys, which I never wear. And an ermine coat that Delia used to wear every cold day. And she'd wear it up to Harlem, they say, to go slumming and listen to that 'Negro music.' And you know what? Add them all together, and they don't make it one bit easier to live here."

Keevan touches her hair, turns her chin so she's facing him. "Would you ever leave him?" he asks.

"No," she says.

"You sure? I have a van Gogh poster I think you'd really like. It's Metropolitan Museum of Art and everything. You could move in with me, share the wealth."

She starts to laugh. "Don't think I haven't thought of it," she says.

"Have you?" he asks.

She looks away, smiles vaguely to herself. "You're scaring me again," she says finally.

"I'm scaring myself, actually. C'mon. Let's go see the famous pink marble bathroom."

The next night, Zoe comes to his house, and they make love. It is slower and warmer and better than Keevan could have imagined. As he thrusts into her, he feels her quickening and slides his hand between their bodies to help her come. His fingers search for the ridge of her clitoris. It grows beneath his slightest touch. Her orgasm is so intense it nearly throws him off. And inside, in the spasm of her pleasure, her muscles involuntarily embrace him, again and again, drawing forward his own orgasm. It seems five minutes that she grips him and lets go, grips him and lets go, and cries out. He thinks of everything he can to postpone his own moment, but finally she pulls him over the top, and it is like a roller coaster ride they share. He clutches her to him, and cries out, and fears the letting go. And she whispers, "Come, I want to feel you."

Later, as she lies in his arms, he says, "I never felt anyone come like that."

"I feel safer with you now. It's funny. Now that we've had a fight, it all seems easier."

"Whoa. I don't get it. Masochism?"

She laughs. "I don't know. It's not a fairy tale anymore," she says. "When things are too perfect, I distrust them."

"I won't have to try too hard to make them imperfect," he says, smiling. He closes his eyes and breathes in the pleasure like an exotic fragrance for a long while. He thinks of how angry he was just two days ago, but pushes the feeling away. I just want to love her, he tells himself. Let me just love her.

"Listen," he says. "Do you think on Saturday we can take Rose to the park?"

"You and I?"

"Why not?"

"Aren't you afraid of what the street will say?" she asks him.

"I don't care. Do you?"

"Would we have to go to the boathouse?" Zoe asks.

"No. We'll go to the Sheep Meadow. Or the carousel or the zoo. Have you been?"

Zoe gets up on one elbow and looks into his face. What is she looking for? She appears both troubled and bemused.

"What?"

"You think if you seduce Rose into loving you, you can have the two of us."

"Seems to me that she needs a father . . . a man in her life."

Humming to herself, Zoe begins to gather her clothes, put them on. He wishes she wouldn't have to leave him at all tonight. "Come again tomorrow night," he says.

"Can't. I'll be working late. I'm getting film in tomorrow with a short deadline. I'll probably have to work tomorrow and Friday pretty late. We'll go to the park Saturday," she tells him.

"You won't come see me before that?"

"I can't. And we'll only go to the park on one condition."

"Tell me." He worries.

"You have to buy us Italian ices."

He laughs. "Any flavor. Any flavor at all."


Saturday is balmy, not nearly so hot as it's been. The park is packed with Little Leaguers, sunbathers, barbecuers, dog walkers. Rose walks between Keevan and Zoe, commenting on everything.

"Look," she cries out with glee. "That dog is big as

a horse. . . . That boy's standing on his bicycle.'' Then: "Oh, wow! They're barbecuing a whole animal!''

"A goat, I think,'' Keevan tells her.

"No! You're teasing me.''

"You never believe me, Miss Rosie. Come right over here and see.''

Together they walk up to the family amusing themselves around the barbecue. Their laughter, their sense of family, make Keevan envious.

"My little girl here is very curious about what you're roasting.''

"Is a goat,'' the man says in a lilting Jamaican accent.

"Thank you. Looks delicious.''

"Come by in aboot an hour and you can taste it for your ownself.''

"Maybe we will. Thanks. See,'' Keevan says as they walk back to Zoe. "You never believe me.''

She moves close to him and whispers. "I'm not your little girl, but I don't mind you pretending, Kevin.''

"Thanks. That's very kind of you. But it's Keevan.''

"I'm calling you Kevin,'' she says, with the authority of someone who on a daily basis names her dolls. He takes her hand. It's small and soft and as insubstantial as a fistful of petals.

"Who am I to argue?'' he says. The Sheep Meadow stretches ahead of them, the grass yellow with August drought. They come up to Zoe, who's breathing in the air as though it's perfume.

"God, it's nice here,'' she says.

Without warning, Rose sinks to her knees and does a crisp forward somersault. Her little A-line top flies away, exposing her back, the top of her shorts. Her long legs hold tight as she rolls forward and stands. Keevan smiles at her and kneels down. The grass tickles his knees and then his neck as he rolls forward; his hands smell sweet from the new-mown lawn.

" 'Anything you can do, I can do better,' '' he sings.

Then Rose does a cartwheel, perfect and graceful. He

cannot believe how lithe and delicate she is. Keevan does the same, wheeling sideways, unsure how he'll balance. How long's it been since he's done one? How satisfying it feels! Zoe watches, laughing, her face lit with sun and pleasure.

Rose skips, Keevan skips. Rose spins. Keevan spins. Then, standing behind her, he says, "Make your arms stiff," and, lifting her, tells her to flip backward. She does, just touching the ground with her toes, and flips forward again.

"Mommy, did you see that?" Rose calls. "Did you see what Kevin and I can do? A circus trick. Just like the circus. Let's do it again, Kevin."

"Keevan," Zoe says.

"I'm calling him Kevin. Let's do it again, Kevin. Come on."

Later, he buys them ices. Both Zoe and Keevan choose piña colada. Rose chooses cherry, and soon her lips look as if she colored them in with red crayon. Sitting on the bench, licking the last drops of syrup from the fluted paper cups, they eye one another, all three of them, and begin to laugh.

# ELEVEN

◆

Now, in the heart of the summer, when evening brings the first and only breeze of the day, the citizens of Eighth Street leave their dinner dishes in the sink and sit out on the stoops. At Maggie and Jack's, young and old share the stoop. Corey goes home to get a six-pack of beer. Someone says he's seen Jim O'Connor on Seventh Avenue with that flashy new girlfriend of his, wagging her hips like a peep-show dancer. And what do you suppose is happening with Patty now? they wonder. Keevan? No way, the men say. Maybe, the women speculate. Someone saw that new woman going over to the O'Connor house late one night. Another says, I've seen her with Keevan in broad daylight. More than once. . . . And did you know she's married? With a little girl. Did you know—honest to God—she's married to a Finney. One of *the* Finneys.

Patty is a mess. Today she saw them all going out together: Zoe and her little girl and Keevan. Walking down the street to Seventh Avenue. Patty was cleaning her bedroom windows and stopped when she saw them, so happy and certain together it gave her a chill. She noticed, for a moment, how Keevan's hand settled on the small of Zoe's back and eased her tenderly forward.

She hated him then, even more than she hates Jim. And she sat down on her bed and had to bite her lip to keep from crying. All summer she's worked hard to hide her feelings for Keevan, give him time to see her as a single woman. And there are days when she feels he cares for her. Once, as they sat in the garden talking, she looked up from her ice tea and he was staring at her. His eyes were the color of the tea. A weird, pretty color, pale reddish brown, not so different than the color of his hair. She'd never noticed that before. He was smiling slightly, and she couldn't help feeling he'd never really seen her before. Not really seen her. As though maybe she was just some fixture like the kitchen sink that he'd known all his life and was not worth the effort to notice. But in the garden that day, his eyes took her in and appreciated her. Her heart beat so wildly she wanted to laugh aloud. She felt herself blush.

For weeks, she held on to that moment, reminding herself, when she was in low spirits, that Keevan felt something for her then that he never felt before. Or he saw something new in her.

And there is something new to see. She feels changed, renewed. All that's been jammed up and miserable in her is beginning to drain out. Since Jim's moved, the world has seemed full of possibilities. Now, when Brooklyn College sends its catalog, she looks at the classes and wonders which ones she might like to take, although she has no intention of going to school in Brooklyn. But there are lots of colleges in New Jersey, and she thinks that out there she might be able to count on her mother to look after Michelle and John so she could go to school and learn to be something. She doesn't know what, exactly. Perhaps a chef. Why not? Her kitchen experiments are coming out so deliciously these days, it seems a shame there's no one around to really appreciate them, except maybe Keevan. She's good enough to cook in a restaurant, she thinks. She imagines herself in one of those high white hats. Keevan tells her it's called a toque.

"Toke?" she asks. "Like a puff of marijuana?"

He laughs at her. "What would you know about marijuana?"

"What? You think they reserved that stuff only for college kids? Jimmy used to get high all the time when we were dating. He used to make me join him. It made me stupid, though."

In fact, Jim used to make her smoke so she'd be willing to do things in bed she wasn't normally willing to do, because when she smoked, everything felt good. Keevan must be gentle in bed, she thinks. Tender.

But now she can't stand what's going on. Keevan back with that Zoe. All summer not a peep from the ice queen, and now, suddenly, she's back. Patty heard her up there one night this week, making noises. And not just talking. Noises that couldn't mean anything else but sex. And he's been so curt to Patty lately, like he used to get sometimes before. Huffy and rude.

Now she hears him stirring above her. There are no voices, and his movement is occasionally suggestive. He must be alone, she thinks. The children are in bed, and she checks on them as she goes by. They sleep floppy and open. She remembers how she used to go up and watch Keevan sleep. Since Jim's left, she hasn't had the nerve to do it. As though Jim was her protection from Keevan's knowing how she felt.

She climbs the stairs now, trying to think up a good excuse to see him. It takes a moment for him to answer her knock, and she wonders if he's purposely hesitating.

When he opens the door, she knows instantly that he is not pleased to see her. He sighs loudly, impatiently. He does look weary. He is wearing a torn T-shirt. He's barefoot, and his jeans are unsnapped.

"Can we talk?" she asks.

"I'm beat," he says, not even letting her in. "How 'bout tomorrow?"

"Just for a few minutes. We've gotten three appraisals on the house now. And I want to talk about the asking price."

"You know how I feel about that."

"We've got to agree on a price."

"Six million dollars," he says, sighing again. He lets her in now, but she knows it's only with reluctance.

"I don't understand why you're not happy to sell the place. If we get four fifty for it, that's two hundred and twenty-five thousand dollars in cash for you. You could afford a great little bachelor pad," she says, sweeping potato chip crumbs off his coffee table and taking them to the garbage.

"Don't clean up. You're not my maid."

"I'm only trying to help."

"Sit down."

She does, but uneasily. It's easier to be in motion when her emotions are flying around the way they do with him. "I mean, even if you use it just for a down payment, think of what you can buy. An apartment on Prospect Park West, with a doorman, even!"

"I don't want that." His stare is cold and angry.

"Or if you're so hot for a house, you could afford one of those little limestone ones up on the next block. They can't go for more than three, if that."

"I don't want that either."

"What *do* you want?"

"I want to stay here."

She shakes her head at him. "Are you just trying to be impossible or what?" She never knew she could feel this way about Keevan. So distant, so angry, as if he's the enemy. It's the way he's treated her in the last week or two. With no respect, with no patience. Ever since Zoe came back.

"And what about what *I* want?" she asks suddenly, surprised by the power of her own voice. "Doesn't that count to you? I won't be able to move to New Jersey if we don't sell this place. It's all the money Jim and I have, in this house. We haven't saved much, what with parochial school and all."

"Jim has plenty of savings. Ask him about the mutual

funds and some sort of convertible insurance. I don't know. Ask him. I know he's not as poor as he's telling you. Besides, why can't you stay here? You've lived here all your life too. Michelle and John don't know any other place. You have friends here.''

Patty sits on the couch, shaking her head and feeling small. Jim could always do this to her, reduce her to muteness with questions she should be able to answer. But she's never felt this way before with Keevan. Still, if he doesn't see, what can she say? If he doesn't know, what's the point of explaining?

"What?" he asks, after a while.

Then it spills from her, what she really wants to talk about. Without warning, she is surprised by the words that come out of her mouth. "Why are you seeing that Zoe again? I thought you weren't going to see her anymore. All summer you stayed away—"

"She stayed away from me."

"Am I wrong, or is she married?"

"Not strictly speaking," Keevan says. He tosses his coppery hair in a haughty way that drags at the pit of her stomach.

"What in Mary's name does that mean?"

"I don't think I need to explain."

"I think you do."

"Who the hell do you think you are, Patty? You waltz in here and clean up my coffee table and try to tell me I have to sell the only house I've ever lived in and that I shouldn't be seeing the woman I'm in love with."

She feels the color drain from her face, and it's as though lead shot is flowing to all her extremities, so that even though the thing she wants most is to get out of here, she can't move at all. Still, she stands, and she hears her voice waver, making her sound like Katharine Hepburn.

"I'll be going," she says, the tone fluctuating. "The agents all came in around four fifty. I was going to say we should ask for four seventy-five. That's what I'm going to tell them tomorrow, whether you agree or not. And if your true love is so unmarried, why don't you just move in next door with her?''

Keevan is already at the door, opening it for her. His cheeks are flushed with rage, his jaw especially flames with anger, and his neck. Suddenly she leans forward and kisses him full on the mouth intensely, unexpectedly. She feels the soft, vulnerable insides of his lips, and is hurt by the sharp intake of his breath as he steps back. She can't believe she's done it, doesn't know why she did. And then, just as quickly as she's kissed him, she slaps him. Her hand makes an incredibly hollow sound on his cheek.

''Jesus, Patty, are you out of your mind?'' he asks.

''No,'' she says. ''You are. You're out of your fucking mind to be fooling around with a married woman right under her husband's nose. And right under *mine*, you asshole bastard.''

She skitters down the stairs as fast as she can, feeling the heat of her anger all the way down. It could practically set the house afire. As she opens the door to her own apartment, she hears from above Keevan muttering, ''. . . a fucking lunatic,'' and she slams the door behind her, nice and loud, so he'll hear.

Rose Finney can't sleep. She can't stop thinking about their last few weekends together, going to the park, taking a walk on Seventh Avenue, and today, walking all the way to Grand Army Plaza for the Caribbean Day parade. Never in her life has she seen such costumes. Like jeweled birds and living flowers. The pounding rhythm of the music still makes her body sing. She and Kevin danced in the crowd. He twirled her round and round, while her mother clapped and laughed. Rose can't remember her mother ever being so happy.

As her mother was putting Rose to bed, Rose asked her, ''When are we going to see Kevin again?''

''Soon.'' Her mother smiled at her, her eyes soft and dreamy.

"Could you marry him?" Rose asked her, and her mother frowned.

"Oh, Rosie," she said. "You know perfectly well I'm married to Jamie."

"Keevan's much more fun than Jamie."

"Jamie's sick. He won't always be."

"Yes he will," Rose told her.

Her mother changed the subject then, talked about how school was going to start in just two weeks and how she'd be going to a new school, just blocks away. How she needed shoes, and whether Homer has begun to like Park Slope.

Rose couldn't wait until her mother left so that she could lie on the cool sheets and think about the dancers and the music and the way Keevan's twirling her made her feel as though she could take off like a bird. When he kissed them goodbye, he told them that next weekend, if the weather was nice, he'd take them to Coney Island. There's a big Ferris wheel there, he said, and when you get to the top, you look over the ocean and feel like you could dip your feet in it when the Ferris wheel comes down. And there's a water flume that makes your tummy tickle. And he said he'd win stuffed animals for Rose if she likes. Rose imagines it all as though she's watching TV.

# TWELVE

◆

When autumn comes, Eighth Street is a different sort of place. The children wake earlier, and the Saint Agnes uniforms, smelling of mothballs and old plaster, are taken from the roof-access closets at the top of the houses and aired. The girls appear in pleated plaid jumpers, the boys sweat in plaid pants and blue blazers. Everybody seems busier, and by October 1, stoop sitters stop sitting out unless the nights are unusually balmy, and neighbors know they probably won't see each other much until spring. The impatiens, having filled the gardens to capacity, droop and wither. The autumn mums replace them, rarely having time before the frosts to establish themselves and stretch out from their pot-bound stiffness. Halloween decorations show up in the Kilkenny windows: An electrified full-size witch moves back and forth, straddling a broom; Jack has wired a speaker so that her cackle can be heard on the street. Cotton webbing stands in for cobwebs. A jolly orange pumpkin flashes on and off.

Now, nearly every night, Zoe comes to Keevan's house to make love. One October night, when the temperature is more appropriate for August, they climb up to the roof. She is already excited as he follows her up the ladder, reaching out to touch one of her ankles.

"Keevan, you'll make me fall," she whispers, laughing.

When the hatch is open, they climb out to a warm, inky world of stars and a shocking view of all Manhattan—the Statue of Liberty, the Empire State Building, the Chrysler Building, lit for their pleasure.

"I never knew this was up here. I never knew you could see all this." She steps over the foot-high wall to the roof of her house. Odd to be standing atop her own house. Odd that beneath her feet, Jamie lies half awake.

"Come back," Keevan calls her. "You're at my house tonight." She wonders if Keevan saw the look on her face as she thought about Jamie. She climbs back over the wall with a sense of relief and helps him spread a quilt upon the black roofing. Kneeling, he pulls her down, undresses her, and presents her skin to the bathwater-warm air, touching her with special reverence. Nuzzling her neck, her breasts, the dent of her waist, he lays her back on the quilt. Through it, she can feel the heat of the black roofing, which, having absorbed the unseasonably hot sun all day, now radiates soothing warmth. Naked, in the open air, Zoe feels so full of life she wonders if her skin will split.

Lovemaking with Keevan goes beyond anything she's ever imagined. Often when they make love, he narrates in her ear what he is doing, and she is surprised at how it excites her. "I'm inside you," he whispers. "I'm hard inside you, sliding in and out of you. Do you feel it? Do you feel how much I want you?" She comes much faster when he talks to her. His voice insists that they connect, that she knows he's thrilled by her pleasure. "My God, Zoe, you're coming. I can feel you coming. Come for me. Come for me." She has never known this level of intimacy before. Sometimes he is very dirty in the words he chooses, sometimes poetic. Both excite her. In the end, his words, the slender strands of his words, connect her to him, thrill her. And sometimes, though she has come two or even three times, he draws her desire forward with his lips and tongue yet again before he allows her to go home.

This night on the roof, after they kiss for a long time

on the heated quilt, he rolls over and pulls her on top of him, asks her to straddle him. With her breasts and back exposed to the cooling air, she is wild with desire.

"Don't move," he tells her. "I just want to look at you against the skyline." She arches her back, pulls her blond hair from her eyes. "My God. The two most beautiful things in my life, side by side," he says.

"My flat breasts?"

"You and the view," he says, laughing. After a moment of silence, she sees his eyes glistening with pleasure.

"What is it?" she asks.

"I've never been this lucky," he tells her.

She wants to reassure him that she loves him too. She doesn't give him half what she's always given Jamie. But somehow, though she is happier than she can remember ever being, she can only smile, and smooth his coppery hair. Then she rides him wildly, until they both come. She literally sees stars beneath her eyelids, and then she opens her eyes to real stars.

"I don't think there is anyone in all of Brooklyn as happy as I am tonight," he tells her, holding her spoon style afterward, petting the arc of her hip and the hollow in front where her thinness makes a cave.

She finds her hips moving with longing at his touch, and soon he is running his hands along the backs of her thighs, the opening of her buttocks, the swollen nub of her clitoris, and they are making love again, with Zoe on her hands and knees.

"Are you happy?" he calls out to her, when she is close to coming yet again.

"Yes."

"Tell me you're happy."

"I am. . . ."

"Tell me you love me."

"Oh, Keevan."

"Tell me."

She tries to escape the declaration by moaning.

"Tell me," he calls out even louder, more insistently. "You do. You love me," he says.

"I do," she whispers. She is surprised how much his insistence excites her.

"Tell me."

"I love you," she whispers, but the second the words leave her lips, her desire leaves too. And she feels unbearably bereft. Revolted with herself, with this act, she feels her body freezing up, and revulsion for him overtakes her like nausea. She knows he senses it, because he slows down and soon stops. Pulling away from her, he lies silently beside her, and when he touches her, she can't help but flinch.

"You don't love me?" he asks. She hears hopefulness in his voice, and kindness and innocence.

"Please don't ask me to tell you anything aloud," she tells him finally.

Later, as she kisses him good-night, she whispers in his ear, "I never knew I could care this much for you."

Zoe feels as though she's been tangled in a net and now is free. Everything seems suddenly easier to her. She is astonished to find that the urge to steal is ebbing away, and not having to fight it gives her renewed energy. She begins to look for things for the house. At lunch time, she goes down to antique shops in the Village. In a small shop that smells of licorice, she buys a Victorian mahogany side table with a white marble top. The cool solidity of the marble seduces her hands. The certainty of the piece seduces her psyche. When it is delivered and set beneath the window in Zoe's front parlor, it gives off the faint blue-grey scent of licorice for days. She buys quilts and chairs, an old pine trunk with flowers and "Jane Thomas, her trunk" painted on it. Rooms begin to fill; the house begins to feel more and more like hers.

One Saturday, at a flea market, she and Rose find a blue stoneware vase entwined with tulips and marked with a signature and the date 1883. "It's the color of sky before

it snows," Rose tells her, fondling it. "I'm so glad it's
ours. I like all the things in our house now. Even more
than the stuff we had in Sutton Place." With all the money
Jamie's brought into her life, she's never been able to give
herself such pleasures before. She'd always wait for him
to initiate any purchase. Now she even buys a few indul-
gences for herself: a jar of ocean-scented bath salts, the
blue-green of the Aegean. A silk bra and panties the color
of blue plums. A tiny antique silver picture frame, which
she fills with a picture of herself and Keevan and Rose
laughing, taken in a photo booth at Coney Island. Also
jammed into the picture are five stuffed dogs that Keevan
and Rose have won together. Zoe keeps the little picture
in her desk at the office and takes it out only when she
is alone.

Alicia says, "Look what you're doing to the place. It
changes every time I see it. And you too. You seem so
happy."

"I love the autumn," Zoe says, nervous that Alicia
might guess she's fallen in love. "You're the one who
seems particularly happy, Alicia."

"It's Manny," Alicia confesses. "He's been coming up
to see me nearly every weekend."

"Really? You didn't say a word. This is wonderful.
You deserve Manny."

"Do you think so? It was you who told me to write
him back. I think he's crazy for loving me so much." Zoe
is grateful Alicia's distracted by love. Otherwise she'd
surely guess that something in Zoe's life has changed.

For one thing, she's never home anymore on the weekends. Keevan takes them to wonderful places: to a petting
zoo in Connecticut; to Bear Mountain State Park, where
the air seems almost sticky with the scent of pine. At the
Jersey shore, though it's too cold to swim, they chase
seagulls and collect shells. Rose holds his hand and flirts
with him. She wants to sit in his lap after dinner, to show
him her drawings, her books, her new underwear. The
Oedipal flirtation she never could have with Jamie, Zoe

thinks. Zoe feels that together they are more like a family than she's ever had, more like a family than Jamie and Charlotte and she were in the early days. For even then, Jamie was quiet and serious. Even then, there was no holding hands, no laughing and running. The joy she experiences now makes her feel she's turning her back on him. The more it grows, the more it betrays her marriage. But how can she stop when they are all so easy together, when the days slide one into the other with the pleasure and precision of a movie montage? When she suddenly realizes that her urge to steal is gone entirely, for the first time she can remember. She is uplifted by the realization and feels that somehow, with Keevan loving her the way he does, she is maybe safe from its ever returning.

Stuart tells her, "Zoe, you've changed." One night when they have worked long and hard, she kisses him on the mouth to thank him for staying. She is so full of joy, so full of her own sexuality, she can hardly bear not to share it. He kisses her back, hungrily. And she lets him, realizes, with shock, that she wants more. When he locks the door to her office, still she does not stop him. It isn't until he has half undressed her, drawn her hand to his swollen crotch, that she understands what she is doing. She is trying to put Stuart between herself and Keevan. Trying to protect herself from something real and intense and worthwhile with something that means nothing at all.

"I'm sorry," she tells Stuart, red-faced, nervous with shame. "I didn't mean for this to happen. Forgive me."

Pushing back his disheveled hair, he looks baffled and frustrated, but he says, "As far as I can see, Zoe, it's just a matter of time."

Lois comes over one evening and, with a curt nod to Zoe, walks straight up to Jamie's room. Afterward she walks through the front and back parlors in her high heels and geranium-colored knit suit, looking from object to object.

"Where did you get these things," she asks coolly.

"All over," Zoe says. "Antique shops."

"It looks like a secondhand store in here," she says.

Zoe bites her lip. "Rose and I like it," she says.

"None of this is nearly the quality of what Delia had, you realize." Lois sits down, and Zoe is shocked to see her bring out a silver cigarette holder and light up in front of her. Maybe she just doesn't care what I think anymore, Zoe tells herself.

"Listen," Lois says. "I'll get to the point. I'm not going to wait much longer for you to put Jamie in the hospital. If he's still like this by Christmas, I'm going to take him there whether you like it or not."

"Even if it's not the best thing for him."

"Well, I suppose what you're doing is the best thing? Do you see him improving?"

Zoe bites her lip.

"If I have to bring in a lawyer to do it, I will. I want you to understand. I've let this go on too long. What do you think people would say if they found out we were letting someone in our family go without treatment so long? Do you have any idea what kind of scandal it would be?"

"Is that all you care about—a scandal?"

"You know better than that," Lois says. "After all, there could be a scandal if anyone found out he was in the hospital too. It's his welfare that matters most. And I can't leave his welfare up to you anymore, it's obvious."

Keevan's love for Zoe grows daily. His capacity to adore her astonishes and pleases him. So he *is* capable of loving a woman deeply; he just never met the right one before. She tells him about her fears about Jamie, or her encounter with her mother-in-law, and all he needs to do is hold her and reassure her, and she's able to throw off her sadness. His words can transform her. He can make her laugh, change, bloom. All she asks of him beyond the affection, the lovemaking, is his interest in her. And stories. She wants to hear stories of his new class of students, stories of his childhood in the neighborhood (she never seems to get enough of these). "What was it like then? Tell me more," she begs as they lie in bed. "Every detail."

He recalls for her his memories of the tree men who came one summer and dug up squares of bluestone all along the outer margins of the sidewalk, smashing them in the street and then carting them away. Keevan was sad. No one on the street had been warned. No one was sure what they were doing. The next week, they came again and brought a truckload of sad little Norwegian maple saplings, their roots wrapped in diapers. That whole first year, tied to stakes, they seemed puny and miserable. No one thought they'd live through the summer, let alone the more than thirty years they have grown and thrived. "That one, and that one," he tells her, opening the shutters, "and the one down by the Kilkennys', and the one down by the Costellos'."

He tells her how every Saint Patrick's day when he was a child, no matter how cold or snowy it was, the entire population of the street would gather in front of the Reillys' house, and Mrs. Reilly would cook sausage and hamburgers over a Weber grill. The boys would form teams, the Saints and the Patricks, and play stickball in the blocked-off street, no matter how high the snow or slippery the asphalt. At the end of the day, Mrs. Reilly would give every child a green handkerchief she'd dyed herself (if you used it, your nose would turn faintly green, Ralph was the first to discover). She filled each handkerchief with jelly beans and red hots, and a little prayer typed on school paper, for the children to say when they went to bed. And tied it with a white ribbon printed with green shamrocks. Keevan remembers one prayer that read: "Dear Lord, please let me be grateful for what I have, though it may be little, though others may have more; for what I have is what you wish me to have, and what I want is only human folly."

"How can you remember that?" Zoe asks in awe.

"Because I kept it. I have it still somewhere."

"Why did you keep it?"

"Because it soothed me to think it was God who didn't want me to have parents." They lay silent after that, holding hands, Zoe breathing as though she's crying, but when he turns to her, he sees no streaks of tears along her cheeks; only her eyes, glowing too brightly in the dark.

"What?" he asks her.

"I'm just so happy to be with you," she says. He is infused with joy. He hates it that she still rations her declarations of affection, but he can't help being pleased when she bestows them upon him.

One day, Rose says to Zoe as she pours her a glass of milk in the kitchen, "Watch, Mommy," and she takes her wadded-up Kleenex and drops it in the trash.

"You threw it away!" Zoe says, trying to contain her excitement, not wanting to make too much of it.

"I still might save some things," Rose says solemnly.

"Of course," Zoe says.

"But I think that saving Kleenex is stupid."

"Are you sure?" Zoe asks.

Rose rolls her eyes. "I threw it away, didn't I?"

Zoe can't help but laugh. She hugs Rose tenderly, knowing that she owes this to Keevan. She tells him that night, and they share the pleasure of their triumph, the joy of loving their golden child.

Later that week, they are at the aquarium, and an older woman whispers to another (but not so softly Zoe can't hear), "Isn't that a pretty family? Just lovely." Zoe turns, to see that the woman's staring at Zoe and Keevan and Rose. The woman smiles an old wise smile at Zoe, and Zoe smiles back, as if to say, yes, aren't I lucky? Since she seems to have lost her urge to shoplift, this is the only thievery in which Zoe partakes.

While playing jacks on the wood floor of the shed out back, Rose tells Michelle, "Your uncle's going to marry my mother."

Michelle looks up, dumbstruck. "No he isn't. Your mother is married."

"Your uncle and my mom are in love, though. And they are definitely going to get married."

"You can't be married to two people at once," Michelle says. She frowns at Rose. "Unless you don't really have a father."

"I told you he's upstairs, sleeping."

"All day?"

"All day."

"Fathers don't sleep all day. I would have seen him sometime."

"Mine does."

"I don't believe you," Michelle says. Rose sees that she's gathering up her jacks.

"You want to see him now?" she says. She's never let anyone see her father before.

"Okay."

Michelle follows her up the stairs. Rose hates the way the room smells, hates the way Jamie smells. Like earthworms. She feels embarrassed, but she's taken it this far.

"See?" she says, opening the door to Jamie's room and trying to pull Michelle in. "There he is." But Michelle hovers at the door.

"I think I have to go home now," she says.

"Yeah," Rose says, closing Jamie's door behind them and heading down the stairs. "The whole thing is definitely pretty creepy."


On Sunday, Patty takes the children to Carroll Gardens to see Jim. He has seen them only twice since he moved out. He's come over to the house and sat in the TV room and talked to them as if he doesn't know them at all, sitting in a chair he rarely sat in when he lived there, as though his favorite chair was too familiar. Sitting on his hands like a schoolkid in an interview, using none of his endearments for Michelle, like "honey" or "sweet," he uttered such inanities as: How's school? And to John: Did you play baseball this week? Patty wanted to swat him. She went into the kitchen and tried not to listen to his voice.

Michelle, seeming not to recognize her father's stiffness, talked on and on about Henry, their new grey kitten, one of five Hal and Donna Shea begged everyone to take last week. "Aren't we lucky? He was the smartest, handsomest one, Daddy, and he climbed right into my arms." (Patty noticed that Henry, usually friendly as a dog, was avoiding Jim entirely.) Michelle went on about her friends and some school project Sister Edwin wanted her to complete about ocean life. John might not have been in the room. He said nothing at all.

When Patty came out of the kitchen, Michelle was sitting on Jim's lap, tickling his neck. John was sunk into the armchair, fiddling with his sneaker laces. For a moment, Patty felt sad because she realized that not only was Jim a stranger to her now; he always had been. And he added so little to the family. Michelle, so full of love for everybody, was easy to love; but John needed someone to stir him up, break through his sulkiness, and Jim would never be patient enough to do it, would never have the know-how, to bring him to life, to get him to respond. And Patty is beginning to realize that she is the same. She needs someone to bring her to life too. Jim never could. No one ever has. Except Keevan.

Now Jim's asked if Patty will let the children come to his house. He offered to pick them up, but Patty likes having an excuse to go to Carroll Gardens to buy some fresh vegetables at the green market there, some exotic spices, and that bread stuffed with prosciutto and cheese her mother always used to buy at Canero's bakery. And she wants to see Jim's place. Ugly, she hopes, and small, and pathetic. She will be disappointed if it isn't all of those things.

On the subway, the children sit in silence, looking very small, their arms folded in their laps. Once in Carroll Gardens, it isn't difficult to find Jim's apartment, half a brownstone floor. Someone has put cheap plastic flowers in the first-floor flower boxes, the color of orange juice. As they climb the stoop, Patty flicks them with her fingers. The stems are painted green, with Day-glo orange showing through the scratches. Cheap. The entrance, she sees glee-fully, is filthy, with broken and chipped tile on the floor. The stairs smell of garlic and oil. His door is painted blue, and the number is upside down, so she checks the other doors, to make sure that it is six, not nine. He deserves this.

"You live here?" Michelle asks in a whisper as Jim lets them in.

"Welcome to the Magic Kingdom," Jim says.

She looks around mutely, then asks, "Where's the bedroom?"

"You're sitting in it. And that's the bed." He points to a linty green sofa.

"Is there a bathroom?"

"Of course." He opens and closes one of the doors quickly. Patty sees a pink chenille robe hanging on a hook near the shower, and she is surprised at how the sight of it makes her mouth dry. Michelle and John aren't stupid. They'll understand. But what can she do?

"So now you've seen everything. Every bit of it. Before your eyes," Jim says.

"I'm leaving," Patty says. Her children sit there, stunned, perhaps by their father's child-size apartment. They say nothing as she goes out.

"Bye, Mama," she hears Michelle say through the closed door.

She walks along Kane Street, her heart slamming. He deserves every bad thing that can happen to him. They should cut him up and serve him to the Knights of Colum-bus for dinner. Let the Rosary Society pick his eyes out. Usually, these days, she doesn't even think of him, doesn't realize how angry she is until she sees him.

The first chill of autumn fills the air as the clouds cover

the sun. She pulls her sweater tight. The green market cheers her, though, with beautiful zucchini and Bartlett pears, pumpkins that could fit in your hand and giant ones high as her knees. She buys portobello mushrooms and saffron, arugula and Granny Smith apples.

At the bakery, she can't wait to get her hands on the cheese-stuffed "lard bread." Deep into deciding which flavor she wants, she hears a vaguely familiar deep voice. She looks up, surprised to see Terence Beaumont, a classmate from Saint Agnes. He's standing in the corner of the bakery, talking to the owner. Terence was always considered a bad boy, the school's official juvenile delinquent. But he looks like he's doing well enough now, in a classy leather jacket and neat grey slacks. He was a good-looking boy, and she used to feel an urgent attraction for him, the way young girls are always drawn to bad boys. Now, she can't seem to stop looking at him; the transformation is so striking. She forces herself to focus on the bread, glancing over at Terence now and then, hoping to catch his eye, sure he won't recognize her with her auburn hair. While she's making her final choice, she hears, "Well, well, if it isn't Patty Costello."

She looks up into his black Irish eyes.

"Um . . . I don't . . ."

"Terry Beaumont. St. Agnes."

"No kidding."

"You remember me?"

"You stole Sister Joan's rosary in third grade."

"I borrowed it."

"I thought you left Brooklyn."

"Been in Jersey for years. You married Jim O'Connor, right?"

"Yes, but . . ." She struggles, thinking of what to say. In her own neighborhood, everyone knows all about her and she never has to explain anything.

"But? You would rather have married me, right?"

"But Jim and I aren't living together anymore."

"No? I'm sorry. What a pity." He doesn't look like he

thinks it's a pity. He has laughing eyes. She always thought so. She used to wonder what the police thought when they caught him, up to no good, and he flashed those laughing eyes. "Recently?"

"In the spring."

"Maybe we can have a drink sometime, and you can tell me all about it."

Patty shrugs. "I can think of things I'd rather talk about," she says. She eyes his left hand for a wedding ring and sees none. She wonders if he ever married.

"Well, we'll talk about those things, then. Do you still live on Eighth Street?"

"For a few months more. We're selling the house. Moving to Jersey."

"You're talking to the Jersey expert. I dabble in real estate, among other things. Where in Jersey?"

She tells him about her mother's town house, the way she feels there. He bounces back her enthusiasm, and she's warmed by his interest in her.

"Can I find you in the phone book?"

"Still under Jim's name."

"Good enough. Guido, we'll talk tomorrow, my friend," Terence says to the owner.

"Gotcha."

Terence winks at him. He has big white teeth when he smiles. Patty remembers that too. Even as a kid. A million-dollar smile.

After he leaves, Patty just stares through the glass at the bakery counter. She can't even think of ordering until she catches her breath. And now she's lost her interest in the lard bread. It's probably too fattening anyway.

"I'll take a plain loaf," she says finally.

"That all?" the counter boy says, clearly disappointed.

Alicia comes to Zoe's house for dinner, with a cake in the shape of a rose, for Rose, and, for Zoe, an antique gold chain that belonged to her grandmother.

"It suits you much better than me. I can't imagine wearing it. And it's rather pretty, isn't it?"

"It's lovely." Zoe imagines how Keevan will rub his finger over the braided gold when they make love, when she wears it and nothing else in his bed. "I'll wear it constantly," she says. She is wondering if it will be too late to see him tonight, after Alicia leaves.

"Just tuck it in when you're on the subway," Alicia says. She's wearing bell-bottom pants the color of tiger lilies, a midriff top that exposes her navel, and above it, a chain belt with a fake-leopard-covered buckle. Zoe smiles. It does seem lately that high fashion corresponds rather too closely to prostitute wear.

"Here, Rosie, check out this cake," Alicia says when Rose throws her arms around her aunt enthusiastically. "I figured that since everyone always wants the roses on a birthday cake, it would be more fun to have a cake that was all roses. Only roses. For my Rose. Should we eat it first? Before dinner?"

"Aren't you going up to see Jamie?" Zoe asks.

"Not until after we eat. It upsets me. I truly came to see the two of you."

At the dinner table, they joke and share. That's when Rose tells Alicia about Keevan.

"We have a friend next door," she says. "His name is Kevin, and he's very handsome. He takes us everywhere. He's in love with Mommy."

Zoe feels the heat to the roots of her hair. "Don't be silly. He's just our friend. He loves us both," she says. "He's a very nice man," Zoe tells Alicia as coolly as she can. "He's crazy about Rose. He's a teacher, you see. He loves kids."

"Uh-huh," Alicia says. But her eyebrows are cocked. Zoe's mouth is so dry it makes a clicking noise when she opens it. She decides to say nothing. It never occurred to her that Rose would tell Alicia, though it probably should have.

Through the rest of the meal, Zoe barely hears. She

keeps thinking up stories she might tell Alicia to allay her suspicions about Keevan. He's gay. He's terribly shy. . . . But Rose chatters on and on. About the aquarium and the carousel ride, about Bear Mountain and the Jersey shore, and how Keevan does cartwheels "just like you do, Aunt Alicia."

"I'll have to meet this fellow," Alicia says, smiling. "He sounds like Cary Grant."

It isn't until Rose is in bed that Alicia agrees to go up to see Jamie.

"I feel like I'm going to a funeral and I'm required to view the body," she says.

"Maybe he'll respond to you," Zoe says. "I'll come up with you."

Alicia walks into the room cautiously, as though an uncaged animal might be there. Zoe was careful to be sure Jamie had a shower today, that his hair was combed, that she'd brushed his teeth. But even so, he looks disheveled and miserably atrophied when she turns on the light.

"Christ, James. You look like *Night of the Living Dead,*" Alicia says in full voice. Zoe realizes how often she whispers in this room. She whispers. She tiptoes. She tries not to roll over too much in bed. Jamie opens his eyes and looks at Alicia. Whether or not he recognizes her is hard to tell. "Why can't you get out of this joint and make a living, you slug," Alicia says. She jabs him in the arm.

"Alicia!" Zoe says.

"Oh, what the hell. He doesn't hear me. Jamie, do you hear me?" She waves a hand over his face. "God, Zo, I don't know how you take it."

"He knows when I'm here. I'm sure of it. It makes him feel better. I talk to him a lot. I know he hears."

Alicia sits down gingerly on the side of the bed and smooths Jamie's hair back from his brow.

"Zoe thinks you hear me," she says. "She thinks you know I'm here. Well, if you know it, I want you to know

I love you. You're my baby brother, and I love you. But frankly, you're acting like Aunt Delia.''

Alicia is silent for a long time. And Jamie's eyes stay open. But they don't focus on her, and finally they close.

She gets up slowly and looks up at Zoe.

"You're a saint or a fool," she says. "I don't know how you take it." Zoe pulls on her arm to leave the room. She doesn't want Jamie to hear this.

Downstairs, she makes Alicia coffee. Alicia lights a cigarette, her twelfth of the visit.

"So tell me about him," she asks, blowing a plume of smoke. Zoe wonders how she can bat it away from her face without offending Alicia.

"Jamie?"

"No. The man next door."

"Oh . . ." She swallows hard, trying to gain composure. "Nothing to tell. He's very nice to us. That's all."

"Is he great in bed?"

"Alicia!"

"Come on. You're talking to *me*. If you're not sleeping with him, you're mad. Jamie's been like this far too long. And even when he's better, he's not really okay. I hope to God you've got someone to put his arms around you and give you some pleasure. You said I deserve Manny? Well, this fellow sounds like Cary Grant and I think you deserve no less."

"I . . ." Zoe is so stunned and shamed she can only bite her lip and stare at the table. She knows she's blushing. She wonders if Alicia can see her hands shaking, her heartbeat slamming in the artery of her neck.

"I'm giving you permission, stupid." Alicia draws a circle in the ashes on her saucer and looks up pointedly at Zoe.

"I want you to meet him," Zoe says suddenly. "He would like you."

"Sure. I'd like to meet him. Listen. Let me take Jamie and get him into a hospital. I won't abandon him. A really decent hospital. A good doctor. It could be totally different than last time. We'd keep them from utilizing the shock therapy. That was a disaster. But he'd be off your hands. You could visit him all you want, but you could breathe, for God's sake.''

"He needs me.''

"God knows what he needs. He's up in the ozone layer somewhere.''

"He almost died last time.''

"You don't know if it would be the same. He's worse now. A lot less communicative. I tell you, we'd insist that they don't give him shock therapy. I know that would kill you. They could try new things. We don't know what they've come up with. . . .''

"Your mother's been trying to get me to hospitalize him. She came last week and said, 'I'm not going to wait much longer for you to put him in the hospital.' ''

"Oh, well, Lois just wants to ship him to Mars, where she never needs to worry about him again. It's not out of the goodness of her heart. But it is out of mine. I'll interview a million places. I'll ask people I know.''

"No.''

"You just don't *want* to be happy, do you?''

Zoe is struck dumb by Alicia's words, and Alicia doesn't look at her, merely sips her coffee and stares into space. It's easier when Alicia doesn't look at her. Her manufactured face always makes Zoe nervous.

"I want to be happy,'' Zoe says finally. "I just have a commitment to Jamie. To love him for better or worse. This is worse.''

"You've had nothing but worse.''

"But I've made a commitment,'' Zoe says.

Alicia looks at her. "I've got to run. Manny and I are meeting on the Vineyard in the morning. I'll call when I get back.'' She stands and straightens the belt on her bare, toned stomach. Every movement of her body says she's annoyed with Zoe.

Nevertheless, at the door, she reaches out and hugs her. Zoe feels truly held. She smells the cool dry scent of Alicia's French perfume, the strength of her long, slender arms.

"Think about what I said," Alicia insists, then breezily descends the steps and walks a few doors down to her car. As she climbs in, she waves. "I love you," she calls.

Astonishing, Zoe thinks, as Alicia drives away, that two siblings could be such polar opposites: Alicia embracing life, Jamie trying to hide from it.

That night, Zoe wonders about leaving Jamie. It seems an easy choice now. Keevan loves her so much. Rose loves him. Jamie sleeps through it all. Yet Zoe can't forget that she has spent years loving Jamie and that for many years he loved her back. She remembers the night she gave birth to Charlotte. Jamie, following the Lamaze instructor's suggestion, rolled frozen Coke cans on her back for hours to ease her back labor. He breathed with her, held her up when she needed to be held. He told her stories to make her laugh in the respites, wiped her brow with cool cloths. When Charlotte's head was crowning, he coached her, cooed to her, helped her breathe. Other women told her that their husbands were useless during labor, didn't understand their pain. Jamie knew her pain and more. They were bound in a way no other couple she ever knew were bound.

Together they have survived grief and illness, silvery joy. No one has ever needed her the way he does. No one.

That night, though she hasn't spoken to them in over a year, she calls her parents. Mostly, she just writes them. Once a month, she sends them checks they won't cash, photos, a long letter. They rarely write her back. They say they are embarrassed about their English, that Zoe can't read Polish well enough for them to write in Polish.

"Why you call, Zosia?" her father asks. "Is something wrong?"

"No," Zoe says. "I just wanted to speak to you."

"Long distance. It costs."

"I can afford long distance, Father," she says.

"You throw money away. Someday you need it. Your husband, he is still sick?"

"Yes."

"You tell him he should get up. Work."

"You don't understand, Father."

"I understand. I understand he sleeps all day. I put your mother on. I no talk anymore."

"You. You are well?" her mother says.

"Yes. And you?"

"I have much pain these days," her mother says. "My back. My stomach. I only have broth now. And crackers. Otherwise I be sick in the toilet."

"You should see a doctor."

"No. You know I no like doctors, Zosia. They just want money. This year is not so good for us. A new shop opened on Central Avenue. They steal our business."

"You should cash the checks I send you. It will pay for whatever you need. If you just cash the checks—"

"No. No. We are fine, Zosia. Fine. You buy the shop on Central and close it. That will help. No. Better you burn it to the ground. They kill our business."

"What do you do with the checks I send?" Zoe asks in exasperation.

"Your father keeps them."

"Keeps them?"

"If we need to cash, we cash."

Zoe chews her lip. There isn't any point in arguing with them. There never has been.

"Rose is growing so big," she tells them. They haven't seen Rose since she was three, and though Zoe writes about her and sends them pictures and even notes from her, they never mention her name until Zoe brings her up.

"She is a healthy girl," her mother says.

"Yes. A happy girl too." Zoe wants them to know she

cares about Rose's happiness, the way they never cared
about hers.

She thinks about her mother being ill. For all she knows,
her mother could have stomach cancer. Who knows how
long they will live. She would like Rose to remember
them a little before they die. Funny, she thinks, that she
should feel this, when she would most like to forget them.

"Maybe we could come see you soon," she says.
"Rose and I."

"No. Plane tickets are too much money," her mother
says.

"I *have* money, Mother. I want you to cash the money
I send you."

"Keep it," her mother says. "You never know what
will happen to your money. Keep it. You should listen to
me, Zosia. I know. Once I had money too."


Four-fifteen the following Tuesday afternoon, there is
knock at Keevan's door. He's come straight home from
school with tests to grade, a task he never looks forward
to. When he opens the door, there's a middle-aged woman
with hair dyed too dark for her wrinkled face, and an
anxious-looking couple, holding hands, not more than
thirty years old.

"Janet Thompson, Shatner Realty. And this is the Mar-
golins," she says.

"Yes?"

"They want to see your house," she says, annoyed that
he hasn't already guessed.

"No," Keevan says.

"No? They've already seen the downstairs." Her voice
is huffy now.

Keevan stares at them, feels his fists clench.

"No," he says.

The couple turn and look at each other.

"They're very interested, Mr. . . . ." She consults her
papers. "O'Connor."

"Well, I'm not," Keevan says, and closes the door in their faces. He hears footsteps trailing down the stairs. Two minutes later, he hears footsteps stomping purposefully up the stairs.

A fist pounds on the door. He hesitates. He doesn't want to speak to these people again. "Keevan, open the door, damn it." It's Patty.

When he opens the door, her face is red, the fine hair at her hairline damp.

"What's up, Pat?" he asks as nonchalantly as possible.

"You asshole. They're waiting downstairs. They want to see your apartment."

"Well, forget it."

"How can you do this to me?" The whine in her voice makes him want to swat her.

"How can *you* do this to *me*?" he asks very softly. "I've lived in this house all my life."

"Yeah? Well, this part of your life is over. Your brother's who you should be mad at. Jim doesn't care one bit about this heap. Unless you can come up with the cash to buy it from him."

"Maybe I will." Keevan hears his own voice quavering.

"What are you going to do, rob a bank? Let the people walk through, at least," she says. "They're here. It's rude to send them away."

"I'm not letting them come through here."

"Keevan!"

Her face is getting redder and redder. He shakes his head. "No," he barely whispers.

"I hate you!"

"I'm sorry you do," he says.

"Oh, God," she wails. She's crying all the way down the stairs, and he does feel like a bastard. And yet he mutters, in the safety of what is still his part of the house, "I was here first."

One night, Zoe notices that Jamie is watching her, his eyes clearer than usual. She pushes his hair from his forehead, and he reaches out, takes her braid in his long fingers, and holds it tight. A sound comes from his throat.

"Jamie?" she says. Her heart is pounding. She thinks she sees him barely nod. "You want your dinner?"

Again, she thinks she sees him nod.

Her hands shake as she assembles his tray. But when she comes up to serve him, he appears to be fast asleep.

He woke and she was there. Now she is gone. He lies in the dark, his eyes tracing the patterns on the ceiling. Not his room. Yet she is here sometimes. Not his room. Yet his bed, his sheets, the smell of her. Her. His beautiful wife. More beautiful than he deserves. He remembers the weight of her silvery-gold braid across his palm, his fingers closing around it. A skein of silk. The dark, heavy pressure is parting. Soon he will swim up toward the light. Swim up to her. She has waited for him. She will be there to help him break the surface, to help him learn to breathe air again.

Three nights later, she falls asleep in Keevan's arms and wakes only because the sounds of a cat fight cut through the night silence. Amid the yowling and hissing, she untangles herself from his long, entwining arms and, after dressing, shuts the door behind her quietly, so she won't wake him. It's past 2:00 A.M.

Coming wearily home to her sleeping house, she puts on the alarm, turns off all the lights, climbs the steps to her bedroom, and peels off her dress, which she throws lazily on a chair.

"Where have you been?"

Zoe jumps. The voice is dry and unpracticed. Brittle as kindling.

"My God!" she says. "You spoke."

Jamie is sitting in the dark, his eyes aglitter. He nods, belying that he's spoken at all.

She approaches the bed but suddenly finds herself unwilling to get too close, unwilling to touch him. Awake, speaking, he is a different creature, requiring of her something that she may no longer be able to give.

"You're feeling better?" she asks tentatively.

"Yes." His body is perfectly still. Too still somehow, in a way that reminds her of an animal's stillness when it stalks, and she shivers.

"Can I turn the light on? Just the little one?"

He nods.

She clicks on the lamp by the mantel, and its syrupy light defines his gaunt, squinting face. His skin wears the sickly yellow tint of months without sunlight. His lips are white as chalk, like the lips of someone who's been drinking Maalox, but she knows it's just the dry skin lifting away from the blood flowing beneath. Still, his eyes no longer have their dullness, or the feverish look they sometimes have. They're focused, and behind them is somebody, a soul. What does he know or remember? All those nights she recited her memories to him, hoping he was absorbing it all. Has he noticed that lately she has stopped the anxious monologues, that these last few weeks she never comes home until late?

"How are you? How do you feel?" she asks, not sure how to phrase the question so that it's not a criticism.

He shrugs. "I wanted to talk to you. . . . You weren't here."

She begins to cry in her own way, her throat twisting into pain. She doesn't know whether it's from happiness at his return or guilt for making love to Keevan while Jamie waited in the dark. "Are you hungry?" she asks. Her voice sounds odd and strangled.

"You've been gone . . . a long time. . . ."

Zoe's breath catches. "I was at a neighbor's," she says. "There are wonderful people in the neighborhood."

"Yes?"

She is hauntingly aware of Keevan's scent still on her,

the slow seep of him inside her. She shivers and turns away to get her robe. Has Jamie noticed the time?

"Don't go," he says to her.

"No. I'm just getting a robe and going to the bathroom. I'll be right back." Her hands shake as she washes her face, brushes her teeth, and even these rote tasks are broken down into chores in her nervousness: pull the toothbrush from its holder, pick up the toothpaste tube, remove the cap, squeeze the gel onto the brush, not too much . . .

She is immensely relieved to discover when she returns that he's asleep. His face is drawn but innocent, like a little boy's. His dark eyelashes, glossy in the warm light of the small lamp, make perfect arcs on his hollow cheeks. She kisses his brow, which is as cool as a corpse.

When Zoe wakes, Jamie's eyes are open, but once again his body is rigid and silent.

"Jamie?" she says softly. His eyes light on her.

"Are you hungry?" she asks, hopefully. He shakes his head and closes his eyes.

"You spoke last night," she says softly. "Do you remember?"

His only response is to roll away from her. She is choked with her own relief.

She checks on him again when she is dressed and ready to leave for work. She pets his forehead this time, kisses his brow.

"I miss you," she says tentatively. "I miss you the way you used to be."

He opens his eyes and looks at her. His eyes are wells of sadness. His bottom lip bleeds. He reaches out his hand and touches her knee. Just his touch stings her, with longing or guilt—she is not sure how to identify this churning heat inside her.

\*　　　\*　　　\*

That evening, she calls Keevan. "I don't think I should come," she says. "Jamie spoke last night."

Keevan is silent for a long time.

When he speaks, his voice is thin. "How do you feel?"

"Confused. He asked me where I'd been. I don't know if he realized how late I was out. It was two in the morning when I left you."

"And today? What did he say today?"

"He wouldn't speak to me this morning. I tried to talk to him, but he turned away. Tonight he was sleeping when I got home. Still is, I think."

"You've got to come over," he says. "Even if only for a while. We need to talk about this. If Jamie's going to wake up . . . we need to discuss this and see how we feel."

"I can't."

"Why?"

"It just doesn't feel right. Not if there's a chance he'll talk to me. I don't want to leave him. I don't want him to even suspect about us."

"And if he does get better, what about us?"

"I don't know," she says. "I just don't know."

After she puts Rose to bed, she goes up to Jamie. His eyes are open again, but no matter how much she cajoles him, asks him questions, or talks to him, he responds with no more than a nod. As soon as he is asleep, she finds herself putting on her shoes, her jacket, and ringing Keevan's bell.

He looks startled and mussed when he opens the door.

"You were asleep," she says.

"I fell asleep in my clothes . . . on the sofa. I think I was upset you weren't coming. Come on. Come upstairs. I'm relieved you're here."

She is wild tonight. Wilder than ever. She doesn't want small talk and wine. She wants to get into bed and hammer her feelings away. She doesn't want him to be gentle with her. She wants somehow to be overpowered, all the decisions out of her hands. But he won't take her cues, and she can't seem to focus. Nothing feels quite right. His touch, which is so often knowing, only irritates her. And Keevan, confused by her response, exposes his nervousness, his vulnerability, in trying to please her.

"Please. Don't touch me anymore," she says finally, in a voice that is so cool it seems to hang like an icy cloud between them. "I want to go home."

"What's happening, Zoe?" Keevan asks her while she dresses.

"I don't know."

"Why are you angry at me?"

"I'm not angry at you," she says, though she feels she could kick him in two.

"I didn't make you come over here," he says as he lets her out.

She turns to him but somehow cannot see the man she loves. He is a stranger to her, a tall, naked, redheaded stranger, and she cannot wait to get away from him.

When she wakes the next morning, Jamie isn't in bed with her. The bathroom door is closed, and she hears the whisper of the shower. She wonders if she should go in, check that he's all right. Opening the door slightly, she sees him moving behind the glass, soaping himself, looking like an ordinary man showering for the day. She can't decide if the idea of another adult in the house is comforting or terrifying.

When he comes out, wrapped in a towel, he moves slowly. Standing, he appears even thinner than she imagined. And his muscles are shapeless and weak, like an old man's. He sits wearily on the bed, takes her hand.

"I'm sorry for everything," he says. She looks closely at his face, this face she has known so long, can read so well. He looks penitent and truly sad. But not tortured, not fearful.

"I know," she says.

"I put you through . . . so much."

Zoe just bites her lip. Her hands are shaking.

"You didn't leave me. . . . Thank you for that. Or put me in the hospital. You didn't . . ."

"I didn't think it was the best thing for you. Not after last time."

"You moved us. Where are we?"

"In Brooklyn. I wanted us to be where it's quieter. Remember, we'd sometimes talk about how we wanted to be somewhere quieter. This house is so beautiful, I was sure you'd like it."

"Did we buy it?"

"Yes."

"What about the co-op?"

"I sold it."

"I think I'll lie down now."

"Are you angry?" She realizes afresh how brash she's been, moving them when he was unable to voice an opinion. Right before his eyes, but as though behind his back. "You never did like Aunt Delia's."

"No."

"I thought it would be more soothing here for all of us. More restful. The neighbors are so kind."

"Whose house were you at the night you were late?"

Zoe swallows. "Our next-door neighbor's. It's all one family. One man sells insurance. His brother's a teacher. The teacher reads lots of books. You'd find him interesting, I think." She wonders if he would. Jamie seems like such an old man compared to Keevan.

"I'm glad you've found friends," Jamie says. He lies down and stares at her from the bed. "I'm so tired," he says.

"You should take your time at this."

"I knew we weren't in Sutton Place anymore. But I was just glad . . . just glad you were with me," he says. His voice is distant, soft. Then it seems he is looking into her. Going far deeper than the surface. "I love you. More than ever now," he says.

"I know you do." She is swept with emotion for him. A flood of forgotten feeling. Its intensity is almost painful.

"Get some rest. I'll call in and say I can't come to work today. I'll stay with you."

"No," he says. "I'm not ready. . . . I don't want to talk much. Go to work. I want to be alone still."

"Tonight. We'll talk tonight," she says. "If you have the strength. We'll talk about everything. Okay?"

She feels close to him when she kisses his cheek, feels as though she could recapture what they once had, and more.

It's eleven-thirty, and Zoe still has not come over or called. She usually arrives by ten; sometimes by nine-thirty. And always, if she thinks she might be late, she calls. Keevan considered her behavior last night temporary madness, confusion over Jamie, but now he doesn't know what will happen.

I deserve this somehow, he thinks. I was an asshole to Patty, I convinced Zoe to make love to me. She told me she still loved Jamie. The thoughts revolve in his head like the crown of stars around a cartoon character after a fight. His temples throb. He pours himself a glass of beer, but it does nothing for the nervous flutter in his abdomen. He can't contemplate a night without Zoe.

He is astonished by the grip she has on his heart. By expecting nothing, she has unlocked his need to give. It's her imposed distance that has made her safe enough to love. That's it. She has no desire to consume him. It's because she always keeps a piece of herself away from him, the piece that loves Jamie. How perverse the human heart is, he thinks. If only he had money . . . the things he would give her. Jewelry and beautifully bound books. Dinners out. Paintings. Weekends at country inns. Weeks in England and India and Kathmandu. Just because he can't own her.

When the phone rings, he is startled.

"Don't tell me," he says, without even asking who it is. "You got hung up, and you're coming over now."

"No." Her voice is whispery, even softer than usual. "He's speaking again. He's awake for real now, I think."

"Are you okay?" His chest grips up with worry.

"I'm okay."

"Are you glad?"

"Of course. Of course I'm glad." He is astonished and wounded that she *does* sound glad.

"I don't feel I should talk to you. Not tonight," she says. For a long time, Keevan is silent. He hears Patty closing shutters downstairs, the maple tree sweeping against the window.

"When, then?" Keevan asks. His voice sounds weak, and he hates it.

"I'm confused. Give me time."

"To decide what?"

"I don't see how I can keep this relationship going, with Jamie awake. And yet . . ."

"What?"

"You said you understood when we started. You said you knew there was no commitment. . . ."

"How was I to know we'd feel the way we feel?" He's angry. He has always thought of her as fragile. A slender piece of iron, he thinks now. "Don't do this to me."

"I don't know what I'm doing yet. Don't be angry at me, please."

"You've got to come over tonight," he says.

"I can't. He's awake upstairs. He's waiting for me."

"You've got to come over to talk this thing out. I need you."

"No," she says. "He's the one that needs me."

"Has he made love to you yet?" Keevan asks.

"Come on. He's weak. He's still sick."

"Don't let it happen. Not ever. Don't let him touch you."

"He's my husband, Keevan."

Keevan is silent, choked with feeling.

"Well, I'm going. Goodbye."

The room seems thick. His limbs ache. His head throbs

more than ever. He can't move from his chair. He thinks of the park. He's considered going there sometime in the early morning. He looked forward to the wet grass and the verdant air, the eerie glow of the boathouse, the moonlight like an ice cap on the water. He doesn't have the heart for it now. Or for anything. He barely finds the strength to raise himself from the chair, brush his teeth, and go to bed.

Zoe lies in bed with Jamie. She is astonished at how unfamiliar he feels to her now. She touches his wrist, his gaunt face. He smells of toothpaste now. Of soap. His jaw is smooth from shaving.

"Did you hear me all those nights?" she asks him. "I used to talk to you, even though you wouldn't speak to me. I used to tell you so many things. Remind you of the way things used to be with us."

"I don't remember," he says. "I don't think I could hear you. Just knowing you were there is what mattered."

She finds herself disappointed, remembers how carefully she wove each memory, wishes she had written down every word. For herself. Maybe she remembered all those sweet good moments just to remind herself why she stayed with him, to give herself hope.

Now hope has paid off. He's awake. And yet she's lying here talking to him, touching him, and a part of her can't stop thinking of Keevan O'Connor.

On the other side of the wall, Keevan has a terrible dream: He's standing on a high floor in a tall building, a penthouse maybe. And at the far end of the room are two beautiful French doors, open to the night, which flows into the room like velvet. The cool air calls him forward, and he crosses the room, carpeted and silent, and steps out to the balcony, but there is nothing there—no iron railing, no concrete slab—just a rush of cold air and the sidewalk below. Like a cartoon, he stands for a moment on the cushion of air, treading, and he wakes in the midst of a heart-stopping fall.

Zoe lies awake, trying to hear Jamie breathing. He is as silent and motionless as a dead man. "Jamie," she says softly, gripping his arm, shaking him. "Jamie?"

"What!" He sits up, his eyes wide from some dream, then turns and looks at her. "What's wrong?"

She feels sheepish. Her mouth is dry. "I just wanted to know if . . ."

"If what?"

"If you'd wake when I shook you."

He stares at her for a moment. How can she tell him she thought he was dead. What made her think that?

"I'm sorry. Go back to sleep. I didn't mean to wake you." They lie down again, Jamie rolling to his stomach, Zoe still on her back, watching the patterns of light through the slats of the shutters. She wonders if Keevan is awake next door. Jamie sighs and settles his bony wrist over her wrist.

The next morning, Rose stands by Jamie's bed and stares at him. At breakfast, her mother told her he is awake and has been speaking, but to Rose he looks just as asleep as ever. She holds Homer tightly under her arm. She clears her throat.

Jamie opens his eyes.

"Hello," he says. She steps back from him. His voice is scratchy. She sees him smile. He almost never smiles. Almost never speaks directly to her. Not even when he's feeling completely well.

"Hello," she says.

He sits up. The way he looks is frightening. The few times she's come to see him before, the shades were down. She knew he'd grown thin and ugly, but she couldn't exactly see how strange and Halloween-like his face had become.

"Did you come to see me?" he asks.

She nods.

"I'm glad you did," he says.

"You are?"

"How's Homer doing?" She is surprised that Jamie has remembered her dog's name. She squeezes Homer more tightly.

"He's got a cold," she says.

"I'm sorry. Does he get colds often?"

"Usually in the autumn."

Jamie smiles again at her. She doesn't want to like him, doesn't like that his smile makes her feel shy inside.

"Has school started?" he asks.

"Yes."

"What's your teacher's name?"

"Miss Holiday."

"That's a happy name."

"She has three pierces in one ear, and she plays the guitar."

"Really?"

Rose bites her lip. "I should go downstairs and see Mommy," she says. She doesn't know what to think. Jamie is almost never this friendly, this nice. "I gotta go."

"Okay. Will you come up and see me again?" he asks.

"Do you want me to?"

"Yes. I would like it very much."

Rose finds that her heart is beating hard. She doesn't want to come and see him again. For one thing, next time she comes, she figures, he'll probably be acting dead again.

He watches her leave the room. This child who has been the center of his fears. Beautiful, except that her face is too similar to his own. And too serious, too much like him in every way. I need to get out of this bed, he thinks. I need to be there for her. The way I've never been before. I won't make any decisions for her. Too dangerous. I won't let myself be alone with her. Not like Charlotte. But I'll get to know her. I'll learn to make her smile. He rises and goes to the window, looks down the street. Brooklyn. He says the word out loud. "Brooklyn." A prettier word than he ever realized before. And the street itself is pretty, the tall, narrow houses standing shoulder-to-shoulder, the trees. But Brooklyn. Why did she bring us here?

In the next few days, Jamie dresses and comes downstairs twice; he starts and finishes a book; he even takes a walk down the block and then haltingly back up one night when the weather isn't too cold. Walking with him past Keevan's house, Zoe feels her neck grip with tension. She's afraid that at that moment, Keevan will be watching out the window and see them walking. Jamie is like a skeleton now, frail and slow. People stare at him on the street, wondering about his age, probably, and what he is sick with. Did the rumor about his having AIDS ever spread? Zoe wonders if he will ever not look sick, will ever be normal, even for a time. Because she knows that it could be only for a time. Again and again, she's held out hope that each depression would be the last one. Now she no longer even hopes. Again, sooner or later, he'll slip into the anxious mornings, the long naps, the restless nights, and she will be excluded, at first a little and then entirely.

She has spoken only briefly to Keevan each night, telling him to give her time to understand her feelings for Jamie, time to allow her to figure out what to do about Keevan. He tries to sound calm on the phone. Tries to make their conversation as nonchalant as that of two lovers separated by a short business trip. But she hears his worry, his restlessness. Soon she must go see him. If only she knew what to say.

For Jamie seems very different this time. Sweeter, more open. He even has been going out of his way to speak to Rose. How many times since he's awakened has he told Zoe how beautiful she is, how much he loves her? Zoe is moved now when he touches her. She remembers how gentle and sensual his touch once was.

Jamie's mother comes over on Thursday night and sits on the pink sofa, jangling her heavy gold charm bracelets. Lois poses as the devoted mother, holding Jamie's hand and calling him "darling." She talks to him about social events, the fall antique show. Too bad that Alicia is in Italy. She'd be so pleased to see him well. After Jamie goes upstairs to lie down—for he's still weak and not anxious to put on a show of strength for his mother—Lois turns to Zoe.

"I was discussing with my lawyer a court order to have Jamie moved to the hospital. If he hadn't started feeling better, I would have gone ahead." She is looking down at her hands, twisting her diamond ring.

"I'm glad it didn't come to that," Zoe says.

"You're very devoted to Jamie, aren't you?" Lois says, looking up now.

Zoe is surprised to hear what sounds like a compliment coming from her mother-in-law. Yet she feels guilty, thinking of Keevan.

"I love him," she says.

"I know I haven't been very fair to you," Lois says. Zoe wonders why she's being so magnanimous. Because she's pleased that Jamie's going to be well again? Zoe has no idea how to respond to her confession. Lois doesn't seem to expect a response anyway. She gathers up her cashmere coat, takes her leather gloves from her quilted handbag, and for a moment, Zoe glimpses her pack of unfiltered cigarettes right at the top. "I'll come again soon," Lois says. Zoe is surprised to find she believes her.

Lois stands at the top of the stoop and calls out to her limousine driver, who's parked across the street at a fire hydrant.

"LeMott." Her voice is high and affected. "Come. I'm ready."

Zoe, embarrassed, wonders if anyone on the block has seen her. Yet when the limo door closes, and the flare of a lighter appears in the back seat, when the wheels move forward toward Manhattan, Zoe actually feels a pang to see her go.

# THIRTEEN

◆

On Thanksgiving, a light snow falls on Eighth Street, sugaring the stoops and the bluestone. Darlene dresses her baby in a snowsuit and takes him outside to play in the snow. His blue eyes fill with wonder as he touches a rail dusted with snow and rubs the snowflakes on his nearly bald head. Michelle and John and Rose make snow angels in the O'Connor's backyard. Patty isn't a very friendly mother, Rose thinks. But she likes sharing the snow with friends. And Michelle has a new grey kitten, which fits in her hands like a sandwich. She asks Michelle if her uncle is upstairs, but Michelle says they're not allowed to go see Keevan right now, because he and their mother are having a big fight. She wishes she could spend Thanksgiving with him, could invite him over for dinner with her mother. She can't understand why her mother hasn't invited him herself.

Zoe, not entirely comfortable that Rose is playing next door, watches the snow accumulate on the pavement and wonders if Keevan can hear Rose's voice in his house. At noon, she pays a homeless man, who rang her bell with the offer, to shovel the walk and stoop. Keevan once told her that when it snows, brownstone owners must have the walks clear by 11:00 A.M. or face a fine. She isn't sure that the rule applies on holidays, but she wants her walk clear anyway. She watches as the man eagerly shovels every bit of walk. He does a far better job than she expected, and she wonders why he doesn't have a steady job.

She reheats the turkey Teresa left them, and when Rose comes home at three, right when she's supposed to, Jamie descends the stairs to eat with them.

Patty drives the children out to her mother's house, departing at four, worried about traffic.

Keevan spends the holiday lying on his bed, staring at the ceiling, angry and lost. He is so bruised by Zoe's retreat that he's found it hard in the last week to do the simplest things: get up in the morning, pay his bills. And the hours seem to tick by second after second, at a lagging, exhausted pace, like a ninety-year-old man running a marathon. Time may simply never pass.

Zoe has changed him. He's a boat that's lost its rudder, and he spins round and round, having no forward motion, no direction. He can't read a book. He forgets to eat. And he's drinking too much, which even in his miserable state worries him.

He's exhausted all day, then, at night, he can't sleep. His body aches and gets in his way. His arms seem too long when he tries to nestle into the mattress. And the mattress, which he never really thought about before, feels like a bed of hard, unforgiving knots.

At midnight on Thanksgiving, he realizes that he hasn't eaten all day, that he's drunk two six-packs of beer, that he has nothing to be thankful for.

Patty is in the process of ripping a page out of *Gourmet* magazine when the call comes. She's asked Keevan to dinner, to try and talk sense into him about the house. And besides, he's been looking so miserable, drinking too much, she thinks, and she can't help worrying about him. She feels bad she didn't invite him to her mother's for Thanksgiving, that she's even been keeping the kids from him. This morning, she saw him on the stairs and asked him what he did for the holiday. He glared at her. "I got drunk," he said.

Tonight the children are spending the night at Jim's, sleeping on the floor in sleeping bags. She agreed to it only if he promised that Kim would stay away. But she's just talked to John and Michelle, and even to Jim, who grunted and said, "Of course they're fine. What am I— an ax murderer?" So she thinks the call must be from Keevan, trying to cancel. The bastard. It's only six o'clock. Who else could it be?

"Is this Patty Costello?" the voice asks.

"Well, I was," she says.

"You might as well be. You've hardly changed."

"Who is this?"

"Terry Beaumont. I thought you'd recognize my voice instantly."

"Sorry," she says. She's glad she didn't. It gives her power, she thinks, to make him feel she's cool about him, hasn't been waiting by her phone for him to call. And she hasn't, much to her surprise. She's been thinking about selling the house, and getting Keevan to see things her way, and applying for cooking school. She's sent away for a few brochures, even one from the Culinary Institute, though she doesn't know if she has the guts to go there.

"I've been thinking of you," Terry says. "Wondered if you might have dinner with me tomorrow."

"Tomorrow? Well, yes, I guess I could. . . ."

"Thought we'd drive up to City Island for lobsters. Ever been to the Lobster Box? I haven't been there much since I've been living in Jersey, but I figured if I'm coming out to see you, it'd be a straight shot up the Whitestone Bridge. . . ."

"I've never been there," Patty says. It's comforting how easy it is for Terry to go on talking without her encouragement. Jim was such a moody son of a bitch. She had to force words out of him.

"I know a real courteous guy woulda asked you maybe on Wednesday. I know it's a lotta nerve asking you for a Saturday night on a Friday. Frankly, I thought I had to go up to Albany to see my kids this weekend, but my ex

says her parents are coming in from Altoona—she's a
Pennsylvania girl—and we switched weekends. Being a
Saturday night, when a pretty girl like you could get asked
out by just about anybody . . ."

"The person I was going to have dinner with canceled,"
she says, not wanting to sound too available. "So I don't
mind this time."

"The Lobster Box is sensational! I'll make reservations.
You ever been to City Island at all?"

"No. I hear it's nice."

"I'll pick you up at seven. I've been waiting for this
for—what?—twenty years? Deck yourself out."

"Do I need to dress up?"

"You don't need to. Just do it for me. You got some
pointy heels? I'm a sucker for pointy heels."

Patty remembers Donna always calling that type of
pump "fuck-me shoes."

"I think I can dig out a pair."

"Well, put 'em on tomorrow night. Seven o'clock."

When she hangs up the phone, she sits for a few minutes
with the cookbook in her lap, trying to think what she
might wear, how she might do her hair. She is startled
when the doorbell rings. She can't imagine it's already
time for Keevan to come over.

He stands at the door, running his fingers through his
hair. He looks like hell. Really like hell. His eyes are
bloodshot and sunken; he appears to be in pain.

"Come in," she tells him. "I haven't even started cooking. Somebody called me."

He shuffles in, throws himself down on the sofa, but
says nothing, so she goes on. "An old friend of mine.
You know Terry Beaumont?"

"Is she from around here?" he asks listlessly.

"He. Terry Beaumont. He went to Saint Agnes."

"Oh."

"You must remember him. He was a real JD. He got
kicked out of school for three days because he was sent
to the principal and before the principal arrived, he'd lit

up a cigarette and was smoking. Right in the principal's office. Do you remember?"

Keevan shrugs. "Guess not."

"What's been bothering you lately?" she asks, though she's certain it must be that Zoe.

"I just have some stuff going on," he says, not looking at her.

"Well, come into the kitchen while I start the chicken. It won't take long. I bought breast filets. I'm going to bread them, then sauté them with mushrooms and wine."

"Don't bother for me," Keevan says.

"I *want* to bother for you. So," she says, pouring flour into a bowl for dredging, "you having trouble with the princess next door?"

Keevan is silent, and when she turns for an answer, his golden eyes flash at her angrily.

"I told you that was trouble right from the first."

"Don't start," he says in a measured way. "I came down here because you said we have to make peace about selling the house. You want to persuade me to see things your way. I want to persuade you to see things mine. This is probably a total waste of time, and I certainly don't need you needling me now of all times about my relationship with Zoe."

Patty, hating just the sound of Zoe's name, turns to look at him and finds herself feeling pity. His eyes have such a sad light in them. His shoulders are drooping. He obviously feels miserable. Suddenly she begins to wonder if, in such a tender state, he might let her in, might show her how much he's always really cared about her, though lately they are enemies.

"Let me get you a drink, Keevan," she says. He's going to drink anyway. Why not with her? "I'm sorry I was teasing you. It's an old habit."

He shrugs.

"What do you want? I've got vodka, scotch, wine, beer."

"Scotch," he says.

"She musta really broke your heart," Patty says, searching the drawer for the jigger. She throws two ice cubes in a glass, gives Keevan a double jigger of scotch. "Water with it?"

"No."

"Do you want to talk about it at all?" she asks.

"No." He slumps in the kitchen chair. His skin is ashen. He drinks the scotch as though it's water, barely noticing the kitten that's jumped up to his lap and is now pawing a fray on his left cuff. The kitten scratches him. "Damn," he says. "Go away."

Patty takes a deep breath. "Well, I hope you're hungry."

She adds Parmesan and bread crumbs to the dredging, checks the garlic she's already started on the stove, slices the mushrooms.

"I've never seen you like this," she says after the chicken breasts are dredged and sizzling in the pan, the green beans steaming in a pot. She touches his neck, which is always rosy and vulnerable-looking. "Poor baby."

"Don't make me sell the house," he says in a childish voice. "Please. It's all I have left of my grandparents, of the parents I never knew. You can't understand this. You've lived here only as Jim's wife, and God knows that must have sucked. But Jim and I have memories of so many things . . . of Ralph."

The foreign ring of Ralph's name makes her shiver. She goes over to the kitchen window and closes it.

"I'm not doing this to hurt you," she says. "It's Jim you should be talking to. He doesn't care about the house. He'd be happier to see it sold."

"Patty, we all used to be happy here," Keevan says. He sets down his glass. It's empty. Patty pours him another double. What the hell. He needs it.

"Things change," she says. "You can't hold on to old things just because you're afraid to go forward."

Keevan looks at her, frowning. "It's funny hearing that from you."

"Is it?" She wonders what he means.

"You're the one who used to be so protective of this neighborhood. You're the one who'd get mad when new people moved in. Or when anything changed. You said everybody was Jewish or yuppie or whatever."

"That's why I don't mind moving. It doesn't feel like my neighborhood anymore."

"What's made you change so much?"

"You think I've changed a lot?" she asks, flattered.

He nods. "Totally. I don't recognize you anymore."

"I guess I got sick of being who I was. I was stuck, and nothing felt right." He sees I'm different, she thinks. He sees me!

"There was a time you never would have thought of selling this house. Think of all the wonderful times we've had here."

We. He said "we," she thinks with satisfaction. She wonders for a moment if she could bear not living near him.

"Where are the kids?" Keevan asks.

"You just noticed? They're at Jim's."

"I thought his place wasn't big enough for them to stay."

"They're managing. They've done it twice before. I'm surprised how much I like it, just being alone, not having to take care of anyone."

"You didn't have to invite me over," he says.

"Oh, stop," she says. "You know I like doing things for you." She touches his upper arm, squeezes it. His muscles excite her. He's more muscular than Jim, more masculine.

"I haven't been very nice to you," he says suddenly.

"We've been having a disagreement."

"I forget how nice you've always been to me," he says. "You were always the one who thought of me when no one else did." He's getting weepy, the way some men do when they've drunk too much. She's thrilled. Her father used to get like that, before he got just plain mean.

"I care about you," she says. She squeezes his hand. She longs to touch him all over. For a moment, she imagines running her hands over his naked chest, and that alone sends a charge through her. Over dinner, they are easier with each other. Easier than they've been in a long time. She doesn't care if it's the liquor. She's always thought liquor brings out the real person underneath the mask.

After they eat, he settles on the couch as though it's his apartment, lying with his hands behind his head, eyes open, staring up at the ceiling. It warms her that he feels so comfortable. He is never this comfortable around her when he isn't drinking.

"When my grandmother lived down here," he begins after a while, "she had this room painted bright green. I hated it. She said she did it for Grandfather, to remind him of Ireland."

"I remember," Patty says. "It seemed very dark."

"Grandfather said he couldn't care less what color rooms were painted, as long as they were painted."

Patty sits down on the rug beside him, cross-legged, and tentatively touches his hair. It's so thick, so silky, the texture Oriental hair must be, she thinks, only his color is luminous, as though it's grabbed a piece of the setting sun.

"That feels good," he says, closing his eyes.

"I'm glad." She continues stroking his hair for a few minutes, touching the skin along the roots with just the tips of her fingers. She wonders if he is asleep. Just being this close to him makes her happy. His odor, pale and fresh compared to Jim's, is seductive. She longs to put her face into his hair. Dear Jesus, she'll never stop loving him, never stop wanting him.

"You're nice, Patty. Really," he says after a while, still not opening his eyes. She kisses his forehead, his cheekbone. He seems to purr, an assent, as she trails her lips down his cheek to the hollow where his jaw is strong and smooth. Why not? Why can't she do this? How long has she waited for the right moment? When she reaches his lips she hesitates, though, remembering how he's always rejected her before, but instead, as she plants her lips on his, he murmurs, reaches for her with his arms, opens his mouth. His eyes are still closed. But his kiss is hungry and active. She wonders if he knows who he's kissing. She doesn't even want him to think about it. She kisses him more, and his hands reach for her breasts, squeeze them through her blouse. She worries about her padded bra. What will it feel like under her blouse? False. So she pushes his hand away and opens her own blouse, unsnaps the hook. Better he should know how she really feels; no matter how flat, it's better than the lie. But she is surprised at the roughness of his touch. He's making her wince. She had always thought he'd be tender.

He's absolutely wild as he kisses her, lets his hands map her chest and shoulders. There is a tangible anger in his touch. She tries to deny the disappointment she feels. She tries to concentrate on him, what he's feeling. Even though he's clearly drunk, she can tell he's excited, can see his swollen penis pushing up against his jeans. She surprises herself by letting her hand cup it, squeeze it lightly. He moans and, much to her surprise, reaches down to unzip his own jeans. His penis unfurls longer than Jim's, harder than she would have imagined for a man with so much scotch in him. She touches the skin tentatively with her fingers. She's never much liked touching a man's privates. But this is Keevan, she tells herself.

"Squeeze it," he says, squeezing it himself. And so she does, taking its thickness into her palm, letting her fingers encircle it. He starts to pump his hips, absorbed in his own pleasure. "Squeeze it harder," he says.

She is bewildered. This isn't how she thought he'd be. But she doesn't want to stop. She wants that between them: the fact that they've had sex, even if he wasn't himself when it happened.

"Come down on the floor," she tells him.

"The floor?" he asks. His voice is distant and self-absorbed.

"Yes," she tells him. If she asks him to come up to

her bedroom, she'll lose him, she knows. If she gets up for her diaphragm, he'll be back in his apartment in no time. It doesn't matter, she thinks. She just finished her period. All she knows is that she wants him. Any way she can have him. Still, she never imagined, all those nights, watching him sleep, longing for him, that it would come to this. She always thought it would be tender, knowing. That they would look at each other when they made love. That he would really see her. See her.

She undoes her own jeans, clumsily, yanks her panties down. She takes his hand to touch her. She's wet already. She can't remember it ever being like that with Jim. He doesn't seem to know what to do with his hand.

"Touch me," she says. "Touch me."

His fingers, the ones she was certain would be gentle, clumsily explore her, drunkenly slide up into her, but she is still excited by him, can't help it. It's been months since Jim left. Months since anyone has touched her. His fingers find her clitoris, and she pushes against them. She is excited because it's him. It's Keevan. But another part of her is disappointed, sad.

She wants to wake him up somehow. Suddenly she does want him to know it's her. It matters now, the more excited she gets. She takes his penis in her hand, and leaning over, she brings it to her mouth. She's never been able to stand this with Jim. Always hated it. Just the thought of it. But with Keevan . . . with Keevan it will be different. Still, after a moment, he pulls her head away and settles her back down on the floor, gently. It's the one gentle thing he does do. For a moment, he stares at her, she thinks. And then he mounts her, and she feels him sliding into her. So easily. So deliciously. Inside her. Jim's brother, her brother-in-law, thrusting and breathing hard. She wishes he would speak to her. Just to say her name would make everything all right: "Patricia . . . Patty," the way she always thought he would.

Instead he groans. And his thrusting is unrestrained. Like Jim when he was seventeen. Violent.

"I love you, Keevan," she says. "I love you." His whole body stiffens, and then he comes inside her. She feels it. And the sound rising from his throat is more mournful than any she's ever heard. A banshee sound. A weeping sound. As he pulls from her, she sees his face is stricken.

"Oh, Patty," he says, shaking his head. "God, Patty." He pulls up his jeans and underwear, and before he's even zipped his pants, he puts his hand to his head in a gesture of shame. "God. I didn't want to . . . we shouldn't have."

"I wanted to," she says. "It's all I ever wanted."

Next time will be better, the way she's always imagined, she tells herself. She comes toward him to kiss him. But his face is deeply red, and he gently, and with a shiver, pushes her away. "I think I'm going to be sick," he says. He stumbles out the door, and she hears his footsteps charging up the stairs, then the sound of his own door opening and slamming.

His shoes are still here. His scent lingers. She wonders if she should go up to him. Hold his head. No, that would put her in the role she's always been in: his older sister. She feels equally worried and insulted. She shouldn't have made the last one a double.

But time passes, and she hears the plumbing, and when he doesn't come back, she goes up to him, carrying his shoes.

He's on his sofa, half sitting, half lying down. His eyes are narrow slits.

"Don't come near me," he says softly, but it's like a dog. A growl, a warning.

"I came to see if you're all right." She comes toward him. His face is pale, and his skin tone a faint shade of green.

"Don't," he says through his teeth.

"Keevan. Jeez." She steps closer, kneels beside the couch, reaches to touch his cheek. And then he lashes out. The heel of his hand strikes her shoulder and throws her back. She lands hard on her hip. She can't believe he's just pushed her. She's bitten her tongue, and she can taste the blood.

"Please just go away, Patty," he says. His head is turned from her.

"Keevan . . ."

"No."

"Keevan . . ."

"Get out!" His voice is nastier than she remembers it ever being. Drunk nasty. Like the stories of his father. So handsome, Brian O'Connor. But a nasty drunk, her mother used to tell her.

"You wanted to, Keevan. I could feel it. You've always wanted me."

Again she tries to touch him. She doesn't know why. Maybe because she is terrified by the sudden gulf between them. By the cold look in his eye.

"Get out of here, you cunt." His voice is solid ice. She feels sick herself now.

She doesn't know how to get out of the room with any grace. She doesn't know what she's feeling. It's so jumbled up, confused, painful. She stands and turns her back on him, goes for the door.

"But you love me," she says weakly before she closes it.

"Love you? I've never loved you. You're always stalking me. Watching me. Listening. Telling me to stay away from Zoe. I love Zoe. I love her. Not you. I'll never love you."

"Shut up," Patty cries. "Shut up." Her voice is louder than she's ever heard it, and as it spills from her lungs, she truly hates him. "If you think there was any way I wouldn't sell this house, you've just lost your chance," she says. "I'll sell it around you. I'll go to court. I'll do anything not to have to live near you." Her words still echoing, her feet find the stairs, her hand the banister, and when she gets to her apartment, she can only sit and stare and shake for a long, long time.

*    *    *

Zoe, putting Rose to bed, hears Keevan's sister-in-law shouting. At first her words are muffled, and Zoe assumes she's yelling at her children, but then she hears, "I'll sell it around you. I'll go to court."

"She's yelling at Keevan," Zoe mutters to herself.

"*Who's* yelling at Kevin?" Rose says.

"Sounds like Keevan's brother's wife."

"She sure sounds mad."

"Yes."

"What do you think he did to make her so mad?"

"I don't know," Zoe says. "She's mad a lot." Zoe closes her eyes and takes a deep breath. It's hard to think of Keevan now, and yet he comes to her often, any moment her brain is free. He haunts her.

"Aren't we going to see him again?" Rose asks.

"Keevan? Well, sure," Zoe says, attempting cheerfulness. "After all, he lives next door."

"But we didn't go anywhere together this weekend. And he promised he'd look at my science project."

"Well, we have to think of Jamie now," Zoe says. "We have to spend our time helping Jamie to get well."

"I hate Jamie," Rose says.

"Rose, don't say that."

"I do. He's not fair. He wouldn't talk to us, and now why do we have to be so nice to him?"

"It isn't his fault he didn't talk. He was sad, and he couldn't—"

"I'm sad sometimes, and I still talk to you."

Zoe sighs, thinking of all the times she and Rose have had this discussion.

"Things are going to be a lot better with Jamie now," she says. "He's been spending more time talking to you than ever, don't you think?"

"He asked me dumb questions. He thinks I'm still a baby. He mostly just asks me about school and stuff."

"He hasn't spoken to you in a long while. He'll learn. We have to give him a chance."

"I miss Kevin."

After a long while, Zoe says softly, "Me too."

She thinks of Jamie, waiting for her downstairs. She's been touched by how he lights up when she comes into the room these last few days. He needs her more than ever. But sometimes—and she finds herself ashamed to recognize it—the sound of his voice scrapes her spine. She isn't used to Jamie's having a voice.

It's Keevan's voice she longs for. Last night she told him on the phone she still loves him. She couldn't help it. He begged her to come over. She said no, it would be impossible. And he yelled at her that she was teasing him, killing him. He even called her a cunt. It stung her. She thought he must have been drunk to call her that. She felt so bad that after Jamie fell asleep, she actually considered going over to see Keevan. But what could she do to make him feel better? Sleep with him? Tonight she will go anyway. Tonight she must go see him.

Keevan wakes with a hangover and hears his bell. He won't answer it. Doesn't care who it might be. His head feels like a cannonball. His mouth is so dry that even if he had the strength to bear the pain in his head and get himself some water, it wouldn't quench him. Twice since he fell asleep he's awakened and had to take deep breaths not to vomit again. Hot waves swept him, made him take off the clothes he had fallen asleep in. In the dark closet of his brain, he knows there is something he doesn't want to remember. But his head hurts too much to let it come to mind. Even his hands feel stiff and swollen.

In time the memory comes to him anyway. My God. Patty.

"Oh, Jesus," he says aloud. "Oh, God."

He remembers only vague pieces of what happened: the way her padded bra felt like a quilt beneath his fingers. The way she pulled down her own panties and drew his hand to her. He literally shivers when he thinks about how wet she was. How had it ever gotten that far? She was the last person he should have fooled around with. The

last in all the world. She's goddamn in love with him.
And then he knows there were words after he ran upstairs
to escape her. He knows that if he thinks hard enough,
he'll remember them. But he doesn't want to. Can't. He
feels sick at heart. The bell finally stops ringing. Sickening, swirling sleep sucks him down, pulls him under.

Jim opened his eyes as the first light came into the
room, and now he waits for the kids to sit up in their
sleeping bags and ask for breakfast. He really likes having
them visit. He likes hearing their noisy breathing as he
falls asleep. He likes hearing them—well, especially Michelle—go on and on about school projects and Sister this
and Sister that. He likes helping them pick outfits to wear
from the few things they brought with them. He likes
making toast for them in the morning, and scrambling eggs
the way Kim showed him. In a way, it's weird having
them instead of Kim around. He's almost gotten used to
her, though it's taken a lot of patience. Bottom line, she
can be pretty annoying. The way she talks on the phone
and does her nail polish about five times a day and moves
her lips when she reads books and watches stupid TV
shows when he'd rather watch sports on ESPN. There are
plenty of times he's sorry he let her bully him into living
together. He's glad when she goes back to her old apartment in the Village every other weekend, when the kids
come. It'd be better if she lived there full time and let
him do her a few times a week, over his desk in his office
or in her apartment. It was more exciting then. Now she
won't even let him kiss her at the office. And the sex at
home has slackened off, lost its dirty thrill.

It's a funny thing, but being around the kids actually
makes him think of Patty. The last few times he's seen
her, she's looked far hotter than she ever did when they
were married. For instance, since when did she have
breasts? And the way she walks. He knows she's taunting
him, but he likes sassy women. Pushing her chest out,

wiggling her behind in jeans that are tighter than he ever remembers on her. Her body's really pretty nice.

Sometimes he actually thinks about going back to her. She'd be grateful, probably, and the kids would certainly be. Hell, he'd even consider moving to New Jersey with her if she was intent on that. Why not? Maybe she's changed. Maybe she'll be looser in bed than she used to be. Give him a blow job now and then. Even Kim doesn't seem to want to much lately.

After all, it wouldn't be hard to get all romantic. Tell her that Kim is nothing compared to her. It was a fling that taught him a lesson, and now he begs her forgiveness. Jeez. Maybe that's going too far, but hell, it would be awfully comfortable. He misses her stew and pot roast. He misses the way she always took up so little room in bed. And she had real nice hands. He misses how delicate and soft they are, even though she washes floors with them, does the dishes. He's probably never told her he likes her hands. Maybe he was an asshole in that way. Maybe it was partially his fault that there was no passion. He hears Michelle rustle in her sleeping bag. God, he loves her. She's quite something. It sure would be nice to have his family back.

Patty feels surprisingly good when she wakes up. For some reason, no matter how badly Keevan treated her last night (and it was worse than she could have dreamed), truly hating him is a delicious release. He's a worse pig than Jim, she thinks, probably always was. I was just too blind to see it.

Feeling angry is easy for her. A lot easier than loving him ever was. Never knowing how he felt. Hoping he was thinking of her, being disappointed that he wasn't. And getting back at him will be so ridiculously easy. She contemplates the times when she can have people come see his apartment when he isn't there. She'll call a lawyer. She'll find some legal paper that will say if he can't buy Jim's half, the house will be sold out from under him.

She doesn't care if she ever sees the bastard again. She is astonished by the glee she feels.

Taking the bus to A&S, she looks out the window but sees nothing. She is thinking of her date tonight, of Terry Beaumont with his dark hair and eyes, his confident swagger. Screw both the O'Connor boys, she says to herself. Neither of them could ever live up to Ralph anyway.

At the department store she takes the escalator up. She feels young and pretty, like she's sixteen, shopping for clothes for a date. When was the last time she went out on a date? Twenty years ago, maybe. She tries on three of the spikiest, sexiest shoe styles she can find, one pair cut so low it gives her toe cleavage. Like in the Frederick's of Hollywood catalog. Once, she bought a purple teddy from them, but Jim thought it looked silly. Anyway, Frederick's sold shoes like this. And she always thought they'd show off her slender legs. She finds the heels difficult to balance on, but hell, how much walking will she do? Terry no doubt has a car. In the mirror, with her calves elongated by the high heels, her light-auburn hair newly touched up at the roots, her T-shirt showing off the effects of her push-up bra, she looks pretty damn good for a thirty-eight-year-old, and whoever doesn't think so, well, that's their tough luck.

Zoe and Rose are drawing pictures together. Jamie sits on the other side of the room, reading. Zoe is aware of him, can't help thinking of him as an intruder. All she can think about is Keevan and where he might have been last night when she rang his bell.

"Do you think I should make the house pink?" Rose asks.

"Pink would be nice," Zoe tells her. She is surprised that Rose's representation of a house is narrow and four-storied, with a flat roof, a cornice, a stoop. Just weeks ago, she drew them square, with triangular roofs.

"It looks like ours," Zoe says.

"It *is* ours," Rose tells her. "Hey, Mama," she says,

pointing to Zoe's doodle. "That looks just like Kevin. Just like him."

Zoe looks at the doodle and knows Rose is right. The sienna hair, the long legs. She feels her stomach tighten. Where was he at one in the morning?

"It does look like him, doesn't it?"

"We should give it to him. I know he misses us, because we miss him."

Zoe looks up to see if Jamie has taken note of their conversation, but his head is bowed with concentration. He doesn't even know they're there.

"I'm sure he does miss us," she tells Rose softly. Since last night, she has blamed herself for shutting him out. If he was out with someone else, what reason did he have not to be?

"Let's go see him tomorrow," Rose says.

"We can't do that. I told you. Not right now."

"Jamie won't mind," she says too loudly. Zoe watches her glance over at Jamie meaningfully, clearly hoping he's heard what she's said. But he's deep in his book.

"C'mon," Zoe says. "Let's go find that book we were reading." She takes Rose's hand. As they start up the stairs, Rose says again, too loudly, "I want to go see Kevin."

Patty starts getting ready at five. She can't help it. She's been planning it all day. God, she wishes she could have a cigarette. She quit in the middle of July, and usually she doesn't miss it, but now, Boy, could she use one! While she puts on her underwear and makeup, she hears Keevan tromping around upstairs. Dragging around, actually. He probably has the hangover from hell. Serves him right. He sure was a disappointment in the lovemaking department. All those years and years of wanting him, and for what? Well, who cares.

She's ready at six and spends fifteen minutes looking at herself in the mirror, making sure there are no cat hairs on the short, raspberry-colored dress she bought this afternoon, modeling the spiky shoes. Then, because it's still so early, she decides to go up the street and show Maggie.

Darlene answers the door.

"Hi," Patty says. "You visiting? I just wanted to see your mother."

"I moved back in," Darlene says. "For good. I'm not going to spend my life with an alcoholic."

Patty thinks of her own father. "Well, you're doing the right thing," she says. "Maggie here?"

"Yeah, she's upstairs. Daddy's not feeling a hundred percent."

"What's wrong?"

"I'll let her tell you. *Ma!*" Her voice could file your nails, Patty thinks.

"What is it?" Maggie comes down, looking worn out, old.

"Patty O'Connor. God bless you. You look like Princess Diana, I swear."

"I just wanted to show you. I have a date."

"Well, maybe it took getting rid of Jim O'Connor to bring out your natural beauty. I just don't know. Aren't you something! Look at her, Darlene. Ain't she a sight?"

"Yeah," Darlene says without much spirit. "A real sight."

"Thanks to you," Patty tells Maggie.

"Now, who are you dating? I'm a little afraid to hear it."

"You might remember him. Terry Beaumont."

Maggie shakes her head. "Terry the Terror. Lord! You sure know how to pick 'em. He was a troublemaker from day one."

"He seems pretty successful now. He's into real estate, though I'm not quite sure what he does."

"Okay. You know what you're doing. Anyway, come sit down and have a cup. I'll be grateful to sit down myself."

Patty follows Maggie into the kitchen. "What's wrong with Jack?" she asks softly.

"Sit down, take a load off," Maggie says. She puts the water on to boil. "It's his heart, actually. Doctor says it's the size of a melon. So big it's barely doing its job. He's only got a few weeks, Patty."

"Maggie. You didn't say anything."

"We didn't know till the beginning of last week. He had some pain in his chest. Not a lot. I thought maybe he was having one of those mild heart attacks, even though he was sure it was indigestion. The way he eats . . . Anyway, I took him to the emergency room at Methodist. They said it wasn't a heart attack. Worse, in a way, they said. They gave me the name of a heart specialist in Manhattan. We got in fast, because they told him it was serious."

"Isn't there anything they can do?"

"Have a heart transplant, I suppose, but fact is, because of his age, he'd be way down on the list. There aren't so many hearts floating around you know. They give them to young people, or people with young families. It's only right, after all. God gave Jackie a good life. And me with him. Now he can go to his reward."

His reward. What kind of reward is it to die? Patty wonders. She realizes that lately she's hardly gone to church. She doesn't want to confess things that don't seem wrong to her anymore. And she's not so sure about heaven. Who wants to wait until heaven to be happy? She did that for years, and what good did it do her? You wait and wait for something that just might not be there.

But she looks at Maggie's face, still pretty in its own way—a kind face—and is sorry she'll lose Jack soon. They always were so happy, in their teasing, bickering way. Why is it some people get what they want, and others don't? Maggie always seemed to have everything, but now her life won't be the same without Jackie.

"Isn't there anything I can do?" Patty asks.

"Nothing anyone can do," Maggie says, lifting the whistling kettle off the range, pouring water over the tea bags. "We just have to wait. And love him till we can't anymore.'' She sighs, and Patty hears a sound that could be a sob, but Maggie goes on. ''I'm just glad I have my job. It's a comfort to me.''

''I'm glad you have that.''

''You ever going to get one?''

''Let's not talk about me,'' Patty says.

''I want to. It's easier not to talk about Jackie. So, a job . . . you ever going to get one?''

''Yeah. I'm thinking of going back to school. I'm thinking of lots of things. I just want to thank you for getting me to cut my hair and everything. You know, I was kind of blue in those days. It was like I never knew there were possibilities. I never could see beyond the front door. You helped me in that.''

''You must have been ready. You were blue for good reason, I'd say.'' Maggie shakes her head. ''That Jim O'Connor redefines slime.''

Patty laughs. ''I guess you couldn't come out and tell me then.''

''Oh,'' Maggie says, a twinkle in her eye, ''I did my best. How's Keevan?''

Patty feels herself coloring. ''Oh, he's slime too.'' Just remembering what he called her makes her want to take a shower.

''Not Keevan,'' Maggie says. ''Not like Jimmy. Keevan's always been a good boy in his own way. Though I've seen him with that Finney woman lately. So I know why you feel the way you do.''

Patty is relieved Maggie's interpreting her anger with Keevan as being about Zoe. But she'll get back at him. In her own way. She'll get back at him.

Maggie serves the cups of tea.

''After . . . after Jackie . . .'' Patty hesitates, then: ''You going to stay in the house?''

''I don't know,'' Maggie says. ''Darlene will be awfully mad if I don't. She's crazy about the free rent and baby-sitting. But I'm thinking of Arizona, if you want the truth. I'll miss the neighborhood, and Monsignor Patrick and

Saint Agnes and all. I just get the feeling I'll be happier with more sun. Darlene can come along if she likes.''

"We'll all be gone soon," Patty says, holding the warm cup in her hands.

"Well," Maggie says, drawing her sweater around her, "things change, and you gotta let 'em."

Patty nods. "That's what I've been saying." Then she looks down at her watch, startled. "I'm late. My date'll be here soon."

"I'm glad you came," Maggie says. "You cheered me up some."

Patty hugs her. "Seems the least I could do. Plenty of times you've cheered me up."

"It's always been kind of nice," Maggie says, "the way we've all been here for each other."

"It's more than nice," Patty says. "It's the only thing I've ever known." She sighs, knowing it will all be gone soon.

Zoe dials Keevan three, four times, late into the evening. She can hear his phone ringing on the other side of the wall. She thinks she even hears him over there, walking around, opening drawers, climbing up and down the stairs. She has learned there are many reassuring sounds you can hear between the houses. But these sounds aren't at all reassuring when Keevan won't answer his phone.

# FOURTEEN

◆

Now, just a few weeks before Christmas, Eighth Street seems silent and expectant. Though the last of the roses still rest on their stalks, drying as perfect orbs, never losing their petals, a few houses are already graced with lighted, heavily decorated trees in their windows, shimmering in the early dark. Donna and Hal Shea have trimmed their windows and their maple tree out front with tiny glittering Italian lights. And the O'Neills have put electric candles in every window. And a wreath with blue Christmas balls on the overhang above their front door.

Old Mrs. Reilly has been trudging up Eighth Street to Saint Agnes every day, looking sadly at the new decorations, wanting to enjoy them but thinking she's seen them too many years. She walks slowly so as not to slip, then, once at the church, prays that God will let her die before they cart her off to New Jersey, now just a month away. Her family has already sold her house to a young couple with babies. After the contract was signed, the couple came for a last-minute walk-through. Mrs. Reilly watched the wife measure the front-parlor windows. As her sleeves fell back, Mrs. Reilly could see her arms, slender and still brown from summer. That used to be me, she thinks. My arms were strong. I thought I would live forever. She remembers herself in her shirtwaist and skirt and apron. The perfect housewife fresh over from Ireland, scrubbing the windows. Afraid of her husband, worried about the baby in her belly. Scrubbing and coddling and punching this old house into something resembling a home. She thought of the house as old even then. Just thirty-five years old it was, in 1921. Now, almost seventy years later, she wonders why Jesus won't heed her call, won't take her now before the moving van does, plucking her from the only home she remembers.

Up the street, Darlene's baby has the croup. And in the next bedroom, Darlene's father is dying. It takes a great effort to die, Jack Kilkenny thinks, and he hears himself, though it seems from a distance, groaning and sighing. Inside, he feels young, and he is bewildered that the man in the bed is him. He lies in the very bed he's slept in since the day he married Maggie. But now, he has a rented bed tray parked by the bed with water and a fluted papercup of pills, and Maggie's been sleeping in their son Derek's room, which hasn't been slept in for—what?— maybe ten years. She says she doesn't want to disturb him, but Jack thinks that somehow she fears his dying is contagious. And he knows he groans now in his sleep, and wheezes, and has trouble turning over. He misses the heavy certainty of her. And realizes he will never know it again.

When Zoe asks Keevan why he didn't answer his bell or his phone for two days, he tells her he went out of town to see an old friend. She knows her hesitancy in acknowledging his answer means she doesn't believe him. He's always been a terrible liar. But what should he have said? That he was too hungover and racked with guilt about the incident with Patty to see or speak to Zoe?

After the lie, Zoe's calls aren't as frequent; she tells him less about Jamie and herself. But what can he do? He can't barge into her house and tell Jamie what went on between his wife and Keevan all those months. He can't demand that Zoe leave Jamie. He has to wait until she decides for herself.

So Keevan tries to live a normal life. That is his goal. Just be normal. Normal. But nothing seems normal at all. In class, his enthusiasm is at low ebb. His students, responding, slump in their chairs, talk to each other during class, don't read the books he assigns. But he can't help it. The world seems dull and far away. And his books no longer give him solace.

"If you really loved me," he says one night, feeling angry at what the situation is doing to him, "you wouldn't leave me dangling. It's really unbearable. Christ. It would be better if you told me it was over."

"Is that what you want?" she asks. He wonders if that *is* what he wants. In a way, the relief would be delicious. And yet he can't say yes. Not if there's any possibility at all that she'll someday choose him. Because that's what it's going to have to come down to: a choice between Jamie and himself. He suspects she wishes he'd disappear, let her slide back into the half-life she lived before. But he can't. He won't.

He misses Rose nearly as much as Zoe. Misses their Saturdays together in the park, at the aquarium. Her flirtatious laughter. The feel of her arms around his neck when he gave her a piggyback ride. He hears Rose's voice sometimes, playing downstairs with Michelle. He almost goes down to see her, but can't imagine how to speak to her gracefully in front of Patty.

One afternoon, he comes home from school and sees a bright-red piece of paper stuck under his door, and somehow he's certain it's from Rose. The paper is grimy and a little dog-eared, torn, he thinks, from the envelope of a Christmas card. (He can see the edge of a postmark.) On the top is a drawing of a man holding a little girl's hand, with a simple inscription: "I love you, Kevn. Rose." Below it is a little postscript: "I was plaing with Mshell." He hopes Rose knows he misses her, that he isn't staying away from her on purpose. It seems cruel of Zoe to be keeping them apart, for Rose's sake if no one else's.

After dinner one night, he hears a hollow, rhythmic

noise, which disturbs his paper grading. He looks out his back window and sees that Rose is bouncing a ball in her garden in the dark, with just a single light illuminating the red ball. She is wearing a lavender coat and mittens, for it has grown quite chilly. And she swings her leg over the ball with every third bounce, chanting, "One, two, three, O'Leary."

He opens his window and calls out to her. "Rosie!"

"Kevin!" She starts to jump up and down. "Kevin!" Her delight is so obvious, and so unconstricted, that a flood of feeling warms him. Patty is home, and he can't go through her apartment to get to the fence.

He leans out and calls to her. "I love you. I miss you."

"When can I see you?" she yells up at him. "Come over right now."

"I can't."

"Why not?"

"Your mama might not like it."

"I want to see you," she says. She balls up her fists with frustration. This is just how he feels.

"Tell her you do. Tell your mama you do," is all he can say.

She cups her hands around her mouth, and suddenly her voice is very small and private. He can barely hear what she's saying, with the wind pulling her words from him. And then he hears: "Mama loves you too."

"We'll find a way to see each other," he calls. He blows a kiss. She blows one back. He waves, then closes the window. Later, he looks out, and, bouncing the ball listlessly now, she's still looking up at his window. She waves at him, and once again he waves back.

That night, as she gets ready for bed, Rose tells Zoe, "I want to see Kevin. I saw him today. He was in his window. He talked to me. I want to see him."

"I know. But we have Jamie back now. It's very complicated, darling. It would just be very hard right now—"

"I don't care," Rose says. "I want to see Kevin. I want to see him."

She hates her mother for not understanding. "He wants to see me too. Even if you don't want to see him. He wants to see *me*."

Her mother bites her lip as she squirts toothpaste on her daughter's toothbrush, watches quietly while she brushes her teeth. Rose keeps her sad, staring eyes on Zoe, trying to make her feel guilty. It isn't hard to look sad. Missing Kevin is worse than missing her old doormen, or her old neighborhood and school, or even Mary Ellen Axner. Every night when she goes to bed, she imagines what it would be like if Kevin were her father. He would rock her to sleep. He would read to her. He might give her piggyback rides. He might bring her presents when she had the flu. She imagines calling Kevin "Daddy." She's never called Jamie "Daddy." At least not that she can remember.

She suddenly feels so angry her arms and legs stiffen. She wants to punch something. Instead she grabs the toothpaste and twists off the cap and starts squeezing. The gel flies from the tube in glossy ice-blue worms, starts to fill the sink.

"Rose, for heaven's sake," her mother says. "Stop that." But Rose strangles the tube right up to its missing cap. Then she kicks Zoe in the shin.

"You stop that." Zoe, outraged, grabs Rose by the shoulders. "That is not acceptable behavior," she says in a very high voice.

"Not letting me see Kevin is NOT ACCEPTABLE BE-HAVIOR!" Rose yells back. She runs to her room, throws herself on her bed, and won't say another word to her mother, though Zoe asks her questions about Homer and even tells jokes. But Rose, in her anger, is not even tempted to talk. She turns her face to her pillow and doesn't move an inch until Zoe finally leaves.

*     *     *

Patty can't believe her luck in finding Terry Beaumont. He wants to be with her all the time. He tells her she's beautiful. He brings her flowers. He likes her cooking. He enjoys spending time with the children. And he is so wonderful to her in bed. She didn't know sex could be so exciting. He makes her feel beautiful. He calls her "my little seal" sometimes, because, he's told her, she makes noises like a happy little seal when she comes. She wishes she could tell Jim. She wishes she could tell everyone.

Last night when they were making love, he used his mouth to make her come. She didn't know men ever did that. At first she felt embarrassed, worried.

"It tastes so sweet," he told her. Then that strong mouth she's become so crazy about kissing teased her, stroked her, and had her bucking up and down on the bed till the box spring sang. She came so hard she thought the light had switched on in the room.

"Well, you're a regular little hot tomato, aren't you?" Terry said. Patty blushed. "How would you like it if I did that again?"

"Please," she whispered. "Now."


Jamie sees that Zoe has changed. He senses it long before he understands it. But he is still so tired. Still so weak. He tries not to think about how it disturbs him. The way she jumps sometimes when he speaks to her, as though he's intruded on a good dream. A new secretiveness. Sometimes when he comes into the room, she is on the phone and hangs up without saying goodbye. Her eyes are more distant, her touch less frank. Still, every night when she comes to bed with him, her presence is kinder and more soothing than anything else in his life.

One night, he says, "Do you wish I still weren't speaking? Was it easier for you when I wasn't?"

"Easier? I was miserable that you were suffering."

"But you had more of a life then?" he asks. He searches her face for confirmation, clues.

"I don't know what you mean," she says. She bites the back of her right hand.

"You told me there are wonderful people in the neighborhood, and yet you haven't gone out or done anything once since I've been better. I don't want to keep you from that," he says. "I don't want to see people yet, but I don't want to keep you from doing what makes you happy." The truth is, he fails to understand why she's moved them here. Brooklyn still feels foreign to him. And this house may never feel like home.

"But I want to be with you," she says. "I like staying home to be with you." He looks at her. Her eyes seem transparently honest. But when he takes her right hand in his, the teeth marks, the raw skin, tell him the truth.

"What does Rose think of me?" Jamie asks one night.

Zoe jumps. She's been sewing a button on Rose's coat, a task that reminds her far too much of working at her parents' dry cleaners. She sets the coat down in her lap.

"You startled me," she says.

"Did I? I'm sorry. I just wanted to know."

"About Rose?"

"About what she thinks of me."

She hesitates. She can't tell him the truth. That Rose resents his taking Zoe's time away from her. And keeping the two of them away from Keevan. "She feels as though you're a stranger in some way," Zoe says.

"I guess I can't blame her," Jamie says. "Do *you* feel as though I'm a stranger?"

The question prickles the back of Zoe's neck. She looks up at him. He is gaunt, and though some of his natural color is coming back, he is wan and ghostlike. A concentration camp victim, she thinks, and shudders, envisioning the number on her mother's arm, which she used to stroke sometimes, wishing it would miraculously disappear. She bunches up Rose's coat, tries to find composure in the fabric gathered on her lap.

"Yes," she finds the courage to say. "Yes. You seem like a stranger sometimes."

"I thought I did."

"Why?"

"You're different to me now," he says. He looks sad, and his green eyes are muddied with the thought.

"I didn't realize I was," she says. "I've tried not to be."

"I've put you through so much," he says. "Anyone would have resented it."

"Let's not talk about it," she says.

"You deserve better than what I've given you. Better than me," he says.

She finds she can't look at him. "Don't say that."

"I've probably never said anything truer in my life," he says.

"I love you, Jamie," she tells him, but her voice comes out low and odd, and the words echo insincerely.

He doesn't answer her. And for a long time there is a silence that keeps her from picking up her needle again. That keeps him from opening his book. They sit there, avoiding each other's eyes. Suffering.

"Maybe loving me isn't enough," he says. "To survive what I put you through."

"We're sitting here, aren't we?" she asks. "We've survived."

He stands up and shakes out the legs of his grey flannel trousers. He squeezes his book so tightly in his hand she can see white haloes on his knuckles. Hands she has loved for so long.

"I'm not certain," he says. "We're here," he says. "But maybe we haven't survived."

Someone's bought the house, Patty tells Keevan. A couple named Dancer. The name is a nasty incantation. Dancer. Dancing right over his heart. They want to be in at the beginning of the year. They offered the full price if Patty and Keevan will accommodate them.

"Full price!" Patty says, her eyes aglow. It's the first time in nearly a month she's spoken to him. She stands outside his door in a short wool skirt, cigarette in her hand. Smoking again; serves her right, he thinks. But she looks too good, too confident. Sexy, even.

"Do you want to come in?" he asks, not wanting her to.

"No. I just wanted to tell you. We sold it for four hundred and seventy-five thousand. That's over two twenty-three five apiece after commission. More than I expected. The agent was real happy about it. Said she never expected it."

"When?" he asks numbly.

"We got the bid last night."

"No. When do we have to actually be out?"

"January fourth we close," she tells him. "It's like being rich."

"What are you going to do?" he asks her.

"Move in with my mother if we don't find a place before then. But I'm going to buy a town house. Something really nice. Terry's been taking me around. He owns a lot of real estate out there. Knows a lot of agents."

"Terry?"

"Beaumont. The man I've been seeing."

"Oh."

She smirks at him, holding a tiny ceramic plate under her cigarette to catch the ashes.

"You're rich, Keevan. You can do anything you like. Buy a littler house. You could get a mortgage, use the money as a down payment."

"Yeah."

"You could."

"Thanks for telling me," he says, and starts to shut the door. He wants her gone.

"Wait," she says. Her face suddenly changes; she looks less confident, more like herself.

"What?"

"What *will* you do?" she asks. Her voice is sweet and pleading. He can tell she wants to be friends again.

"Why do you care?" he says, and shuts the door in her face.

His whole body sings with fury. He can't contain it. Drawing his leg back, he slams his booted foot into the desk chair. It falls heavily and skitters halfway across the floor. A bolt of pain shoots all the way up to his thigh.

He feels as though his life's in ruins. He's lost Zoe, Rose. He's even been a crappy teacher lately, his mind not on his class. Yesterday one of his favorite students, Luz Sanchez, asked him if he was all right. She stood there, nervously clutching her books to her chest. She's the sort of student he's lived to teach. Who lights up at big ideas, loves literature. Since Jamie's awakened, he feels he's been able to give her nothing. Nothing. And soon even the one thing that's been certain in his life— his home—will be gone.

Alicia, back from Italy and glowing, stands at the front door in a chartreuse minicoat, puffing her cigarette and peering down the street.

"I think I'm going to move to Brooklyn. Even after Florence, this place is Disney picturesque. Manny's parking the car."

"Manny's here! I'm so glad. You didn't say he was coming."

"He was interested in seeing a dead man risen. How's the resurrection going?" She steps into the foyer, begins unbuttoning her coat.

"Jamie's so much better. You'll see. He'll be thrilled to see you."

"He'd better be. It took forty-five minutes to get here. They're having a street fair or something on Flatbush Avenue." She calls up the staircase. "Are you up there, Sir James?" Zoe has always been charmed by Alicia's certainty and rebelliousness. But today the combination seems like rain after a long drought.

Jamie comes down the stairs slowly, putting a bookmark in his book. "Alicia?"

With Alicia watching, Zoe is extra aware of how stiff he seems, how unsteady. How uneasy his face appears, as though he worries Alicia may be more than he can handle.

"You look like hell," Alicia says.

"Well, thanks," he says softly. He kisses her cheek.

"Zoe says you're on the road to recovery. You look like you should hit a tanning salon."

"It wasn't on my list."

"Is Rosie here?" Alicia throws her coat over the banister. Her skirt, made of something stretchy, is the color of Pepto-Bismol and even shorter than the coat. A pink Band-Aid. Her purse is just like her mother's Chanel chain bag, except that it's clear plastic, embedded with colored condoms, rolled as they might be in their package and lined up to create rows of multi-colored polka dots. "I brought her something." She pulls from her purse a tiny china dog that looks astonishingly like Homer.

"I bought it off a friend of mine's daughter. It was sitting on her dresser. 'I'll give you ten dollars for this. I have to get it for my niece,' I told her. She knew a sweet deal when she saw one."

"I'll call Rose," Zoe says. "She'll love it."

"No. Let me talk to Jamie first. Come into this room, young man. What do you call it again, Zoe?"

"The parlor."

"What a charming tree. White lights and gold ribbons." Alicia rearranges a golden bow on one of the branches. This year, Zoe put up the tree for Rose because she felt she had to, but she was listless as she tied the wired ribbons to the boughs. And the sight of the cockeyed bows now makes her weary. "And you've hung mistletoe," Alicia says, trying to reach for it, touch it. "Quaint. Mother would love it. If it were in Manhattan, that is. Sit here, darlin'. You've been rather a bore, you know. You have a lot of nerve, not speaking for months like that."

"Give him a break, Alicia," Zoe says softly, watching Jamie's face for signs of pain.

Instead he chuckles softly. "Yes, I'm sure I was awful."

"And why shouldn't he know it? You baby him, Zo. He drove you practically mad, not talking."

"I know I drove her mad. She told me yesterday I seem like a stranger. And I can't blame her."

Zoe feels herself blushing. "I only answered your question when you asked. I didn't tell you—"

"Every time you're better, you won't see a psychiatrist. Won't talk to anyone. And she's your ally. Lets you get away with it. Well, I'm not going to let it happen this time. You have to think of her and Rose for a change."

Jamie looks up at Alicia with eyes like a child, sheepish yet agleam with respect. "You know I . . . I've never been comfortable . . . talking about myself with anyone."

"Too bloody bad," Alicia says. "You just will have to get over your shyness. And they've got a new drug a minute these days—you'll be a poet or a politician in no time. They get depressives right off their flabby asses and into life with a bang. Ah, here's Manny," she says to the ring of the doorbell. "Go let him in, Puss," she says to Zoe.

Zoe is happy to see Manny at the door. Clear-faced, kind. Simply dressed. The only man Alicia's dated that she cared for. Oil paints under his fingernails. No smile was ever more genuine.

"Dear Zoe," he says.

"I'm so glad to see you," she says. "How was Italy?"

"I was there with Alicia. How could it be bad?" He grins, hugging Zoe hello.

"Here he is," Alicia says to Manny. "My dead brother, walking and talking. A miracle."

"Jamie, good to see you," Manny says. Zoe notices that after shaking Jamie's hand, Manny comes up next to Alicia, slides his arm around her, and that Alicia lets him, smiles at him.

Now she turns to Zoe and, with a voice like honey, says, "May we have a drink? Seltzer for me. You too?

Yes, Manny wants seltzer too. And something to stick this damn butt and these ashes into. I don't think you want me to squash it out on your Victorian floor.''

"No. I'm sorry. I should have offered.''

"Good old Aunt Delia looks quite grand presiding over the parlor, don't you think?'' Alicia is saying as Zoe runs down the stairs for a saucer and the seltzer. As she quarters a lime, she finds her hands are shaking. She doesn't know why.

When she returns, Jamie's actually laughing. Zoe can't remember seeing him laugh once since the onset of this round of depression. Not even since he's been better. She hands the seltzers to Alicia and Manny, lets Alicia stub out her cigarette on the saucer, and takes it from her. Then sits quietly in a nearby chair. If only she were as breezy as Alicia. If only she could rush through life and feel just the good parts—for wasn't that Alicia's secret? She enjoyed herself. Always. She enjoyed life. And didn't run away from pleasure. She had a way of seeking it out. And, when it wasn't there, creating it. God. What a talent! To do that. To not only be able to stand pleasure but *create* it. Thrill in it.

Later, after Alicia has charmed Rose by standing on her head (it reminds Zoe of Keevan) saying, "See, isn't it wonderful. This skirt is so tight you can't even see my undies,'' and made Jamie promise he will go to see the psychiatrist she's interviewed for him, she corners Zoe down in the kitchen as she pours more seltzer for everyone.

"Well, he looks like hell. But not as bad as you do. What on earth's happening to you, lovey? Is it more of a strain having him better?''

"No. Of course not,'' Zoe says.

"I think it would be. When he's sick, you can always imagine that when he's well he'll be normal. The way it used to be. He'll never be really normal.''

"Don't say that.''

"Why not? It's true. If he goes to a doctor, maybe there

will be some new medicine that will actually help this time. But chances are, considering his history, it won't keep him out of a depression forever.''

"Why are you telling me this?" Zoe says.

"I told you before. When he was sick. It's not fair to you.''

"I don't want to talk about this," Zoe says.

"Fact is, I don't think you're helping him, not if you get yourself all depressed too. What's happening with him?" Alicia points her thumb toward the opposite wall.

"Who?" But Zoe knows. Alicia has often asked on the phone: Are you still getting laid? Are you happy?

"Cary Grant."

"He still lives next door."

"I hope you still see him."

"I haven't. Not since Jamie woke up."

Alicia shakes her head. "You put too much store in Jamie, and it will kill you, Zoe."

Zoe chews her lip. "If you ever tell Jamie . . ."

"I wouldn't do that. Christ. I'm on your side, stupid." She takes another cigarette from her condom bag and lights it. "Did you fall in love with him? The man next door?" She looks up through her dyed lashes. "I bet you have."

"Why do you say that?" Zoe asks, trying to keep her voice neutral and steely.

"You do everything with sincerity. I envy you, in a way. But it's a failing too. You have no self-protection. You don't have my cynicism, or even Jamie's self-centeredness. So you did fall in love with him?"

Zoe nods and looks away.

"Well, then, for God's sake, don't give him up. You need someone, Zoe. Someone who can give you something. For the first time in my life, I know what that means. Manny scares me, he loves me so much. Sometimes I think to myself, How can he think I'm beautiful? How can he love me? Sometimes I actually hate him for it. I look in the mirror and think he should have better taste.''

"Alicia . . ."

"No. Listen. It's just that lately, most of the time, I forget to ask myself why he feels this way, and Zoe, I'm happier than I've ever thought possible."

"You're always happy, Alicia."

"Ah, naive child. Believe me. It's a smoke screen. A lie. If you can't be pretty, at least be lively . . . you know. But this time—with Manny—it's different. It's real. The only time I ever saw you the least bit happy and normal and lit up was that time when you were seeing this guy. Listen to me: if you love him, let him be in your life. Leave Jamie for him. *Have* a life, for God's sake. You deserve it."

"I appreciate what you're saying—"

"Hogwash. You hate my saying it. You'd rather hide away with Jamie and never come up for air. That's clear as day." She grabs the seltzer glass and drinks half of it down. "This was mine, wasn't it?"

"Yes."

Her silver bracelets clattering, she puts her hand to Zoe's cheek. "Listen to me," she whispers. Later, Zoe can't get the sound of her words out of her mind. "If you love him, let him be in your life."

That night, Zoe wakes to a rhythmic pounding. She presses her ear to Keevan's wall, then she realizes she is hearing it better from the hall. It is only midnight, but feeling oddly exhausted lately, she's been going to bed early. She's groggy now in the way you are when you've slept only an hour and have been snatched from the deepest sleep. And she's painfully stiff. Lately, every time she rises from sleep, she is so stiff she can barely move. She must be clenching up in her sleep, she thinks. Fisting up to be as small as possible. Then waking crumpled as a linen suit. So now she has to hold hard to the railing, as her stiff back and legs feel unreliable. She limps into Rose's room and is so startled that at first she merely watches, as Rose, in her nightgown, but wearing the cowboy boots that Alicia brought her from Phoenix last Christmas, kicks the wall by the fireplace. Each kick is fortified with an astonishing amount of intent, venom even, as Rose hauls her leg back as far as she can before kicking. So far she has managed only to chip the butter-yellow paint and a few flakes of plaster and to smudge the wall.

"Rosie! What are you doing?" She isn't even sure that Rose is awake. The vision of her in her lace-edged gown and cowboy boots is so dreamlike, so surreal.

"I'm going to see Kevin," she says. "I'm going to see him."

"Well, how does kicking the wall help?" Zoe asks, putting her arm gently around Rose's chest and arms, trying to draw her back without a struggle. But Rose does struggle, kicking the wall even more furiously despite Zoe's effort to hold her.

"I'm going to kick a hole in the wall," she says. "I'm going to see Kevin," she says. "I'm going to kick the wall down. And you can't stop me."

The intensity of Rose's feeling envelops Zoe, and the desperation to see Keevan overtakes her as well. It jolts her like a dentist's drill hitting a nerve.

"We'll call him in the morning. Before he leaves for work. We'll arrange to see him."

"No," Rose says with certainty. "Now. I want to see him now."

Zoe looks at the clock on Rose's wall, a duck whose legs swing like a pendulum. It is ten minutes past midnight. She holds her breath a moment, wondering if she has the courage to call him. But the look on Rose's face galvanizes her.

"Come on. Follow me," she tells Rose and, taking her hand, crosses with her through the dressing room into the guest room, where there is a phone. Taking a deep breath before she presses the last digit, she simply prays he won't be too angry to see them. Or too tired. Or purposely remote.

"Hello?" His voice is an odd mixture of annoyance

and curiosity. Who could be calling him at this hour? it says.

"It's me," Zoe says. "It's Zoe."

"Zoe."

"I know it's late," she says. "Did I wake you?"

"No. I was reading."

"Tell him we want to see him," Rose says loudly.

"Did you hear some pounding coming from our side of the wall?" Zoe asks him.

"Yes," he says. "I was asking myself how many pictures you could possibly be hanging at this hour."

"It was Rose," Zoe says, "trying to kick the wall down. Wanting to kick the wall down to see you."

She can hear him heave a sigh. "Poor baby. Is she there? Does she want to speak to me?" Zoe is nearly made insensible by the tenderness of his voice.

Rose is staring, waiting, wanting to be part of the dialogue. "Tell him," Rose says.

"Can we come over and see you?" Zoe asks. "I know it's late . . ."

"Oh, Zoe. Come. Come now," he says.

"In ten minutes."

"As soon as you can," he says. His voice is so thrilled, so open. She hangs up.

"Go brush your hair. Brush your teeth," Zoe says. "I'm going up to do mine."

Upstairs, she closes the door between the bedroom and the dressing room so Jamie won't wake. She reties her robe, a pretty one Alicia gave her last Christmas. She brushes her teeth, stares at her face without makeup, picks up a lipstick but decides not to. She is doing this for Rose, she tells herself. Just so Rose can see him. Still, thinking about what Alicia told her, she smooths her hair back into her braid. If you love him, *let him be in your life.* Could she do that? Why does it frighten her so?

Downstairs again, she bundles Rose into a robe, a coat, and puts on a coat herself. The air is biting. A night of frost. It feels as though it might snow. The gate seems to clank even more loudly than usual in the cold and silence of the night. The house lights are haloed with the damp air.

He is waiting at his door. When she sees his face, she stops dead still on the sidewalk. He is smiling. And standing calmly, watching them, two refugees in robes and shoes and coats. Escaping to a benevolent country.

"Come on, Mama," Rose says. "Come on." She drags Zoe forward, then lets go of her hand and runs up the steps to Keevan. Keevan folds her into his arms, lifts her high into a long embrace. Zoe watches from the gate. The way he closes his eyes when he holds her daughter. The way he opens his eyes to find Zoe. She climbs the steps slowly.

"Oh, Zo," he says, still holding Rose but drawing Zoe toward him, so his cheek can rest on her head. She tries to keep herself stiff. She's afraid to let him think this is a change in the way things are. Jamie still needs her. She has to step back so she doesn't cleave to Keevan. But my God! His face breaks her heart with its beauty, its clarity. The pale brows, the solid chin, the mouth, a strong line softened by the sight of her.

She steadies her voice before she speaks. "Keevan," she says.

"Come in," he tells them. She can tell he's rattled by her seeming coolness. Yet she feels that if she so much as breathes in his scent she will drown in feeling for him. She lets him climb the steps first, with Rose snuggling against him, tries hard to keep her distance from him.

When they reach the landing, the very color of his apartment seems to invite them in. The lighting, the books. A volume lies opened and upside down on his ottoman.

"*Wuthering Heights*?" she asks. "Are you teaching that this year?"

"Yes. I thought it was a good thing to teach."

"I thought you said it was sentimental."

He smiles at her, doesn't take his eyes from her. "I guess I've become a sentimental kind of guy." He shrugs. "Tell me how you are, Rosie," he says, lifting her chin.

She sits on his sofa in her nightgown, her cowboy boots crossed at the ankle, as prim as an old-fashioned portrait.

"Fine." She yanks off her boot and looks at her toes. She has on no socks.

"Do you have a sore toe?" Her big toe is red and tender-looking, mottled beneath the tiny pearly nail. He takes her foot into his large hand and kisses it. The tenderness of his lips on that grubby set of toes bruises Zoe's heart.

"Did you know it was me trying to kick through your wall?" Rose asks proudly.

"No. I thought it was King Kong. I'm very relieved it's you."

"Who's King Kong?"

"A giant man-eating ape."

"For real?" she asks, wide-eyed.

"No. It's just a story. But I'm still glad it's you. I don't know what King Kong and I would have talked about."

"Zoos, maybe, if he didn't want to eat you," Rose says.

"He probably would have an opinion on zoos; you're right," Keevan says.

"I don't think he'd like them. I've been meaning to ask you, have you been to the zoo or Coney Island lately?" Rose blinks her eyes with interest. The grown-up phrasing of her question makes Keevan and Zoe look at each other and smile, as conspiratorially proud of her as two parents. His smile sets off another click of the tumblers inside her.

"I haven't been to either," he says. "The zoo is no fun without you. And Coney Island is probably closed for the season. It's too cold by the beach for carnival rides."

"They should put it in a huge house," Rose says. "All of it inside, under glass."

"It wouldn't be as much fun in the summer, though," Keevan says. "It wouldn't be the same on the Ferris wheel, looking over the ocean, if it were under glass."

"I guess not," she says. "Can we go back when it opens again?"

"I'd love to."

"We can win some more dogs," she says. "We did pretty good winning those dogs."

"We practically wiped the guy out, we won so many dogs."

"We practically wiped him right out," Rose agrees, turning to Zoe.

Keevan looks up. "Do you want something to drink?" he asks Zoe.

"Yes," she says. "Hard liquor."

He laughs. "Me too. You want Coke or cream soda, Rose?"

"I can't drink that stuff. Mama says it's bad for my teeth." Rose looks over at Zoe with accusing eyes.

"We'll make an exception," Zoe says. "You want cream soda?"

Rose nods.

"When the cream soda's done, that will tell us it's time to go home," Zoe says. "Okay? It's a school day tomorrow."

"I'll drink it reeeeeeeeally slow," Rose says.

"No you won't."

"Okay. I'll try not to. But I have to drink it kind of slow so the bubbles don't go up my nose. If you drink it too fast, it can come out your nose. And that would be gross."

"I once saw a man on television who drank milk through his nose and squirted it out of his eye," Keevan says.

"Eeeewww!" Zoe and Rose say together.

"Really. It was on a late-night show. People doing stupid tricks. I think he had some kind of hole in his bottom eyelid. He pulled his eyelid down and—"

"Don't give her ideas," Zoe says, laughing.

"I wish I could have seen that," Rose says. "Did it really squirt?"

"Like a fountain."

As they talk and laugh, Zoe tries to reconcile the giddiness she feels with the strictures she's put on seeing him.

Maybe they could see each other sometimes. Maybe Alicia's been right that she still needs him as a lover. God knows, just sitting near him, seeing the rosy skin of his neck, the crisp corner of his jaw, the pale-fawn color of his eyes, she is painfully aroused. Inappropriately aroused. What the hell can she do with this kind of feeling now? She would sell her house right now just to feel his arms around her.

"Can I get you another drink?" he asks her. She is surprised to see how fast she's emptied the last one.

"Better not," she says.

"Why not?"

"Okay."

"Did I tell you Patty sold the house?" he tells her, handing her the drink. "The contract came today."

"You must feel awful."

"I can't stop her. I can't buy her half from her. God, if I only had the money! It's the one time I wish I weren't a teacher."

Zoe bites her lip, wishing she could give him the money to save his house. Her money means nothing to her and would mean so much to him. But no matter how long she's been married, it's not really her money. It's Jamie's. And Keevan would never take it.

"What house?" Rose asks.

"This house," Keevan says.

"They're selling your house?" Rose asks. "You won't live next to us anymore?" She looks so stricken Zoe takes her arm, smooths her robe beneath her fingers.

"The new people want to be in by January. They're coming from Chicago."

"What will you do?" Zoe asks.

"Move into our house," Rose says. "We have a guest room."

"I wish I could," Keevan says.

"Why can't you?"

"I don't think . . ." Keevan looks to Zoe for a reasonable answer. His smile seems lethal.

"We couldn't do that. Jamie doesn't even know Keevan."

"Who cares?" Rose says.

"We can't," Zoe says.

"I want to go home," Rose says suddenly.

"You didn't finish your cream soda yet."

"I want to go home." Her face is red, and then she's crying. "You didn't tell me Keevan was moving."

"I didn't know it was really happening," Zoe says.

"I want to keep the napkin," Rose says. She holds up the napkin Keevan's given her with the soda, damp, limp, and torn.

"Okay," Zoe says. "You can keep it."

Keevan pulls a tissue from a box in the bookshelf. Rose is sobbing now.

"Here," he says. He dries her tears. Makes her blow her nose. "It sucks, doesn't it?"

"*Keevan,*" Zoe says. But censuring his language now seems ridiculous.

"It sucks," Rose says, sobbing even louder. "I want to keep the Kleenex too."

"I didn't want to move. My mean old sister-in-law is making me."

"Let's kill her," Rose says, hiccuping with tears.

"No. She doesn't deserve that. It's not really her fault. Not really."

"I hate her."

"Don't cry, baby girl," he says, smoothing Rose's hair behind her ears. "I'm going to find a place close by. So I can see you often. Now that your mommy knows how much you want to see me, she'll let you come see me whenever you want. Right, Zoe?" He looks at Zoe pointedly.

"Right," she says. How could it not be so now?

"Come here." He lifts Rose to his lap. Zoe watches her fold into him so effortlessly, so willingly. He rocks his body, and she sways in the pod of his arms.

"Whenever you want, you can see me," he chants to her. "Whenever you want."

Zoe closes her eyes and feels her own throat close and spasm. She can feel Keevan looking at her. Even through her closed lids, she can see him.

After she has brought Rose back home and put her to bed, she goes to her window and looks out at the street. She wishes he lived across the street, so she could see him in his window. See what he's doing. Has he gone back to his book? Is he pacing and looking out the window too? Jamie stirs when she gets into bed beside him. They have kissed and hugged in bed, but they have not made love yet. Now she turns to him. His shoulders are so bony beneath her fingers.

"Jamie," she whispers.

"What? Zoe? Are you all right?"

She kisses his forehead, his sharp cheek, his chin. Her hand reaches for his penis and gently takes it from between his legs. Her heart is pumping wildly, and her hormones, aroused by Keevan, spill into her body, make her treasonous. Even if it isn't Keevan, she will pretend. She will take what she has. His eyes open wide as she slides her hand along the soft shaft, causing it to stiffen almost instantly.

"I thought you didn't want me anymore," he says. "I was afraid to ask if you did." His voice is plaintive and childlike.

"I still want you," she says. She isn't sure if it's true. The longing she feels has all come from Keevan. But it is so strong, it carries her along, though Jamie feels unfamiliar in her hands. Still, when she straddles him and draws him inside her, the feeling is tremendously keen, a simultaneous slice of pain and pleasure, and she moans so loud she worries briefly if Keevan will hear, will know.

"Oh, sweetheart," Jamie cries out as she rides him, making him come with a tremendous shattering yell of pleasure. But she can't let out her own moan of pleasure as an orgasm splashes over her. For her moan is suddenly blocked by the spasm in her throat. And for once she is grateful that she cannot shed tears.

The next day, Zoe goes to a discount perfume and makeup store on Twenty-sixth Street. When the woman at the register turns away to help another customer, Zoe palms handfuls of eye shadows in tiny tortoiseshell cases and slips them into her bag, lipsticks, whatever she can grab out of the display, tiny perfume bottles, towering cobalt-blue towers of Italian eye-makeup remover. She walks out, her bag's strap cutting into her shoulder. Mine. All mine, she thinks. Later, at the office, she pours them into her brown paper lunch bag to throw them away, trying not to even touch them as they spill from the recesses of her purse. One of the perfume bottles slips, shatters against her chair leg. And though she gathers up the glass from the grey office carpet, blots away all she can, the scent lingers.

"Jeez," Stuart says later. "You opening a whorehouse in here?"

That night, after Keevan thinks Rose must be asleep, and maybe Jamie too, he calls Zoe. He did not sleep all the night before, he was so wild with Zoe, with Rose. Never has he wanted anything so much as their presence. Their absence has reminded him day after day of losing Ralph, of having to remember that he would never see Ralph again, no matter how intense his longing. But his loss of Zoe is a grief he can reverse. And he knew it last night when he looked at her. There are tendernesses even her coolness can't hide.

"Zoe, please, can you come over? I know it's hard to now, but . . . you did last night. You managed."

"Jamie was sleeping."

"Is he sleeping now?"

"I don't know."

"Come when he is."

She is silent for a moment. "There's nothing wrong, is there?" she asks.

"Nothing you can't fix."

"Maybe it would be better if we took a walk, then," she says. "It's safer."

"If you need to feel safe from me."

"I'll call you when I leave."

A half hour later, they agree to meet. He waits on the stoop for her, in his coat, wishing he'd brought gloves. In two weeks it will be Christmas. And hard on its heels, New Year's Day. This fall, when things were going well, he had imagined he would spend Christmas with Zoe and Rose. He had imagined that they would be his family. And that Jamie would lie in his endless coma upstairs while they shared presents and ate turkey and put logs in the fire downstairs beneath the portrait of beautiful Aunt Delia. Now he knows that Christmas will mean packing boxes and imminent change. He dreads going down into the cellar, sifting through the cartons of family things that have accumulated since 1917. But if he lets Patty or Jim do it, they will discard it all. They have no sense of history or rootedness. He will have to begin soon. Hundreds of mementos lie down there in decaying cardboard. Old striped suitcases of photographs. Trunks of baby shoes and tattered letters, dance dresses, board games, and christening gowns.

Zoe comes out of the house, pale in her grey coat. When she passes through the gate, he takes her hand. She doesn't pull it away. Her knitted glove feels fleecy beneath his bare fingers.

"I'm scared to be alone with you," she says.

"It's just me. Your old pal Keevan," he says gently. He is instantly warmed by her presence. Walking up toward Eighth Avenue, he notices the gardens, all dormant now, the soil frozen, only the evergreens giving color. Maggie's rosebushes are covered with protective Styrofoam cones. The McNallys' metal pillar, which in summer supports a tangle of morning glories, is bare and shaking in the wind.

He will never spend another winter on this street. He will never be a citizen of this block again. If he weren't holding Zoe's hand, he would feel as bleak as the gardens.

"It's so hard to think I won't live here anymore."

"For me too," she says softly. "I don't know what it will feel like knowing you're not next door. But I don't know how long I'll be here myself. I don't think Jamie likes it here. It's possible we'll end up selling our house too."

"Leave him, Zoe."

"How can I?"

"How can't you?"

"Is it right to do things just for pleasure?" she asks. "I think that's what everybody thinks these days. Everyone just wants to be happy. Isn't there such a thing as duty? I married him for better or worse . . . and this is worse than I bargained for. Still, he's my husband, and I've loved him for a long time. It's not his fault he's sick. Shouldn't I stick by him?"

"You've constructed a faultless argument," Keevan says dryly. "Now, if only you believed it."

"It's a reasonable argument. It's the right thing to do."

"And you're making him terribly happy, being there? Is he happy?" He watches her carefully. How tentative she looks, how confused. Maybe he has a chance. "Is he happy?" he asks again.

Zoe shakes her head. "I don't know. No. He's wary of me. He thinks I don't love him anymore," she confesses.

"Do you?"

"I love you," she says. Her words light the sky for him. Blind him.

"Oh, Zoe . . ." Her blond hair is slipping from its braid; it catches the streetlight like a halo. He takes it in his hand. The thickness of the silvery braid, the weight of it, makes her so real to him somehow.

"It was easier before I met you," she says softly.

He would like to wrap this braid around his very veins, so fierce, so intense, are his feelings for her.

"If it weren't for Rose . . . ," she says. "You've made things so much better for Rose."

"You have a right to be happy too, you know," he tells her softly, turning her toward him. He feels her trembling. "I think you're just afraid to be happy. Someone told you a long time ago you don't deserve it."

"Yes," she says. "I know that now. My parents made me feel I deserved nothing. Lately, I think about how much I want to be happy. I was happy when we had that time together. But how can I leave him? He depends on me, Keevan."

"He has his family. And he needs care you can't give him. You don't have to abandon him. You can still stay close, see what happens."

"He might kill himself, for God's sake," she says.

"Or you might kill yourself by living with him. You once told me that you used to feel dead, living there with him."

She pulls her hand away. "How can we be happy, stepping on his bones?"

"If he's not happy now, thinking you don't love him . . . would it really be stepping on his bones? Maybe he'd be relieved."

They've reached Prospect Park West now and turn around, back down Eighth Street, walking again past the small limestone houses that Patty recommended to him. But this block is nothing like their block. One side is all apartment buildings, and these small houses don't have the daunting grandeur of the brownstones. A few are lit, and Keevan attempts to see inside, but all he can make out are ceiling trims and curtains. The bare trees sway in the wind. The branches scuff the night sky, mournfully soughing.

"I could make you happy. Even if I don't have any money," he says. "Not like you're used to. Are your doubts about the money?"

"I don't care about money."

"Rose would maybe have to go to public school."

"Jamie's family would pay for private school. They might not even blame me. His sister wouldn't. She's already encouraged me."

"I love you. I don't know how you can turn away from that. We could be happier than anyone I know. The way we were for a while. Rose would be so thrilled to be my little girl."

"She thinks she is already. You know that."

"Just look at it this way. Now four people are unhappy. If you left Jamie and came to me, three would be happy. Jamie, it seems, will always be miserable." He feels he has her now. She's looking at him, considering it. Hope flushes over him, hot and prickly.

"Even if I said yes, there are things you don't know about me," she says, her face darkening. "Things that would change your mind."

"Come on."

"They would."

"What? Do you snore? Do you bite your nails? Do you watch soap operas? Even that I could live with, if it was you."

"Don't joke."

"I can't imagine anything that would change my mind about you," he says. But he looks at her face and sees that she is truly troubled. That it's something besides Jamie that's been keeping her from him. What secret could she be hiding? Whatever it is, it could not sway him. Nothing could sway him.

"I want to go home now, please," she says softly.

"I want to know what your secret is. Tell me."

She parts her lips as though she might tell him, then, instead, she shakes her head.

"I just want to go home."

"Come home with me," he says. "Come to bed with me."

"I made love to Jamie last night," she says bluntly.

"You did?" He feels remarkably stung. Angry. He wants to say, "After being with me?" in a hurt, childish voice, but he holds back. "How was it?"

"Not so good. I tried to pretend it was you. He was happy, though."

"Christ!" is all he can say. She is so distant, so cool, throwing it out to him to see if he will trip. Well, he won't let her see it. But inside, he's seething. Maybe if he leaves town he can actually forget her. Maybe he can see other women. For a moment, he concentrates on all the things he can do to break her heart.

"I slept with Patty," he says hoarsely. He's been walking around with a stone in his throat over this. Why not spit it out now?

"You slept with Patty?" she asks, breathlessly, her eyes pained.

He touches the sharp dip of her cheek.

"I've been miserable over you. You wouldn't see me. I got drunk one night. The next thing I knew . . . It was the stupidest thing I've ever done. She was in love with me, and I hurt her. She'll hardly talk to me now. I was an asshole. You would have hated me if you saw how I acted."

"Keevan." Zoe shakes her head. She's biting her lip. Now he's sorry he told her. But then she takes his hand.

"I was miserable," Zoe says. "I've made you miserable. You made Patty miserable."

She leans her shoulder against him as they walk. He lets go of her hand and puts his arm around her. He doesn't know how she feels, if she is angry or hurt, but he knows she forgives him.

"What will you do for Christmas?" he asks.

"Teresa will cook a turkey. Or I will. Maybe Jamie's sister, Alicia, will come. His parents go to Baltimore for Christmas, to be with the rest of the family. And you?"

"I'll be alone, I guess. Patty won't have any part of me now."

"Have you talked to her, apologized?"

"I've been a coward. I haven't even been able to face her. The only time we talk is when we're discussing the deadline on leaving the house." She is staring at him. What is she feeling?

"So what will you do alone on Christmas?"

"I'll try to hear you through the wall. I'll be thinking of you."

They have reached her house. The lights glow on her parlor floor. Through the lace curtains he can only barely see the beautiful rooms, the sad rooms where she lives without him.

"Won't you come to my house?" he says.

She touches his cheek, then leans forward and kisses him with a hunger that throws him off balance.

"Come home with me, Zoe, please," he whispers. "I want you. I need to be with you."

But she looks at him with sorrowful eyes and shakes her head.

"How can I?" she asks.

For two weeks, Rose sees Keevan every other day, usually in the evenings before her mother comes home. Just being with him fills her up with happiness, the way a balloon fills with air. At first she had to beg Teresa to take her, but now Teresa says she's happy to bring her over and leave her there, so she can go back and cook dinner in peace. Rose hopes every day that Teresa will forget to pick her up and leave her there forever. She loves how Keevan reads to her, sometimes even really hard books, and talks to her like a grown-up, explaining things, asking her opinion. How he cuddles her in his arms and pulls her hair playfully and calls her "missy." How he lets her play with his books, stacking them like blocks; with his sofa cushions, making forts. He climbs through the forts on his hands and knees, pretending to be characters with silly names like Chief Wanna Be Fed and Fat Harry the Tuna. He helps her do flips, hanging from his arms, teaches her to do a handstand against the wall. And afterward, while they are eating a snack together, milk and cookies or oranges or raisins, he asks her lots of questions about Jamie and her mother.

"Are you in love with my mother?" she asks one day while they are playing tic-tac-toe. She suspects that he lets her win, but she's glad anyway.

"Yes," he says very quickly.

"Would you marry her if Jamie wasn't there?"

"Yes."

"I wish we could just kill Jamie," she says.

"You read too many violent fairy tales. You can't just go killing people."

"I want us to live together."

"Me too," he says. He looks far away, as if he can see it: all of them together. She shakes his hand to get his attention.

"We should think up a plan," she says.

"Unfortunately," he tells her, "I don't think there's anything we can do. I don't think it's up to us."

"You have a bad attitude," she says. "We should be able to think of something."

Still, she goes home that night defeated. Not a single plan has come to them. At the dinner table, however, she looks at Jamie, cutting his chicken. He has such a sad, skinny face. He looks like a mean old man. Even though she knows he's been trying to be nice to her. Yesterday he asked to see some pictures she'd brought home from school. He showed her the compass he had as a little boy and told her about how he and his uncle used to go camping. But he's always so slow and tired. And he never laughs like Keevan or wants to take her anywhere. He can't do flips and won't get down on the floor with her. "You're a wonderful girl," Jamie told her yesterday. She didn't like it that he said that. It made her feel guilty. It made her angry.

"I visited Kevin today," Rose tells him. Her mother looks up from her plate and glares at her.

"Kevin?" Jamie glances over at Zoe.

"Keevan, actually. You know, I told you, the man next door," Zoe says.

"I visit him all the time."

"As long as you don't disturb him," Jamie says.

"He wants me to visit him. He asked me to. He loves me. And he loves Mommy. He told me so."

Jamie stops eating and puts down his fork. "Did he?" Jamie asks. He looks over at Zoe.

"Stop that nonsense," Zoe says.

"Mommy loves him too."

"Rose." Zoe's voice is hard as a hammer. It hits Rose, but she doesn't want to stop, now that she's started. Her mother's already mad. What difference does it make?

"When you were sick, we were all together. All the time. We were happy being together."

"I see," Jamie says. Rose watches him. He looks uncomfortable. Zoe looks furious.

"Rose, go up to your room," she says.

"No," Jamie says. "Let her stay. She's only telling the truth, isn't she? She has the right to tell the truth."

"He was very kind to us when you were ill," her mother starts to explain. "He took us places. Showed us Brooklyn. That's all."

"This is the one that's so well read, isn't it?" Jamie asks. "The teacher?"

"Yes," Zoe says softly.

"Well, it was nice of him to be kind to you. You needed someone, didn't you? You needed some kindness." Jamie frowns when he says "kindness."

Rose knows she shouldn't say any more. She sees that her mother's face is very red and her eyes are staring straight forward, not at anyone at all. She sees that Jamie's stopped eating. Maybe she shouldn't have said what she said. But it was the only plan she could think of.

So that's why Zoe seems so removed from him somehow, Jamie thinks. While he was ill, she had a romance with their next-door neighbor. He can't quite absorb it:

Zoe with another man. She has been there for him for so
many years. Loving, patient, through everything. He tries
to imagine Zoe laughing, kissing, making love to his face-
less rival. Someone else touching her, someone else knowing her. Yet how can he blame her for finding another
man during all those months when he essentially left her
alone? He can't even feel angry.

Ever since the shock treatments during his last depression, he hasn't been able to see the world in the same
way or feel the things he once was able to feel. It's as
though there's a wall of glass between himself and all that
goes on around him. And now he observes his own jealousy with surprise, interest, and acute detachment. I am
jealous, he thinks. I don't want her with anyone else, he
thinks. But his thoughts don't seem to translate to intense
feelings. He could bury all these thoughts in an instant.
Forget. Isn't that the best thing to do?

He feels suddenly, strikingly weary. Climbing the stairs
to his room, he hates himself for being ill, for putting Zoe
through all he's had to put her through. Bed. That's what
he needs. Bed.

That night, Zoe knows she must talk to Jamie about
what Rose said at the table. He went to bed directly afterward, and she's worried he won't get up. He has the covers pulled to his chin when she comes in. His eyes are
open, his mouth is slack.

"You probably want to know," she says. "About
Keevan."

"I think I know," he says dully.

"I was lonely. He was simply very nice to us."

"Please don't tell me more," Jamie says.

She can't bear to hurt him. Still, how can she leave it
like this? "I want to tell you," she says. Maybe if she tells
him it will dispel the distance between them. Heal them.

"You were lonely. You slept with him. Rose was en-
chanted because he gave her what I can't. Perhaps you
were too."

"I . . . we . . ."

"I don't want to know more," Jamie says. "I'm sure you slept with him. You did what you needed to do. Anyone would have done the same. If you do love him, I don't want to know. Please don't tell me." He doesn't look at her. His fingers trace the scallops on the top sheet.

The coolness of his voice frightens her. She goes to the window, sees a few flakes fly in front of the window, against the night sky. She feels hollow and defeated. Jamie's been different since he woke this time. He's tried harder to be warmer, more affectionate. Perhaps that will all be gone now. Perhaps he'll fold back up and go to sleep for another six months. Would she regret that? Then there would be no decision to make. She could bring Keevan back into her life just as before.

"Zoe."

"Yes?"

"I don't blame you for anything. Let's just start fresh. Let's just start over."

She goes to the bed and sits down. Touching his still too gaunt cheek, she can't think of anything to say to him. She wishes she could tell him about Keevan, wishes that she could use her time with Keevan as a template for how their relationship might be—hers and Jamie's: doing things together with Rose; comfort, sex, teasing, excitement. Could she and Jamie ever have that together?

"Give me time to get strong again," he tells her. "I'll be able to give you what you need. We'll have fun again."

"I know."

"Someday I'd like to meet him."

"Who?"

"Keevan." It's odd to hear his name come from Jamie's mouth.

"Why?"

"If you cared for him, he must be someone special."

"Oh, Jamie . . ." She can't look him in the eye. For a moment, she is painfully aware of how kind he is, how good inside. She squeezes his hand and gets up to leave. She is startled to find him getting up too.

"Can we light a fire?" he says. "In the back parlor? Does the fireplace work? Are there logs?"

"Yes."

"Come on, then. Come sit with me by the fire."

# FIFTEEN

◆

Christmas week, three inches of snow falls on Eighth Street and freezes over. The early mornings are marked by the sound of shovels scraping and chopping before people go off to work. Business people skid down the icy, puckered sidewalks or take mincing steps to keep from falling on the slick bluestone. One of the Methodist Hospital interns falls in front of Donna and Hal Shea's house at 6:00 A.M. and calls and calls for help, until Hal opens the door in his robe and peers out. An ambulance is summoned to take the man around the corner to the hospital where he works. Just a precaution. The Sheas didn't want to move him without professional help. Turns out he suffered a broken ankle and collarbone. Donna tells Patty, "Good thing we have insurance."

Another ambulance comes down the street at noon one day to rush old Mrs. Reilly to the hospital, but to no avail. Her daughter found her lying at the foot of the stairs and assumed she must have fallen. But the coroner says she must have been standing there, thinking of going up, or just having come down, and simply died, very quickly, not long before her daughter arrived to help her pack boxes. Her daughter told everyone who could listen how sad she was, since she had just found her mother a wonderful nursing home, where she wouldn't have to be alone and isolated. A place she would truly have loved. In only a week's time, she was to have moved there. In New Jersey, where there were trees. They even had senior citizens' aerobics classes. It seemed like a tragedy her mother never had a chance to know it.

Patty invites Terry Beaumont and her mother for Christmas, and even Maggie and Darlene, who have found a nurse over at the hospital willing to sit with Jack while they come for dinner. She debates whether she should invite Keevan. It is, after all, the last Christmas they will share in this house. He looks so lost and lonely lately. She watches him come and go, his shoulders rolled forward, his head down. She's had to let him into her apartment a number of times recently so he could go down to the cellar, where he is sorting out the family things to keep, the things to throw away. He never looks her in the eye anymore and Patty doesn't feel the same about him now. She still loves him, but she sees him as pathetic and lost, someone she is glad she won't have to see much once they've moved.

But now she goes down to ask him to Christmas dinner. He's sitting on the cement cellar floor with a box of letters. Bundles and bundles of them, wrapped in faded blue ribbon.

"Whose letters?" she asks him softly. He is lost in reading, hardly acknowledges her.

"From my father to my grandmother during the war. Before he was injured. He was so enthusiastic. So worried about everyone at home. 'How's Pop doing at the body shop since Earl was drafted? I hope he can hire someone as capable. I thought of your Indian pudding this morning when I was eating powdered eggs and watery porridge. Make some and eat six helpings for me. Ma, I miss bedsheets. I miss the sound of the mantel clock in the parlor. I miss the smell of the oil in the body shop and the jokes Earl used to tell every Thursday that he got the night before at the Knights of Columbus meeting. I miss Lolly's flute playing, and mostly I miss your smile. Gee, I'd pay a million dollars to see all of you right now. I'd give up the chance to be a millionaire just for that.' God, I wish I'd known my father then.''

"I always heard he was a nice man before the war. Before he was injured,'' Patty says.

"His letters remind me of Ralph. It's funny how Ralph went off to war so easily, knowing how our father lost his arm in the war. He even remembered Father a little. He used to tell me about him. He remembered touching the stump of his arm. It was one of his most vivid memories. But Ralph went off so willingly. He accepted it as his fate to go, and he told me he thought life was just like one long opportunity to be surprised. Stunned, he said. 'Life is to be stunned.' ''

Keevan looks miserable, leaning over those letters. She wants to pet his pretty hair, or hug him, but she doesn't dare.

"I can't throw this stuff out. Any of it. It's all I have of them, all of them, now they're dead. My grandparents and Ralph too.''

"You could put it in storage. Or buy a house. You can afford a smaller house. Put it in the cellar of that house.''

"I don't want to leave this house. The history of this house is the history of this family.'' He looks up at her. She can feel his anger.

"It's too late now,'' she says, not unkindly, but sadly. Even though she is glad to be moving, she is sorry to see his pain. Hates it that he's angry at her. "Look,'' she says, "will you spend Christmas with us? I'm having Darlene and Maggie and everyone for dinner Christmas Day.''

He hesitates, looks at her just as he did the night they made love, confused and miserable.

"The children will be disappointed if you don't come. It's our last chance to all be together. Besides, I want you to meet Terry.''

"This is the man you're seeing?''

"Yes. Look, I'm willing to just put what happened behind us. . . . I don't want us to not talk anymore. I don't see the point.''

All this time, he's never been gentleman enough to mention it, to apologize to her, but what does it matter now? Soon they won't see each other every day, or be together at all. And she still wants him in their life somehow. For the children. For continuity.

He looks down at his hands. "I'm sorry," he says. "I've been a coward. It never should have happened. You deserved better than that from me."

"I did," she says, and believes it. "Will you come, though? Please come. It's the one thing I ask of you."

He looks into her eyes now. "I'll be there."

Patty looks forward to Christmas dinner in the worst way. Making lists of what she wants to cook: sausage-and-cornmeal stuffing, acorn squash with ginger and lime. Broccoli soufflé. She will dazzle them all with her meal. And mostly she wants everyone to meet Terry Beaumont. Jim hears about Terry from the children and seems wildly jealous.

"What do you see in this clown?" he asks her on the phone.

"Everything," she tells him. And it's true. He's all she could ask for. Lately, she's noticed how he flirts with nearly everyone: waitresses, counter girls, female traffic cops. But his flirting is innocent, she thinks. He makes it clear in every way that he loves her. And she's gotten much better on her high heels, not tottering nearly so much.

Terry says he's going to help her pick a school to go to. Already he's found her a town house, with three bedrooms and a new kitchen. As soon as the money's free from the house, she'll buy it if it's still available. Terry wanted to make the down payment so she wouldn't lose it while she was waiting, but she wouldn't let him. She wants to do it on her own.

"After you're all happily settled in the house, we'll go

to Italy. In the spring when it's warm," he tells her. "To Tuscany. You ever been there?" She tells him she's never been anywhere. "I'll change that," he says.

"You know what I really want to do with you?" Patty tells him one night at a restaurant when she's had a few drinks and feels loose and happy.

"Whatever it is, baby, I want to do it. Tell me."

"I want to rent a changing room at a beach club in the Rockaways. And I want us to do it there."

"Do what?" he asks.

"You know," she says, punching his arm lightly.

"Oh. Well, we'll rent a cabana. Why stop at a changing room? I've got friends at the Shamrock Club."

"No. I want to rent a changing room. It has to be a changing room."

He looks at her thoughtfully. "Oh, this is a fantasy of yours?"

She nods. He laughs. "It's a done deal," he says. "We'll do it in that changing room so many times next summer, we'll rock it right off its foundations. The people in the adjoining rooms will think we've penned a live seal in there." She laughs and blushes, and feels as though she's won the lottery.

Ever since Charlotte was born, Christmas has been important to Zoe. She never celebrated Christmas when she was a child. Her parents, though they rejected Judaism, still would not embrace the Christian holiday, but all around Zoe, the world made it key to year-end happiness. So she celebrated with friends, wishing she could be truly part of the celebration, wishing she could believe in it and understand it. Even the part about Santa Claus, and the stockings and green and red candy, were foreign to her. She doesn't want Rose ever to feel so disenfranchised. In Zoe's mind, it's become more of a secular celebration anyway, and Jamie, though long a lapsed Catholic, has always seemed pleased that she insists on dragging home a tree, putting out silver candlesticks and wreaths and gar-

lands. Still, Zoe wishes she felt more for the carols and
the crèches, that some church might feel welcoming and
familiar to her, that the holiday, like everything else in
her life, wouldn't feel so "stolen."

This year, she has decked out her new house as never
before. Since Alicia came and admired the tree, she has
gone further, twisting Scotch pine garlands down the front
rails of the stoop, hanging wreaths on the double doors.
She's even elaborated the tree trimmings with candy canes
and blown-glass ornaments she found at an antique store
on Seventh Avenue. If I make it seem cheerful here, I'll
feel better, she tells herself. Rose has helped her, twisting
the garlands around the iron railings and up the mahogany
banisters, hanging the fragile angels only on the sturdiest
branches, leaving a glass of milk and an oatmeal cookie
for Santa.

Christmas morning, Rose shakes Zoe awake.

"C'mon," she says. "It's Christmas." Jamie stirs, rubs
his eyes like a little boy.

"Mama," Rose says, "do you think Santa came?"

"What time is it?" Jamie asks.

"Six forty-five," Zoe tells him. He groans.

"Let's find out what Santa brought," Zoe says, getting
up, pulling on her robe. Her head aches. She was up late,
wrapping presents, and then had a hard time falling asleep.
She kept thinking about Keevan. She misses him and feels
ashamed. Since Rose told him about Keevan, Jamie's been
loving, kind, working hard to give her the attention he
hasn't been able to offer for so long.

Nevertheless, the first present she wanted to buy was
for Keevan, and now she's not sure when she can give it
to him. It's a grey cashmere robe that cost her six hundred
dollars. She found the price outrageous, and yet the fabric
was so silky against her fingers. She knew how beautifully
his red-gold hair would contrast with the simple oxford
grey, how the deep, plain color would light his milky skin.
And she couldn't help imagining how his muscles, his
erection, would feel through the sleek cashmere. As she

handed the saleslady her credit card, though, she had a pang of guilt.

"Wait," she told her, and pulled an identical robe off the rack for Jamie. She knew that Jamie's boniness, his sallowness, wouldn't benefit at all from the soft grey material, but oddly enough, buying the same robe for Jamie assuaged her guilt.

Keevan's robe is wrapped and tucked away in the back of Zoe's closet, the final present she wrapped last night. But before she did, with Jamie sleeping, Zoe locked herself in the bathroom and drew the robe over her naked skin, tied the sash tightly beneath her narrow waist. She was only going to try it on, to know how it would feel to him. But she couldn't help imagining again how thrilling his muscles would feel through the delicious fabric, how his stiff silky cock would press out against the rich stuff. Her own breasts felt incredible to her hands with the robe pulled taut over them, her nipples hard knots pressing up through the knit. With the cashmere teasing her skin, and her thoughts about him hotter, wilder than ever before, her desire was soon flowing. She could feel its stickiness on her thighs. If only he were here. If only she could take him into her, feel the exquisiteness of the erection she imagined, filling her, sliding deeper in her than anyone else had ever been. She came so hard that she bit her tongue, as she arched her back while the pleasure repeated and repeated itself inside his cashmere robe.

Her tongue is sore even now as Jamie lifts his package from beneath the tree. She feels mortified about the matching robes, wonders how she could have done it. Jamie takes the silver package onto his lap, tentatively touches the red ribbons, the plaster cherries.

"For me?" he asks.

"For you," she says. She might have wallowed in the shame of her choice, if Rose weren't already screaming with joy over her first gift: a wooden doghouse for Homer that Zoe had a woodworking shop make specially for her. Both the inside and the outside are painted in pinks and

blues (Rose's favorite colors), and there are shingles on
the roof and curtains inside—this is no mere doghouse. It
has windows, a counter with dog food on it, a closet full
of bones. Homer's name is lettered on the front in gold.
Rose runs up to get him, so she can show him his new
home.

"She's so beautiful," Jamie tells Zoe. She thinks it
might be the first time he's ever noticed Rose's beauty,
doted on her.

"Yes," Zoe says. "She gets more beautiful every day,
I think. Go ahead—open the box," she coaxes him, wanting to get it over with.

But he shrugs. "I want to open it slowly," he tells her.
And he opens one fold of wrapping paper at a time, waiting while Rose, back downstairs for more presents, unwraps hair combs from Santa Claus, a stuffed cat, a box
of lined stationery. Jamie lets the present from Zoe linger
in his lap while Rose explores a gift from Zoe's parents:
a dull navy cardigan sweater that arrived two days before
in a flimsy cardboard hanger box, unwrapped. Zoe
wrapped it for Rose last night in pale-blue paper adorned
with angels, resentful that she had to lift it from the skin
of newspaper her parents put it in. (They had declared
wrapping paper a waste of money long ago. The nicest-
looking gift she can ever remember receiving from them
was wrapped in the Sunday funnies.)

Jamie still waits. He insists they open the presents from
his parents first: A fat F.A.O. Schwarz package for Rose—
an audiocassette player. One from Abercrombie & Fitch
for Jamie—a black and burgundy paisley umbrella with a
sterling handle. Strange choice, Zoe thinks, for a man who
rarely goes out. And hematite beads from Tiffany's for
Zoe. Jamie's parents are generous in their own way, Zoe
supposes, but over the years, she has become certain that
they use a hired shopper. Lois never seems to know what
Zoe's thanking her for.

"I think it's your turn," Zoe says, pointing to the silver
box, but Jamie insists she open her gifts from him: a black

wooden picture frame, a sweater with flowers on it, both bought through the mail. They are simple and pretty, and they suit her well enough. She wonders if Keevan has bought her anything, though it really doesn't matter to her. It's always been much easier for her to give rather than accept gifts. And she is certain he will love the robe.

Finally, just as she's becoming curious at his reluctance, Jamie lifts the cover off the box and pulls out his look-alike robe.

"It's beautiful," he whispers, and taking off his old plaid flannel robe, he tries the new one on. The draping fabric shows too clearly his skeletal shape, his stooped shoulders. But he seems pleased, standing for a long while in front of the pier mirror in the parlor, looking at himself wrapped in his new present. Zoe turns away, can't bear to see him so happy about something that shames her.

When the presents are all opened and the wrapping papers are stuffed into a D'Agostino's bag, Rose goes up to play with Homer's new abode, Jamie picks up a book, and Zoe goes down to the kitchen. Alicia's coming to dinner, and Zoe's decided to do the cooking herself for the first time in a long while. She discovers as she chops and simmers how much she's missed these simple meditative tasks. Cooking was the one thing she liked to do when she was first married to Jamie, because the food, unlike that at her parents' house, was fresh and top quality, the cost of ingredients didn't seem to matter, and she could cook whatever she wanted. Jamie loved her cooking and told everyone she was the best cook he knew, better than the ones his mother used to hire for fifty thousand a year.

When Charlotte was born, then when Jamie got ill, Zoe just gave up the cooking. His mother hired them a cook, and the cook's meals were far more elaborate than Zoe would ever have had time for. But now she's excited about spending time in this kitchen, an entirely new place to cook. Not once since they moved here has she done more than heat soup. Teresa's gone to her sister-in-law's in Queens, and the kitchen is entirely Zoe's.

As she minces thyme for the green beans, the phone rings.

"Merry Christmas, Zoe." It's Keevan, his voice soft and intimate. The joy of just hearing it slides through her.

"Keevan."

"What are you doing?" he asks.

"Cooking."

"Have you opened presents?"

"Yes."

"But not all. I have one for you."

"I have one for you."

She talks softly, not wanting Jamie to hear, glad he's a floor above her.

"Last night I thought of you," she tells him. This is the gift he really wants, she thinks. "All night I thought of you."

"Oh, Zoe. Tonight. Can we meet late? Can we give each other gifts?" They plan it, but still Zoe feels uneasy. She doesn't like the idea of sneaking out, of trying to fool Jamie.

Then she tells him, "Rose told Jamie about you."

"What about me?"

"He knows. Everything."

"Everything?" Keevan is silent for a long time. "Then you must have told him. There's plenty Rose doesn't know."

"He guessed after Rose told him. He knew."

"Was he angry?" Keevan asks hopefully.

"He was forgiving. He was incredibly kind." She feels Keevan wince. Feels it right through the phone wires.

"I wasn't just some guy you picked up off the street to sleep with, Zoe. Does he know that? It wasn't just lust or pent-up sexual energy, for God's sake."

"He knows. Rose told him."

"She told him what?"

"That you love me. And that I love you."

"So . . . what did he say to that?"

"He says he doesn't want any details. He doesn't want to think about it. But he's been all right since."

There is a moment of silence. What is Keevan thinking, feeling? "What are you going to do for Christmas?" she asks him finally.

"I'm going to Patty's," he tells her. "She's been nice to me. I think she feels sorry for me in a way. . . ."

"Why?"

"Because I'm losing the house. Because she said I look like hell . . . because of you."

Zoe winces.

"Anyway," Keevan says quickly, as if to avoid the subject, "she invited me. Her new boyfriend will be there, and Maggie, our neighbor up the street, too. Patty's mother. Our last Christmas here. I've spent every Christmas of my life in the same dining room, Zoe. And now . . ."

"I'm so sorry," she whispers. She wishes she could have bought him the house for Christmas. A house instead of a robe. The one gift *she* truly wants for herself is the answer to a question she feels she can never solve: how to leave Jamie, with dignity, with respect for him, feeling right about it. I'm ready for this, she thinks. I'm ready to make Rose happy. To make myself happy. She might even be able to tell Keevan about her stealing. But even if he accepted her terrible secret, how can she leave Jamie at all?

"I wish you could come for dinner here," he says. "I wish . . ."

"I wish you could come for dinner *here*," she says. "I'm cooking. I wish I were doing it for you."

"When you come tonight to get your gift, make love with me," he says hoarsely. "Please."

She can't deny herself this, she thinks. At least she can have this one pleasure. "Yes," she says.

He is silent for a moment. "I never expected you to say that."

"Are you sorry?"

"My heart's palpitating. I'll never make it until tonight! Come over now."

"Hang in there."

"I'll wait for you. Even if it's very late. No matter how late it is tonight, be sure and come."

"I'll be there," she tells him.

All through her cooking chores, Zoe is giddy, thinking of Keevan. About three-thirty, with the turkey already browning in the oven, she realizes that she's forgotten sweet potatoes, Rose's favorites. She tells Jamie she's going out to the Korean vegetable market to get them, that she's leaving Rose with him.

She puts on her coat and revels in the snowy street as she walks down it. The houses, dressed for Christmas, take on a less solemn, more individual air. Someone's wrapped a front-yard gas lamp with red and white ribbon like a candy cane. There are double wreaths on many oak doors, just like hers, a moving angel with a wand in one parlor window. And someone has flocked his windows with jolly Santas and sleighs and candles. But as she walks carefully along the slick sidewalk, she thinks of Jamie, and the impossibility of leaving him. No matter how much she wants or needs Keevan, she'll never be able to free herself from the tangle of her commitment to Jamie.

At the Korean market, she walks the aisles, listlessly picking up the sweet potatoes, more milk for Rose, and looking for things for the table. She aches that Keevan won't be there to enjoy them: a box of rolled chocolate-covered crepe cookies from France; some navel oranges, fat as grapefruits. As she comes down the health food aisle, her eye is stopped by a tiny metal-mesh cage, like an old-fashioned milkman's carrier, filled with minuscule glass ampoules of ginseng, a dozen of them. The ginseng is imported, expensive. The whole carton is twelve dollars.

Saddened and weary, she is surprised to feel the heat of desire slide up her back and over her. She doesn't even know what ginseng is for, but breathing hard, in the grip of a cold sweat, she grabs the tiny metal package off the shelf and thrusts it into her pocket.

"Stop there," a voice says. She wheels around. The Korean store owner is staring at her with eyes that could shoot fire. "Thief," he says.

"What?" she asks. Her heart pounding like a timpani.

"I'm calling the police."

"What do you mean? You haven't given me a chance to pay," she says, holding up her plastic basket of groceries.

"The ginseng. You steal it. Soo Yung, call the police."

"I'll pay whatever you want," Zoe says. "For God's sake, don't call the police. I was going to pay for it."

"You put it in your pocket. You no pay for it."

"I would have."

"Call the police," the man instructs his wife. The woman, whom Zoe has spoken to a hundred times, nervously turns to pick up the phone.

"Maybe we no call," she says. "The lady pays."

"I'll pay whatever it costs. I always intended to—"

The Korean man snatches the phone from his wife's pale hand. "You give me. I call. We lose too much money to thieves. She the worst. She no need to be thief. I see her steal from here before. I no believe it. Now I believe."

Zoe leans against the vegetable bin. She feels she's been kicked in the stomach. Her lungs feel collapsed and sticky. Her head is throbbing. This is the terror she's been courting for a very long time. Now everyone will know what she is. Heat stains her face. She feels she could have a stroke. Right here at Kim's Market.

"You stay there. You try to leave, I shoot you. I not afraid," the man says, producing a gun from beneath the counter.

"I won't try to leave," she says weakly. She thinks of her turkey in the oven. Of Jamie and Rose waiting for her to return. Of Keevan. How she wishes he were here now. He's the one she wants. The only one who can help somehow. The only one who makes her feel safe from herself. When she had him, she no longer needed to steal.

A policeman comes sauntering in. No wailing siren, as she expected, no screech of tires. The policemen walk their beats now, ten blocks apiece in endless circles.

"This her?" the officer asks the owner, incredulous. He's a young man with a mild face, a crew cut, a trim body in the fitted uniform.

"She a thief. A bad thief."

"What did she steal?"

"Look." He holds up the ginseng he took from her.

The policeman approaches her warily. "Is what he's saying true?" he asks her.

For a moment, she thinks she will tell him what she told the Korean man, that it's a mistake, that she intended to pay. But somehow she can't lie. Her tongue is heavy as lead in her mouth. The young officer looks at her with imploring eyes. He wants a good excuse. He wants her to go home and have a nice Christmas.

She closes her eyes.

"She steal before. I see. I no believe I see right. Now I know."

"You make a habit of this?" the officer asks her.

She says nothing.

"Are you a—what is this stuff called—a ginseng thief exclusively, or do you steal other stuff?"

Zoe just shakes her head.

"Come on, then, I gotta book you. My partner's outside. I gotta cuff you. That's policy." The metal cuffs clank on her wrists. She feels she can hardly walk.

"You okay?"

She nods.

"We gotta read you your rights. Jeff, you want to do it?" he asks his partner, who's just walked in.

"This the thief?" Jeff asks.

"Seems to be," the young officer says.

"Christ. It never makes sense to me," Jeff says. "Don't you have better things to do on Christmas Day, lady?" She nods sadly. "Come on," he says, pushing her gently forward, rattling off the list of her rights.

"How much does this stuff cost?" she hears the young officer asking the owner, as the other marches her down the street. Between the babble of her rights, she hears the word "charges." She hears the word "theft," and then they turn the corner to Ninth Street and the place where the officers have parked their car.

"Get in," Jeff says kindly. "It's a little uncomfortable with the cuffs. Watch your head." His voice is soothing and fatherly. He protects her head with his hand as he ducks her into the car. Once there, she looks down at her braceleted hands and just closes her eyes.

Maggie kisses Jack on the cheek and tells him she'll bring him back a taste of Patty's meal. Darlene will be around for another few hours if he wants anything, and then the nurse will come, and he's always liked this nurse best. Maggie's going early to Patty's to help her get things arranged, to set the table. She's relieved to get out of the house, she discovers with a subtle rush of guilt. The doctor has told her that Jack could go any day now, and she is so tense with anxiety half the time she can't seem to do normal things like sort the mail or iron clothes. Her ironing bag is full of crumpled things. Her pile of mail keeps spilling over the kitchen counter, full of bills she has yet to pay. Being forced to leave the house and go down to Patty's is a godsend. Her body simply aches as she walks down the street.

Michelle answers Patty's door, braided and fresh-faced.

"Hi, Maggie. Uncle Keevan's coming too."

"Well, that's nice for you, isn't it?" Maggie asks her. "You love your uncle Keevan."

"Mom and him have been having a fight," Michelle whispers. "A real nasty one."

"So I've been told," Maggie reassures her.

"In the new town house, Mom says I can go out with my bike and I don't have to have an adult with me."

"Won't that be nice for you! You'll feel so independent and grown up."

Patty bustles out of the kitchen to greet Maggie, takes one of Maggie's hands between her two.

"Oh, Maggie, you're such a peach to come early. I've got a million things for you to do. How's Jackie?"

Maggie just shakes her head. Patty squeezes her shoulder. "Well, maybe it's good for you to have a break." Maggie, watching Patty, so full of life, fly around the kitchen showing her the small chores she wants done, thinks: She's a completely new person from what she used to be. Happy and so much more confident. The bitterness seems to have lifted from her entirely. Getting rid of Jim, forgetting Keevan, has done Patty a tremendous turn. If Maggie had run into this Patty O'Connor a year ago, she doubts she would have recognized her. But poor Keevan. He's changed too. She's watched him lately, looking all sallow and sad.

"What's wrong, darlin' boy?" she asked him last time she saw him on the street, though she knew, since Patty had told her. "You used to tell me all your secrets." She wanted to hear it from Keevan himself.

"You'll just say 'I told you so,' " Keevan told her petulantly, "and I don't want to hear it."

"Okay," she said. "You've got my number. Tell me anyway. I'll hold my tongue."

So he told her, eyes on the sidewalk, shaking his head. He was a good boy, she thought. Just misguided, poor lamb.

"It'll pass," she told him. "Before you know it, you'll forget. And you won't soon run after another married woman, I'll bet." But he turned away, hunched over, a shadow of himself, and went on down the street. It was like one of those science fiction movies Jackie used to watch in the fifties, as though Patty had sucked the blood right out of Keevan to bring herself back to life, and left poor Keevan pale and empty. It was the very oddest thing.

Terry Beaumont pumps Keevan's hand with a bit too much energy. He's noisy and full of bravado, not unlike Jim, Keevan thinks. Only he does seem very fond of Patty. And he's nice to Michelle and John. Patty looks pretty in a purple dress. Keevan watches Terry admiring her as she hurries back and forth from the kitchen to the dining room, swinging her full skirt. Once, Terry stops her and gives her a kiss. The children stare; John, in fact, glares.

"This is the nicest Christmas I can remember," Terry says when Patty brings out the turkey. It is picture perfect, golden brown and fat as any Keevan's seen. Patty's mother applauds. The whole house smells of Patty's exotic cooking. He is glad to be here, after all. If it hadn't been for this, he would be home pining over Zoe.

"I wish Jackie could see this," Maggie says, with tears in her eyes. "One last time. He would have loved it." She's grown plumper in the last few weeks, and more grandmotherly, since Jack's illness. Keevan puts his hand on her neck. It is cool and soft. She leans gently toward him, telling him without words she's glad for his support.

"We'll make a small package of food for him, Maggie. The things he's allowed to eat," Patty says.

"Yes," Maggie says. "I told him we would."

Darlene comforts the baby. Maggie conducts the grace before they eat. Michelle and John get the drumsticks. The dishes are tasted and commented on. Keevan looks around the old room and thinks of all the Christmases it's known. The Christmases of his childhood and his father's childhood. The Christmas after his father came home from the war, wounded. The Christmas he brought Keevan's mother, Violet, to dinner for the first time. Keevan has heard about them all, from his grandmother, from his grandfather. And the house has contained the memories like a neat filing cabinet. But this is the one Keevan will remember most, he thinks. His last. His loneliest.

When the phone rings, Patty sighs and, swinging her purple skirt, says over her shoulder, "It's probably Jim, calling to talk to the kids." But she comes back a moment later, looking perplexed.

"It's for you, Keevan. A woman."

Keevan scrapes back the chair from the table so fast he nearly tips it over. And he almost trips over Patty getting past her skirt.

"Hello?"

"Keevan?" she says in a squeezed voice.

"Zoe!" he whispers. "Are you all right?"

"Do you remember," she says, in a choked, controlled way, "I said there was something you wouldn't like about me if you knew?"

"Yes."

"Look," she says. "I need you to come down to the police station. I've been arrested."

When they hang up, he calls Jamie. Having only one phone call, she asked him to do this one thing for her. He dreads speaking to Jamie, having to explain who he is and why he's calling. He tells Jamie what she's told him to say: that she's had a small problem, an accident, nothing serious. Keevan will bring her home. Jamie sounds vague and unsure. "Well," he says. "Okay."

"Oh, and she told me to tell you to turn off the oven."

Keevan's mouth is so dry that when he finally stumbles back into the dining room he can't speak. Everyone is watching him as he takes a sip of water from his grandmother's crystal goblet.

"I have to go," he says.

"Why? What?" they ask together.

"I just have to go," he says. "I'm awfully sorry. It's an emergency."

"Who's had an emergency?" Maggie asks.

"Zoe," he says softly. Patty sets her own water glass down, right on her knife. It falls with a thud, sending a plume of water across the damask Christmas tablecloth, which distracts them all just long enough for Keevan to leave.

Zoe is sitting at one of the officers' desks. Though the room is unpleasant, lit only by ice-cube-tray fluorescent lights, Keevan is grateful they've let her sit there to wait for him, and not in some cell. A paper Christmas ornament dangles from the ceiling above her head.

Gusts of heat blow from the radiators all around the room, and the few officers—everyone at all senior is home with family, turkey, and toddies—are wiping their brows. Zoe looks like a scolded child, sitting in her heavy coat, her pale-pink hands folded in her lap. He has already paid her bail, after asking questions about her arrest, the charges, the implications. Four hundred dollars. They asked to see three IDs before they'd accept his check.

"You can go now," the officer tells her. Zoe rises, and Keevan reaches out for her. She comes into his arms with such force it nearly knocks him off balance.

"There now," he whispers.

"I didn't know if you'd come," she says hoarsely into his shoulder.

"Of course I'd come. Why not?"

"You must be so ashamed. Just to know me."

"No," he says.

"I steal things all the time. All the time. Stupid things . . . everything. Combs and candy and magazines and socks . . ."

"Shh," he tells her. "They'll hear you. Come on. We'll go outside." He ushers her out into the night air, warmer than it's been all day. Snow is melting along the curbs. But after the hot, stale room, she's shivering beneath her coat.

He helps her into his car. He's ashamed for her to see it. He rarely drives it, an old Chevrolet with a fender missing, the perfect city car: it runs, and it's ugly enough that nobody thinks of stealing it. But he is newly aware of its shortcomings as he closes the door on her side and goes around to his. She may be a thief. He still sees her as a queen.

"I'm a kleptomaniac," she says before he has even put on his seat belt. "I fit all the symptoms. I've been doing it since I was a kid."

He is still reeling at the thought of her arrest. What must the officers have thought when such a woman turned out to be the alleged perpetrator?

"Have you ever been caught before?" he asks.

"It's almost like I tried to get caught sometimes. Sometimes I've tempted fate. I was caught once but I got away. I didn't even tempt fate today. I just wasn't thinking. I was thinking about you."

"So I'm the culprit," he says. But light words do nothing to dispel the mood.

"I don't know why I do it," she tells him. "I hate myself for it afterward. I'm ashamed you had to find out."

"Shh," he tells her. "I slept with Patty. You steal. How can we love each other if we're not perfect?"

She looks up at him. Her eyes are almost as clear as water now, reflected off her pale-grey coat.

"You think you have to steal just to have something of your own, don't you?" he says.

She stares at him, then nods.

"I love you," he tells her softly.

"I don't know how you can," she says.

"Well, I do. Does Jamie know? About your stealing?"

"No."

"You never told him?"

"No."

"Why?"

"I was too ashamed."

They are silent for a long time as he maneuvers through holiday traffic. He reviews the events of the last hour: the phone call, the overheated precinct, Zoe hunched in her coat. He wonders briefly if there is any danger of her going to jail, but then he remembers the Finney family clout. First offense, something small, the most she'll get is a short parole. And not a word will reach the papers. He feels immensely relieved. Does Zoe realize it too?

"Did they take a mug shot?" he asks.

"Yes. They took my picture."

"Did you smile? In the mug shots you always see, everyone looks like a bulldog."

"You really love me?" she asks softly. "Despite this?"

He knows how hard it must be for her to believe him.

"More, I think," he says. "I want to help you. I want to be here for you."

"What did you tell Jamie?" she asks.

"That you were in an accident. Nothing serious. I'm glad it was me you called," he says.

"I never thought of calling him. I didn't think he'd be able to handle it. Didn't think he'd be able to come."

Keevan turns down Eighth Street and finds a parking place up by Maggie's. It's nearly 9:00 P.M. He wonders if Patty's guests are still there. He's surely missed opening presents with them, the pie à la mode. Michelle must have been disappointed. He looks up at Jack's window and sees the light still on, wonders how much longer he'll live. Compared to that, this is nothing.

Taking Zoe's hand, he feels oddly happy. Maybe it's the way her hand grips his, as though she never wants to let it go.

"Do you want me to come in with you? To help you tell Jamie?"

"No."

"What will you tell him?"

"The truth, I guess. I need his lawyers. I need his family to get me out of this."

Keevan nods. "I thought of that."

"I didn't steal when we were together," she says, stopping before they reach her house, looking into Keevan's eyes. He nods. "I didn't feel like I needed to steal then," she says.

He pulls her toward him, holds her tight against his body. He never knew he could love anyone so entirely.

He hated Helayne for every fault. Tina's quirks enraged him. But Zoe's need to steal combs and candy and ginseng only makes him love her more, for it tells him how much she needs his love.

"Will I see you later?" he asks.

"I don't know," she says. "We've waited so long. I want it to be right. It wouldn't be good tonight."

"I just want to give you your present, then. I just want to hold you."

She looks small and lost.

"I want that too," she whispers. "Please just let me get through this part. I have to face Jamie now. I have to tell him. And then . . . and then we'll see."

Jamie is waiting in the front parlor while Zoe hangs her coat carefully and slowly over the mahogany hall tree. He clears his throat, as if to indicate that he's there. But she takes her time, terrified to face him. She is limp with shame. Feels almost feverish. And imagines herself bruised all over, like an overripe peach. One touch, and she's certain all her sadness will ooze out, leaving empty skin.

"Jamie . . ."

Jamie lowers his book and stands. His hair is tousled, his face drawn.

"What happened? Are you all right?" he asks.

"Yes."

"Was it a car accident? What?"

"Where's Rose?" she asks.

"I told her you got delayed, couldn't come home until late. Alicia came and didn't know what to do with the dinner. She just turned the oven off and put it all away. We ordered pizza. She left a few minutes ago. Rose asked to go to bed early. I thought telling her you'd been in an accident would scare her."

Zoe imagines how disappointed Rose must have been, wondering how her mother could have abandoned her on

Christmas Day. At least if she thought Zoe had been in a minor accident, she would have understood.

"What kind of accident was it, Zoe?" His face accuses her. His lips are milk white, his nostrils flare.

"It wasn't an accident," she says. She hears her voice shaking.

"Oh," Jamie says, sitting down again. "You were with *him.*" His words are controlled, but his voice drops, as though she's deflated him.

"It's not what you think."

"Look," he says. "I understand. You said you were going to the store. I'll pretend you did." Zoe hadn't thought about how Jamie might interpret the lie about the accident—that she had sneaked off to see Keevan while the turkey was roasting in the oven.

"No," she says. "I did go to the store."

"With him?"

"I went alone. Just like I said. Only something happened."

"What happened?"

"I was arrested."

"Arrested?" And then she tells him. She has no choice now, and the truth might at this moment seem preferable to Jamie, so it spills from her. All the times she's stolen since she's known him, even with him nearby; the close calls; the misery of her shame and how lately it's gotten worse and worse. She tells him until she's soaked in a cold, weakening sweat. She feels both relieved and nauseated. She searches for his reaction, but she can't read it. He is staring at her, as though longing to understand. Then he looks at his hands, stares at her again. What is he thinking? Is he shocked? Disgusted? She tells him how she was arrested. Handcuffed. How she called Keevan. How he bailed her out.

"Why didn't you call me?" he asks very softly. She sees hurt in his eyes.

"I didn't think you were strong enough to come get me. I didn't think you would have been able to face it—

finding a car service, coming to the police station, all that. Would you have? Would you have come?''

He is silent for a moment. He shakes his head. His eyes are distant, troubled. "I don't know if I could have."

"I never wanted you to know," she says, feeling more miserable and defeated than she can remember.

"My God, Zoe," he says. "All these years you were troubled too, and you never told me. Never trusted me to be able to help *you*. Or understand."

"I was ashamed. Too ashamed."

"I haven't been much good to you, have I?" he asks suddenly.

"Jamie." She reaches out for him, hugs him. He feels bony in her arms, awkward. She steps back. Looks at his face. She never expected him to be so understanding.

"There'll be some kind of a trial," she says. "I need a lawyer. I need your family's help. To protect them as much as me."

"Alicia will tell you. She has all the names."

"I'll go call her."

"Wait." He stops her by gently grabbing her elbow, then takes both her elbows in his hands. "Listen. I want to know: Do you find yourself stealing most when you're unhappy?"

"Yes."

"You said it's gotten worse lately. Is it since I've been better that it's gotten worse? Since you haven't been with this man Keevan?"

She bites her lip. She hates telling him. Hates hurting him. Still, she sees in his eyes that he already knows the answer.

"When you were with him . . . when I was ill. Did you steal then?" he asks.

"No," she says. And that's when she feels it. Her throat twists, burns. The sensation that means she's crying. And then a new heat rises behind her eyes, turns liquid. And suddenly real tears are rolling down her cheeks. Tears that run along her nose, quiver in salty pools at the edges of her lips. She is crying for the first time in so many years. Her burning eyes are cooled by the tears. The relief is delicious, and terrible. Relief that the truth is out. Recognition that her feelings for Keevan are more intense, more real, more special than she dared believe, and that now Jamie knows it.

"You're crying," he whispers. "My God. Really crying."

She nods. "I'm sorry."

She tries to hide her face in her hands, but he takes her hands and brings them to his lips, kisses each palm. He kisses the tears from her face.

"Oh, Zoe," he says. "I'm the one that's sorry. I'm the one that's truly sorry."

Keevan finds Patty in the kitchen, washing dishes. Patty's mother is upstairs with John. Maggie and the others are gone. Michelle is playing with a new doll at the kitchen table.

"Hi," he says. He feels relieved to be in the golden kitchen light, the smells of her good dinner still mingling with the scent of the Christmas tree and cinnamon candles.

Patty smiles vaguely at him. "Did you see your friend?" she asks.

"Yes."

"What did she cook up to pull you away from Christmas dinner? I can't wait to hear it."

"It wasn't funny, believe me."

Michelle sits at the table, tired, her head leaning on one hand, her braids coiling onto the table.

"You missed all the presents, Uncle Keevan. I loved the ball with the balloon in it, and the book, and the Clue game especially. Thanks."

"I figured we wouldn't live near each other anymore. You used to play it sometimes. I thought you needed one of your own."

"There's still presents under the tree for you," Patty

says. But Keevan can't imagine anything he wants. Not this Christmas.

"Later," he says. "Terry gone?"

"He's waiting up in my room for me," Patty tells him, with a subtle smile and eyes narrowed to cat slits. "You have to go to bed, young lady," she says to Michelle. Michelle gets up slowly from the table. Keevan hugs her as she passes.

"I'll miss you, Mich."

"Me too," she tells him. "Will you come see us anymore?"

"Of course. We're still family," he says. But he wonders if it will ever feel that way again.

"What's going to happen with you and Terry?" he asks when he is sure Michelle has climbed the stairs. Patty turns to him and seems to be looking him up and down. He feels like a stranger around her now. She emanates a new strength, a sense of purpose.

"I don't know," she says. "I think eventually we'll get married. We've even talked about it."

"What about divorce, though? You've always been so religious."

"You know . . ." Her eyes become unfocused and sad for a minute. "It's funny," she says. "I used to find a lot of comfort in all the ceremony and rules of the Church. It made everything so easy and certain. I love the Church still. It's just . . . I don't know. Maybe I've got my own rules now."

"I'm sorry I hurt you," he says. "I wish that night had never happened. I took all my hurt and anger out on you. All these years . . . I guess I was selfish. I didn't think much of your feelings."

She smiles at him. "And I thought too much of yours."


Jamie wakes early and watches Zoe sleep. He wants to shake her hair, to kiss her brow, but he doesn't want to disturb her. He's never been very good at physical affection. Now he wishes he were, wishes he could give her what he's never been able to give her. All these years, he's been intimidated by her ability to face everything so squarely. How little he knew about her. How little he's tried. He gets up and showers, then again watches her sleep as he dresses quietly. It's only seven-thirty. Because of Christmas, Zoe is taking off today and tomorrow as well. He'll let her sleep.

Deciding to take a walk in the snow, he puts on his hiking boots, his parka. The air feels surprising on his cheeks. Wakes him. His boots bite into the icy tops of the drifts. He feels more in touch with the world today. More present to all that's around him. For the first time, he'll go all the way around the block: to Seventh Avenue, up Ninth Street, and along Eighth Avenue. It's time to get stronger, he thinks. To be more normal.

As he walks, he stares at the houses, sturdy, side by side. He knows no one here. This neighborhood will never feel like home, the way it clearly does to Zoe. Especially now that he knows what happened here while he was ill. Here, on this block, he has lost the loyalty of the only person he's ever loved. And how can he blame her? He longs to go back to Sutton Place.

The cold air exhausts him, and the thought of Zoe in love with another man makes him dizzy and weak. Only a handful of houses until he gets back to their house, and yet he needs to rest. He finds himself leaning against a gate to keep from falling. Black patches float before his eyes; his lungs burn. Just as he sees no choice but to sit on the snowy bottom step of the house where he's stopped, a woman comes out. He doesn't even get to see her face until after he feels her competent hands steadying him.

"Are you all right?" she says. She smells of apples, and cooking. She's a middle-aged woman, with a kind, round face.

"I'm sorry. I just felt dizzy."

"I saw you. Come. Come into my house," she says. She lets him lean on her, and he does, noting her solidity, her comforting heft. He feels foolish, has never been easy with strangers. He's surprised someone he doesn't know should have rushed out to help him.

"Please sit here, Mr. Finney," she says as she ushers him in through her door. She leads him to a sofa, and he sits with relief, bending forward to ease his dizziness. "I'm sorry I don't know your first name." Her house smells of cooking too, and apples. It's warm and colorful.

"Jamie," he says. "How do you know who I am?" He is suddenly conscious of how he must look to her. He has avoided mirrors as much as possible, but he knows he's ugly these days. Frightening.

"You look like you could use some water," she says, not answering his question. "I'll be right back."

She returns, bringing him water in a pretty old emerald-green glass. It's cool on his lips. He sips, tries to rise through the darkening halo in his brain. Relax. Breathe. He likes this house, this warmth. His head is clearing, his lungs are easing.

"You asked how I know who you are. I know most of the people on the block. Your next-door neighbors have told me about you."

"Do you know my wife?"

"I've seen her. Zoe, right? I'm afraid we've never really met. I'm Maggie Kilkenny, by the way."

"Thank you for taking me in, Mrs. Kilkenny. I'm embarrassed to cause you any trouble. If I just sit awhile . . ."

"As long as you like." She has a warm face, a sweet smile. She is totally genuine, he thinks, and somehow wise.

She pulls up a rocking chair to sit by him. "It's good to see you walking about," she says. "I know you've been ill for a while. Then I heard you were better, though I haven't seen you walking outside much. Just once, with your wife."

"Yes. I probably shouldn't have tried to walk so far alone. I thought I had more strength." He thinks of Zoe, the walks she has taken with him, the patience she has offered him time after time.

"My husband, he has a bad heart. He hasn't long to live. To me, compared to him . . . well, you look the picture of health," she says.

He smiles. "Well, it's good to be healthy in a relative way, then," he says. "I'm sorry about your husband."

"Oh, me too. Though I'd say all in all he's had a splendid life. That's what you want. To find you're dying and to be able to say 'Ah, but I've had a splendid life.' "

He smiles at her and thinks how he has never expected a splendid life. Not since the accident. Not since Charlotte. He figures his chance to have a really splendid life is long past. But Zoe . . . he has done nothing to give her a splendid life. She deserves better. She deserves it from him.

"You said you know my next-door neighbors," he says.

"All their lives. Well, not so much the people on the uphill side, the Epsteins. Barely know them. They're out of town half the time. He's a lawyer, I think. I hear they have a house in the Hamptons and she's out there most of the time. Imagine, having two houses. My.

"But Patty, Keevan, and Jim on the other side I knew when they were babies. Of course, they won't be your next-door neighbors for long. They've sold the house. I'm sorry to see them leave. I'll miss them. The O'Connors have lived in that house seventy years or more."

"They're moving? I didn't know."

"Oh, yes. Patty's divorcing Jim. Best thing she ever did. He was always trouble, that boy. She tells me she's newly in love. A changed woman. And Keevan . . . well, I'm not sure what he'll do."

"What is he like?" Jamie asks tentatively. He wants to know, wants to know everything about him.

Maggie looks thoughtful, then smiles.

"I think," she says, nodding with conviction, "I think he's one of the best human beings I know. A good man."

"Is he? Is he a good man?" When he looks up at her, he knows that she knows all about Keevan and Zoe. She knows why he's asking about Keevan. "A man who could be trusted?" he asks.

"With the most precious things you have," she says squarely, leaning back, crossing her arms, observing him.

He feels heat rising up the back of his neck. There is no question what he must now do.

"I should go," Jamie says. "I'm feeling better now."

"Are you certain? You can sit all day if you need to. I enjoy the company."

"No. It's just down the street. I'm sorry to have put you out."

"No trouble at all. I must ask, are you really one of the Baltimore Finneys?"

"Yes."

"My great-aunt worked for the Finneys once. She had great respect for them, I must say. And I've always followed what goes on with your family. And always found them quite remarkable."

"Thank you," Jamie says. He hates comments about his family. But he feels nothing but kindness toward this woman who was there to help him when he needed it. He rises, tests his steadiness. The black patches have cleared. The dizziness is gone. "Mrs. Kilkenny. Thank you so much for taking me in," he says.

"Come by anytime," she says. "Let me get my coat and walk you down to your house, though."

"Oh, no. I'm all right now, really."

"Are you sure?"

"Yes. You've been very kind."

"Oh, no," she demurs. "Nothing more than you'd expect from a neighbor."

Halfway to his house, he turns to see Maggie Kilkenny still standing in the cold, pulling her sweater tighter around her, waving to him, watching until he's safely home.

When he closes the door behind him, he hears voices in the kitchen. Zoe and Rose are at the table, Rose drinking cocoa, pushing down on a marshmallow with her index finger, trying to sink it into the warm chocolate.

"Where were you?" Zoe asks. "I was worried. You were gone so long."

"I took a walk around the block. I'm sorry I worried you. I guess I still don't walk too quickly." He won't tell her about his dizziness, about Mrs. Kilkenny. This is not the time to make her feel concerned about him.

"Rose, would you mind going upstairs to play with Homer for a little while? I want to talk to Mommy," he says.

Rose looks startled. She turns to Zoe to see if she agrees. Zoe, too, appears surprised. "Go ahead, darling."

"But I'm not done with my cocoa."

"Take it with you. But hold it carefully. Don't spill it on the stairs." Rose lifts the plastic mug, gives Jamie a frown, and starts up the stairs. Jamie can't help smiling at her. A beautiful little girl, and yet, in so many ways, he has made her a stranger. His own child. He waits until he hears her footsteps start up the staircase to the third floor, then he turns to Zoe.

"I've done a lot of thinking." He sits in the chair where Rose has been sitting, feels her warmth still radiating from it. "Zoe," he says. He takes her hand. He prays his courage won't let him down now. She is biting her lip, staring at the table. Her hand is holding his too tightly. Does she think he's going to scold her, shame her? He takes her chin in his hand and makes her look at him. How long since they have really talked, since he has had the strength or focus to know her. "I love you," he says.

"I know," she says. Jamie has always thought her beautiful. And yet these last years, how little he has bothered to take her in. He hasn't troubled to know the brush strokes of age that have defined her, deepened her eyes, rendered her cheekbones more elegant. He's never noticed how her mouth has softened and filled out with maturity. The opposite of his mother, whose lips have thinned and grown angry with time.

"Do you love me?" he asks.

"Yes," she says. He sees alarm in her pale eyes. Last night she cried. How vulnerable she seemed to him then. Odd that he should love her even more when she's vulnerable, though he has always forced her to be strong as he has allowed himself to grow weaker and weaker.

"Then I'm asking you to understand what I'm going to tell you."

"What?"

"I want to go back to Manhattan," he says.

"Manhattan?" He sees her blanch. Her voice quavers. "Sell the house, move back there? But Rose is in school . . ."

"No," he says, evenly. "Not you, darling. Not Rose. Just me."

"But, Jamie . . ."

"I'll find an apartment in Sutton Place. You know Mother. She'll call out all her resources. She'll find me something fine."

"I don't understand," Zoe says.

"I want you to stay here in Brooklyn. I want you to be free."

"You need me," she says. "You won't be happy being alone. You've never liked being alone."

"Alicia and my mother will be right there. Listen, I'm asking you to do this for me," he says. "To let me go back while you stay here."

"I knew you weren't really happy here. Maybe it was wrong of me to decide to move us when you were ill. I thought you'd want to get away from your mother. I'm sorry if—"

"No, no," he says. He is proud to hear how soothing his voice sounds. How even. This is the most courageous thing he has ever done in his life. And how unexpectedly exhilarating it feels. He senses himself lighten. Even the residual gloom in his heart seems to scatter, to let in daylight. "I want you to be free, Zoe. Even if I'm better now, how long until I'm ill again? Stay here. For Rose. She loves this man next door. And you love him. I'm trying to give you this. This chance to do what's best for you. For once, let me do something for you."

He can't help noticing that light is easing into her troubled face, that some glimmer of hope is straightening the line of her brow. For a moment, he feels a cramp in his soul, tastes acid in his mouth. How can he live without her? She has been all he's had for far too long. And then he reminds himself how he wants her to be able to say someday, "I've had a splendid life."

Zoe goes to her room and opens her jewelry box. One by one, she lifts the deco diamond ring, the antique gold chain, the pearl earrings, that Jamie has given her over the years, for beneath them all, in a small velvet compartment, is Junie's eye. She lifts the glittering glass bead, presses the clip deep into her palm. Until last night, this doll's eye has held her tears, has been her reminder that her feelings do not come first. For the first time in her life, she has an opportunity now to be truly happy. And, she realizes with equal impact, an opportunity to be sad without shame.

She thinks of all the hopes she had when she married Jamie, the times when they were close, the times they laughed. She thinks of Charlotte's birth, and of the loneliness of Rose's birth, when he wouldn't even come into the delivery room. Of how tied she once felt to him, and how tied down she's felt recently. Holding Junie's eye tight in her fist, she weeps with no strictures. Not as she did last night, with equal parts of guilt and relief; last night was only an experiment in crying. Today she cries unabashedly, with a sorrow she did not know she owned.

At nine-thirty that night, when Keevan comes down the street with a late dinner he picked up at the deli, he finds Zoe on his doorstep in a parka, her cheeks flushed, just ringing his bell. She's got a package tucked under one arm. Snow is falling in fat white flakes around them. And the clouds producing it reflect the light of the streetlamps, so that the sky is pearly. Her hair is coming out of her braid, and already snow glazes it, a translucent scarf of white over the silver gold.

"Zoe," he calls to her, climbing the steps to join her. She smiles as he nears her, looking different somehow, sturdier, stronger.

"Keevan, I have something to tell you," she says.

"What?"

"Let's go inside."

She climbs the steps to his apartment. She stamps off her boots on the landing. He slips off his own shoes, sending crumbs of snow in all directions. What could she have to tell him that excites her so? He expected, the next time he saw her, to hear that Jamie had turned from her or grown angry with the news of her arrest. Not this. He bends down and helps her unzip her boots, takes them off, holding the tender backs of her ankles in his hand, and sets the boots on the mat. What if something Jamie's done has made her very happy? What if he could lose her because of this news she's about to tell him? He can feel energy emanating from her.

"What happened when you told Jamie last night?" he asks. "Is that what this is about?" His hands shake slightly as he unlocks the door, hangs up their coats.

"He was kind," she says. "More than you know."

"That's good." But Keevan feels deflated. "And so . . . ?"

"Well, first," she says, drawing her hand through her dampened hair, melting the flakes beneath it. "Did you mean that yesterday, Keevan? That you love me even though I steal?"

"Of course."

"But even if I could never overcome it, would you feel the same?"

"I'm not saying I wouldn't want to help you, wouldn't want to try and get you help. But I love you. Your problems are mine. I'd still love you, no matter what.'' He knows it's true.

"But why would you want to marry a thief?" The look in her eye is defiant.

"I'd only marry you. Other thieves need not apply." He smiles at her, sees how her eyes are gleaming, how their color has deepened to a dusky blue.

She lifts the package from the floor beside her.

"Before I tell you, open your Christmas gift," she tells him. She sets it in his lap.

"I have a gift for you too."

"Open mine first." He tears the paper away, whistles when he sees it, the color soft grey like a storm cloud. He lifts the robe from the tissue, knowing he's never held anything so soft, so fine.

"Zo," he says. "What is it? Cashmere? It's incredible. It must have cost a fortune."

"Maybe it's the last outrageously expensive thing I'll ever be able to buy you."

He looks up, worried. "What do you mean?"

And then she tells him. "Jamie wants to leave me."

"*He* wants to leave *you*?"

"He wants me to be with you. He wants me to be happy. At first I couldn't believe it, didn't think I should let him go. He's been my responsibility so long."

"And then?"

"And then I thought and thought about it." She leans forward. Her eyes glisten. "And I realized he's giving me something precious. Something he wants to give me. I don't want to be unhappy anymore. I don't want Rose to be unhappy."

Everything expands for him. His heart, the room.

"Zoe."

"You're still sure?" she asks. "That you want us to be together. You don't have to commit yourself really. I could be alone at first."

"You know what I want."

She smiles a smile that seems more open, more relaxed,

than he's ever seen. To live with that smile, her kindness, to have Rose as his daughter . . . There's nothing more he'd ever ask for.

"I still have a Christmas gift for you. Though it seems small now," he says.

"Let me see," she says. Her eyes light up, remind him of Rose's eyes when she's truly happy.

"It's not much," he says, bringing back the package from the kitchen. "It's just something I found when I was cleaning the cellar."

She unwraps it carefully, sliding her fingers under the tape, barely disturbing the paper. It's an old photo he had framed for her in a beautiful burlwood frame. The frame alone cost fifty dollars.

"Before I had it framed, you could see that on the back, in pencil, it said 1917. That's the year my grandfather bought this house."

Side by side stand two brownstones. Lace curtains in the windows. Gaslights out front. Window boxes on every sill of the house on the right, all the way up, all four stories bedecked with flowers. No trees. There is a wagon parked close to the camera. It says "Fanelli Dairy."

"It's our houses," he says.

"How do you know?" she asks. "It could be any house on the street, couldn't it?"

"But it's not. Look." Stenciled elaborately on the side of the front door of each house is an address. She squints to see: 645, 643. Those numbers have now been washed away by weather, by time, by repair.

"It *is* our houses. Oh, Keevan. It's a wonderful gift. When I miss my house, I can look at this picture and remember."

"You're going to leave your house? Won't Jamie give the house to you? I mean, you could fight for that in the divorce settlement."

"He'd give it to me happily," she says. "And money too. But is that what we want? Living next door to your house, which is no longer yours. Won't that hurt you? And living in mine—doesn't it hold just too many memories? It does for me. I want a house that's just ours. Here, somewhere in the Slope. A house we buy together. A house we love."

All these months, he has done nothing to firm up his living arrangements for the future, having spent all his time denying he'd ever have to move. Now he sees he has waited for a reason.

"I would like to buy a house together. I hadn't thought. But you're right. It would be better to do that," he says. He can't believe how hopeful he feels, hungry for the future in a way he's never known. Choosing a brownstone together, making a new home for them, for Rose. He could not ask for more than that.

"I feel lucky to have lived here, though," Zoe says, leaning back into the sofa. "I walk around the Slope, and some of the houses are grander, but you know, there isn't a street I like better."

"We'll always own this street," he says. "In a way, it will always be with us."

Zoe lifts the photograph of the houses again, and Keevan leans close to her, staring at the elegant shapes and shadows of their houses, side by side, lifetimes ago.

"Look!" Zoe says. "Did you see? There's a little girl in the upstairs window of your house. Right there. Peeking out."

"Really?" He takes the smooth frame into his hands and holds it close. In an upstairs window, above the window boxes spilling with petunias, he sees the tiny face of a little blond girl in braids, looking out at the street, at the photographer. "It must be my grandmother," he says. "I didn't notice her before. It looks like her." His heart is warmed by the sight of those steady eyes, the arched brows. His grandmother. The only woman he ever truly loved before Zoe.

"It looks like she's looking out her window at us," Zoe says.

"It does," Keevan says, focusing on the face of that

little girl so long ago. Without her, he wouldn't be here. In his body, two generations later, he still carries her tastes, her fear, her hopes. What did she think, looking out the window that morning? Was she imagining her own future? The future of the street? Could she have imagined a street where horses would no longer walk? Where giant trees would filter the sun into thousands of half-moons on the bluestone, where lives would come and go many years after she was gone. No. She was probably looking out at her father, with his clumsy old camera. She was probably listening to the milkman's clanking bottles. She was probably wondering what her mother would be cooking for breakfast.

"I'm hungry," Keevan says. "Come sit with me while I eat my dinner. Come tell me what's going to happen next."

If you walk down Eighth Street now, you will not be aware that much has changed. You'll be lulled by the clip of your feet on the old dark bluestone sidewalks. And if it rains, the Norwegian maples will still shelter you better than an umbrella.

The houses march up the hill the same as they have for more than one hundred years, locked in their cool symmetry. It is inside that things have changed. The O'Neill teenagers no longer rock the walls of 664. The eldest is off at college. The youngest never seems to come home anymore. In 652, Darlene Kilkenny's toddler cries, and his grandmother Maggie does too. For her, tears are release and pleasure, in the privacy of the room she shared for so many years with her late husband. The house is for sale. The real estate agents predict it won't be on the market for long. She folds bright, thin clothes to wear in the desert, where she imagines she will take up knitting again and go to exercise class and maybe even flirt.

In 643, the new owners talk of the crocuses breaking through the thin crust of snow in the front yard. A bonus, they tell themselves, though the workmen have already trampled some as they carried out sagging lath taken from the soon-to-be-replaced ceilings. How had that O'Connor family lived here so long and done so little in the way of major repairs?

And from 645, with the double oak doors pried open like a patient's mouth in a dentist's office, the movers carry out a candy-colored sofa; a box full of a child's cowboy boots, stuffed toys, picture books; a wardrobe of woman's clothes. They have only to move it, and some select contents of the house, to a smaller house a few blocks away, a pretty little limestone with a round bay window, where Keevan O'Connor is busy filling a crystal vase full of tulips and irises and baby's breath. He's waited over a year for the arrival of his new wife and stepdaughter. He's painted every room himself, soaked the paint off every piece of hardware. He even paid for a man to paint a mural on the wall of what will be his stepdaughter's room: a bird's-eye view of Coney Island's Wonder Wheel: below, the booths and rides made tiny by distance; beyond, the vast blue ocean. Already his little girl has walked over half her stuffed animals, her doghouse, her favorite pillow, and, curling up in a chair with him, has fallen asleep in his arms. It is for her he's turned this flaking jumble of a house into a home. For her mother too. Amid the paint fumes and plaster dust, he's dreamed of this house as a place where they will live when they are old, where his little girl and maybe more children will still live when he and his wife are gone, where their children will live when the memory of all of them is just a pile of photographs in the basement.

Spring smells of mud and stone on Eighth Street. Soon the older boys will throw footballs between rows of parked cars. The littlest girls will chalk the sidewalks, the stoop sitters will come out again, to watch their children and wait to see their neighbors, to find out how each of their winters have gone. If you walk up the bluestone to the top of the hill, you will look down on a row of houses as symmetrical as soldiers. And try as you might, you can't

help but let the facades lull you. Row after row of brownstone stoops line up, row after row of wrought-iron gates
mark the entrances with fleurs-de-lis. You could easily
walk by your own house and not know it. People do
every day.

Fall Victim to Pulse-Pounding Thrillers
by *The New York Times*
Bestselling Author

# JOY FIELDING

## SEE JANE RUN
71152-4/$6.50 US

Her world suddenly shrouded by amnesia, Jane Whittaker wanders dazedly through Boston, her clothes blood-soaked and her pocket stuffed with $10,000. Where did she get it? And can she trust the charming man claiming to be her husband to help her untangle this murderous mystery?

## TELL ME NO SECRETS
72122-8/$5.99 US

Following the puzzling disappearance of a brutalized rape victim, prosecutor Jess Koster is lined up as the next target of an unknown stalker with murder on his mind.

## DON'T CRY NOW
71153-2/$6.99 US

Happily married Bonnie Wheeler is living the ideal life—until her husband's ex-wife turns up horribly murdered. And it looks to Bonnie as if she—and her innocent, beautiful daughter—may be next on the killer's list.

# SUE HARRISON

"A remarkable storyteller...
one wants to stand up and cheer."
*Detroit Free Press*

"Sue Harrison outdoes Jean Auel"
*Milwaukee Journal*

## MOTHER EARTH FATHER SKY
71592-9/$6.99 US/ $8.99 Can

In a frozen time before history, in a harsh and beautiful
land near the top of the world, womanhood comes
cruelly and suddenly to beautiful, young Chagak.

## MY SISTER THE MOON
71836-7/ $6.99 US/ $8.99 Can

An abused and unwanted daughter of the First Men
tribe, young Kiin knows that her destiny is tied to the
brave sons of orphaned Chagak and her chieftan mate
Kayugh—one to whom Kiin is promised, the other for
whom she yearns.

## BROTHER WIND
72178-3/ $6.50 US/ $8.50 Can

## SONG OF THE RIVER
72603-3/ $6.99 US/ $8.99Can

Experience the world of Hannah Trevor —
widow, mother, and midwife in colonial Maine
by
❦ MARGARET LAWRENCE ❦

## HEARTS AND BONES
78879-9/$5.99 US/$7.99 Can

Nominated for the Edgar and Agatha Awards
for Best Mystery Novel

"The narrative is woven together with entries
from Hannah's journal, pieces of the trial transcript,
letters, reports and local gossip to provide
a convincing sense of period."
—*Minneapolis Star Tribune*

## BLOOD RED ROSES
78880-2/$6.50 US/$8.50 Can

"Suspenseful, complex...Lawrence's primary theme
is the remarkable strength and fortitude
of the women of the era."
—*San Francisco Chronicle*

### And coming soon in Hardcover

## THE BURNING BRIDE
97620-X/$23.00 US/$30.00 Can

Avon Books Presents
*New York Times* Bestselling Author

# KATHRYN HARVEY

# BUTTERFLY

Every Woman's Ultimate Fantasy
70835-3/$6.99 US/$8.99 Can

# STARS

The rich, the glamorous,
the powerful all come to Stars
71504-X/$5.99 US/$6.99 Can